" *Was that her fate, too? Her bones polished and cleaned by the sun and the winds and buried by the sands on a distant planet?*

CLAUSTROM

Breaking in is the only way out

A novel by
JAMES SLATER

www.jamesslaterbooks.com

Copyright

Dedicated to my family and friends, all of whom have their own visions of the future.

1

NEB LOUNGE

THE VIEW WAS BREATHTAKING. The Cain Nebula was a swirling mass of blue and purple curtains swaying in a random display of reflected light that defied description by words. It was something you had to experience. Nik shivered involuntarily. Partly from the viewing gallery where the nebula took up the better part of her view and partly from the memories of her first time here a few hours before.

It hadn't started as anything out of the ordinary, but it ended with mind-bending spasms of pleasure that had shaken her into a self-examination of priorities. She wondered absently how long it had actually been since she'd had someone other than herself. Yes, she thought, she could get used to that kind of exercise, and she felt herself shudder involuntarily again and smile with what she knew was a dreamy, goofy smile.

The steam rising from her hot tea was the only thing between her and the reaches of space. The viewing platform was enclosed in a transparent, station-generated field that maintained the fresh, always circulating air of New Manhattan and sheltered her from errant radiation and random space particulates. She inhaled the delicate aroma and gazed into the vacuum beyond.

Durt. She thought it was a stupid name when she first heard it. You couldn't work for the company and not know who Durt Larson was. The company pilot who had gotten himself, and whatever company assets he had with him at the time, out of more tight spots than her G-string. The stories were legendary. She smiled each time she heard one of these stories. They were all similar, but each time she heard them repeated they changed a little, edging toward the fantastic.

So when he showed up at her desk, clipboard-in-hand, to personally confirm her status, cargo, destination, health and a pile of other pre-flight details, she was surprised at her own embarrassment to meet him face-to-face. He was all business. Gathering the mandatory data from her, he'd rarely consulted the checklist that floated above his left hand, making only a few notations here and there. Stopover on Midway. Return to Earth. Routine.

Nik answered as quickly and as honestly as she could, trying not to stare. He was handsome. Movie-handsome, even. It was the scar that ran diagonally across his cheek that caught and held her gaze, and she wondered which of the fantasies she'd heard about him might have left him with that memento. It had faded to white and was not the disgusting kind you have to force yourself to watch for fear of offending. Just the opposite. It seem to compliment his sharp features perfectly. His dark, close-cropped hair framed the unnaturally pale blue eyes that watched her intently. She wondered what woman could tell those eyes no. To anything.

Pre-flight complete, he'd closed his palms. The clipboard dissolved back into his flight jacket, and he turned abruptly to leave. He caught himself on a random thought and turned back with an inquisitive look on his face. He was on his way to the ship, the Raven, he said, but was going to stop by the the Neb. If she'd not been before, the Nebula lounge was something pretty amazing, and she should consider herself an invited guest.

Just like every other woman before, she imagined. But she didn't tell him no. To anything.

Afterward as she sat motionless, literally staring into space, she acknowledged to herself that she was much less enamored with Durt the man than she was with the thought of Durt. Durt the swashbuckler. Durt the pilot. Durt the hero. All of those visions were put aside now, and she would have to play tricks on her own mind to retrieve them. Which she would at some point, but not now. For now, she was going to bask, and as she did, her focus was on her true love, numbers.

Numbers didn't lie. They didn't cheat. Were anything true in the universe, it would be numbers, and that was something she could hang on to. Something she could count on. Numbers told stories, and numbers talked to her. For the better part of her life, her ongoing relationship with them had earned her a comfortable living, and if she ever wanted to be alone with her true love, this remote edge of the galaxy was heaven. For weeks at a time, the numbers told her the ongoing story of New Manhattan's construction, expansion, of arrivals and departures, of debits and credits, of inventories and schedules.

But just like everything else, now and again she needed a break from her obsession, and tonight had been exactly what she needed.

Durt had left her alone with her thoughts in the privacy of one of the Neb's crash pads. It was amusing, she thought as she sat, still entranced by the Cain Nebula's never-ending visual variations, that pilots would use that term for a sleeping area. They seemed to her a pretty superstitious bunch. At the same time, the ones she'd known anyway, were a pretty brazen bunch as well, and Durt didn't seem too concerned about jinxing his flight plans by using one of the pads.

Truth be told, she'd expected it to be smaller and more utilitarian, but the pad was actually a well-appointed apartment, and there were a number of them that adjoined the Neb's lounge and viewing area. Here on the edge of earth-explored space, size and space no longer clung to earth's overpopulated minimalist design mentality. Here, few limits existed, either financially or spatially, and the construction of a palace took about the same effort as a standard earth apartment.

Yes, thought Nik, *she'd enjoyed her crash. It was delicious.*

***

Thirteen decks below the loading terminal, the constant motion of activity in support of the construction and development phase was in full swing. Automated pallets on hovering vectors made navigating the passages a tricky operation of timing and agility.

Jata was used to it. She skipped around a container-stack a good three meters tall. Its digital marking identified it as tubes and valves, and it was hitching a ride on an old auto-wheeled pallet. She dodged and ducked into the primary dry cleaner on that level.

She looked at the aging east-Earth man behind the counter.

"Picking up for Lance Mader, please."

The old man peered over his old-style reading eyeglasses to get a better look at his next customer. The few wisps of hair that remained on his balding head were slicked flat by sweat, the light reflecting brightly off the sheen of his head. She could feel the heat emanating from the ongoing cleaning operation behind the counter. He slid his hand across the top of the counter, shuffling the hundreds of cards that floated above it and began to check his inventory.

Jata wondered, with all the health technology available today, why he wouldn't have his eyes adjusted or his hair replanted. It wasn't that painful, and the cost was…well, she thought considering, maybe that was it. The cost was significant. Most things here on New Manhattan were ridiculously expensive, but dry-cleaning wasn't one of them, and she always figured the company subsidized that service as part of their ongoing image effort. This was a future where everything was perfect. Almost.

The old man stopped his search abruptly as he processed her pickup request. He took off his glasses and took a second, harder look at her and saw her for the first time. She felt his eyes survey her slim and muscular form. Were it not for her clothing that hugged every well-formed curve, her buzz cut might have suggested a man standing before him. He threw a couple of inquisitive glances beyond her at the stream of activity that continued outside.

Apparently satisfied, he pulled a shimmering garment from the high rack behind him, pointing out something and nodding imperceptibly, inviting her behind the counter. She followed him, straining to appear nonchalant while trying not to lose the man's trail as he swished left and right through a dizzy maze of hanging uniforms and clothing.

Suddenly she stopped. The old man was nowhere to be seen. Racks of hanging clothes stood on either side of her, and a dead-end wall blocked her progress ahead. She turned hesitantly to try and retrace her steps, but then remembered what the message had said. *Follow the dry-cleaner.* She mentally slapped herself. *She had one thing to do. One thing.* Time was running out, and she had none of it to waste before she had to check in and board her Earth-bound flight.

Follow the dry-cleaner. Fair enough. The old man had gone through the wall, maybe? So would she. She moved forward and touched the cool metal surface of the black, almost invisible wall. Left to right, she ran her hands across the entire surface. Her fingers felt a sudden warming area, and she instinctively pulled her hands back. Nothing happened.

Slowly, she retraced the arc of her search until she came to the warmer section, first with a finger, then with her full palm, joined immediately by her second palm. Yes, this area was significantly warmer. As she moved her two hands in unison across the back wall, she watched it change. Still dark, but then transparent and then nothing. It simply disappeared.

An arched doorway appeared, beyond which she could begin to make out shapes as her eyes adjusted to the darkness. She stepped through, and as she did, the doorway closed behind her. There was no door that slid open or closed. It was again a dark wall of metal.

The darkness in the room melted into light and revealed a well appointed office. Corporate Earth style with an expansive desk backed by shelf after shelf of books, their spines a rainbow of colors and textures, with some jammed haphazardly on top of others where space allowed. She stared, unmoving, marveling at the collection and couldn't help herself from wondering aloud.

"Are all those real, actual books?" she asked the figure behind the desk.

"Do you think they are?"

"I'm not sure. It's just that I've never seen real books. I don't think they are, but they look so—"

She paused as she recognized the voice as that of the east-Earth shop owner, but saw his face was no longer east-Earth. Gone were the glasses. His hair was white with streaks of grey and close-cropped, much like her own style, and his face was similar but strangely different. While she saw similarities, she would never have recognized the two faces as the same, had she not seen them in logical, sequential order.

"Maybe they are and maybe not," said the man. "Things are not always what they seem. But I don't think that's what you're here for is it?"

"Look. I don't have much time. I have to be upstairs in a few minutes. I'll keep my end of the bargain. I just need to know you'll do the same."

The man behind the desk opened a drawer and pulled out a thin sheet of what appeared to be transparent glass and placed it on the desk. He placed his palm on its surface, then pulled back as a transparent green holographic image jumped from the glass and began to rotate. Eagerly she stepped forward for a closer inspection. It was a castle. In reality, it was a luxury dwelling with more space inside than she and the rest of her extended family could ever fully occupy. Not that they'd be invited to stay, or visit even. But once you had a house like this, you could have your pick of friends and visitors. She marveled at its amenities. Full landing port with a pair of shuttles. Sports complex with courts and a ridiculous-sized pool. On its second full rotation, the green faded to actual color and texture details, dissolving and reforming as it progressed on its rotation, offering a clear vision of the interior layout.

She was almost drooling and caught herself quickly. "This is it?" she asked.

"150-year lease. High Earth orbit. All services provided. Give me what I need, and I give you what you crave."

"Facelift, too?"

"Yes. Your choice of identity. Same as before."

She smiled. This was it. In a few weeks, she'd have a new appearance, a new house and a new life. She was finally going to get what she deserved.

"I like you. You see what you want, and you don't let anything stand in your way. I think we're a lot alike. The two of us together? Unstoppable."

The man smiled. "I think you can find your way out."

She nodded and turned toward the back metal wall.

"Just one more thing," she said, turning again to face the man. And stopped dead. The room was empty. A couple of empty crates stood at the back of an empty room. No desk. No library. No man. A quick bolt of fear ran through her as she turned quickly to find the warm section of the wall and let herself out. Outside the shop, the passage buzzed with its continuous activity, the life-blood of New Manhattan with construction parts, repair tools and various bot techs still riding whatever was going their way to ensure the constant expansion of the thing itself. Bot ships arrived from near Earth, docked and began their mechanical disassembly and reassembly. Just another part of someone's idea of an exclusive Earth colony with a heavenly night sky.

Jata jumped a low rolling trolley carrying some flat construction materials that made a perfect ride for her and hitched up a few hundred yards before skipping into a rare gap in the tunnel's traffic and making her way into an elevator bay. It was a pain, but it was something you got used to here, she figured, but all that was about to change. She'd put up with too much for too long not to take advantage of an opportunity like this. She should be giving the orders instead of taking them. *This wasn't chance*, she thought. *It was her destiny.*

***

Guyal was shaking. From the look of him he was tired of laughing but couldn't seem to stop, his grin keeping his face creased. It looked exhausting to Durt. His navigator and engineer stood outside the Raven's cargo hatch facing one another, each with his own unique stance and attitude. Guyal seemed to find something humorous in just about everything. Jolly was probably the right description. White hair and plenty of him to go around, give him a sleigh and a beard, and he'd be a dead ringer for Santa Claus. He had a zoo of kids at home and a real talent for navigation. They hadn't flown together for what seemed like ages, now that he thought about it, and it was good to see his old friend again.

If there was an opposite of Guyal, it was Truman. They were similar in size, but they were shaped differently, both physically and mentally. If Guyal were a jolly elf, then Truman was a crotchety hermit. If Guyal was everyone's friend, Truman had one friend. Two, actually. Their ship the Raven and Durt. Mostly the Raven. Truman was thick and powerful. When his hands weren't pulling up the latest status reports from Raven's engineering plant, they were somewhere on the ship, ensuring full functionality. His eyes were dark and sharp and what hair he had left did little more than keep his ears company. He was an engineer's engineer. He found machines logical and people difficult. Unlike Guyal, he didn't have a family, unless you counted Raven, which, Durt thought, would not raise a disagreement from Truman. In function, she was an older executive shuttle, but in form, she and Truman were one—he, her caretaker; and she, his ticket to the stars.

The trio stood in the shadow of her open cargo hatch, the horizontal metal surface providing a temporary roof above them in the vastness of the larger transportation terminal where New Manhattan's shipping and transport activity was forever in motion. Thousands of meters above them, the outer shell of the station ended offering a view into empty space beyond, a view interrupted now and again as arriving and departing craft of dissimilar shapes were vectored to their destinations.

Truman wasn't laughing and apparently didn't find it funny in the least. He was defensive, and his face still reflected a mix of surprise and incredulity.

"Alright, what is it?" asked Durt as he approached. "What happened?"

Truman looked at him without speaking, his face now stone. He didn't seem sure of how Durt would take the news of his faux pas.

"You won't believe it, but your engineer just assaulted one of the richest men on Earth," said Guyal.

"What?" Now Durt was fully engaged.

Truman remained silent.

Guyal, still smiling, recounted the story. "So he's just getting back to the ship—pre-flight preps, I presume. Who's sitting right here, his back to the Raven? It's a kid. A fully grown kid, but a kid still the same. Hair all over the place, earring, dark glasses. Butt on the ground, back against the hull. He's got his arms flailing around in front of him like he's possessed by some kind of space demon. Like he's got a convulsive sickness where he bites his tongue off or swallows it."

Durt grew his smile a bit more. "Don't tell me."

"Yes, Truman to the rescue. He comes screaming in from the side like some half-deluded bird of prey, grabbing the kid's arms and pinning them to the deck. All the while, he's shouting in his face, *calm down* and *relax* at the top of his lungs."

Guyal couldn't help himself and let go an additional snicker before he could continue.

"At first, it looks like Truman's doing some good, and then the kid overcomes his shock, thinks he's under attack and starts to pummel poor Truman."

Durt was grinning broadly now. "Bam?"

"Exactly! Our very own celebrity passenger neck deep in his latest virtual combat game."

Durt looked more closely at Truman's cheeks. He wasn't just embarrassed. His red cheeks retained some scarlet streaks, some finger texture still remained.

"Jesus," said Truman at last. "The least you could have done was tell me we had an heir to the Bambaci fortune on board."

Durt rolled his eyes. They all had access to the passenger manifest, but Truman rarely reviewed it. Typical. He'd invent critical mechanical problems to be solved, then set to them immediately to avoid even the potential for human interaction. If he had his choice, Durt was certain he'd choose to be a machine over a man. He knew his friend better than anyone. His love was the inner workings of their space propulsion plant. Spaceships made sense to him. They didn't disappoint him. He could count on them to react appropriately. Not people. They were way too twitchy for his taste.

"C'mon. We've got work to do," said Durt, still smiling as he led the Raven's crew aboard. "Let's get to it while we still have a ship."

***

Truman watched their progress through the viewport. Shortly, he'd close it and move to video display. Not that there was any real need anyway. In space, aside from stellar formations that provided navigational bearings, there just wasn't that much to see. Standard transponders coordinated the trajectories of the various transports arriving and departing from New Manhattan, its jagged edges of construction now clearly outlined against the backdrop of the Cain Nebula. What a sight. From this angle of illumination, New Manhattan was a back shadow, a giant spherical mass with thin snakes and odd-shaped mounds and sharp protruding edges that stretched from one end of the viewport to the other. Construction in progress. It was an amazing accomplishment of human ingenuity, an ever-expanding settlement, fantasies made to order for the right price.

Eventually, New Manhattan would meet itself in a completed sphere once construction was completed, but according to current planned schedules and sales trends, that wouldn't happen for another few years. Not that it mattered as each individual creation was guaranteed its own unique environment and ecosystem, and they were delivered as soon as they were completed, whether the larger orb was complete or not. These weren't the temporary ones created for the amusement of visitors on Midway, these were family and municipal investments as varied as those of any time period on Earth.

From castles with hunting grounds and forests to fantastical architectures only possible in the managed gravity of these creations, everything was available for those with imagination and money to burn. Truman had not visited a single one of them, but he'd seen the promotions and understood what was now possible with matter and field manipulation.

He watched as the silhouette receded behind the Raven's viewport, passing his hand over the controls to close the port and ignoring the display as it popped on to his right. He had work to do.

Keeping the Raven in flight-ready condition was a labor of love for him, and he had a good day of work ahead of him before they'd be ready to make the hyper-gate jump. He had no desire to visit any of the New Manhattan creations. Not that he minded the enterprise itself. The matter engineering and manipulation feats were amazing, and it was the business and success of New Manhattan that kept him airborne.

He and Durt had developed themselves as a go-to team over the past 20 years, just by doing what they said they were going to do. Their reputation as that team paid regular dividends, and with Durt's growing fame—Truman smiled at the thought—also grew their opportunities. Durt didn't even have to do anything now. Their exploits together were enough of a base to self-generate new and creative "myths" that he'd heard retold at pretty much every establishment they'd walked into for years. Those legends translated into business, security, and of course, his ability to keep flying while someone else footed the bill. Anyway, the company was bound to upgrade their shuttle fleet sooner or later. Despite its age and shortcomings, though, Raven had her advantages. Truman's intimate familiarity with her inner workings was one of those, but automatic hyper-gate preps and calculations were not. As the New Manhattan construction project, its fantasies in progress, receded from view, Truman took no notice as he made his way to the interior of the ship.

2

THRUGATE

"CAPTAIN, WE'RE BEING HAILED. Looks like a security check. Customs maybe."

Guyal rubbed his eyes. It used to be, he had no trouble recovering from hyper-jump stasis, but in recent years, he struggled with recovering quickly enough to make a decent systems inspection that wouldn't slow the ship's schedule. It was usually wickedly routine, which didn't help a bit with any type of a quick wakeup.

"It's Durt," came the reply from the front seat of the command cabin.

"No, the signal's actually pretty clear. And the signature's a valid one."

"Call me Durt."

"Oh, right. Sorry Durt. It just seems so...undignified."

Guyal flew with a lot of crews, but he hadn't navigated with Durt Larson for a couple of years now. Each captain was different, but most were like "Sir this" and "Sir that." It was stupid and awkward, but it was so commonplace that by now he couldn't help himself. It had become his annoying second nature, he realized. "Anyway," he continued, "there's no way to get a visual until the outer hull thaws. I'm guessing 90 minutes or so."

The Hawk glided forward through empty space, under no

power other than the post hyper-jump inertia. This was the most tedious part of the voyage, but also the most critical. Rebooting an entire ship's system was no picnic, especially on an older shuttle like this one. A good portion of the cross checks and systems verifications had to be done manually.

Durt was disconnected from all of his electronics, lounging in his bare feet and underwear, and Guyal caught a wisp of smoke rising from the front-facing pilot seat in his peripheral vision. It slowly wound its way up from between Durt's fingers, meandering toward the cockpit overhead before making its escape into the vent. His navseat was placed behind and perpendicular to that of the pilot, giving him access to the full visual display of the control console. He turned his frame, a tighter fit in the navseat than he remembered it being the last time he sat there. His easy-going manner that had made him quite popular with the shuttle pilots had expanded both his wallet and his belt size. He caught sight of the cigarette hanging from Durt's lips.

"I'm not surprised," said Durt, the cigarette bobbing up and down as he talked. "There's been a solid increase in smuggling over the past year. Even some piracy reported. If I were a cop, this is where I'd do my checks. The choke-points."

If Guyal could handle a cigarette first thing in the morning, he'd probably smoke, too. The healing effects of the cigarette went directly into the bloodstream through the lungs, the most efficient way of repairing any hyper-jump injuries and returning the brain and body to peak operating condition.

He smiled, thinking of the way hi-tech manufacturing had given him new options in just about every aspect of his life. He was tired and achy from the jump, but he was only maybe ten minutes behind Durt in recovery. The thin strip of gum between his cheek and gum were about to do wonders. As he watched the various navigation, propulsion and life support systems return to life on his monitors, he was working his way through breakfast, his chosen way to wake up. Eggs, bacon, hash browns. One at a time, the flavors of each filled his palette as the healing chemicals made their way through his mouth and into his bloodstream.

There was a time, he knew, when this feast was considered unhealthy, when these delicacies were filled with actual fat from animals and could kill a man with an unbridled habit like his own. *Cigarettes, too. Imagine, cigarettes being bad for your health.* He smiled again.

"Acknowledge on the thaw time. Ask Truman to do a focused thaw and see if we can get these guys onboard in half an hour or so," said Durt. "We can finish our jump checks, do their walk-through while the hull thaws, and depart on schedule. No delay."

Larson was nothing if not efficient, thought Guyal as he keyed his headpiece for Raven's engineer.

"Truman, we have guests who are going to want a walk through. Can you do a redirect and have the boarding hatch open in 30?"

Truman responded in typical Truman style. "Stand by."

Even if he knew the answer, Truman could never just say, *yes* or *sure thing* or *no* or anything a normal person would respond with. Truman always had to check. Truman always had to be right. Truman had pretty much the same personality as the machines he worked with. But at least you could count on Truman being himself.

"No way," said Truman, "but I can do it in 35."

Guyal rolled his eyes and shook his head in a single motion. He shouldn't have expected anything else. "Thanks Truman."

"35," said Guyal. "Truman time."

He watched Durt smile and nod. *30 it was.*

"Advise our guests," said Durt.

***

Jata reached for a cigarette as the cover of her stasis unit slid open. She had work to do. She ran through her head once again the plan she'd agreed to execute. The passengers would be eager to get out of their confined spaces as the Raven made its near-Midway stop for document review and vector assignment before descending to the planet below. The official, her inside contact, would find some inconsistencies with the documents or cargo or whatever. The motivation wasn't shared with her, but the end result would be a temporary quarantine. The gracious official would offer luxury accommodations for the crew, but require a representative to remain onboard. While Captain Larson would demand to stay with the ship, his presence would be required at security central to sort things out. And since they were on a jump schedule, the engineer would also need to replenish his spare inventory. And this engineer, she knew, always insisted he do that himself. In person. No arguments. Her status as a company employee and willing volunteer would put the ship in her hands. Paying off the bent official would be easy, but not as satisfying as killing him. Maybe she'd do both, kind of a two-for-one deal. That part of the plan was still flexible.

She inhaled deeply and felt the recovery and rebuilding process inside her body kick into high gear. Naked bodies emerged from surrounding units and began their own recovery rituals.

"Something's wrong."

It was Nik in a nervous, uncertain voice.

You have no idea just how wrong, but you'll never realize the extent of it. You'll be stupid and happy, drink in your hand, pining away down on Midway for some Prince Charming who's never going to show up. She was weak and disgusting, thought Jata. She deserved what she got in life, which couldn't be a lot.

"We're not supposed to stop on Midway for another two months."

It was Nik again. Jata's eyes shot to the stasis control panel and scanned the readout data. Shit. She was right. They'd been on board only about a day or so. Maybe enough time to clear the hyper-gate, but certainly not enough to make it to Midway, whatever its orbit was this time. She stared uncomprehendingly at the readout for a long moment. Waking up in an unfamiliar place was disorienting, and her mind raced trying to make sense of the disconnect between her expectations and the numbers in front of her. She took another long pull from the cigarette and savored the healing, calming sensation, feeling it seep into her body. Either they'd missed their hyper-gate slot time or there was some thru-gate issue. She figured it was the latter. *Son of a bitch. Now what?* She had to find out. She set down the cigarette, momentarily balancing it on the edge of the stasis equipment shelf, as she pulled on her top and rolled out of the unit, walking bare-assed toward the intercom console in the center of the circle of stasis units, cigarette in one hand and pants in the other.

"Truman, it's Jata. What the hell is going on?"

Cigarette clenched between her teeth, she pulled on her pants, dancing from one foot to the other. The deck of the pod chilled her feet, and she returned to her unit to slip into her boots as she waited for the reply.

No answer.

"Truman. I'm coming up there now. I want an explanation."

Still no answer.

"Perfect," said Jata to no one in particular. "On my way."

She walked through the open end of the semi-circle of stasis units configuring the pod and toward the ship's door that connected the passenger pod with the central galley. Pressing her hand against the wall pad, she paused and waited for the red sensor to turn green and the door to slide up.

Nothing happened. The sensor remained its bright red shade as if mocking her. Daring her to try again. First once, then twice, and then a flurry of forceful pounding as she realized it wasn't going to yield.

She turned on her heel. *This was bullshit. Locked down on a commercial shuttle? They had no right.* The remainder of the passengers were in various states of wake up. Nik was in her pants and bra, combing her hair mechanically with that pre-wake up stare on her face, staring at nothing in particular. Bam was in his shorts

Thrugate

now leaning over the console.

"Truman, this is Bam. What's our status?" He tilted his head as he listened for a response.

Nothing.

"What the fuck, Truman? I let you slide once today already. Honest mistake. I appreciate your trying to save my life. But unless you're trying to do it again, I need to know what's up with our early wake up."

That did the trick. Truman's voice came on.

"We've just cleared the hyper-gate. We've been clipped for a security check. Durt should be there shortly. Should be a simple document and cargo check. No idea what they're doing way out here, but should be fairly routine. He may have more for you."

Bam nodded, but uttered no audible acknowledgement. He stared a minute straight ahead into space. Jata wondered at his wild, unkempt hair. *Was it styled like that on purpose or was it just a function of pre-wakeup?* She guessed the latter as it looked pretty much the same as it had when she'd seen him at the preflight check-in. *Was it possible for it to be more chaotic than it had before? Was there a point, if he left his hair to its own devices, where it reflected less of a distracted video game junkie and more of an up-and-coming leader of a major corporation?*

Not that it mattered. The image of the virtual rotating mansion above the desk at the dry cleaner popped into her head again, and she swallowed the taste of her desire and longing. Security check. *Was her planned crime not unique? Were there others who had failed? Or succeeded? Were security forces aware of other stolen shuttles? Was her cover blown, her plan compromised before she even had a chance to execute it?* That was doubtful. She'd committed no crime yet, only conspired to. Just a bump. A delay. An annoyance.

Bam was backed up now against his stasis unit. He'd pulled his pants on and now was wearing dark glasses and making some odd hand motions. *Some type of east-Earth meditation or martial art?*

Who knew? There were a million ways to wake up. Nik was spraying perfume at her neck. *That prissy bitch. That was certainly one way, but not a way she'd ever be caught doing.*

Behind her, the outside door opened and Durt stood before them, cigarette between his fingers, and his face lacking any expression whatsoever.

Jata checked him out. He was handsome enough that she had a hard time not admiring him as he stood before them. What a specimen he was. There were a few things she could think of doing, were it not for the remainder of the crew and passengers.

"If you haven't figured it out yet, we're short of Midway orbit by at least two months," said Durt. "We've been hailed, and we're now required to pass a security inspection before we move on."

They stared mutely at him, expecting something more of an explanation.

"I know this isn't normal procedure, but there's been regular piracy of company vessels in the past months, as well as high-value theft from New Manhattan. Looks as if this is one of the steps they're taking to address that."

He took a long drag from his cigarette and rubbed his forehead, apparently running through the rest of his vessel tasks as he finished his required passenger briefing.

"They'll want to inspect you personally, so be easy with your documents. In reality, we have to thaw the hull anyway before we re-vector for Midway, so I'm hoping we'll be done with this inspection by the time the ship's ready to go."

He looked up at Bam who was now fully dressed with his wild mop of hair as wild as ever, arms crossed and listening intently.

"Bam, I know you've got an engagement on Midway, and you don't have a big time window. Things go as planned, this won't make a dent in our schedule. Now, if you'll excuse me, I've got some inspectors to greet. We'll be back shortly. I'm hosting a Captain's meal in the galley as soon as we're done with this. I think you'll enjoy it. Something to get you back into a stasis mood."

Without waiting for any response from his passengers, he did an abrupt about face, the door sliding silently closed behind him, and the little red light taking up its vigil as before.

Jata watched him go. Not a crisis, she thought, just a delay. She'd have her opportunity to call the shots soon enough.

***

Durt grabbed the bar above the hatch for balance as he descended into the cargo bay. They hadn't taken on a lot of cargo. Usually returning shuttles were packed tight with passengers and equipment returning to Midway or Earth, and he guessed Bam was the primary reason for their light load. Only three of the 12 passenger stasis units were in use. This, certainly was no passenger bus, but with the company's optimization policies for just about everything, this trip was in clear violation. Made sense that a high-level company exec could do as he pleased, especially the son of the chief executive.

Why even bother, then? He knew the executive fleet was more than capable of making the trip, and he'd seen three of the new, sleek vessels at the New ManhattanVIP dock. *Why hitch a ride on an aging bird like the Raven?* Probably something to do with the splash he wanted to make on Midway, he thought. One of those company rigs would be mobbed, but no one would bother to check out a standard arrival in the public bay. *Easy enough to figure.*

Durt passed his hand over the Raven intercom interface mounted on the side of the loading bay and used two fingers to identify the pilot cabin.

"Guyal. Any updates from the security team?"

Guyal's voice came back through the plate beneath his hand.

"Durt. Nothing yet. Hang on. OK, I do have something. Their shuttle is now detached and broadcasting a docking code. Should be ready to dock in about three minutes. They're not wasting any time."

Durt changed to a single finger, ready to call engineering when Truman's voice came on.

"That's it, Durt. The loading bay door is ready for action. Be there in a minute."

Durt looked over their loaded containers and equipment and took a quick inventory of what would likely be their first stop in the next hour or so as they made their way methodically through the ship. Some was specialty mining equipment that came with the mechanized construction ships. Most of those ship's parts were manufactured as prefabricated units that would become integrated into the New Manhattan structure, but not all. Some of the more delicate instruments were returned to the ongoing mining operations on the asteroid belt and would make the trip over and over again until they were either damaged or made obsolete with something more efficient, at which point they'd be atomized and become a part of the structure as well. In the vacuum of space, even the basic atoms and molecules of their matter was a valuable commodity. In the new world of New Manhattan, nothing was available for building and construction that wasn't transported from some other place.

There were planets in-system, Midway's system, that might one day be useful as well, but in the culture of efficiency, New Manhattan, this exclusive luxury outpost on the edge of space that kept them all employed, had yet to turn a profit. He'd presumed it, and Nik had confirmed that presumption. Not that there wasn't a huge market for luxury on Earth where medical science continued to extend the human lifespan, while shrinking Earth's capacity to maintain it. But soon enough they'd be moving their mining operations closer. A few more estate sales would probably increase the revenue stream enough to finance the migration, he guessed.

Containers of various sizes were packed and secured in the bay. Most notable were the shiny silver rectangular containers, about the size of sleeping mattresses, stacked neatly on one another, their field locks blinking in assurance that whatever was inside was secure. Without the authorizing retinal scan, no heat, cold, impact—or anything really—could open those things. These were what Bam was transporting. He wondered if this was maybe another reason for the supposed nonchalance of the transport.

He felt the impact of the security shuttle's coupling bump their grav field and saw Truman swing down the ladder and take position behind the hatch's control panel. Truman shot him an inquiring glance, and he gave a quick authorizing nod. The seal locked; the pressurized door slid open, and a man stepped in through the opening.

Durt was confused, and he reflected it openly in his expression. One eye squinted, and his brow furrowed as his brain processed the scene.

Something wasn't right.

The man wore no security uniform, just a plain flight suit and a patch that said he was security. And he looked familiar. Something tickled the back of his mind.

Who was he?

Truman was unfazed, business as usual, waiting expectantly for the second set of footsteps to board the Raven. None came.

"No recorder?" asked Truman.

A standard inspection party included a security officer and an assistant to make notations, quote regulations and serve as a body guard.

"No, gentlemen," said the newcomer. "Not today. Allow me to introduce myself. I'm Strober Uti. You've no doubt heard of our heightened security posture along this route. You've read the reports and taken the precautions. That's what you're supposed to do. You're supposed to be efficient with company resources."

Truman was nodding, but Durt watched him strangely. *What was it about him? Where did he know him from?*

Strober looked at Durt, pausing momentarily as a flash of recognition splashed across his face.

"Jesus. Look at who we've got here. Durt Larson? I've heard so much about you. I—"

He stepped forward, his mouth searching for the right words.

"I want to shake your hand," the man called Strober said, extending his hand in front of him in a gesture of genuine interest.

Durt began to extend his hand, when the clarity of his face came into clear view, and he realized he'd been duped. He now recognized the officer. His hair was worn differently, and he was clean shaven, but the nose and the eyes gave him away. He continued smoothly, not betraying his recognition. *When in doubt, play along. This wasn't a security inspector. This wasn't legit at all. This was something much worse. This was a hijacking.*

3

PRISON

THE GIRL WATCHED THE WIZ stare into the depth of the desert. Somewhere far beyond the prison boundary lay a particular point where the desert stopped being desert and turned into sky. Some days it was a clear, distinct line that ran from one edge of the horizon to the other, uninterrupted. Not today, though.

Today, Claustrom's desert winds whipped sand into the air, creating a hazy feel to the horizon, softening the clear line. The desert temperatures during the day could be deadly, but from the perch in the prison's lookout tower, a controlled breeze kept the air cool and comfortable. The tower overlooked the few white, odd-shaped structures that made up the prison complex. Not a square corner in the lot.

It was the same scene they'd seen yesterday and the day before. And for so many days before that.

Curves and bumps of brilliant white looked like random cubes melting in the sand. The oddness of the exterior shapes masked the interior layout of each building. Quite a sight from the air, the girl was sure. Not that she'd ever seen it from that angle. Prisoners arrived here in restraints in the secure interior of a prison transport, naked and shivering. That initial blast of Claustrom heat so shocked their systems, they usually fell to the ground helpless, before being mechanically herded and prodded into their new prison home.

Simms was here, she knew, not so much for what he'd done, but for what they'd feared he could do. He'd made a name for himself on Midway, jacking the Casinos for millions. He'd evaded security for years, living off his wits and his "winnings." She'd heard the story many times, each version slightly different. Most folks couldn't wait to get to Midway for the gambling and entertainment. Wislon Simms, or The Wiz, as he was better known, saw things differently. She didn't dare ask, but she'd heard. His philosophy was common knowledge here. The Wiz figured the Casino's odds were stacked in favor of each and every house. If that wasn't stealing, he didn't know what was. Of course, the Casinos didn't see it that way. They provided entertainment, and those odds were the cost of doing business.

He'd spawned a cult following, sharing his talent and creating a corps of hacker clones, disciples and followers who continued to help "unbalance" the Casino's house odds, at great benefit to themselves, of course. The Wiz, was really something of a folk hero. The Casinos had wanted him, and would-be hackers wanted to be him.

She watched him and wondered what he thought about. Transfixed by the desert scene before them, he spent hours lost in his own thoughts.

The problem with the Casinos was their tenacity. You could run, but they'd never quit. Simms was a write-off on the wrong side of their balance sheet and hunting him became both a business and a corporate quest. She knew they'd eventually caught up with him. He'd recounted to her in one of their regular conversations that he presumed they'd just "disappear" him, but they turned out to be savvy marketers. They'd turned him over to the prison system and showcased his capture whenever possible. "We caught the Wiz" was their deterrent to would-be Casino thieves, and they played it up whenever they could across Earth communication networks.

Caught he was, but his talents had freed him from his prison status a number of times. The way he told it, he broke out, really at will, until he became more of a liability than an asset in the eyes of the Casino's marketing strategists, and they'd sent him here, where even, should he make his break-out, he'd have no place to go but to die. He told her he thought about that, too. Sometimes on a regular basis, but he said opportunities always seemed to present themselves sooner or later, and usually all he needed was patience and a watchful eye.

She realized she was pacing now and had been pacing back and forth for minutes before he became aware of her restlessness.

"Oh, sorry," he said. "Rehearsal is tonight isn't it?"

She flashed her brilliant smile and nodded enthusiastically, her eyebrows up in a unspoken anticipation she couldn't hide.

He waved her off.

"Go. I don't know what you all see in him. Enjoy."

She was ready to dive back into her explanation of how the music made her feel, and how it was an enjoyable diversion for everyone, but it didn't look like he cared. She'd lost count of the number of times she'd tried to explain her appreciation of Moot's music. He'd called it a damned waste of time. He couldn't understand the words. She agreed. No one could. That was the beauty of it. The music was not for understanding, but for feeling and Moot was so…so mysterious and wonderful and…. She began to make a mental list of things he was as she skipped out of the room, leaving the Wiz to himself and his desert panorama.

***

Durt took the extended hand and shook it warmly as if this Strober character was an old friend. He put on as genuine a smile as he could manage.

"Strober, is it?" he asked.

"Strober it is. My friends call me Stro."

"Be careful with that one," said Durt with a feigned smirk. "Sounds like a four-letter word."

Strober took a step back and looked Durt up and down, sizing him up. Considering his next words. There was something genuinely friendly about this fellow, Durt noticed. Something in the easy motions and steps he used. He wasn't worried about a thing in the universe. Carefree. It put him at ease—something he wasn't used to—and that made the hair on his neck stand up. Strober or Stro was about to have an attitude change, he figured, courtesy of Durt Larson.

"Captain Larson. Durt. Do you mind if I call you that?" asked Strober, not waiting for an answer before quickly continuing. "I'd like to offer you and your crew—your passengers, too, if you see fit —what I like to call significant financial compensation to relinquish your ship."

Durt stared at him, surprised. But not too surprised. His eyes narrowed as his brain processed what he was hearing. Truman had come up behind Strober and wore a look of puzzlement on his face as well.

"No, don't say anything. Hear me out. I think you'll like what I have to say. I'm willing to offer each of you enough to live the rest of your lives in luxury. You like New Manhattan? Luxury dripping from every piece of that palace in the sky. You like Earth? I can get you a place inside the Park Service boundary. Off-world. Midway. Whatever you want. All you need to do is turn over control of the ship to me. No worries. No fuss."

Durt's face tightened.

"Don't give me that look," said Strober with a smile. "It's a company ship. What do you care? They'll give you another one. You're Durt Larson. There's a thousand pilots standing in line behind you, just waiting to take on your route and recreate your legend. What about Truman here? I'm sure he saves your ass on a regular basis working his engineering magic. He deserves something more than the pittance of a pension the company promises, presuming he even makes it that far. I know the company accountants aren't immune from what they call their culture of efficiency."

He said those last words through tight lips, the words dripping with sarcasm, his voice almost a hiss, his good natured banter abruptly turned foul. Then he broke back into a grin.

"It's my special gift to you. You got a girl? You got a dream? Sure you do. We all do. We spend our whole lives chasing those things. But most of us are technicians. Working stiffs. We'll slave our lives away waiting for a break and dreaming what we'll do and how we'll handle it when it comes. Ever win the lottery? Today's your day."

Durt looked directly into his eyes. He saw no animosity whatsoever. Strober was sincere and believed each and every word he was saying. Actually, there was a lot of truth in what he said. His eyes shifted to Truman who was watching him curiously. At least one thing was right. Truman did pull his butt out of some tight squeezes now and again. He figured that was the standard relationship between most pilots and engineers. He did owe Truman a recurring debt of gratitude that he could never really repay. His gaze shifted back to Strober.

"That actually explains a number of things," said Durt, "so I have to thank you."

Strober tilted his head slightly, waiting for the expected capitulation.

Durt's fist caught him in the left corner of his jaw. Strober crumpled, unconscious before he hit the deck. Truman jumped back, startled.

"What the hell was that?" asked Truman, suddenly out of breath.

"That, my friend, is the heart of our inventory issue."

"I thought the two of you were just joking around."

"I wish it were that simple. No joke. But first things first. You're head of security, so get some restraints on him before he comes around."

Truman looked at him quizzically, searching his memory. "OK. But we've never had any use for them before. I guess they have to be around here somewhere."

"If we did our pre-flight," said Durt, the emphasis on the "we" in the sentence, his head nodded forward as if playing Truman's mother. "If *we* did our pre-flight properly, *we'd* know where onboard restraints are."

Truman's face reflected a moment of clarity. He said nothing, but turned quickly, passing the hatch control console and quickly passing his hand in front of an equipment locker a meter away from the external hatch. It looked more like a bench seat than a locker, but inside were tools, spare parts, and safety gear that came out quickly and randomly as Truman found the bottom.

Durt watched Strober's eyes blink and his arm move as his senses began to return.

"Truman," said Durt.

"On it," replied Truman, unwrapping a plastic-wrapped package and reading the label as he walked back toward Durt and the prone Strober.

"Leg restraints. One each. Composite steel. Mechanical lock," then added his own update. "Never used."

He discarded the plastic on the deck and deftly clamped the metal claws around Strober's ankles, pulling the mechanical key out with a flourish over his head and stepping back a pace. Strober sat up, his weight braced on his hands behind him, and looked at Truman's handiwork, then up at Truman. He smiled.

***

"I want you to light them up. So when I tell you, initiate the pulse-cannon. The EMP will weaken them, and that will knock out most of their systems. I need full power on the shot. No shields. Everything we have. Aimed—and discharged—directly at that bird. We're turning it into dust."

He stood before the control console of their so-called security vessel. Watching control screens and energy levels over the shoulder of the seated pilot, he anticipated the shot with tight-lipped anticipation.

The pilot turned and looked at him, eyes wide, a look of supreme surprise painted across his face.

"But that wasn't the plan you discussed with Strober. We're supposed to wait for his signal from the shuttle, just like last time."

The man who stood behind him smiled slightly, but said nothing. He really needed to retain a more sophisticated class of pilot, he thought. *This kid is annoying, even if he is a competent pilot, and he's clueless to boot.*

"New plan," he responded. "Just do what I say when I say it."

He now knew two things for certain. There was no honor among thieves, and he was about to become a rich one.

***

Durt released his grip on Strober and pushed himself backward on the cargo bay deck, letting out a huge breath of air, almost whistling as it left his mouth. He and Truman faced the sitting Srober, the rigid metallic restraints both grabbing his legs and keeping them apart. They weren't designed to allow walking like chains that might allow small steps. The only way to move in these was to swing one foot while the other was planted, or hop, of course, neither of which Strober was doing right now. He sat grinning on the deck, his legs before him, his arms behind, propping himself up.

"Really, gentlemen. This isn't necessary at all. But I don't mind," said Strober. "We have a little business to conduct, and each of us will be on our respective ways, each one of us leaving with what we want."

Durt stood up and turned to Truman who stood behind him. "What do you make of this? He seems pretty confident that we'll offer him something he's interested in. I'm pretty sure my fist told him no."

Truman looked past Durt to Strober sitting behind him. "I don't like it. Not even a bit. Look at that grin. We haven't heard the whole story. Not even close."

Durt nodded. "You're right about that, Truman. But let me take a guess. Strober, tell me how I'm doing. He turned back to Truman. "Strober here," he said, nodding to their prisoner. "Stro. Do you mind if I call you that?"

Strober closed his eyes and smiled again.

"Stro has found a ready market, a lucrative market, for company property. The Raven here is not the newest vessel on the market and has her quirks, her personality. Those little things we do here to keep our lady in the air. Things that are routine to us. Things we're comfortable with. Those sleek looking VIP transports and executive shuttles are ten times the ship of this one. In fact, the company doesn't even purchase this class of ship anymore, so why the fuss and the excitement over a ship only its crew could love?"

Truman looked at him, a slight squint as he considered the question. "It's the field drive isn't it?"

"Exactly. These things will last forever. Now take the newer models. They're fast and they're sleek and they look like they should, but they're quirky, too. They don't always work when they should. They can't always depart when they're supposed to. Bottom line, they're unreliable. No, his buyer likes these field drives. In fact, I'd bet that at the core of that security vessel that stopped us is the twin of what we've got here in the Raven."

"Because of the monopoly," said Truman, nodding.

"Because of the monopoly. The company keeps a tight reign on this technology. You can use it, but you've got to pay for it. Everything reverts back to the good of the company. The good of the human race," he said, rolling his eyes in sarcasm. "So Stro here has a buyer who buys ships with crew payoffs. While they may be our wildest dreams, they're actually getting a discount."

Truman watched Strober with renewed interest as Durt continued.

"Now I don't know verbatim what the company policy is on obsolescence, but when one of these ships goes missing or is reported crashed or abandoned, they happily make their reports, adjust their accounting entries and smile because their maintenance costs just went down. They don't ask too many questions because they don't have to. They run contract crews on pretty much every transit. Certainly, those of us with the established records get first crack at whatever comes our way, but I'm betting you could fly this ship through their accounting standards."

He glanced down at Strober. "How am I doing?"

"You're right on track, Durt. Your company's thirst for efficiency is ravenous, and the size of its operations have allowed a fundamental flaw in its execution. I ride into town, make an offer you can't refuse. You report your ship damaged, missing or inoperable. I enrich your financial status, and you go on about your business. Your company is happy because their modernization goals are on track, ahead of schedule even."

Durt walked around behind Strober, lost in thought, rubbing his chin. "No," he said. "There's something more. There has to be another motivation. I can see the development of a new shipping enterprise, but I just don't think there's that much opportunity. The market's not that big. What could you possibly do with a hundred of these ships?"

Truman looked at him uncomprehendingly, apparently stuck on the vision of a hundred Ravens.

"Unless," he said and paused with sudden concern. "Unless they're being militarized."

He looked into Strober's now serious eyes. Strober was no longer smiling. He stared straight ahead into Durt's legs and Durt knew he was right.

"Jesus," said Truman. "We're sitting here, pants down, and we allow a pirate in a security getup onboard. Meanwhile, we've got a ship next door with a loaded gun pointed at our naked butt?"

Strober nodded slowly.

"Maybe we deserve what we get for being so sloppy. But if that's the case, I think I'm getting my licks in now." Truman turned toward the open equipment locker. "I bet I have something here that can wipe that smile off his face."

Durt ignored Truman's sorting and threatening commotion, working through what weaponized could mean.

"Modified construction equipment, yeah?" he asked the sitting Strober. "Maybe the SK20s?"

Strober nodded again. "21s actually. But right on the money, Durt. Right on the money. And that's really what we're talking about here. We have nothing but the best intentions for you and your crew. Whatever you've always wanted is just around the corner. I'm your new best friend."

"Not mine," said Truman, advancing with a manual hatch wrench in hand and a scowl on his face. "You're not a friend of mine at all."

Strober's even face now bore a look of concern, and he began retreating the best he could, sliding his hands and butt backward across the cargo deck.

Durt held up his hand in Truman's direction. "Hang on Truman. First we get to the bottom of this. He tells us what he knows. Then you can give him a makeover. I highly doubt they'll destroy the prize they've worked so carefully to capture."

Truman stopped short, his ears listening to Durt, but his eyes locked on Strober.

Durt turned to face Truman and smiled. "Well played, friend. I always get a kick out of Badass Engineer."

Durt watched Truman's understated expression and detected the beginning of a rare smirk. In an instant the smirk vanished, replaced with wide-eyed surprise.

Durt felt the emotion of surprise surge through him, too. The edge of a blade pressed against his neck. He hadn't heard or felt Strober, but there he was still the same. He was impressed. That was some kind of skill—slight of hand, or maybe slight of foot was a better description. Strober stood directly behind him, arm looped around his neck with blade placed expertly above his jugular. Struggle meant damage and probably death in these circumstances, he thought. Some situations were won by physical strength. This was not one of them. This required finesse and careful consideration.

Truman shook his head side-to-side, worry and dread seeping from every pore in his face.

Durt spoke. He said the only thing he could say. "Well played, Stro. I'm impressed. You now have my full attention. You were talking about financial compensation?"

Strober seemed almost apologetic. "This has never happened before, so you'll have to excuse my improvisation. I've had heated discussions before, but none have come this close to spilling blood. Not really necessary, so we'll have to do things nice and slow for a few minutes, so we all walk away from this. He shifted uncomfortably behind Durt in his leg restraints. "Let's start over again. First, Truman, I'll need you to remove these things from my legs."

Durt nodded his assent with his eyes, and Truman moved behind Strober, using his key to free Strober's legs and tossing the restraints behind him.

"Next, and we're going to do this slowly, I'm going to release you, Durt, and then maybe we can have a smoke and talk." Strober rotated Durt around, his cold steel knife flush against Durt's neck, until they both faced Truman. "Very slowly now, I'm going to back off. No sudden movements."

He was lying, of course. In an instant he'd put a good two meters between himself and Durt's back. Durt's hand immediately went to his neck as he turned to face Strober. No injury. The knife had not broken the flesh.

Strober stood before them, a blade the length of his foot in his right hand, his body in a fighting stance. Now he moved slowly. He slid the knife back into its holster inside a fold of his flight suit with his right hand and dug into a pocket with his left, producing a pack of cigarettes.

"Smoke?" he said, tossing the pack to Durt.

Durt caught the pack with his right hand, flipped the top open with his thumb and with a deft, practiced motion, pulled a cigarette from its container with his lips, using the bottom of the pack to light it before passing the pack to Truman.

Truman waved it off. "So talk," he said.

Strober nodded. "OK. I'll tell you what I know."

Durt tossed the pack back to Strober who caught it mid-air. "You're pretty close on your rundown of my operation. But I'm less a pirate than an agent really. I don't know why these ships are so valuable to our client. I don't ask. What I do know is that my relationship with them is strictly business, and it's based on my hatred of the company. This huge Casino empire knows no bounds, and this is my contribution. I'm well compensated, as you might guess, but that's not why I do it. I hate this corporation with every molecule inside of me, and this is my way of doing something about it."

"So let me ask you this," asked Durt from the corner of his mouth that wasn't occupied by the cigarette. "What if you find a crew who won't give up the ship?"

He squinted as the smoke curled into his eye.

"Never happened before. Nineteen times. Nineteen ships," said Strober. "I always found a price point that would make all of us happy."

"Humor me. Just say that you did."

"Fair enough. If I met my match and couldn't make a deal, I'd walk away. Not that it would make a lot of difference in the end. The people I work for are what you'd call single-minded. If I fail, there's someone else on my heels."

Durt noticed the effect the cigarette was having on Strober. The adrenaline was wearing off and his stance was now relaxed. He felt it himself. That cellular healing that now ran through his bloodstream always brought with it a mental calming as well.

"In fact," continued Strober, "I'd be surprised if there wasn't someone waiting on Midway to welcome you and relieve you of your ship. Knowing that, it makes a lot more sense to come to what I like to call a mutually desirable accord."

Durt recalled the corporate advisory he'd received as part of his pre-flight download. HQ knew they were having issues with the ships in their fleet inventory, but they weren't sure why. Ships reported navigation troubles or propulsion issues, then they'd just not show up at their destinations. Search vessels were dispatched, but without success. Hard to analyze engineering issues without an example. They suspected hyper-gate issues, but repeated unmanned testing verified the integrity of the transport gates. Ultimately, they'd discover the truth. It was just a matter of time. In their realms of efficiency, this had slipped through. Corporate thinkers believed everyone thought like them, and they were skilled at optimizing their business operations to satisfy their investors. Apparently they were equally poor at anticipating the breadth of human invention and the impact of their own efficiencies.

"Alright, Strober, say we do believe you. Which I don't. But I think it might amuse me to hear your pitch. Go ahead. Impress me."

Strober smiled again. It was that same, I-knew-you'd-come-around smile he'd worn a few minutes before. He was genuinely happy—that was something you couldn't hide, not from Durt anyway.

But Strober's pitch was not something they'd hear in the cargo bay. As Strober took another drag on his cigarette, the trio was suddenly plunged into darkness.

4

COUNCIL

THE INSIDE OF THE PRISON COMPLEX was as bare and utilitarian as the outside was sleek. Apparently the structure's architect exhausted his vision on the elegant exterior, that, ironically, almost none would ever appreciate. Inside, the vision left a gaping creative void. The walls and cells were a singular grey color, if grey was even a color, rather than the lack of one.

Grinder's arrangements for the council were in place, and he met Simms at the entrance to the common area of the main prison complex. It was a circular area, hundreds of meters across, with railing and cells towering above it like spectator seats at a sporting event. He noted that at the opposite end, the band equipment remained, instruments leaned against equipment at haphazard angles, waiting for their performers to return. Band members had joined the assembled crowd, their rehearsal curtailed by the council. The arena now transformed into a forum for inspection and the ambient conversations echoed faintly now within the grey circular structure, magnifying every sound and sending it along virtually unhindered. No secrets in this prison. The central arena was devoid of anything other than its murmuring human occupants. Their footsteps punctuated the spoken sounds and brought them to silence as he and Simms approached.

"Six today, Wiz."

It was Grinder's standard intro to kick off the council. He ran things. Everyone knew Simms counted on Grinder to complete the details of his various biddings.   He told Grinder that it freed his creative mind and allowed him a real sense of focus when he needed it. Sometimes Grinder conducted the council, but today, Simms was taking a personal hand in the proceedings.

"All have passed their medical and debrief quarantine. They've been briefed on what to expect. Pretty standard. Scared shitless."

Simms nodded his assent as he and Grinder made their way toward the assembled crowd. The group formed a loose semi-circle and left a barrier of five meters or so between them and a straight, evenly spaced line of six prisoners. The six—four men and two women—stood rock-still, arms at their sides, eyes unblinking and staring directly forward. Unseeing, as they faced the group of prisoners.

Simms made his way to the front of the crowd and deliberately walked the length of the line. Grinder trailed, pausing briefly to inspect each individual. Simms said nothing, and the crowd behind him kept its silence. Some had crowded to the front to watch the spectacle. Others were content to listen. With all the time they had on their hands, there would be plenty of time to see them face-to-face later. That was just the way life was on the inside.

At the end of the line, Simms turned and walked back behind the prisoners. Slowly and carefully making his observations, only the sound of his echoing footsteps broke the silence as he made his way along the line. As he rounded the end and began his second pass, he stopped short suddenly, peering closely into the face of the second in line before taking a step backward and placing himself before a slim young man.

"Tell me about this one," said Simms, not removing his gaze from the man.

"This is Wa Velen," said Grinder, "He goes by 'Vee.' He's the odd one of the bunch. The rest are fairly low level thieves and hackers, each one I'm sure, with a foolproof plan to take their own slice of Casino pie."

Laughter and comments erupted from the crowd behind and quickly fell silent as Simms raised his left arm.

Simms watched the man's face turn from stone attention to fear and disgust. The comfortable temperature that hung over the arena didn't help hide the line of sweat that appeared on the prisoner's forehead as he caught his breath.

Standing before him, Simms' right hand was on his hip, but the end of his raised left ended in a stump. The slim kid swallowed hard, the icy look of dread tempering his expression.

"Vee doesn't have a record of crime against the Casinos," said Grinder. "He's clean. We haven't seen anything like this in a while. Apparently the arrest and processing papers are valid, so it's not mistaken identity. The in-processing documents don't say anything that would justify his being here, so that only leaves a couple possibilities."

Simms nodded slowly, now holding his stump in his right hand.

"A sinner or a saint? Which is it, Vee?"

Vee moved his lips to speak, but was cut off like the crowd before him with a raised stump again.

"That doesn't require an answer. Anybody in your position here under your conditions? I'm not sure I'd believe anything you might say anyway."

He turned to Grinder. "It doesn't matter. In time, the truth will reveal itself. For now, take his hand."

***

An electrical arc sparked in the cargo hold, and Durt saw a flash of Strober's face for an instant before it went black again. He saw surprise. Confusion. The charge hung in the air and pulled the hair from his body.

"EMP," he heard Truman say behind him as emergency lighting flickered and lightly illuminated the bay. "Fucking pirate. Listen to me. Don't touch anything and get the hell into the passenger pod.

Flight boots insulate your feet, but we don't have gloves. Move!"

Durt moved instinctively toward the ladder to the deck above. Truman's even demeanor, that of an engineer with a problem to solve, was evident, but Durt heard the urgency and sensed an undertone of fear. That wasn't like Truman at all. Truman was the answer man, the option provider, the rock of logic in an ocean of uncertainty. If Truman was concerned, he had Durt's full attention. He was acutely aware and suddenly still, taking in what Truman had already processed. EMP, electromagnetic pulse, and a big one, too. *Nothing else could play such havoc with the ship's fields, but from the other ship?* He thought for a second, how would he do it? That wasn't something the SK-21s could do. He wasn't familiar with the 21s, but that didn't seem like a function miners would need in their excavation efforts. *No, it was—. Son of a bitch. It was on the shuttle and docked to the skin of the Raven. It had to be.* Strober had brought the thing over with him, and the exterior hyper-gate ice had served as an insulator to keep the EMP's power inside the ship. *What damage had it caused? Why? Would Strober really damage the ship he was attempting to take?* He couldn't make sense of it. Truman was moving forward in the dim light.

"I'll go first," said Truman. "Keep shit-head in the middle. If he tries any of those fancy moves, just push him into something. His own handiwork will take him down. Strober, you say a word, and I'll do it myself."

Hands raised, cigarette still in his mouth, Strober fell in behind Truman as they made their way up the ship's ladder. The trio climbed with hands raised, moving slowly, oddly.

Strober protested. "This is not my handiwork. This is not my plan. I want a functioning ship. A ship with damaged circuits is worth about as much as—"

He didn't finish his sentence. Truman cut him off. "Shut up," he said, and gave him a solid shove. Arms flailing for balance, Strober caught the top of the ladder handrail, and a bright spark arced over his hand shocking his body into a frozen paralyzing stance. Durt caught him as he lost consciousness and fell backward.

Durt shot Truman a questioning glance.

Truman shrugged. "He was pissing me off."

***

The door to the passenger pod slid open, and Nik watched with curiosity as Truman entered. Behind him came Durt, back-first, the limp arms of a third man she'd never seen before, the security inspector, she presumed, extended loosely on either side of his shoulders, his boots following, dragging on the deck behind him as Durt's awkward back steps pulled him into the pod.

This can't be good, she thought, moving quickly forward without thinking to examine the prone form.

"Is he dead?" asked Nik.

"Not yet," said Truman, standing over Nik's kneeling posture. "But when he wakes up, I may change that."

All eyes locked on Durt.

Nik looked up from her kneeling position on the deck beside the security official. The eyes of the other two passengers stared back at her, brows furrowed or heads tilted. Bam and Jata looked uncomprehendingly at the scene before them. The access door behind them opened, interrupting their surprise again as Guyal made his way into the pod, hands held up, still hesitant to touch anything. On the deck beside her, the man in the security suit blinked twice. He moved his neck slightly as he began to come around.

"What the hell did you do, Durt?" asked Nik. "You can't just knock out security inspectors when you don't like what they have to say. You're in some real trouble now."

"We're all in some real trouble now," said Durt, "but not for the reasons you might think. And you might not believe it, but I would never knock out a legitimate security inspector. They're our primary line of defense between the law and lawlessness. This, however," and he gave Strober's shoulder a light kick for emphasis, "this is not a legitimate inspector. This is a fake one. An imposter. A wolf in a sheep's flight suit. This is Strober Uti. His friends call him Stro. I'd like to jack him out of this ship, but before I do, I need some information out of him."

"If he's not legit, what are we even still doing here?" asked Nik, examining the quickly reviving man. He was lithe and fit, his nose maybe a bit too big for the rest of his face, but there was some grace and dignity to its profile. His eyes were a dark shade of brown and while his flight suit said security, his hair was a little longer than the security inspectors she'd seen before. Cops, security professionals, bodyguards, the majority of them anyway, had that cop look. The short hair and air of authority always exuded a sense of power. This one had something different. Not that there wasn't power there, but it was something else. He wasn't clean shaven, but he wasn't shaggy either. Handsome with a tinge of sadness in the eyes. "Let's just go," she urged. "We can turn him in to actual security forces on Midway."

"It's a little more complicated than that," said Durt.

"I agree with Nik." It was Bam. Looking even slimmer than before in a skin-tight T-shirt, he walked toward the group gathered near the door. "I've got business. I'm sure we've all got business on Midway. We're wasting time with this clown."

"So here's the complicated part," said Durt. "Strober here brought us a little present aboard his shuttle, an EMP."

"A what?" asked Nik.

"An electromagnetic pulse. A magnetic bomb, really."

Nik heard Bam let out a low whistle.

"He detonated it five minutes ago," Durt continued. "And it's paralyzed the ship. It's anybody's guess how soon we can assess the damage, much less get ourselves back on course."

"I didn't feel anything," said Nik. The other passengers nodded in unison.

"You wouldn't inside here. The stasis pod has its own field generator and is sheltered from pretty much everything. That's why we're all in here. The rest of the ship is still hyper-charged and, as you can see," he nodded at Strober, "a bit dangerous for us to be wandering around and bumping into things."

"But won't we have company through the hyper-gate, the next jumpers behind us?" This time it was Jata who spoke from behind the group, half standing, half leaning against her stasis pod. "We can report it, make repairs and those on a tight schedule can hitch a ride."

"Theoretically, yes. We'll have another jumper behind us in about an hour. But there's more. Strober's come aboard with a proposition. He wants to buy the ship."

Nik looked down at Strober, now fully awake. She watched him prop himself up on his elbows and stretch his neck from side to side.

"More accurately," continued Durt, "he wants to pay us off to look the other way while he takes the ship. Says he's acting on behalf of someone with ridiculously deep pockets."

"That doesn't make sense," said Nik. "Why would you go through all the trouble to get your hands on a ship and then do this to it?"

"Exactly. And that's why he's still here with us and not fried like an egg or floating outside the ship. According to him, he's been quite successful at what he calls negotiating for ships. And I saw his face when the EMP went off. There are some things your face can't hide, and that was one. I don't think he set off the EMP. He was as surprised as I was. But you know what? He knows exactly who set it off."

Strober spoke from the floor, shaking his head. "That son of a bitch. I gave him everything. He's too smart to pull something like this."

"Don't tell me. You've been usurped by your apprentice pirate," said Durt.

"Get him on the net. I can talk him out of this."

"No you can't," said Durt. "No, I think from his point of view, he knows everything he wants to know from you. I think he's going to report an accident with you as the unfortunate victim. Body disintegrated. Strober was getting old. Not the same man he used to be."

Nik felt a shiver of fear as she realized what Durt was saying. Somehow, the security vessel needed to see Strober dead. With him here in their midst, that probably meant they were expendable as well.

"But we're safe here in the pod, right?" the beginnings of a desperate tone tinged her voice. "That's what you said. We can just wait it out here. Right?" Nik's sentence ended with an almost pleading tone, as if she knew there was more to the story, and she was afraid to hear it.

"Do you know what SK-20s are?"

Oddly enough, she did know. Of the millions of pieces and parts that go into world building, SK-20 was a name that stuck out, tagged by the noticeably huge price tags from financial statements she'd reviewed. They weren't used on New Manhattan, but they had something to do with raw mining, primarily in the asteroid belt. "They're big-ticket items used in mining operations."

"Exactly. SK-20s generate superheated blasts that turn solid mountains into piles of rubble. For decades, asteroid mining has been an awkward, inefficient procedure, but because it was automated and excavation was done by mining bots, there wasn't a lot of incentive to modernize. But with New Manhattan sales starting to catch on, the volume of those sales is limited now by the pace of construction, which is, ultimately, all driven by how quickly ore can be transformed into settlement ships, those huge flying building blocks. So, in the name of efficiency," and here Nik watched his eyes roll and his head shake, "like everything else in the company, they've been working on the SK-20's little sister, the SK-21, a real step forward in the mining business model."

As Durt paused for a breath, Bam's voice joined the conversation. His area of expertise, Nik realized. "Our estimates now are that our through-flow with the 21s will more than double, maybe triple, once we get the mechanics of New Manhattan's settlement ships reprogrammed and migrated to the Midway system."

The whole mining conversation seemed oddly out of place for Nik. "I'm not following you. Why does any of this matter to us here?"

"Follow me just a little longer," said Durt. "The 21s are efficient because they're able to generate the same energy as the 20s, but they're focused. They don't heat and blast, they scan and cut. They use a focused beam to cut blocks to their exact specification, skipping the disintegration, sifting and compression steps. It's a lot more complicated than that, but that's the gist of it. Our problem today is that, as far as I can tell, the galaxy's finest pirate has a mutiny on his hands, his ambitious lieutenant is now in control of some kind of hybrid patrol craft that's got a 21 mounted on it, and he's taking this opportunity to promote himself—by disintegrating his captain and anyone nearby."

***

The quizzical look on Vee's face melted into fear. The phrase, *Take his hand,* could be taken a couple of different ways, including to actually hold his hand, but with a man standing before him with a stump for a hand, Grinder watched the intended meaning make itself clear.

At first, Vee's response was whispered. "No" escaped from his lips as the realization became apparent in his mind. He repeated it once, then more quickly, each syllable uttered in a tone rising both in pitch and volume.

"No. no. no. no. NO!"

He was screaming it as two of the prisoners detached from the now silent crowd, and one on either side, restrained him by the arms.

Any normal human would have pitied the poor soul destined for mutilation as he was dragged, stumbling and resisting across the open arena, his protests echoing back from the surrounding cells that towered above the now dispersing crowd. But Simms was not a normal person. Pity was never an emotion he'd had any use for. When he needed something, he took it.

Grinder knew the Casinos had taken a lot from him. And Simms always swore he was going to have it back. With interest. That was no secret.

A few minutes later Simms and Grinder stood alone in the center of the circular complex. From above they looked like two fleas in a flea circus. "I know what you're thinking," said Simms. "Don't. You're with me or you're not, and you'll be well rewarded for your loyalty. Make it clean. I need him cool, clear and calculating in a week. I need at least two solid weeks of planning time."

Grinder shook his head slowly. "A week is pushing it. He's just a kid." But his tone changed as he reconsidered, reading Simms' face. "But a week should be fine. A week it is. Two things I need, Wiz. If you can mention them to the warden when you interface this afternoon, I'd appreciate it."

Simms raised his eyebrows without a word, looking almost annoyed at the request.

We're out of fabric. We'll be creative, but we'll only make it through about half of the new arrivals. This isn't the first time we've made the request, but this is the first time we're actually thread-less.

Simms nodded and Grinder watched him smile, a slight smile, but a smile nonetheless. He was sure Simms was up to something. That was Simms. The white material was easy to come by on Earth, a real commodity and a big business for some guild or family. But here on Claustrom, it was non-existent.   For whatever reason, Simms or maybe the Casino suppliers had opted not to keep a full inventory. What that probably meant was a full restock on the next inbound shuttle. Yes, he thought to himself, that was what would happen, but why?

"And?"

"Also, we're overdue for a circus. It's that season. After today's review, and all the other reviews just like it, we really need something to recharge the group. I think a circus announcement would be just the thing."

Simms nodded. "Yes. I think you're right, Grinder. It *is* time for a circus."

Circuses were one of the few mental welfare relief valves provided by the prison system. The virtual technology from Midway coupled with trained human performers made for spectacular entertainment. This was the bone the Casinos threw them occasionally. With it, the show brought not only performers and staff, but other opportunities as well. Simms didn't keep a woman here in prison, though there were plenty of willing and likely candidates. Not that he didn't enjoy the company of women, just the opposite, Grinder knew. But for Simms, women came with a price tag, and that tag was usually distraction. There was, and always would be, a time for women, Simms liked to say, but Claustrom's obligations meant distraction in the form of a female relationship was not in the cards. The circus, however, in addition to bringing a superb entertainment spectacle, would also be accompanied by staff, some of whom would serve a conjugal role. Others were retained for their Casino debts, and some came just for the party. The arena complex often served as the venue for the devolved after-parties, the prisoners fulfilling their appetites for whatever their collective minds could invent.

"Wiz, I'm off to have a word with Vee. Anything else you need?"

"Come see me later this evening. I'll let you know what the Warden says. Also, I've got some other particulars you'll need to know about."

Grinder nodded his assent without speaking. He left Simms alone with his thoughts in the arena. *There weren't many like Simms. Always anticipating. Always watching.* He was Grinder, Simms' defense against any adversary. But, he wondered, as he crossed the arena, *Who was his defense against Simms?*

***

Guyal's eyes told his story. Nik watched his wide-eyed expression reflect surprise, dismay and fear at Durt's dismal pronouncement. Of all of them facing a death sentence in space, he was probably the one with the most to lose. Navigating the Raven and any other vessel he could sign on with kept his numerous children in private school, and his wife installed comfortably in society. He was as good-natured as they came, and according to their brief conversation during the pre-flight preps, a conversation filled with family pictures and tales of outings, he played the breadwinner and fun father whenever he got the chance. He didn't seem to spend much time with his children, but when he did, he, like his wife, had a problem with saying no. But that's just what he was saying now. She watched the word form silently on his lips. The thought of abandoning his family by dying in space seemed to terrify him. Ironic, she thought, for a guy who spent the better part of his life navigating across the galaxy. But she felt it herself, too. She didn't have near the equities that Guyal had to lose, and she always wondered if her final day might be in the coldness of space. She just hoped it was quick and painless. Dying, for her wasn't going to be a problem. It was the fear of dying and the curiosity of what lay on the other side that gnawed at her mind. *Was she closer to heaven here? Would her soul know how to find its way home, or would she be stuck in some kind of space purgatory, wandering endlessly through the galaxy looking for heaven?*

Durt raised his arms. "Let me finish. I know all this is a shock to you, and it sounds pretty grim. I can't argue with that, but if there's one thing I've learned, there's an elegant solution to every problem. If we can't think of it in time."

"Sounds to me like what they really want is this piece of shit." It was Truman being Truman who motioned to Strober as he spoke. "Let's give it to them."

"Yes and no," said Durt. "You're right in thinking that what this guy wants is not this ship, but the position. I think he wants to be the new Strober. And he's willing to sacrifice this prize," he said, stomping the deck with his boot, "for that opportunity. But what he can't have is any witnesses to his mutiny. Say we send him back in the shuttle. We're still an open loop and a threat to his enterprise. When that next jumper comes through, we can't be here to report them. He couldn't allow it."

Nik thought for a second. "What if we give them what they want? What if we say yes to their proposal? We can repair this ship and give it to them, right? See if they want both Strober and the ship. How could they turn that down?"

Durt's eyes narrowed and Nik could see the thoughts in expression forming a plan. His head nodded slightly. He had something. His rapid-fire instructions followed without a pause.

"We don't have much time at all, and things are going to happen quickly. Listen closely. I need everyone to do what I say. Don't ask questions. Work quickly, and we may have a way out of this. Truman, I need the shuttle's pilot recorder set to broadcast." He looked down at the deck. "Strober, you're with Truman. Make your best case for calm. I don't care what you tell him, but keep it going. Tell them we agree. We're giving up the ship. There's no reason to be hostile. He can have everything." He shifted his gaze again. "Jata. Go with Truman and Strober. Keep an eye on Strober. He's got a blade and he knows how to use it. Watch your ass." Shifting gaze again, Durt continued. "Guyal. We're at the very edge of non-lethal charges. See how soon you can get comms rebooted. I don't expect a miracle, but the EMP was probably designed for a directional attack, so those functions should be intact in the shuttle. He turned to Bam. "Bam, I need to use your welcome cargo. I know they're supposed to be a part of your splash on Midway, but we need them unlocked and loaded onto the shuttle. I need you with me."

Bam nodded quickly. Nik was still trying to piece together whatever it was that Durt had planned, but Bam already understood. "They're yours."

"What about me?" asked Nik. "What do you need me to do?"

"Stay here," said Durt. He wasn't smiling. His expression and his face were strained with concern. "Stay here and pray."

5

Vee

THE KID'S CONFINEMENT CELL was just like all the others. Grey. Sparse. Practical. In the rear of one corner stood the toilet and dry shower, while the other was occupied by the desk and its built-in read projector. Prisoners had free access to an extensive library, and a good portion of the inmates spent their time watching, reading or listening to various works of literature and so-called literature. It was a closed system without transmit capabilities, as the last thing the prison wanted was to give any type of access, greater than what was required by law, to a community of hackers. Grinder thought that was probably a smart idea. The ancient network technology used by the library's system was hundreds of years old and was chosen specifically for its limited capability. Not that the inmates didn't test the system's limits. They did. But it didn't matter. Its restricted virtual borders made it impossible to access anything beyond its archive of books and films.

A bed with shelves and drawers built into the prison wall behind it rounded out the room. Sitting on the bed was Vee, alone and silent, his head in his hands. The door, like pretty much every door in the prison, was open. The prisoners had no place to run and only closed the doors for privacy now and again. The prison culture respected privacy, but craved and encouraged social interaction. Inmates wandered into any open door for advice, games, films, sex, or discussions on just about any topic in the galaxy. Unlike earth prisons, where violence, intimidation and power ruled, this prison was different by reason of its selective inmate population. The prisoners were not here for crimes of murder, rape and a long list of other primal violations of law, but for what Grinder considered crimes of ego.

Each inmate, at one time, believed he was smarter than the system. And for a time, each had been right. What they collectively couldn't anticipate, from their ego-centric point of view, was the patience and tenacity the system had for identifying them, tracking them down and ultimately placing them here. This was an amazing brain trust locked away in the middle of a desert on a restricted planet, he thought. *If someone ever figured a way to harness and harvest its creative power, it would be a bad day for—* He smiled to himself at that thought. *It was the Wiz who was doing that very thing. He was on his way now to make everyone's dreams come true.* Even if he never said that, that was the presumption of all who knew him well. *Help the Wiz and reap your reward.* Grinder knew he could be quite generous. But no one ever knew his plans or his ultimate goals, only their little piece.

Except for Vee today. His dream was not coming true, at least in his opinion. He looked up as Grinder entered his cell and closed the door behind him. The shaking fear that had gripped him before was replaced now by the look of resigned dread.

"Vee, I'm Grinder, and we need to talk."

"So talk." A tinge of insolence dripped from his response, but it sounded more like the dejected voice of a terminally ill patient yet to make peace with his diagnosis. His face said he couldn't be more than ten years away from his mother's home. Sheltered from the depths of human debasement and desires behind a virtual interface, whatever his talent was, it certainly was not human interaction or courage in battle. He was lithe and slim, but something in his eyes betrayed some superior knowledge or at least a presumption of knowledge.

"The Wiz is counting on you to do your part. There's something special about you."

"I'll tell you what's special," said Vee, his voice sharp. "He's going to cut off my fucking arm."

Grinder nodded. "

Let me tell you something about the Wiz. He's a man of his word. He does what he says he's going to do. If he says he's going to take your arm off, he means it. What he said was your hand, but I understand your concern."

"My concern? My CON-CERN?" he repeated, articulating each syllable. "I didn't do anything to deserve that kind of mutilation!"

"Vee, this is not about you. This is about him and about the larger us," said Grinder, extending his arms to indicate the entire prison community. "And whatever he has in store for us outweighs what he has in store for you, but ultimately, all of us, you included, will benefit from it."

Vee stared at him, saying nothing.

"For each of our crimes against society, we're stuck here at least for now. No one is going anywhere, and while we're here we don't do a lot. But we do two things well here on Claustrom. We wait, and we make prosciutto."

Now Vee was puzzled. "What, like ham?"

"Yes, it's like ham. But it's cured meat instead of cooked meat like you're probably used to. And unlike the fake stuff you find in Earth supermarkets, this "like ham" actually comes from the meat of pigs. So when we're not hanging around in this palace, we're killing, butchering, curing and packaging pig parts. Prosciutto isn't the only product that comes out of here, it's just the most notable. I know you've heard of Brecas."

Vee look up at him questioningly.

"Plate of the Gods?" he asked.

Grinder smiled. "So you've seen the advertisement. Yes, Brecas, the most exclusive meat in the Galaxy, sold on Earth, but produced primarily for those Midway and New Manhattan customers who can afford to pay their ridiculous prices. There's a unique combination of soil, vegetation and air on this planet that makes this meat like something you've never tasted. One of our little pleasures here. The name is actually an inside joke. It's an abbreviation of "Bred by Casinos," but we produce it, and if you put the accent on the first syllable instead of the second like they do in their fancy ads, it sounds like "break us," which is really why they've got us here in the first place.

"Real live pigs?" he asked, in near disbelief. "No way."

"Well, they don't live long once they get here. But yes. Real live pigs. No food manufacturing process. Nature does that for us here. If you grew up on Earth, you'd never know what you were missing, but once you taste this, you'd have a hard time not knowing the difference. Pigs are raised in the north country and transported down here. It's our job to convert those pigs into delicacies for the ultra rich."

Vee shook his head, his fear displaced by curiosity momentarily. Then it dissipated, and he put his head back into his hands and lapsed into silence.

Grinder watched him for a minute before continuing.

"So here's how I see it. The Wiz only gives each of us the pieces of information we need to know. We're all compartmentalized, so I don't have a clue to what he's planning. What I do know is, and this isn't of much comfort to you, but he really doesn't care about you or me or anyone else here. And that's not good or bad. It's just him. He has few, if any, emotions, so it doesn't bother him a bit to hack off your hand or take your eyes or whatever. But he always has a reason for the things he does, the decisions he makes. As for you, he sees you as either a strong ally or a serious threat, a spy, an undercover Casino cop. You're just a kid, and maybe one person in a million would think that you'd be able to pull that off. Probably not even him. But he is one in a million, so he may suspect you. Either way, it doesn't matter. If you are, he's sending you back to the Casinos as a sign, with his own personal brand. On the other hand," and he smiled at his unintended pun, "if you're not a spy, then you're here for something similar to what he's here for. Your record on arrival would reflect any charges of crimes against humanity or the Casinos. If it were humanity, you'd be on Earth. Since you're here, it's a good bet that you're some kind of threat either to the Casinos or New Manhattan, even if you haven't done anything. He truly understands that."

Again, Vee shook his head.

"I'm no kind of spy. I don't even have a clue on how to go about that. I think that's pretty obvious."

"Or too obvious. Nothing's obvious here. That's something a good spy might say."

"So if you're right, what does that mean?"

"Without your hand, you're useless on the pig production line. So it's really up to him how he would use you. Here's my guess "If you're a spy, you'll lose your hand and maybe more. If you're a hacker, you'll lose your hand but get it back."

Vee looked up quickly, his face asking the unanswered question.

"Get it back?"

"I know what you're thinking. Who could afford to have that done? Certainly not you or I, and certainly not here in prison."

"So how?"

"There's only one solution if all of those assumptions are right. I think we're breaking out, and you don't know it yet, but you're the key."

The surprise splashed across his face like ice water. "The key? I don't know the first thing about this place, much less breaking out of it. And that's the last thing I need, to be a wanted man. A wanted man without a hand."

"Let me ask you this. What are you in here for? What crime did you commit that would land you here in the middle of this desert wasteland like the rest of us?"

"I already told you. I didn't do anything."

"Right. In fact, nobody here did anything, either. We're all a bunch of misunderstood bastards. Mistaken identity. We're all the wrong guy."

"Look, I know that sounds tired, so let me say it in a different way. I didn't do anything—that I know of—that would get me sent to a place like this. And certainly nothing serious enough to get my hand chopped off."

"Now we're getting somewhere," said Grinder with a nod. "Given the fact that you are here and presuming you're *not* a case of mistaken identity, wouldn't you like to know the reason why? I'm thinking that deep down inside, you know exactly why you're here, or at least who put you here."

"You're wrong. I know less than you do. At least you've seen the file and, I'm guessing, the documentation that allows them the legal right to keep me here. I haven't seen shit but the inside of a prison cell and bad food for weeks now."

"Well, I have seen the file, but—"

Vee interrupted. "But as for knowing why I'm here. Yes, you're right. I'd like to know what landed me here. All I've ever done was do what other people asked me to do. I finish my work. And I always try to give a little bit more than I'm paid to do. It's something my father taught me."

Grinder pulled the chair away from the desk, pulled it over toward the bed and sat down. "Go on," he said.

"He said there's a billion people out there who can do everything I could do—and better. And the easiest way to distinguish myself was to do what was asked of me, then a little bit more. There was something about human nature that was undeniably drawn toward that little bit of something extra, he said, and whatever it was, it didn't matter how big or small—that sometimes the smallest little thing made the difference."

"Was he a programmer? A mechanic maybe?"

Vee shook his head. "Nah, he was a cook. He made pizzas. Always simple, but always good. There wasn't anything really special about them. I loved them, mostly because he made them, and I like pizza, but there was one thing that allowed him to out-sell every other pizza place in the city. His pizzas were just a bit larger than everyone else's. Not a lot. But enough. The others all had fancy marketing campaigns, and they were always reinventing the shape and the ingredients. But not him. He had a few signature pizzas that he never changed. His marketing fund went into extra dough for bigger pizzas. That was it. That simple."

Pizza. Real flour ground from wheat, thought Grinder. There was something that would make your mouth water. None of this molecular manipulation for near-Earth food, but no-kidding, actual food made from Earth-grown plants. What he wouldn't give for that.

***

Nik lifted her head from her hands. Yes, just like Durt had asked, she'd said a prayer for all of them. Nothing better than a word to the divine when death was such a real possibility. She wondered if it had done any good. At the very least, she thought, it couldn't have hurt anything. The stasis pod was now abandoned. Actually, she realized, it wasn't, as she caught the form of Guyal out of the corner of her eye, his back to her in a recessed corner of the pod. It was some kind of secure panel that she hadn't paid much attention to, but it now had Guyal's full attention.

"Guyal, aren't you going to Control and do a reboot? Do you need some help?"

He turned his head to answer, but his hands continued to work whatever controls they were engaged with. "Actually, I am going to Control. I'm just getting there remotely," he said as he worked. "This ship is set up with its own lifeboat—this pod not only protects us, we can pilot it around in an emergency. Give me a minute, and I'll show you."

Nik knew little of ship construction and contingency design, but it made sense. She wasn't sure she understood the risks involved with what they were facing, but Guyal seemed pretty confident, even if Durt wasn't. Maybe she'd just been lucky, but she'd never had even the hint of anything out of the ordinary in all her space flights. Pilots briefed what would happen, and it did. No questions. No worries. The fear she felt now gripped her unreasonably. *What else didn't she know? How many times before had she been on the edge of dying and not even had a clue?* "Ladies and gentlemen, we're experiencing a minor delay." That was a pretty normal pilot advisory that she'd heard regularly for years. Yes. She was now experiencing a delay, but there wasn't anything minor about it. She wondered how often those words had disguised some actual danger she'd been oblivious to. This had to be the feeling pilots had. They knew every little flight detail. They had to as a general responsibility—as part of their position as pilots. *Wow. No thanks on that one.* Nik was good at a couple of things. Numbers was one, she thought. And sex. She should stick to what she was good at. This, someone else's concern, had now become hers. She closed her eyes tightly and took a couple of deep breaths. *Whatever happened, it was going to happen quickly*, she told herself, *so just tough it out.* She wasn't doing anyone any good by worrying.

"There. That's it," she heard Guyal say from his recessed position in the pod. "You can come have a look if you want."

She did. She made her way past the circle of stasis units. There was no corner in this end of the pod. The odd angled wall that formed the back of the area was now open with some type of a lighted console. Guyal was overflowing one of the two seats that now extended vertically from the deck. He motioned to the other.

"Have a seat. I should have full control established here in a second, and we can call up that ship and see if anyone answers."

The monitor before them flashed through a number of system screens, displaying ship schematics, system updates and statuses. Guyal waved his hands before the screen as if conducting an orchestra. Reports and diagrams in various colors popped up before him. Some he read. Others he tossed with a flick of his hand.

"I normally do this with the nav-helmet in Control," he said, "but this works just as well. Sometimes it's the only exercise you get as a navigator. And there it is."

The screen stopped its flurry of motion and displayed a tiny purple circle. Guyal used his hands to direct the circle out of its two-dimensional display and into the space before them where it floated, rotating slowly. "That's not an actual image, as you can see. We can't get visual until we get rid of the hyper-gate ice, but it's a model based on the transponder signature, and that's who we want to talk to." He pushed it back with his hand to its place on the 2D vertical screen.

"Security vessel, this is Raven. Request status." He paused and tilted his head, gazing upward, anticipating a response. Silence. He looked at Nik, shrugged and repeated himself. "Security vessel, this is Raven. Request status."

Again, the pair waited in silence.

"If the transmitter's damaged, we may not have enough signal strength to reach them," said Guyal. He turned to his side and passed his hand over the comm panel mounted on the pod's wall. "Durt, it's Guyal. Systems are rebooted, but looks like some damage to our transmit capability."

Durt's voice crackled from the control panel before them. "Raven, Durt here aboard security shuttle. Last transmission garbled. Try text."

Nik watched Guyal make a slight motion with his hand and repeat the message. The letters of his words appeared before them in green floating text and scrolled from left to right. Again the pair waited.

"Raven. Message received," came the scrolling text reply in the blue shade of an incoming message. "Do you have audio receive capability?"

"Affirmative," answered Guyal.

"Roger. Try all possible hailing channels with the security vessel using your text capability. Tell them we're on our way, that no company ship is worth dying for."

Nik looked sharply at Guyal, disbelief in her voice. "He's not going over there is he?"

Guyal made no response to her question. He repeated the message, and his hands were in motion again, the green message scrolling continuously as his fingers directed the words out through available channels."

What the hell was Durt thinking? Nik tried to use the logical part of her numerical brain to find some sense in what he had said. *Tell them we're on our way.* That could only mean one thing in her mind. Durt had got it in his mind that he had to go over and reason with these criminals. *What kind of person would actually listen to him? And who on Earth would disable a ship, then listen to reason? No one. But they weren't on Earth, were they?* Rules seemed to be different out here, she knew. But what did she know of criminals? To the best of her knowledge, she'd never met one. Not one as brazen as this, anyway. Maybe they thought differently. Maybe they didn't think at all. *What was Durt's intention anyway? Did he think he'd just walk aboard, be recognized, and it would all end amicably?* "Oh, Durt Larson, I've heard of you. I was just kidding. You can be on your way." *Who knows?* Maybe he meant it in some other way, she thought. Maybe he wouldn't try to take the shuttle. Or maybe it was that thing that Bam had. Maybe he was going to bargain that away for their survival. Anybody's guess. She watched the text before her. All green. No blue text of response or acknowledgement. Maybe the thing was damaged, and it wasn't working at all, then the messages wouldn't actually be going out. They couldn't.

"Oh." she heard Guyal say. It was a questioning utterance of the word, almost musical, that trailed off at the end. Like he was seeing something he didn't want to or something he understood but didn't want to share with her. A second circle appeared on the screen. This one wasn't purple. This one was a small yellow circle.

"What is it?" asked Nik. But she knew what it was. The shuttle had detached from Raven and was making its way toward the purple circle at the top of the screen. "Oh no." It escaped her lips in a high pitch before she even realized she'd said it. "This can't be good. Is that Durt?"

Guyal placed his hand near the screen, fingers together over the yellow circle, then retracted it while opening his fingers. The console followed his command pulling the circle into 3D space before them. The rendering of a horizontal disc with two of its sides indented like bites from a cookie floated before them. Her heart jumped with the confirmation and sunk with the realization.

"Not good. Not good at all," she whispered to herself.

"If there's one thing I know," said Guyal, trying his best to be positive, Nik thought. "Sometimes you just have to trust him. His plans don't always work out as he intends them to, but he always has a plan. Usually they do."

Another voice spoke from the console. Strober. He actually sounded cheerful and upbeat. Great news, he was saying, they'd bagged another one, and he was on his way back for his flight bag. This time he would pilot this ship to Midway and make the exchange. They were all in for another big payday. He went on about how successful they were, sometimes repetitive, but always upbeat like they'd just won another game. On the screen before them, the shuttle closed the distance, bringing the two circles closer together. Nik noticed that the shade of the second circle had become brighter, turning a lighter purple, almost pink now. "What does a pink circle mean?"

Guyal's expression shifted suddenly. "Oh my God." His eyes went wide as he spoke. "Shuttle, this is Raven. Durt, get the hell out of there. High energy reading from security vessel. Abort! Abort before you're toast!"

He was shaking. The words scrolled in front of him as he shouted them at the screen.

"What about us?" Nik asked quickly. This can't be right, she thought. This is supposed be about travel and transportation, not some kind of bad dream. "Are we toast, too?"

"Probably, but we're still covered in a thick wall of hyper-jump ice. We'd be damaged, but we'd probably pull through." He paused for a moment, thinking. "If they do have those SM-21s, it's a good bet that it would vaporize that shuttle."

"Jesus," she said, and put her face into her hands, doing her part and saying another prayer. The pod door behind opened, and she heard Truman's voice in conversation with Bam, but when she looked up it wasn't at Truman, it was at the screen. She now understood what was happening and couldn't look away if her life depended on it.

Displayed before them, the purple was gone now, replaced by bright white, the center of its circle filled in—a giant white dot. The shuttle was almost on top of the white dot when it happened. A small streak of white suddenly emerged from the white dot, turning the yellow quickly to white, and Nik watched in horror, unable to move or even look away as the two white circles became one and expanded quickly to engulf the entire display area, flashing white before fading to black.

6

SEA

THE SEA WAS CALM TONIGHT. The ship's engine hummed rhythmically as Cotel listened to the swish and splash of the ship's bow wave below. His forward perch gave him an unrestricted view ahead of the sky reflecting its starry essence on the sea's glass-like surface. Gone was the deep green of daylight sailing, now replaced by the eternal blanket of stars that stretched to the horizon before meeting its reflection and returning to complete itself. The Namian sea was a beautiful thing to behold at night, he thought as he gazed ahead. This trip had gone well. Harvest was abundant and the animals were fat. He thought of his family and knew they would appreciate his gifts. Not so much the elders, but the younger generation would certainly revel in the machines that he would present.

They'd been through lean years before with nearly half their farmlands sold to put food on the table. Raspotua's climate had not been kind to Mudson farmers for a string of years. But the last two years had more than made up for those, and he hoped to never again see them suffer as they had. Farms and grazing grounds would be recouped and expanded this year, thanks to bountiful crops and renewed agreements with Earth traders. He didn't much care for them, with their aristocratic presumptions and their imperialistic views. They even renamed Raspotua, their planet, on their maps and charts. Claustrom, they called it. He had no idea what that even meant. Nothing like the musical sound of Raspotua, or protective mother in their Mudson dialect. He didn't like or envy them, but he did appreciate the benefit of their accord. At one time, Cotel knew, hundreds of years prior, Earth had maintained a presence here in the north, a military outpost of some type. Some had stayed, their ancestors. Steady settlement and technological growth from their Earth infusions, they'd evolved into what they knew today to be Kulan. Certainly, the Mudson had Earth roots, too, but had cut ties centuries before, choosing the fertile ground of Raspotua as their protector and provider. While the Mudson traded regularly with their neighbors, their culture shied away from technology, save for those who used it to increase their ability to farm and herd.

For himself, he'd had little to do with Mudson's culture of planting, herding and the other assorted farm and livestock tasks of his family. He was of Mudson blood, but his spirit lay elsewhere. His family sensed it in him as a boy. Restless and troubled, he'd created as much farm work as he'd accomplished. He never fit in well with his brothers and sisters when it came to working the land and its livestock. Never happy until the first day he'd visited the sea where he found a new world. On the beach in the water, he'd sensed what was missing in his young life. He'd left home a sullen difficult boy, but emerged from the green waters of Namia that day a changed soul. The freedom and the unrestricted possibilities washed over him as he played in the waves. It had changed and awakened something inside of him, and his connection with the sea offered him a new path, a guide which he'd followed and continued to follow today. As soon as he was old enough, he'd begged his parents, and then the town elders, to allow him to apprentice as a seaman. It was a struggle. Becoming a sailor meant fewer hands to work the fields.

His vision had been insatiable, however, and eventually he'd won them over. Today, he knew they had done the right thing, not only for him but for their town as well. His passion for the sea translated directly into a skill for handling ships and a respect, if not an affinity, for the Kulian craftsmen who made possible these ships of metal that rode the waves of the Namian Sea. During the lean years, his position had helped them survive and earned their grudging respect. While he never had the same relationship with his family once he left for the sea, they loved to hear his stories and were grateful, he knew, for his loyalty, even if they never told him that explicitly.

To this day, they held him at arm's length. He was a friend to the Kulian which changed their perception of him. Though they benefitted mightily from his skills at transport, trading and negotiation, they had no love for their counterparts across the sea. While he understood their prejudices, he'd changed his view on the perceptions he'd grown up with. He had crew members who were Kulian. He'd saved lives of his Kulian shipmates, and in turn, they'd saved his, a number of times over the years. By now, they'd developed and become their own unique culture, a seafaring culture. A mix of the two from which they came, they'd become a critical part of the prosperity of both.

His wife especially, thought Cotel, would appreciate the appliances for the kitchen. She'd use them to help prepare the sometimes substantial meals that kept their family fed and healthy. From soups to the delicious and beautiful after-meal treats, her skills were only matched by her energy and efficiency as she tore about the kitchen before mealtimes, barking orders and orchestrating her concert of preparation. Of course, should they have guests, all the Kulian mechanicals would disappear. He had no idea where she would put them, but should he, on rare occasion, walk into the kitchen during such a time, he'd see nothing but the traditional Mudson cooking ware. Their guests would help with the preparation, the men would be shooed out of the house and the gossip, news and laughter would take the place of the whirring mechanicals.

The ship knifed forward, slicing into the liquid blanket of stars, and Cotel knew he'd be soon interrupted by his Kulian mate. Standard ship status report with updates on various ship systems. Hull integrity, propulsion issues, navigation reports, maybe he would share a story or two. He admitted to himself that it sounded mundane, and he smiled. Yes, he would enjoy this feeling for a while. The coming trips would become increasingly dangerous with the onset of winter and its related hazards. No, he'd revel in this quiet passage. They worked continuously to keep the ship and its systems intact and functioning, but while regular passages and constant use was good for business, it took its toll. The ship might be aging, but it was of solid design and construction and had proved itself worthy, surviving the worst storms of the past two decades.

But there was something else. Cotel sensed it before he heard the crescendo of footsteps on the open deck behind him.

"Evening report?" he asked his mate who now stood beside him sharing the darkness of the Namian seascape before them.

"Nothing new to report," said Ruzilan, his face catching the chill breeze that blew into their faces. "Engineering plant needs rest and care. Our port stay will give us rest, and she'll hold together for our inbound trip."

Cotel listened as he walked through the standard list of status reports, amused at the fact that for Ruzilan, any voyage from a non-Kulian port was the outbound trip with the inbound the return. He thought in those terms, too. But opposite. The report finished and Ruzilan lapsed into silence as they stood side-by-side.

"What else?" he asked. "What is it you're not telling me?"

"Probably nothing."

"If it was probably nothing, you would have included it."

Ruzilan nodded. "You're right. Storm to the south. A big one."

"That's not probably nothing."

"It won't impact us. The mountains will see to that."

But Cotel knew Ruzilan's concern wasn't for himself. "They'll be fine."

"Are you sure?"

"Yes, I'm sure. This is the storm season, Ruz. They know it. They're prepared.

"I just keep thinking about—"

"What? The storm of the century?"

Ruzilan said nothing, gazing over the bow and into the darkness.

"It's not due for years. You know that as well as anyone."

Of all the Kulian Cotel had served with, he considered Ruzilan the most earnest and trustworthy, loyal to a fault. But he also wore his fears like a cloak, reflecting them in his conversations, rare as those conversations might be, and in his face, etched more deeply as the years passed. Like Cotel himself, his lot and obligation to his family was as a seafarer, but he shared none of Cotel's restless wanderlust that made nights like tonight magic. Nothing of the Kulian culture and society intrigued him in the slightest. Ruzilan's internal spirit, Cotel had learned, longed for a flock to tend and a family to raise, but his inherited and presumed fortune was that of a trader. He spent his working life between the various cities of Kulan and Mudson, and his family now worked the trade route south to the Earth place. His calling to the sea was, for him, much more an escape than an undeniable attraction, but looking after the waterborne leg of the family supply chain was a responsibility he couldn't deny. He'd been drawn immediately to Cotel and listened first in amazement and then in contentment. He'd ask to hear the same stories over and over, never tiring of Cotel's stories of his youth and family life on the farm and his extended narrative descriptions of Mudson lands and history. Ruzilan was not a storyteller, but a listener and a dreamer. While the two spent countless hours on their voyages discussing Mudson lands and customs, his end of the discussions was minimal, limited usually to questions, many of them repeated verbatim to evoke yet another repeat of an oft-recounted tale. Cotel didn't mind. He was proud of his family and his heritage, and each telling would bring to mind some new, minor detail he'd overlooked before. He'd suggested whimsically that Ruzilan give up his ship duties and join the farming community. Both knew this would never work. The Mudson, especially his own family, would never accept him into their community as one of their own. Nonetheless Ruzilan enjoyed the suggestion and pestered him regularly with "what ifs." But this voyage was different. Ruzilan had an edge to his standard worried self.

"How is she?" he asked Ruzilan, the pair facing toward their unseen Mudson port destination over the horizon.

Ruzilan licked his lips and was silent for a moment. He struggled when he talked of his mother. He'd never married, and his mother was his anchor, his reason for everything. When he said he was loyal to his family, he meant it, but what he really meant was he was loyal to his mother. He was here to today because his mother had believed in him. She'd been the one to encourage him. *Do something for yourself. Don't concern yourself with your brothers,* Ruzilan had recounted. And now, apparently, he believed she was in trouble.

"She's my mother. She's fine."

Cotel turned to look at his stone-faced forward gaze.

"OK, she's not fine. She's getting old. She's frail. I don't know how much more time we have together. Father's been gone for years, and if anything happened to my brothers, I think it would kill her. She lives well because of us."

The two stood in silence again until a new light appeared on the horizon, a pinpoint that grew from a star into a realization.

Cotel touched the coat of his mate in recognition, but Ruzilan was already aware.

"The inbound."

Cotel smiled. "Yes. The inbound. I'm on the bridge for another hour before I turn in. I don't want you to worry, Ruz. I'm not so sure about your brothers, but your mother is a tough bird and has years to live. She's not the one you have to worry about."

Ruzilan's face brightened. "Really? Is that true?"

Cotel smiled again, nodding as he watched the approaching ship. "Maybe tomorrow you can tell me something more about her."

A thoughtful nod from Ruzilan spoke a silent sigh, the relief evident in his stance. "Yes. Yes I will." He turned and left without another word.

Cotel watched the horizon. The light from the approaching ship had ceased to grow, and he could see the ship making its parallel but opposite course to their south, soon to return the night to the stars. He looked forward, across the bow. Out there beyond the edge of the ocean lay Mudson. He could feel the familiarity of home. It was his past. His present. His destiny.

***

Sometimes the noise was deafening. At full production capacity in processing season, the meat processing floor was a ballet of efficiency, its metallic machines in full swing. The pounding, slicing, grinding, packing and cleaning kept a vibration going that could be felt throughout the complex. It was the vibration of Claustrom that buzzed so often prisoners and staff no longer noticed it. For new arrivals, it took some time before the processing machines became an integral part of their waking lives. It ran efficiently, thanks not only to its original design, but also to ideas and modifications generated by its operators, the inmates themselves.

It did seem counterintuitive, Grinder thought, that prisoners could support and improve on technology that served and improved the lot of their imprisoning organization, but for them, they lived a culture of quid-pro-quo, a non-spoken understanding of trade and barter. They provided the best possible product that might be squeezed from this plant. In return they gained respect for their skills and skimmed some benefit when it was available.

But it was more than that, too. In a world devoid of virtual access and tools, the mechanical technology of the plant served as their proxy. Their collective creative energy could be exercised in this meat processing plant. It was their project and their pride.

Tonight, however, the floor was silent. Soon enough cooler temperatures would return it to an around-the-clock operation with the arrival of new livestock and new opportunities to test the modifications and upgrades they'd made during the hot months. The inventory would be cured, packed, sliced and stored, awaiting off-planet transport. They'd finished up the last of the production testing yesterday, and as Grinder walked through on his shutdown inspection, he marveled at the state of the facility. It literally sparkled. You'd never find anything like this on Earth. Too many other distractions. No passion for the operation. Many times, the prison had visitors from Earth who watched the plant in operation, observed its staff and its output, and took notes to apply to their own operations. But they could never approach the levels of efficiency reached here on the prison complex. They couldn't understand why. To them it was a mystery.

Not to Grinder. It was clear to Grinder that the secret to this operation lay it its people and their particular circumstance. They didn't have family or bars or vacations to think about. On this planet, they had their plant and that was it. It was theirs and theirs only. There was no begrudging the Casinos for the profit they made. The community enjoyed the product as much as the latest jackpot winner on Midway or highbrow political guest on Earth. It kept them together as a community, and it gave them substance, around which they could mold their creative instincts.

The rows of of metallic knives, robot controllers and the maze of processing alleys stood silent at attention, awaiting commands and for the next run to begin. This was a fine plant they'd built, a project in continuous improvement. Maybe this is what they were meant to do in this life, thought Grinder. Sometimes the information security breaches, the hacking as they called it, seemed so inelegant, so far beneath the status of their collective mental and physical capacity. This undertaking, at least, did something productive. Maybe it was just the thought of forced isolation here on Claustrom that bothered him. Aside from that, he'd become quite comfortable with his lot in life here.

The battalion of cutting, grinding and slicing machinery that surrounded him now usually gave him a calming feeling. When the system was cleaned, quiet and pristine, to him it was a work of art—a hallowed zone of efficiency, a testament to their collective willpower. He liked to come here and let inspiration wash over him, to remind him that something positive evolved from his confinement here. But tonight was different. Tonight he had actual work to do.

He stopped momentarily and listened, turning his head slowly and gazing through the dimness of the room. Silence. As it should be. He moved quietly through the maze to the piercers and stood, waiting. Of all the equipment on the floor, these piercing machines were the sharpest and most prone to creating injury, even with the veteran line workers. Often, they didn't even feel the cuts until they looked down at a pierced hand or worse. She was supposed to be here by now. He could picture a scene in his mind where she bumbled her approach, set off one of the security alarms or alerted one of the more rabid prisoner watchers Simms used so effectively. She'd be caught. And dead. Him, too, he figured. Processing accident or failed escape—or actual escape where he'd be withered and burned by the heat of the desert and lost forever beneath its sands. Here, investigators couldn't tell the difference after the fact. If there were to be an investigation at all.

"Hey," came the whisper from behind him that startled and snapped him into a flash of convulsion before he realized it was her. Gina. She'd been standing there partially concealed, but looking, in the shadow-filled facility, like a part of the machinery. Maybe he was wrong. Maybe he was the weak link in their two-link chain. Once recovered from his initial start, he didn't waste words and nodded quickly toward the array of piercing blades that descended from their machine mounts. An array of immobile daggers that pierced pig and boar meat—or any meat for that matter—as if it were water.

Gina moved like a ghost, smooth and soundless toward the machine. She examined the angles now. She's spent enough time on the floor to be familiar with the function and operation of the piercer, but now she looked at it differently, as it seeing it for the first time.

"Take your time," he coached in a whisper. "Just like we practiced."

She took a long breath, closing her eyes for a moment, and then nodded to herself. Yes, she was ready. It was an odd angle, and she had to take on an awkward half-standing stance to insert her right arm inside the machine's interior structure. She moved slowly and deliberately.

Had they the whole place to themselves, they could have programmed the machine for a surgically precise movement, but here in the dark, fear of discovery hanging over them in the dim reflected light, it was a different story.

"You've got to do the moving," he whispered under his breath. "I'll guide you, but you have to do it."

He took out a hand lamp with its dim red light, placed it between his teeth and grasped her arm gently with both hands.

She nodded again. "Do it."

It was the worst possible angle. She was half-standing, half-crouching, her arm extended outward and into the machine. Should the power come on now, it would be quickly reduced to ribbons. But it wouldn't. And without power, this was the most likely opportunity for a quick, clean surgical incision. Her arm rotated upward so the inside of her upper bicep approached the machine's descending corner point.

"I'm your eyes," he told her. "Now rock back and forth slightly, so we can get the length right." He held her bicep in his hands. It was slim but firm. His whisper was almost inside her ear. They were entwined as a single, odd-looking mutation with two heads and too many arms. He smelled her sweat and could taste her fear. "Easy, now. Just short, little movements. That's good. Now, I'm going to push up slowly, and we'll cut only once. Ready?"

He felt her tense and nod quickly without making a sound. He watched her extended arm rock one more time, then pressed slightly upward on her pull rotation. The dagger's sharp tip easily sliced into the top layer of her bicep. Her reaction was delayed. She drew a quick breath as the blood began to seep from the incision. Hands still squeezing her arm, he pushed horizontally, keeping her hand away from unintended surgery as he pulled her backward, removing her bare arm from the machine. He kept firm pressure on the incision as he felt her go limp. He knew it wasn't the sear of pain that sapped her will, but the relief of finally getting the thing out of her. Her other arm was now wrapped tightly around his neck. The lamp, still between his teeth, illuminated the small cut, now visible as a thin crimson line. In the dim red light, it looked black, and as he worked the flesh directly beneath the line, a small capsule, shiny in its reflection, emerged. Keeping tight pressure with his right hand, he grasped the capsule between the thumb and forefinger of his left, plucking a white cloth from his breast pocket and dropping the capsule into its place in a single motion. He quickly bound her bicep with the cloth in silence. He felt her body relax as a long held breath slipped silently from her nose and she leaned into him for support. She stayed there for a moment, her slim body refreshing itself from her slim lungs. He listened to her catching her breath, and he could sense her fear drip from her onto the cool composite floor and slip away. Not all of it, but enough that he noticed. She pulled away and stepped behind him, and he turned quickly to watch her go, but she was already gone. She was probably there, but she'd become one again with the shadows. She didn't give herself away. Impressive.

His red light stashed in his pocket, he retreated slowly through the silent maze of processing machinery. He'd probably given Gina her freedom, although he couldn't be certain. For whatever reason, somehow she'd known. She'd profiled him well enough to know that he was someone who couldn't betray her. *How had she known?* Hell, he hadn't decided to protect her until she'd come to him two days before, desperation in her eyes. *Was she that good? Was he that transparent?* She read him like a ship specification data screen, as if his thoughts—his intentions and desires—scrolled down his face as he listened and spoke. Maybe her questions had been a well rehearsed script, some kind of verbal truth serum in the form of a question matrix that gave her the answers she needed to survive, he thought. Or maybe she was a natural, and that's why she was here. She'd confided in him that she was a prison plant, and she thought her cover was blown. Of all people, why she picked him, the Wiz's left-hand man, in both a figurative and literal sense, was beyond him. Had he decided the other way, which he'd considered strongly, she'd likely be dead now, a meat processing accident. It happened sometimes. But he hadn't made that decision. He'd decided to help her as she knew he would, and now the damn transmitter was on him. Half the size of a tooth, he couldn't feel it in his pocket, but he felt it in his mind. It was as big as a second head poking out of his chest and announcing to all that he was a spy. He was the turncoat. Were it true that Gina had been discovered, focus would likely shift to him. Although he discounted the possibility of an electronic tracker within the prisoner population, he didn't discount the level of creative sophistication, and that worried him. *Ground Grinder. That would be poetic justice wouldn't it?* Whoever her contact was, it was outside of the Wiz's network, or the tracking task would have fallen directly to him, and he'd have had to execute it.

He made his way out of the heavily bladed meat facility through its connecting passageway and back toward the larger prison structure. No, he'd hang on to the tiny second head, he thought. For now it was bait. Soon enough he'd need to find it. But who would it be? Whose cell would he *find* it in? Whose pocket would harbor the tiny finger that pointed to treachery? Who would be revealed as the plant? Whose name would head the list of the next industrial accident report? He didn't have a clue yet. But he knew one thing. It wouldn't be him.

7

FLIPPED

NIK STARED AT THE BLACK SCREEN, stunned. "I can't believe they're gone," she said, "It makes no sense."

"If it makes no sense, then it's probably not true."

Nik wrenched her head around sharply, not comprehending what she'd just heard. *It sounded like Durt's voice. But how was that even possible?* She'd seen him vaporized with her own eyes, right there on screen in front of her. But it was Durt. In fact, it was everybody crowded behind her. They'd all witnessed the same thing she had on the screen, the destruction of the shuttle. She shook her head trying to understand it all.

Durt spoke again, addressing the clear disbelief on her face.

"Truman reprogrammed the shuttle's pilot recorder to its transmit channel, and Strober recorded that unending victory message."

Nik was still uncertain. "But aren't we next? Won't they re-charge and blast us, too?"

"Not likely," said Durt. "Bam was kind enough to contribute some explosive crates he'd intended to use for the unveiling of his new gaming program on Midway. Those mattress-sized crates you might have seen stacked in our cargo bay come in handy sometimes on New Manhattan construction projects. Those would have lit up the horizon on Bam's command, impressing his fans and financial backers from their high-priced Casino seats."

"We were carrying high-explosive crates on *this* ship?" said Nik incredulously, her eyes wide and demanding.

Durt nodded with a smile. "Perfectly safe until they're armed. And we couldn't have exploded them if we'd wanted to without Bam's retinal scan."

Both Truman and Bam nodded in unison, confirming Durt's statement.

Nik shook her head and smiled. "Son of a bitch," she said, barely audible. And then she started a smile she couldn't stop. *They'd all survived.* "And the security ship? Is it destroyed, too?"

"Hard to tell," said Durt. "The amount of explosives that went into the ship certainly had the capability to do that, but it really depends on their power balance at the time of the explosion."

It was Truman this time. "We think so," said the engineer, "but it depends on how they set up their SM-21 shot. Technically, the power required to destroy the shuttle could have left enough to power the ship's shields, but the SM-21s are designed for construction duty and not as an integrated part of any ship. We doubt that level of sophistication in the interface between the 21 and the ship."

"And the level of sophistication of the pilot," added Strober.

"Right. But anything's possible," said Truman. "Sometimes beginners get lucky."

A thought occurred to Nik. "Can't you just flip on the scanners and check it out? Shouldn't we be a lot more concerned than you all seem to be?"

Durt smiled again, but his eyes didn't match his smile. They'd turned a distinctly more serious shade of blue. "We are concerned, but not for the reason you think. The size of that blast has knocked us into some random trajectory. Our real saving grace was the hyper-gate ice that gave us a nice layer of blast insulation."

"C'mon Durt," she said, "You're full of it. We're sitting here now, just like before."

Durt lifted his chin, using it to point in the direction of Guyal. "Navigator, can you pull up an external view screen?"

Guyal played his right hand over the pod's remote console, and a new scene appeared on the display.

Nik stared. Small points of white lights screamed diagonally, across the screen. *Stars*, she realized. *Those were stars*.

"We're out of control, flipping like a leaf in a winter wind," said Durt. "You don't feel it because we have our own grav-generator here. The other ship, if it's not destroyed, is at least as bad off as we are—probably worse because it wasn't iced. No, our problem is that we still don't have power or control of things outside of this pod, and we won't know what our actual situation is until our systems are back online. For now, since we can't do anything else, we'll get something to eat. Dinner's on me."

This time she understood. The concern was no longer about being vaporized, but freezing in the unknown reaches of space. A cold and lonely death. Maybe it would have been a better fate to have gone up with the shuttle, she thought. Durt didn't seem too worried. Maybe he knew a lot more than he was letting on. Besides, he was the captain. She thought again what a captain would tell his crew. Maybe there was some unwritten captain rule that forced him not to alarm his passengers.

Conversations among the group surrounded her now, none taking notice she'd not joined in. They were all grateful to be alive and spoke of their individual ideas and theories, from the security ship to their ultimate doom or salvation.

"So we could actually just flip through space like this until we're dead, couldn't we?" she asked no one in particular.

Truman was the one to break from the group and answer her question. "Yes, that is one option. But that's always a risk we take when we fly. That's the damn thing about it. Nothing's certain."

"An option?" asked Nik, "Like something we could choose to do?"

"Sure. But in this case, I think we'll choose not to. Durt and I have been in some pretty tight places before, and we've always figured our way through them. We just got blasted from a makeshift SM-21, and we're still here, aren't we? You look pretty scared. And it's OK to be scared. I'd be lying if I said I wasn't, but this is a solid ship, and I know her inside and out. Before you know it, you'll be sitting on Midway, a fancy drink in your hand and an old east-Earth woman rubbing your feet."

Nik looked at Truman. He was a bit rough around the edges—sophistication was not a word that would normally, in any sense, be attached to his description. His flight suit was well worn as if he had only one and wore it around the clock. Probably slept in it, too. He was a stout man with broad shoulders and a barrel chest. Balding on top, not exactly her vision of the perfect man. What hair he had left he wore clipped short. Given his job, it was a wonder he had any hair at all. His heart was that of a mechanic, she thought, a doctor for machines. Right now, she was a broken machine, and he was doing what he could to assess the damage. That was nice. She'd never seen him smile in the few times she'd talked with him, and he wasn't smiling now. No, it was more of an amused smirk and something of a twinkle in his eye. She had no idea if he was serious about their chances for survival, or if he was just trying to make her feel better. It didn't really matter at this point, but if he was confident, she thought she could be confident. He was probably the furthest thing from a smooth talker, but she didn't need smooth talk now. She needed simple reassurance, and she got that from Truman. She smiled slightly, and his face brightened.

"What's for dinner?" she asked.

"Finest dehydrated crap in the galaxy."

"Mmmmmm. Dehydrated crap."

"You may be surprised."

"Surprised? At this point, I'm going to find it pretty hard to be surprised at anything," she said, standing up next to Truman.

"C'mon," he said. "This one will be pleasant."

They followed the others through the now open hatch to the

pod's adjacent galley. Inside, it was much larger than Nik thought it might be. It was about the same size as the stasis pod itself, a curved, semi-circle shape with a matching semi-circular table in its center. The table had seats at either end with benches on either side of its curved length, a lot more seating than they could fill with their present crew. In a semi-circle surrounding the table were counters, shelves and the standard food prep areas with a small but respectable array of equipment. Guyal had opened two large doors on the right side of the galley, the pantry presumably, and the bright rainbow of canisters and packages packed inside each shouted out its tasty contents. Even if she weren't hungry, the marketing display of dehydrates would have made her so.

"Choose wisely, friends," said Guyal. "Hard to tell when we'll eat next."

Nik looked quickly to Truman with a questioning glance.

"Whatever we figure out, we're a long way from anything right now, so best bet is we'll go back into stasis before we eat again," he said.

Nik nodded. Fair enough, she thought, a nice meal would make her sleepy. Even though it had only been a short time since they'd come out of stasis, the excitement made it seem like days. Whatever lay ahead was uncertain, but she had a new found confidence in Truman. Truman would figure it out. But the big question remained. *What were they going to do with Strober?*

Within a few minutes the galley's discussions transformed into a symphony of clicking, scraping, and chewing as the crowd made it through the meal. The Raven's menu choices were surprisingly varied, and the delicious mix of aromas that wafted through the air reminded Nik of some of the fancier dinners she'd attended as part of her staff duties.   She'd felt terribly self-conscious about her understanding of meal-time etiquette, or if she was actually honest with herself, it was more a lack of understanding. Sure, she'd reviewed the appropriate screen demos, but doing it in person was a whole different universe. She'd felt their eyes upon her, watching and testing. She hadn't really belonged there. She felt it. The food had likely been spectacular, Earth-fare with actual plant and animal ingredients, but her fear had overcome her, spoiling her enjoyment of the rare meal. She was afraid. Afraid she'd be discovered as someone of an inferior class. Someone who didn't know the culture and customs of those she dined with. A single misspoken word or a misplaced utensil would betray her simple roots, and they'd laugh—or worse. They'd say nothing, eyeing one another and nodding amongst themselves with knowing glances, communicating the unspoken language of social dismissal. She could hear it on the tips of their tongues, "If this one didn't have such nice tits, she wouldn't even be here." But she had been there, and she'd performed flawlessly. They'd been kind and gracious, but the experience left her exhausted, and she'd always call in sick the following day, reminding herself over and over again to find an excuse not to attend the next one. But she never did. Her tits always got her an invitation, and her fear of rejection always made her accept. This time would be different, she'd tell herself, but fear always ruled her heart and ruined her appetite.

But not this time. This time it was different. This time the actual food ruined her appetite. *How was it possible that the rehydrated food smelled so heavenly and tasted like chemicals?* The rest in the galley didn't seem to mind in the least and ate with gusto as if it were their last meal. *Who knew? Maybe it would be.* Truthfully, the food wasn't that bad. It just had that hint of manufactured aftertaste that reminded her of what it wasn't. She wondered if the others had forgotten what real food tasted like. Next to her, Truman ate quickly and efficiently. His eyes, unblinking, focused on nothing, and Nik could sense him working through his engineering puzzle that held all of their lives in the balance, the multitude of options scrolling through his mind.

Maybe efficient eating was a technique that overcame the shuttle food's quality. *Take another bite before the aftertaste set in?* Maybe that way you only had to taste it when you'd finished, she thought. Her tastes in food were two things. Simple and expensive. Some manufactured brands were quite refined, and half of her salary went toward ensuring her meals were as near-Earth as money could buy. She ate some of her meal and thought about finishing, but couldn't convince herself, even if it were her last meal. She pushed it toward Truman who took it quickly and mechanically, his eyes never wavering from their unfocused state.

By now the clink of glasses replaced the sound of utensils as pitchers of mead and ale made their way around the table. This was one area where molecular manipulation succeeded. The ale was good, but the mead was unbelievable. Here then, was the right way to eat while in transit. Eat quickly to minimize the aftertaste and quench it with drink. The mead did not disappoint as she sipped its manufactured glory. From thoughtful to pensive, the group's shared countenance turned into itself, considering the significance of choices and chances. If life flashed before your eyes just before your departure, each of them would watch and re-watch a collection of home movies gathered over lifetimes of experiences, she thought. Lifetimes of should-haves and what-ifs. Bam was now wearing his blacked-out glasses. He might be watching actual home vids on those things. She didn't keep up with the ever-evolving technology, but it wasn't out of the question. His eyes were hidden from view, and his face, like the rest, was without expression.

Jata lit a cigarette, and the soothing properties of the smoke became entwined with the combined scents of the meal to usher in the meal's next course. It was not a course of food, but a discourse of conversation, if a single voice could be considered a conversation. From his place at the center of the semi-circular table, Durt's full ale glass gleamed, its contents begging to be sipped. Durt obliged and cleared his throat. Around the galley table, six pairs of eyes watched him in silence. It was hard to tell if they were concerned or intrigued, but all were engaged. Nik was sure it would be a preamble to a death sentence for the pirate. He'd probably be the one this would get pinned on. They'd want blood, and his was as red as any. Not that his face and his faraway gaze betrayed any particular concern beyond that of any of the others. From Durt she expected something dramatic. Something straight out of the adventure film she pictured him in. Swords maybe? She smiled to herself. That would certainly be dramatic, but in none of the Durt stories she'd ever heard was there anything to suggest he knew his way around the handle of a sword. He did have a hell of a scar though. Maybe that was confirmation he didn't, she thought. Durt talked while she listened and sipped, and as she did she realized it wasn't a death sentence he was pronouncing, not for Strober anyway. Durt was talking about himself. His past. His unrealized dreams. A shiver of fear tickled her spine, and she drank more deeply from the mead glass. His blue eyes didn't reflect his signature take-on-the-galaxy look she'd come to expect in the short time she'd known him. This speech wasn't an inspirational one. It was the speech of a dead man. Or a dying one, at least. The faces around the table had turned to stone. None spoke, but all drank and listened as the same realization sunk in to their ears and seeped out of their eyes.

"We don't know what capabilities we'll have, if any, when Raven comes back on line," continued Durt, his reminiscing dissolving into a Captain's practical approach of giving orders, "so the four of you will go back into stasis immediately as an energy conservation measure. Every little bit counts, and out here," he said, motioning with both hands to the emptiness of space beyond their tumbling vessel, "out here, a little might make a big difference."

It wasn't a death sentence for Strober. It was a death sentence for all of them. Without the power to steer or maneuver or even plot a course, the ship might continue its unabated tumble through light years of deep space, its power degrading over a thousand years, their lives and their deaths suspended until the pod's energy field could no longer support their fragile life functions and released them from their extended sleep. Even if they were rescued, everyone she'd ever known in her life could be dead hundreds of years before she woke. She took another drink and lay her head on Truman's shoulder, squeezing his arm as she did. *C'mon Truman. Don't give up. I never really needed saving before, but I do now, so save me. Save us all.* She looked up at Truman's face, ready for a wink, a nod maybe of reassurance—even a mask of fear was something she was ready for. It was OK to die, but not alone, and she readied herself to be much stronger than she felt, not for herself, but for him. Even the galaxy's baddest asses had a mother and needed to be reminded of that fact sometimes with a loving touch, a squeeze of the hand, a sliver of support and encouragement. But his face reflected none of those emotions. Truman's broad face betrayed nothing but intense concentration. He wasn't listening to Durt's soliloquy. He wasn't demanding space justice for the pirate. He gazed straight ahead as before, an intense and unmoving gaze that saw nothing of the galley scene before him, mentally reviewing his ship and his options, or at least Nik presumed that's where his mind and his focus was. She let out a long, soft sigh she hadn't realized she'd been keeping in and put her head back on his shoulder. The intricacies of space travel were beyond her, but not beyond Truman, she thought. Truman would come up with a plan. He had to. Her confidence somewhat restored, if by nothing else, by the inevitability of it all. No matter what she did or how she felt, none of that would make a speck of difference in their survival or their demise. She felt the mead creep into her bones and stifled an involuntary yawn. It brought both comfort and resignation. Durt was still talking, but she was no longer paying much attention. It wasn't time to die. Not just yet, anyway. But it was time to go back to sleep.

8

CRASH

SOMETHING ABOUT THE DECK was off. Its angle was wrong. Jata stretched her arms above her head and turned to read her stasis display. The Earth-day counter showed only 20 days had elapsed since she'd returned to her life pod.

Were they on Midway? It couldn't be. So where the hell were they now?

She surveyed the interior structure of the ship. All pods were open, but none showed any activity. Lazy or dead, she thought, either was fine for her. The list of the deck beneath her feet was noticeable, but not unmanageable, and she was able to slip into her pants and boots. The access door was open, and she made out what looked like sunlight streaming through its opening.

That was odd.

She grabbed her combat vest, slipped a cigarette out of its pocket, and with vest in one hand, she lit the cigarette in her mouth then used her free hand for balance and handholds as she carefully made her way up the inclined deck.

Outside the hatch the Raven's exterior was torn to shreds, and the exterior heat took her breath away. It felt good on her tits, but that wouldn't last long. She shrugged into her vest. Sweat popped from every pore, a sheen forming across her body as she breathed in the oppressive air with her cigarette smoke. She stood momentarily on a section of Raven's hull that was ripped open and hanging less than a meter off the ground. Beneath her, the ground was a mix of sand and small rocks. Above and behind her towered great rocky peaks that threw a long shadow that engulfed the Raven's wretched remains and traced its dark jagged outline horizontally onto the sandy desert scape. She squinted into the brilliant emptiness of a desert floor beyond, the heat turning its surface to a watery reflection, making it difficult to discern the distant horizon. She blinked repeatedly, her eyes still not used to the light of day, and she made out another figure. Truman. She made the slight jump down, her boots landing softly in the sand, and turned around to survey what was left of their ship, walking backward toward Truman and making her assessment of the crash.

The blanket of desert heat that covered her moderated somewhat as she gave the ship some distance, and she realized much of the the heat she felt was not the sun, but the ship itself.

"Holy shit," she said to the grounded Raven, her head nodding back and forth. "We're not getting you off the ground again are we?" She turned to face Truman who had come up behind her, a mining shovel in one hand.

Truman was stone-faced. He said nothing, but shook his head slowly to confirm her suspicions.

"Where the hell are we? I know we're in the middle of fucking nowhere, but just what corner of hell have you landed us in?"

Still, Truman remained silent. She caught a shape over his shoulder and realized its significance.

"Oh no. Don't tell me." She paused, the realization crossing her mind. "It's Durt isn't it? Is he—"

Truman nodded.

"Jesus Truman, that's just not possible." She paused a moment as the reality sunk in. "I'm sorry."

He turned, and they both stared. Beyond the utility sled that Truman had just climbed out of, she saw a low mound in the distance, a grave of sand and rocks marked with two scraps of what she presumed was Raven's wreckage rigged into a simple crucifix. Behind the mound, a low hill and then a flat, barren desert scape. She bowed her head in respect.

Shit, if Durt couldn't make it, what did that say for the rest of them?

"He saved us, didn't he?" She whispered. "Who would have thought it would be him to go first? The man who always had a plan. Or at least that's what they say."

"A lot of what they said, they made up themselves," said Truman. "But that part is true. He didn't give a damn about the Durt Larson legend, but it sure kept us in business. Everybody wanted him, and he always had a way of figuring things out."

He paused, his back to the remains of the Raven, and his eyes locked on the fresh grave. "Welcome to Claustrom."

"What in the devil's name are you talking about, Truman? The prison planet? That doesn't make any sense at all. Tell me the truth. What's going on?"

"Look, here's our truth right now. We don't have enough manpower or time to do what we really need to do here. I'm going to ask you to keep your mouth shut and do what I tell you. You're smart and strong, and I'm in real need of a plan right now. If you didn't notice, we're a man short. If I read you right, you used to be a cop before you signed on here. I need your focus and your balls to get us out of here."

She looked at him oddly.

"Sorry about the balls," he said.

"You're right, Truman," she said with a half-grin. "I spent a lot of time with the security police, and I do have balls. Thanks for noticing. You've got 100 percent of me and my balls for now. But when I ask, I want the same from you."

Truman turned to look her in the eyes and nodded in agreement. "Square."

She watched his face, but he didn't return the gaze. He turned and stared at what remained of his ship. The front of the Raven was cocked up at an angle, the front of its bow extending over the mound of rocks that absorbed the last of the ship's forward motion and now supported it. The ship had carved out a sandy trough as far back as the eye could see, with a wake of sand thrown up on either side of it. Above them, a sheer rocky cliff stretched toward the sky, and tilting her head back as far as she could, she could make out the outline of jagged peaks, a solid, sheer mountain wall. Durt would have been hard pressed to land the ship any closer to the edge of the mountain, and she couldn't tell if that was intentional or not. Hell of a landing, in any case. Where the side cargo door had once opened like a hungry mouth, only a ragged hole now remained.

Truman began spewing instructions and information without interruption. No time for second thoughts. Only first thoughts. Business and nothing but.

"Guyal is already sanitizing the cockpit. He's got the standard company operating procedures to complete, but he should be done in 15. I'm going to unlatch the other sled. This ship doubles as a maintenance courier vehicle and has two equipment and repair sleds used for transporting material at a job site. At this point, they are our only way out of here. It's too remote to walk out, and the devil himself would have a hell of a time with these temperatures. We've got no power to speak of in the larger ship, but these little machines are self-contained. They don't look to be damaged, so I should be able to bring them both online. I need you to round up the sleepers. Get whatever they have in the pod bagged and ready for transport. As soon as Guyal is done in the cockpit, have him activate the manual access to the cargo hold and pull out what we can. We've got space on the sleds. That's not the issue. Bring everything you can pull through that hatch and start packing it onto the sleds. We've only got a couple hours until it's dark, and I need us to be out of here and on our way by then." He paused a minute and a question crossed her face. "Don't worry, I'll explain it all as soon as we're done. Questions?"

She looked at him for a second longer. That was the most she'd heard him speak yet. Maybe that was the most he'd ever spoken, for all she knew. She figured Durt had done most of the talking for him.

"Got the general idea. Anything comes up, I'll figure it out."

Truman's reply, if there was one, was inaudible as he made his way to the back of the Raven, planting his shovel in the rocky sand by his footsteps, a shepherd's staff minding his flock, his mourning on hold.

No one had yet emerged from the open hull in the side of the Raven.

Lazy fucks. Time to wake up, bitches.

She hiked her left boot onto the improvised metal doorstep and disappeared back inside the ship.

Strober looked up from a kneeling position on the deck of the tilted pod, secured his boot and stood, his face reflecting an awareness of their condition. Others were in states of mid-dress and mid-awareness.

"Midway?" asked Strober.

Jata played her best Truman, shaking a negative. "Alright, listen up. We've got a lot of work to do, and not much time to do it. I need each of you to focus. Whatever it is that wakes you out of stasis the fastest, do it now. I'm not kidding." Her hands were on her hips and no one questioned the fact she was in charge. "We're only as fast as the slowest one of you. You don't want to be the one who holds us up. We crashed the ship, but we're alive. If you want to stay that way, move your slug assess. Get your clothes on. Pack anything you want to take with you and exit the ship." She nodded her head toward the open hatch and the edge of the gaping hole visible beyond.

"What happened?" managed Nik, her face and voice still thick with stasis.

Of course. The prissy bitch would wake up slowly and need to have everything explained. She was no kind of experienced space-

farer. She'd be the first one to go.

Of all the people on the ship, she cared about Nik the least.

"Did I mumble? Did you understand anything I just said?"

Jata was now inches from her face, eyes thin and face severe. Nik was like a baby. For a minute, Jata thought she would break into tears. But she watched as realization crept into her face, maybe rewinding the words she'd just heard in her mind. She had a real beauty to her. Not used to folks talking down to her. When you had those looks, people did things for you. Men wanted her. Probably some women, too. Or so she figured. She was the pick of the litter, the cutest puppy ever. Used to taking her time and getting her way. Not today. Today it was listen-or-get-your-ass-kicked day. Not just because she enjoyed kicking some ass, but there was a real crisis, and whatever wasn't done by lazy assess had to be picked up by the rest.

Nik nodded her understanding and her face cleared. She stood up and quickly pulled on her vest, then began with her flight suit.

"Won't need the top of that one," she said to Nik, "Hot as hell outside. But stow it. May need it tonight."

Nik was packed within the minute. Strober was already outside and Bam, glasses on and bag on shoulder, walked up the inclined deck and through the hatch ahead of them.

Ahead of the downed Raven a few yards, against the side of the cliff, sat the first maintenance sled. Behind them, Truman brought the second and maneuvered it forward, setting it down beside the first. They weren't huge, but there were seats for four in each one with a large open area behind. He stepped down from the second sled.

"I know you've got questions," Truman said to the crew, "and I'll tell you what I know as soon as I can. Right now, I need help moving rations and cargo. We've got little daylight left."

Behind them a carton flew out of the side of the Raven and landed in the sand. They turned to see Guyal pop his head out from the opening in the ship and then disappear within.

"I need two of you. You and you," he said, pointing at Strober and Jata. "Give Guyal a hand with the cargo. Our commercial cargo is gone, but our rations and your personal containers are still inside." The rest of you follow my lead, and we'll get these sleds loaded."

True to his word, the daylight faded quickly and the temperature plunged with it. The team worked in silence, most still in a post-stasis stupor, serving as mechanical loading robots. Jata tossed out the final ration container. She shivered as she jumped down. The temperature was actually comfortable, but the evaporation of the sweat she'd worked up inside gave her a quick chill. The rest were already back in full flight suits. She picked up the container and carried it toward the sleds.

"Last one," she said as she joined the crowd. "Now, Truman what happened, and where are we?"

Truman turned to Guyal. "I'll fill them in, but first, you'll need to finish our procedure."

Guyal nodded and reached into a silver shipping container. It wasn't the dark composite material used for the rations and tools. This one was highly reflective. This was the container Guyal brought out of the ship himself. Jata watched him reach in and pull out a metal cylinder. He cracked it across his knee and it came open with some type of indiscernible hinge connecting the two half cylinders together, creating a double-barreled shape. He walked forward to the tip of the Raven's bow that hung above its sandy bed and placed the open ends of the twin tubes against the hull. He depressed the closed ends of the tubes and they seemed to sink into the hull. Guyal stepped back and watched as a green glow appeared around the cylinders, slowly at first, and then forming a bright green line that crept quickly around the hull of the ship. As the green line expanded its reach, the hull and ship's interior dissolved to dust and then disappeared entirely. Within a minute the Raven was no more. Its structure reduced first to a green dust and then into nothing. All that remained was the displaced sand carved by their impromptu landing. Silence followed as the gravity of their situation sank in. No one spoke.

Finally Truman broke the spell.

"Amazing. That's a sight I've never seen before. I hope I never see it again. You'll forgive me if I'm not my usual personable self, but I've just lost my two best friends."

"Where are we?" asked Nik. "And why did we just disintegrate our only way out of here?"

All eyes turned to Truman, all ready for his answer.

"We're on Claustrom, our famous prison planet," he said. "And we're in trouble."

The group was silent for a beat, processing Truman's announcement. *That's what you told me before,* thought Jata, still not quite believing what he'd told her, so she asked the stupid question no one else wanted to.

"But Midway is closer to the gate than Claustrom," said Jata, "Why in the hell didn't we put down there?"

"Navigator, you want to explain?" he asked, turning to Guyal.

"Sure. It has to do with the orbits of the planets. By the time we got some kind of control back, and did a damage assessment, our best, in fact, I think, our only chance of surviving in this system, was to put down here. It was one of Durt's gambles, and it paid off for us." His voice trailed off as he gazed out over the desert and its most recent addition. "Even if it didn't for him."

Again, the group fell silent.

"There's something else, too," said Truman. "While most everyone he knew was a friend to Durt, there's one in this galaxy who wasn't. His name is Wislon Simms, and he's Claustrom's most famous inmate."

A low whistle came from behind Jata, and she turned to see Strober shaking his head.

"Who cares?" asked Jata. "What's the problem? He's in prison, right?"

"Doesn't mean anything to Simms," said Strober. "He's the Wiz.

No prison ever built has kept him for long. And he's been in and out of a lot of them. That doesn't sound dangerous, but in making those escapes, he left a trail of bodies. Indiscriminate sometimes, but he had a real talent for inflicting pain—both physical and psychological. You insult or slight him? He wouldn't kill you. He'd maim you, then kill everyone you ever cared about. Family. Friends. Whoever he could find. And he could find anyone."

"I never heard anything like that before," said Jata. "Who told you that?"

"I'm betting he spent some time on the Inside, didn't you Strober?" said Truman.

"That I did. And no, he never does it himself. It's just that people he doesn't like don't live very long. Way too convenient for him to be coincidences. Best bet? Avoid him at all cost."

"Durt knew it could be a death sentence for all of us, but considering our alternatives, we agreed this was our best shot," said Truman. "When we entered the atmosphere, Durt vectored us into one of the cities on the Northern Sea, but as we got closer to the surface, he realized our route would take us right over the prison. He turned away, putting this mountain range between us and them. But when we reengaged our original direction, the hull damage was too great. Friction through the atmosphere had made it worse and that redirect sapped enough power from the shields that the hull started to break up. He opened the cargo door for some kind of drag and stability once he knew we couldn't make it, and we were able to land, thanks to the sand and his piloting skill, pretty much in one piece."

"Except for Durt," said Nik under her breath.

"Except for Durt," nodded Truman. "It was just something random, a stray piece of debris. He didn't even realize he'd been hurt until we were down. He had that big stupid smile on his face, like he always gets when one of his plans works out. And then he looks down and sees this piece hanging out of him that shouldn't be there, and his smile turns into kind of a 'What, is this some kind of joke?' expression. He stumbles on the deck and falls. He starts to say something, but the pain hits him like a meteorite, and that was it. The end."

He looked up at what used to be Durt, a small stack of sand and rocks heaped before a low hill, like its own natural grave marker in the vast empty desert that stretched away into the fading horizon. The shadows of the sheer cliff that towered behind them were indistinguishable now from the desert's twilight dusk with Claustrom's night quickly approaching.

"That was it," he repeated, "for the man and the legend. A decent end for both."

The group nodded and murmured in agreement.

Out of the corner of her eye, Jata caught sight of Bam. It was an odd sight. In the fading light, he still wore those dark glasses, but his hands were in front of him, moving in an odd, rhythmic dance, sometimes with one hand, other times with both together. He said nothing, his hands doing all the talking.

"What the hell," she said under her breath.

"You won't find anything here," said Guyal. "It doesn't matter how sensitive your equipment is. If we're on Claustrom, you've got nothing but dead air. No transmitters allowed. No satellites in orbit. Just dead."

Bam nodded his head slowly, bringing both hands together above his head, and moving them down quickly together as if to signal the end of his show. He pushed his glasses up, from covering his eyes to sitting amid the wild hair on his head. "I've got a lot more frequencies on these than anything standard, but you're right. There's just nothing there. We're alone."

"Only thing on this planet with any communication activity is the prison, and its broadcasts are rare," said Guyal. "The only way it activates is if it gets a signal from the warden on Midway."

"So the inmates run the prison?" asked Nik, astounded.

"Pretty much, from what I understand," said Guyal. "Things are worked remotely."

Strober agreed. "What it means, is there are no guards to overthrow and no hostages to take. There is a warden in the prison, and they can talk to him any time they like, but it's just a hologram that responds based on a standard conversation protocol. Requests and updates are funneled into a database and retrieved on Midway randomly so the prisoners never have a broadcast capability."

"So even if we made it to the prison, we couldn't send a distress signal?"

Truman nodded.

"For any other survivors, they might put us up like neighbors, and we'd be off of here on the next automated shuttle. But with our history with the Wiz? I doubt he'd allow our distress signal to make it off the planet. Plus the fact we can't allow any of this hardware" he motioned to the sleds, "to fall into prison hands. Especially if the Wiz is there. In fact, I don't even want to think about it. Bam's right. We're alone."

9

VAMPIRE

NIK'S ASS WAS SORE. They'd been riding the sleds for what seemed like hours now. The sun had dipped below the horizon, turning the desert first orange and then to an almost purple hue. The horizon was no longer distinguishable, yet the sleds still drove forward into the darkness. She shifted again, but there was little room to maneuver and no padding on any of their seats to make the ride even bearable. *They obviously weren't designed by a woman. Totally utilitarian.* She was sure they were made for trucking equipment and people around construction sites, not trucking people across an endless desert. But it wasn't a bumpy ride. The sleds floated above the sand as they moved forward. No, it was the sitting in one place and apparently going somewhere, but not seeming to go anywhere. Her new position wasn't any better, and she shifted back to her original one. Ahead of them, the lead sled piloted by Guyal didn't seem to move at all. It just sat out there in front of them, a couple of lights visible on the rear of the vehicle. If she sat up all the way in her seat, she could see the illuminated sand rushing past beneath them, but if she looked straight ahead into the darkness, it looked just like the vehicle was parked there in front of them, not moving at all. Conversation had been sparse since they'd left the crash site. A death had a way of making you think, and she'd done a lot of that, as had, she presumed, her co-passenger Jata. Conversation had been minimal at best and then nonexistent as they had lapsed into their own minds, grieving or worrying or praying or whatever one did when marooned and handed a likely death sentence. She nodded off now and again. Now awake, she was about to break the deafening silence and cleared her throat when she saw Truman manipulating the the console with his left hand and motioning for silence with his raised right. He said nothing, shook his head yes and entered another command on the console in front of him.

"We're going to stop for while," he said.

Nik looked up from the seat beside him and saw the sled before them, the same as before. Around them was darkness and silence. As she looked more closely, she made out sand and rock beneath the sled in front of them, no longer rushing beneath them, but stationary.

"C'mon," he said, "stretch your legs. We've been riding almost three hours now."

With the sled stopped, the protective field above her deactivated, and she stood up, surveying the darkness of the desert night as the sled settled slowly to the ground. Truman stretched his hands and stepped out of the sled. The sled lights formed a dim pool of light around the emerging group who stretched and peered into the darkness as if to make out some type of landmark. *It was a desert, what could they possibly see, even in the daylight?* The wind had picked up a bit, and she could feel pieces of the desert's particulate tickle the skin of her face and arms. She stepped out of the sled and into the sand, gravitating toward the standing group. The sand still held the heat of the day in its grip, and she could feel its warmth through her flight boots as her soles sank into its top layer.

"We're over the horizon from the crash site," said Guyal, as he squinted at the electronic device he held before him. She realized he was talking to Truman who now looked over his shoulder.

"This is as good a place as any," he replied.

While the group stretched and wandered, he and Truman climbed back into the sleds, and repositioned them together, forming something of a wind break, although the wind had now died to nothing.

"The sleds are too hard to be comfortable, but the sand here is still warm from the day, so stretch out and relax a bit," said Guyal, as he kicked a bit of a butt divot into the sand and leaned his back against the side of his sled.

It was dark and silent, and the night air of Claustrom's desert and sand had an oder to it, not an unpleasant one. Nik wasn't sure if it was desert vegetation or the sand and ground itself that gave off the scent, but there was something comforting about it. Out there in the darkness lay the unknown and undiscovered. As far as she knew, none of them had been here before to tell her any different. This wasn't the coldness of space. This was the warmth of a planet's surface. Who knew what wild things roamed its sandy expanse. She worked her ass into the sand a bit, not too far from Guyal's spot, and found it quite comfortable. Much more so than the damn seat in the sled, anyway, she thought. The sand was warm and forgiving, and she couldn't help herself from smiling just a little bit. The others were chatting among themselves. Maybe she'd join in a bit later, and maybe not. Sometimes it took a while for her to recover from her stasis sleep, and sleep began to tug at the edge of her consciousness.

She gazed up at the stars above, the only real thing visible. They covered the heavens in patterns she didn't recognize. An ass sat down close to her imprint, and she felt it make its own wriggling motion. It was Truman's.

"If you feel yourself nodding off, that's normal. Don't worry about it. After a day like we had, anyone would," he said. "And it's not just the crash and run. We didn't really get a chance to come out of stasis properly. It's supposed to be a gradual thing, not an adrenaline, one-two punch. We've also been without real gravity for a long time. The force on New Manhattan is set to reflect earth standards, and the force is as close as we can measure it, but somehow the body knows it isn't. I don't know why. It just does. Add that to the fact that this planet is a bit bigger than Earth—we'll be tired for a couple of days until we adjust. Even if we don't do anything."

Nik's legs felt relieved, now stretched straight out before her. No one felt like eating anything, but a couple of canteens made the rounds. Truman offered his, and she drank from it gratefully, draining it.

"Sorry," she said, handing the empty canteen back to Truman.

Truman shook it and inverted it above his head, catching the last few drops with his tongue.

"Nothing to be sorry about. But we'll need to keep an eye on that tomorrow."

Beyond the edge of the light cast by the sleds came Jata's voice.

"I'm too hyped to do any sleeping tonight." her position in the night was marked by the crimson tip of her cigarette in the darkness, an orange light that moved and revealed her face as she inhaled. "So I'll take the overnight watch. I still don't know why we ran all the way out here in the middle of nowhere, so my mind will be turning circles for days. I've got nothing for a weapon, but I'll be your early warning system if anything comes this way."

Nik turned to Truman. "That's a good question. I figured you had your reasons for what you did at the crash site, so I kept my mouth shut. We all did. Least you can do is fill us in now."

Truman nodded in assent. She watched as he closed his eyes and took a deep breath.

"Sure. We were pretty sure we stayed below the horizon when we re-vectored the ship. Just a bit of bad luck there. We didn't have great control of the ship, and a lot of what we did have was thanks to Durt's manual flying and not just pressing buttons on the console. He was sure that if they did get a glance at us that Wislon Simms would find a way to track us down. I know you think it's hard to believe, but you don't know him like we do. You don't have a history with him like we do," he said, glancing up at Guyal.

Guyal shrugged.

"Sorry. Like we did." He corrected himself, and Nik realized it was Truman and Durt—not Guyal—and now just Truman with the history and the fear.

"Durt wanted to keep you—all of you—out of his problems. This time though, the problem came looking for him. It was like his destiny, and it hunted him down. Just plain bad luck he didn't pull through."

His voice trailed off as he looked up into the star-filled sky. No one said anything.

"Anyway," he said after a minute. "We figured if we could abandon the site, they'd have no way to follow if they did come looking. No way to track us. The desert would see to that. A couple days from now, and that crash site will look just like the rest of the desert around it—a natural formation. As for us. We drive north. Few days from now, we'll be kicking up our feet by the sea."

"A few days?" asked Nik. "Can't we just fly up there in these when the sun comes up?"

"Yeah, Truman," came the voice from behind the cigarette in the darkness. "Why don't we just fly up there?"

Nik understood the sarcasm, even if she didn't understand why they couldn't jump in their cars and get the hell out of the desert. But she didn't pay much attention to it. The sand was warm and the sky above was beautiful. Her eyes were closing and her strength and energy had disappeared. She gave in. She'd figure it out tomorrow.

***

Simms looked up with his eyes, but didn't move his head of white hair to acknowledge Grinder's presence as he stepped into the tower room. The view from the tower was always impressive, with its panorama of Claustrom's barren landscape stretching beyond the edge of the prison compound to its far horizons. The only distinguishing landmark was the range of mighty jagged peaks that ran north, extending as far as the eye could see. Everything else was flat and sand and dead and foreboding. Grinder followed Simms' gaze. He figured there was some type of desert life out there, but nothing for humans and certainly nothing for him. But even in its landscape of starkness in the evening light, with the sky turning a pastel shade of violet, it held its own kind of power and beauty. The desert expended no effort to keep them confined there. It was a force of the planet and cared not if they lived or died. Any escape into it would be an act of submission, a surrender to the desert's strength. This was something prisoners accepted or ignored as was their choice in spending their own allotted times here. That was life. It went on and eventually, each of these guests would return to a life beyond the desert. Unless they didn't.

Grinder would not have normally interrupted the Wiz's gaze, but when Simms called, you answered. For him, it was a regular ritual, business as usual. Only today wasn't usual. Today was most unusual.

"Something you want to tell me?" asked Simms, who now lifted his head to meet Grinder's gaze.

"Sure. I'll give you a quick rundown on the final circus preps. We do have a couple of—"

Simms was shaking his head a negative, cutting Grinder off mid-sentence.

"About the girl. Tell me about the girl, Grinder."

"Nothing much to tell. She zigged when she should have zagged. Slipped and fell. Such a shame. Pretty little thing. Well, used to be, anyway."

Simms stared at him. "Slipped and fell? Into a piercer?"

The edge in Simms' voice raised his uneasiness tenfold. *Gina was dead.* He'd known when he walked into the tower room he'd have to cover his fear. *He was Grinder. Nothing bothered him.* He'd play it off as if it were nothing, he'd thought. He knew it wasn't nothing, but still, he was the Wiz's confidant, and he'd need to play the role of disinterest. *Focus on the circus. Allow Simms to deduce whatever he liked. In all his brilliance, that was his weak spot. He needed someone to tell him he was right.* Grinder knew he didn't need it for logic's sake as his logic was usually impeccable. No, he needed it for his ego's sake. Whether he admitted it or not, he needed an audience for it to be impressive. If a mystery was solved and none were there to bear witness, it was worthless, at least in the eyes of the Wiz. More often than he liked to admit, he played the oaf—Grinder the loyal, short-minded assistant who asked the simple questions. *Ego was a funny thing. Maybe not so funny in this instance, but a strategy nonetheless, and with The Wiz, it was an effective one.*

"Experience is its own safety net," said Grinder.

"What are you saying? She didn't have enough experience? I checked the logs, and that wasn't even her station. She was assigned binding duty, not piercing duty."

"Word is she was covering for a friend."

"A friend? Not likely, Grinder. It doesn't add up. You're right that she didn't have the quals, but even if you didn't have the quals, that's not the kind of injury you'd get from a normal operation of the machine. We've seen them before. Hands and arms impaled on the spikes, yes. That's reasonable. Medbots have treated a few of those now and again. But not head and torso. That's not inattention. That's assassination."

"You could be right, Wiz."

"Of course I'm right," snapped Simms. "The thing that annoys me most is that this is now a distraction. Accidental death? We're good. We toss the bones to the sand, and they're part of the planet's wasteland. No one cares. But she's dead. Dead this morning. I didn't order it; I didn't authorize it; hell, I didn't even know about it until I came out of the Warden update."

Grinder redirected him for an update. "The circus?"

Simms closed his eyes and nodded for the transition. "We're finalized. Now, I'm going to need your help." He looked into Grinder's eyes, a piercing gaze to say the least.

"I'm going to tell you something I've told no one else. I need your trust, 100 percent. You know who I am, and you know how I work." His voice was suddenly low and cold.

Grinder bit the side of his cheek, fearing what would come next, but he held Simms' gaze, cool and steady and just listened.

"You can walk away right now, and I won't think any less of you. Come with me, and your service will be well rewarded. Betray me, and you'll wish I had killed you as you stand here before me."

Grinder licked his lips. He knew Simms liked a thoughtful, measured response, and he tried to think of one, quickly. He nodded. *No fear. Show nothing in your face.* His eyes narrowed, as he pretended to consider the offer and spoke softly. "I know your reputation. It's one of justice. I've put my faith and trust in you, and I've been rewarded well. I have nothing to complain about, aside from the fact that I'm stranded in the middle of a damn desert on a God-forsaken planet, light years from home. But I don't complain. Our operation here, in an odd sort of way, is one of service. Our minds are occupied with our productions, and we actually have some things, like the circus, to look forward to. I'm thankful we're here and not in some Earth-side prison. I've never been, but I've heard the tales. Not a pretty alternative."

Simm's gaze was steady. *Had he bought it? Was it sincere enough?* Then his face cracked into a smile.

"Grinder, I feel your pain. I share your desires, and I thank you for understanding my need for justice. And when the circus comes," he said, raising the index finger of the hand he still had, I guarantee, it's going to bring some good news. But in the meantime, we have a situation, and we're going to deal with it now. We have an assassin in our ranks."

Grinder nodded in agreement, his relief and concern fighting for control of his facial expression. Simms had almost shared what he knew he needed to share, but then pulled back.

What was this one-handed psychopathic son-of-a-bitch going to do next?"

***

The sweet smoky oder of the morning desert seeped from the dry surface of the desert floor and into the warm morning air announcing the new day. A slight breeze stirred the pastel crimson landscape now illuminated by the first rays of the Claustrom sunrise. Truman opened his eyes and stretched. Nik's head was propped against his shoulder, just as it had been the night before. He couldn't move without letting her head fall and decided a couple more minutes wouldn't hurt anyone. For him, women were usually an encumbrance. Women were exquisite but unpredictable, and in his mind, that was a quality he couldn't fathom. Because it made no sense to his logical engineering mind, his tendency was to avoid female entanglements. *Stick to what you know. That was a good, solid motto.* It kept him out of trouble for the most part. *But Nik was different somehow. She seemed different anyway.* Hell, he guessed they were all different for the first few times. *Was it him? Was it them?* It would be nice if he could find someone who truly understood him, he thought. Not that there was a lot of choice in this spacefaring life he lived—and that was something he wasn't willing to give up. This was what he knew. Stranded in the desert was not a place he'd planned to be when they'd left New Manhattan, but their passengers were intact for the most part, and they were not without resources. Truman's thoughts wandered on in the same random, disconnected manner until his eyes made sense of what they were seeing before him. Fifty meters into the desert's morning landscape, Jata lay flat on her back and Strober, his back toward them, knelt over her.

"Son of a bitch," said Truman under his breath. Nik's head fell from his shoulder as he struggled to his feet and stumbled in uncertain steps in the sand toward the pair.

"What the hell did you do, pirate? What the hell did you do?"

There was something odd about them, and it became clearer as he made his way closer. He could begin to make out Jata's face, her eyes wide open and staring upward at the sky. Strober's back partially blocked his view of her, but he wasn't touching her, and then he saw something he'd never seen before in his life. He made out what seemed to be a colored tail that extended out to Strober's side above Jata's legs. It reminded him of a crocodile tail he'd seen in an Earth preserve once. But it was certainly smaller and strangely colorful. He stopped short and tried to make sense of what his eyes were telling him. He walked slowly the last few steps and the rest of the scene came into view. It was some type of odd creature, a fat little ball with an extended tail. Sitting on Jata's abdomen. The round body was a bright ball of color that seemed to pulse as he watched it.

"What in the name of everything holy is that?" whispered Truman in fear and disgust. The creature was hideous, and its bulging eyes immediately trained on him.

Strober looked up at him with a smile on his face.

"You better crack a smile—maybe even laugh a little, Truman, or you'll be right here next to her in a minute."

Truman couldn't make his brain process what he was seeing.

"Is she…is she dead?" he asked in a shaky voice.

"I'm not kidding, Truman. Smile and laugh right now, or our new friend will be all over you."

As if on cue, the creature turned its full attention to Truman, its tail moving like that of a cat ready to pounce.

Strober laughed out loud. At first, it seemed contrived and foreign, considering the situation, but the laughter had an immediate effect on the thing. It shrunk back and flattened itself closer to Jata.

"C'mon Truman. Help me," pleaded Strober.

"Ha ha," said Truman. "Ha ha ha." He felt nothing on the first utterance, but the absurdity of the situation seemed to dawn on him by the second, and it tripped something inside his mind. *This was ridiculous*. But it began to amuse him. "Ha ha ha," he repeated, this time feeling it deep inside himself as a broad grin crossed his face.

Both now were working on good belly laughs, with the fake laughing sounding funnier all the time.

As the laughter increased, the impact on the desert animal was clear. It shrunk to half its former size, and its bright colors faded to grey brown. By this time Nik and Guyal had made their way toward the trio and joined in the odd laughing scene, Nik with a puzzled look on her face and Guyal in full-on laugh mode, a large, joyful laugh hurled across the open desert. That did it.

The creature's tail wrapped completely around itself, turning it into an almost perfect sphere. What had been a smooth pulsing globe a minute before now shrunk into a blob of loose skin that formed hundreds of tiny spines, a small prickly ball.

Truman backed up. *What the hell was this thing?* Its last move looked like a defensive posture, but it had taken down a person. He wondered what else it might do. Sometimes the best defense was to launch an offense. But not this time.

With a final laugh from Strober, the thing shivered, then skittered off quickly into the desert, leaving a slight track in the sand's surface as it receded.

"What in the hell was that?" asked Nik.

"There's probably a scientific name written down somewhere that none of us can pronounce," said Strober. "We just call them sand vampires. They paralyze their victims, and then literally suck the life out of them. They prey on desert animals mostly, but humans work the same. Their poison isn't deadly, but if you don't scare them off, they'll suck whatever electrical energy your body holds—and the human body holds a lot—until you're nothing but a pile of flesh and bones. Sun and desert here do the rest."

"So, she'll be OK?" asked Truman. This was certainly outside normal evacuation protocols, he thought. *This would be where Durt took over. Durt would have known exactly what to do. What the hell am I doing here in charge when I don't have a clue about this place?*

Strober looked at Nik. "Do you use one of the saturated

perfumes?"

"I do," she said, already moving toward the sleds. "I'll be right back."

"Paralyzed, she can't smoke or ingest anything, but she's still breathing, so the perfume might be her best and quickest way back."

Bam had come up behind the group, his glasses now resident above his head, living in his mass of hair.

"What happened to her?"

"Damn vampire," said Strober.

Bam was nonchalant and nodded as if it made perfect sense to him.

"Guyal, can I have a word?" he said. "I have a theory that might help get us out of here."

10

TIRON

BY THE AFTERNOON, an onshore breeze had picked up, and Cotel could smell the aroma of the sea as it joined and became a part of the port of Tiron's essence. The wind blew a chill into the air, and as it funneled through Tiron's streets, he felt it in his bones. He jammed his hands into his jacket and leaned forward as he quickened his pace. The feel of the city was odd and impressive to him. The same hands and technology that built his ship had also put up these buildings he now walked between. Their square edges formed an imposing skyline, and the city's interconnected rail system became a constant background noise, the lifeblood of the city. Ruzilan had presumed they'd take a rail car, but he had other ideas. There was something about walking through a place, especially a place he'd never walked before, that he enjoyed.

He didn't usually leave the ship when it was in a foreign port, he rather busied himself with the business of the ship. The real challenge of operating a transport ship was the constant care and adjustments it needed. Ship readiness translated directly into better profit lines. But it wasn't just the ship. Books needed to be clean with full accounting lines for inventories and salaries. He liked to spend his in-port Mudson time with his family, so making good use of his underway and in-port deployed time for shipping business gave him the flexibility to do that. Not that he hadn't been ashore here before—usually to oversee repairs or meet with suppliers or some other appointment-driven, time-critical task. But he always took the rail cars. He was always on time. That was how business was conducted. This was, however, the first time, he'd ever made a social visit. He knew no one in Tiron, and it was not a normal social convention to invite a Mudson guest into a Kulian home. Today was no exception. The pair was not headed for a home visit, but to one of Tiron's city parks to meet Ruzilan's mother. As his one and only Kulian friend, he'd agreed to ignore cultural standards and meet the woman. Not because he particularly wanted to, but because he was asked to. And he was curious.

The city looked different up close and in the daylight. The skyline had been impressive as they'd anchored in the bay the night before. The Tiron skyline outlined in white lights with the occasional splash of colors of reflected red and blue signs offered a subtle margin of artistic variety to the city's lighted palette. Here and there, the lighted snake of lights of the connected rail cars made their way through the city streets. It was a familiar sight to him now, but so different from his homeport. When the sun went down there, so did the city. The only light came from a lighthouse, its searchlight warning arriving transport ships away from the dangers of the shore and lighting up the port facilities momentarily as it rotated its illumination. Not here. This city was industrious day and night.

Passersby shot him the odd look as they made their way through the streets of the port area and then went on about their business. He was an odd sight here. A good two heads taller and significantly slimmer than the standard short, squat Kulian body shape, he towered over his hosts. It was a practical body shape that supported a mining heritage and had permeated and defined their culture for centuries. His lighter hair and eyes added curiosity to his long stride and reflected the dual emotion of interest and distrust in their faces.

A 15-minute hike at a good pace through the city brought them to an open area that held fountains, tables, benches and the occasional splash of wild greenery, probably the area's natural vegetation before it had been paved over by Tiron's architects and builders. Ruzilan led them to a smooth stone table on the edge of the park nearest the main street they'd just traversed. He checked the time.

"She should be here soon," said Ruzilan.

Cotel smiled. He was enjoying the time away from the ship more than he thought he would. Behind him, the hum of the city continued, but as he gazed past Ruzilan's shoulder across the table from him, the beauty of its clean look and smooth lines, its fountains and gardens—if you could call them gardens—gave off a completely different vibration. A few Kulian citizens wandered slowly, sometimes gathering in pairs or small groups. The relaxed feel was contagious, and despite the fact that this was as foreign a culture as he'd ever really experienced, he drew in the relaxed energy with slow, deep breaths.

True to his word, within a few minutes Ruzilan's expression shifted from concerned anticipation to overt joy. His eyes lit up. A smile creased his face.

"Here she is."

Cotel turned and stood up. A woman descended from the railcar and made her way toward them. Her form was slimmer than he would expect from a Kulian woman. Her hat shaded her face and matched her long dark dress.

Was it black? If not, it was close enough.

While her legs were covered from view beneath, he detected an almost imperceptible limp in her gait as she approached.

Ruzilan beamed.

"Hello, Mother."

The woman opened her arms and embraced her son, gripping him tightly.

"Ruz, I'm so glad you're here. I—"

She stopped abruptly as her eyes fell on Cotel.

"Mother, this is the captain of our ship, Cotel Liber," he said, breaking the embrace and turning to Cotel.

The woman smiled and offered her hand to Cotel in greeting.

"Mr. Liber," she said, looking up into his face and squeezing his extended hand delicately. "I am Martine. It's so nice to meet you face-to-face. Ruz tells me all about your ship and your travels. Thank you for…well, thank you for everything. Please, let us sit and have some tea."

She waved her arm in signal, communicating across the city park. The tea vendor acknowledged their presence with a smile and a half-handed salute. She had another customer and while they waited, Martine assured him they would be served directly.

She sat across from Ruzilan as he quickly recounted the details of their latest leg of the journey. She listened with rapt attention, sometimes interrupting to ask what Cotel thought were fairly sophisticated questions about engineering and navigation, not what he'd expected from what he took to be a refined Kulian woman. She listened patiently as he brought her up to the morning's work of docking and unloading.

He was surprised at the transformation Ruzilan undertook in the presence of his mother. While his standard role was to play an extraordinary audience with a sharp mental focus, with his mother at the table, he became an animated storyteller. To Cotel, she reminded him of her son, listening, apparently fascinated, by whatever Mudson story or history he'd requested to hear again. She sat across the table, nodding and smiling as Ruz recounted his detailed report. To him, the details were so mundane, so oft-repeated over the years, that he found himself stifling a yawn and wondering how long it actually took to make and serve tea. Ruzilan's mother, on the other hand, was absolutely engaged in the minutia of the recounting. She seemed to know the drills and routines of the ship well, and this, clearly, was not the first time he'd told of similar transport trips. Ruzilan stopped in mid-sentence, a sudden realization crossing his face.

"A thousand apologies, Cotel," he said. "You must find this terribly boring. We can catch up later."

Cotel smiled. "Ruz, after the thousands of times I've been the one to talk non-stop while you listened, this is a nice turn of roles. You have a real talent for storytelling, and that's something I only realized in the past few minutes. Why have you not shared this with me before?"

Ruzilan opened his mouth to speak, but no words came easily. "I didn't," he began before he paused awkwardly. "I didn't think I really had anything to say that you might be interested in. This is so —" and he paused momentarily to motion with his arm to the park and the surrounding city, "It's so not worth telling. It's just so—"

"He's a bright boy," interrupted his mother who now saw it was her turn, "but he has this debilitating shyness that makes him think that whatever comes out of his mouth is wrong. Except around me. For whatever reason, he becomes another person. And I love to hear him talk. Not just because I'm his mother, but it's the way he talks. As you can probably tell, I don't have the ability to move around much. Oh, I get around, mind you, but I travel in much smaller circles than you two or my other two sons. I've never really been anywhere special. This is my city. I grew up here. I got married. I raised a family. That's my life, and I'm happy with it. But there's nothing more exciting to hear than the stories and adventures of those who do travel."

Ruzilan said nothing as his mother began a tale of him as a boy and stared at the city's skyline behind his mother's shoulder.

Cotel sensed his silence. *Ruz was afraid his mother would tell too much. In front of the man he respected most in life. Tales of him as a painfully shy young man. His hopes and ultimate failures.* He interrupted the conversation. Not rudely, but tactfully with a look of wonder on his face.

"This is something I would have loved to hear about, Ruz."

Ruzilan swiveled his gaze to see the approaching tea cart and broke into a relieved grin. He waved in greeting.

"Cotel, I'd like to introduce you to my good friend and tea maid, Sala. He stood up and quickly embraced the woman. "Sala, this is the captain of my ship."

The woman, short and slim with dark eyes and a non-flattering uniform that could only be described as utilitarian, bowed low.

Cotel stood and offered his hand in greeting. "I'm Cotel," he said. "It's a pleasure to meet you."

Rising from her bow, she took his hand and squeezed gently. "So nice to meet you. Welcome to our city."

She winked a greeting to Ruzilan's mother and moved a lever on the tea cart to begin the service.

"Three Standards?" she asked.

"Yes, three please," said Ruzilan. "this will be his first."

Cotel interpreted three standards as a request for three standard teas, but as the cart opened and the preparation began, it became clear that Three Standards was a brand of tea. The container and tea cups bore an insignia with three flags, each of which he recognized as representing one of the country's three cities.

The three standards of Kulan flags represented Kulan's major cities. Tiron, the city they were now in represented by a fish on a sky blue background. Cantor, another port city to the north, and a regular stop for their shipping trade was represented with the shape of a black mountain on a yellow background, and the largest and central flag, a red background striped with two white diagonal lines. The Kulian city of Mintero was the country's largest and oldest.

"You're going to love this," said Ruzilan. "It's our specialty."

***

Truman watched Jata come slowly back to life. Not that she was dead, but she looked it. The vampire had done a number on her. A cigarette now hung limply from her mouth, and her eyes stared blankly into the desert, expressionless. The heat of the morning was coming up and the group began to shed pieces of their clothing, tossing them into the sleds or wrapping them around themselves.

Nik waved a hand in front of Jata's face.

"Hello, Jata. Are you in there?"

No response.

"Give her some more time," said Strober. "She's sitting up now, and that's a great sign. She can hear everything we're saying and is following our conversation, but she still doesn't have full control of the rest of her body. Her vocal chords will be one of the last to recover."

"So what's the plan, boss?" asked Nik "I was going to ask you this last night, or maybe I did. I don't remember. Anyway, we have these two mini-ships here, and I understand what you said about the prison. I'm in no hurry to go to a prison, but there are human settlements to the north. Why don't we just buzz up there and call for a ride off this rock?"

This was normally a question Durt would answer, thought Truman. But like it or not, Durt was not here, and with him the de facto leader of this little group, he had to put on his best face and answer the question. *Of course it was a waste of time. His mind should be figuring a way out of here, not baby-sitting.* But given his new responsibilities, he didn't see an alternative.

"You're right Nik. There are settlements to the north, and that's where we're headed, but our real challenge is to get there in one piece. Our mini-ships, as you call them, are really just utility carts. They work fine in zero grav for construction site duties, but here in Claustrom's desert with Claustrom's gravity, they're little more than hover craft that run only marginally faster than a man can run. You saw how fast we were moving last night?"

"I couldn't really tell. It was dark, and the desert all looks the same."

"In Earth terms, we've got a top speed of about 30 kilometers an hour. And while we are heading north, we've got about 3,000 kilometers to drive before we're able to reach the mountain range that lies on the southern border of the northern sea. So if we can bring ourselves to spend 10 hours a day in these things, we should be there in about 10 days. If these things hold together for that long."

"Why? What could go wrong with them? They look brand new."

"They are brand new, but they're built for zero grav, not for this type of a desert environment. Not that I'm saying we will have a problem. I just don't know that we won't. All of this," he said, waving him arms at the group and their temporary encampment. "All of this is new and risky. Nothing's for certain. And I mean nothing."

The look on his face was hard, and he wondered if it was obvious how uncomfortable he was serving as the leader. It was easy giving orders on the ship. He knew how it worked. He knew what to say. Leading a crowd of unknowns into the unknown. That was a plan for disaster. Or at least it seemed that way.

He felt Nik take his hand.

"Look, Truman," she whispered. "We're all scared. Especially me. I know you don't have all the answers, but we're all relying on you to get us out of here. Just pretend you know what you're doing —maybe we can fill in the rest. I think Bam and Guyal are working something now."

She was speaking the truth. He could feel it. Maybe he didn't have to have it all figured out before he started. *How was that even possible? How much of what Durt said was bullshit? Most of it?* But it always seemed to work out. He took a deep breath and nodded.

"I'm probably the dumbest person here. The last one you'd choose on a team to trek across a desert," she said under her breath, "but I know one thing. I know you are one smart son of a bitch, and just knowing that makes me smarter."

He smiled. "I don't think you're the dumbest person here. I thought I was until now, but if I think about it, maybe you're right. Just maybe we'll be OK."

She squeezed his hand.

"Truman!" It was Bam waving at him from the sleds. Guyal had Bam's glasses on and Bam was moving Guyal's arms for him, a demonstration of what was apparently arm control of the glasses, just like Bam's performance at the New Manhattan loading dock. He now looked like a possessed man, too. Bam waved him over to join them.

Guyal had the Raven's flight recorder out of its case and on the back of the sled.

"I tuned my glasses to the output of the flight recorder, and we have full playback of Raven's entry and landing."

Truman turned to Guyal who was still motioning with his hands. He pushed both hands forward simultaneously, then stopped and removed the glasses, smiling. These are something else. Just phenomenal. Truman, you've got to try these things."

Truman waved him off. "Just tell me how it helps us."

"Here's our thought," said Bam. "We know that Durt had some kind of plan when he flew in here. Actually," he corrected himself, "we presume that Durt had a plan, because that's just the kind of pilot he was. Now, the nav system was almost inoperable, but the flight recorder—probably because it's designed as a flight recorder—did its job beautifully. Using my glasses as an interface, we've picked up his entered coordinates, and we should be able to re-fly his vector. Make that vectors, plural. We've got all the telemetry recorded here."

Guyal nodded. "Because he made a course correction, we figure we compare the two vectors. Where they intersect, we think, will pinpoint his intended destination."

"Makes sense," said Truman. "Probably one of the northern cities. I'm not sure how that helps us. Guyal should already have the city coordinates."

"I do. But here's the odd thing. The coordinates of his vector intersection are not in any of the cities. They're in the water."

Truman nodded. *Let them be creative. Don't dismiss them out of hand. Let them talk themselves into a miracle. Because that's what they needed here.*

As they discussed the vectors, Strober led Jata back to the sled. She walked slowly and with difficulty. He hoisted her up and placed her carefully in a rear seat.

"What about off-line conversations? He didn't say anything?" It was Bam asking. "Think back. Even some off-hand comment might help us figure out what he was up to. Everything I know about him makes me think he'd have some kind of plan."

Truman nodded. That part was true. But he had no idea. There was no conversation about what they would do once they saved the ship. It was all about saving the ship. And the crew. He and Guyal were silent, each contemplating the rising heat of the morning desert, playing back the landing in their minds.

"I know this might be difficult, but maybe you can walk us through it? Just the last few minutes."

Truman closed his eyes, remembering. "I was at the ship's coupling joint. That's the mechanism that allows the life pod to disengage from the larger ship," he said for Nik's benefit. "The surge did a real number on that thing fusing the electronics, and I couldn't get the manual override to work for anything. Durt was swearing to himself about all the crappy luck in the world that took our entry too close to the prison. We're all connected on the earcoms, and I remember thinking to myself how he was right, how all of our good luck after all these years had evened out and come back in one gigantic disaster of crap luck to bite us in the ass. So we sucked power from the shields for maneuvering, which did keep us away from the prison, but took a toll on the ship's hull. It started to break up from the heat. We were hanging on and praying. There wasn't a whole lot of talking going on. It looked for all the universe like we were going down in a ball of flame, when all of a sudden the field frees up some energy and we level out. I hear this whoop in my ear. Durt was on top of it again."

Guyal picked it up. "I watched as he re-vectored the Raven. We started laughing and talking at once, none of us listening to anyone else. That went on for a minute or so, but when we checked our console again, we noticed we weren't maintaining altitude, in fact we started to drop sharply. You could feel the planet pulling us in. We started picking up speed again at a dangerous pace."

Truman felt himself back in the ship again. An impact crash was his ultimate nightmare. He was not a good enough engineer to keep the thing flying. They were all going to die, and it would be on him because he couldn't figure a way out of a simple mid-air crisis. And then it came to him.

"I shouted that we needed more wingspan. I think Durt and I probably had the same thought at the exact same time. He said something like, "Here goes nothing" or "If this doesn't work, nothing will." I don't remember exactly, but some comment about it being our last-ditch plan. And he opens the cargo bay doors. Both at the same time. You could feel the difference in your gut. But that little bit of power was the last thing we got out of that ship. I strapped myself into the coupling seat and got ready for a landing. There was this great, ripping tearing sound as the doors flew off— pretty much at the same time. They weren't designed to be wings, and they didn't hold up long, but our forward motion was strong enough that we didn't break up on the desert sand—you saw what happened, we surfed along the top of it. It really was some kind of miracle we didn't burn up on that reentry."

"What about Durt?" asked Bam.

"Once I realized I was still alive, Guyal went to check on the pods, and I made my way back to the cockpit. And there he was, looking at me with this stupid look on his face. I tried to understand what it meant, because I don't think I'd ever seen that expression. And then I look down. He had his hand on his chest, and when he moved it, I could see a piece of metal sticking out of him that shouldn't have been there. Then his whole body tenses up, and I can tell he's in a lot of pain. I hear him say something like "Madonna mia," and that's the last thing he said."

"Not something like, Truman," said Bam. "Think exactly like.

What did he say, exactly?"

Truman concentrated, his brows furrowed. *Why was it so hard to remember? Did he say something more? Was he imagining this? Because it didn't make a lot of sense.* "No, that was exactly what he said. I figured it was some kind of prayer, but I'd never heard him say those words before. Latin, I think. No, he never said anything like that. Not around me anyway."

"Me neither," said Guyal, "I never head him breathe a word of Latin."

"Italian, actually," said Bam. "Was he a religious man?"

"Not that I knew of. He never said anything about it."

Guyal agreed. "In all the times we flew together, that was the one thing we never talked about. You do a lot of flying with a guy, you have a lot of conversations. But in that area, he always kept it to himself."

"So here's what we've got," said Bam. "We've got a destination that is in the water, and we've got a dead pilot whose dying words are in an Earth language that he never spoke before."

"It doesn't make any sense," said Nik.

She was right. It made no sense, but there *was* something else here, he thought. There had to be. The vectors were specific and the oddity of Durt's last words still rung in his head. *What was it? No coincidences. That's what Durt always said. No coincidences.* No, Durt was trying to tell them something.

"Maybe we're just thinking about it in the wrong way," said Bam. "Why Italian? Why the water? What are we missing?"

"Whatever it is, we need to move out of here quickly. In an hour, we'll be nothing more than half a dozen fried eggs," said Truman. He turned to Guyal. "Just go north. You've got the terrain mapped in your handheld. I'll follow. Keep your comms open and —"

Guyal looked at him a second longer. "And?"

"Find us a miracle."

11

Suspect

GRINDER STARED AT SIMMS intently. *What was his game? What did he, and what didn't he know?*

"The girl," said Simms, after an introspective pause. "The girl was my communicator."

That didn't make sense. Not to Grinder. *The girl—the agent he'd help rescue from exposure—was his communicator?*

"I don't understand, Wiz."

Simms looked up, a wan grin on his face. "No, I guess you wouldn't. Grinder, you're the one solid, reliable resource I have. I do a lot of convincing. I guess I have a real talent for that, but I never really had to convince you. You're loyal and smart, and that goes a long way with me. So I think it's time I give you a piece of the bigger picture."

Grinder narrowed his eyes. *This should be good.*

"As I know you suspect, I've been working an escape plan for a while now. I'm done with my chronic escaping for escape's sake—just to show that I can. I can, and I did, so that's no longer a challenge. The Casinos think by leaving me here surrounded by an angry desert, that I've no place to run, but right back here, even if I did break out.

"I guess you have to give them credit for their logic," said Grinder with a shrug.

Simms smiled.

"I give them exactly that. Every decision they've made in recent memory is based on their preexisting assumptions and their flawless logic. It's truly a linear process, the way they put this place together, which is why their security is full of holes."

"Full?"

"OK, maybe not full, but certainly not impregnable, not by Earth prison standards anyway. So here's my opportunity. Our opportunity."

Grinder nodded, but said nothing.

"They've rightly assessed that we have no real way off this planet. To them, that means we're not a threat, and in their unique way of seeing things, that's true, too. But we have something they need here. Something they can't get anywhere else."

"The prosciutto?"

"Exactly. The all-natural, non-molecularly manipulated, and delicious of course, prosciutto. We make it. We control it."

"No we don't. We don't do anything but cut it and dry it and slice it. We don't make pigs here."

"Correct. We don't. But that's one supply line they'll never break."

"You're losing me, Wiz." It still didn't make sense to him.

"We can leverage that connection." He pause before continuing. "The girl wasn't just any girl. She was a family girl."

OK. Now he was getting somewhere. "Family as in guild family?"

Simms nodded. "I've been communicating with them through her. She had an implant that picked up micro-transmissions when she was in close enough proximity to the Warden. It encoded any conversation she heard and picked up anything she sent. With her dead, now, I'm blind. I don't have a clue as to whether she was burned before she was killed. If she was burned, I'm burned, meaning I'm no longer worth much at all. Casino talent may be inbound with the circus. With me in its sights."

"The enemy of my enemy," said Grinder, not needing to finish his sentence. *Simms was conspiring against the Casinos. That could mean only one thing*. "So what's our play?"

"Figure out just who killed her. That has got to be our top priority. Whoever killed her is our Casino man. The way I see it, we find our assassin, we find our Casino leak. We need to cut off their comms just like they did mine."

"Or her."

"What?"

"The assassin could be a woman, too."

"Yes, of course." His hand was on his chin and his head was nodding. "Yes, it could be a woman. They'd probably use the same method of communication that our girl did, an implant with proximity transmissions. And that helps us narrow the field."

Grinder watched him closely. Now he was thinking out loud. His movements were animated as he moved around the room, and his words were not directed at Grinder, but rather at himself. It was like he was feeding information from his data-gathering self to his genius-self, hearing himself speak and processing the incoming information in a new and creative way. He still didn't have him figured out, so he kept his mouth shut and watched as the process unfolded. *Just pay attention*.

"So our man," Simms said and after a pause, "or woman, is someone who would be retained by the Casino and would have near access to the Warden, without attracting attention. Someone, I guess, who we'd expect to see in those areas. Now that can't be more than a handful of people so it can't actually be that difficult. Any rumors and cell talk, Grinder?"

Of course, there had been plenty of cell talk. Most of it creative and opinionated, but little of it plausible, and hence, little of it useful.

"Lots of talk, but no eyewitnesses, far as I can tell."

"He was careful, then. Guess I'd expect nothing less. OK, so nobody sees anything. A girl turns up impaled." He stopped for a moment. Grinder watched emotions play over his face, his anger rising with his speech. The fist of his good right hand was clenching and unclenching, almost uncontrollably. He froze for a moment, then tilted his head to the ceiling with his eyes closed. When he opened them again, he was calm. His voice was even.

"So the first one who comes to my mind is one of the chefs. The kitchen is adjacent to the comm building. Hell, it might even be possible to transmit from inside the kitchen."

"Maintenance tech?" asked Grinder.

The inmates took turns as the duty maintenance technicians for the few items in the prison complex, outside of the meat processing plant, that were actually automated and electronic.

"Techs have free run of the place. Wouldn't seem out of place at all. In fact, you'd expect to be seen at and around the Warden console if you were the tech. Calibrations, heat levels, signal strength, all that crap has to be watched."

"Right. But *that's* a job that changes on a regular basis. You couldn't count on that regularly. Unless—"

He stopped mid-sentence. "Unless you were taking it for others. Check it out. Check out all the cooks and the techs and see if we've got some enthusiastic volunteer who would rather take others' duties than mind his own business."

"One other group that we'll want to look at, too, Wiz."

"Yes. The latest arrivals."

"Exactly. You thought it was Vee didn't you?"

"I was almost sure of it."

"And that's why you took his hand."

"That's part of the reason. I also wanted to keep him off the test line and work a project for me. Less suspicious if he's been injured. Wanted him someplace where I could keep an eye on him and make my own decision about him."

"And what do you think?"

"Too perfect and too easy. Not really Casino style. They'd have somebody with good cover, not some lame hack like him."

"Is he a diversion, maybe? Send in an obvious to cover the actual?"

"It's possible. And that's why we have to take another look at the new arrivals. I don't like being fooled. It didn't end well for our girl, and it certainly won't end well for the one we find at the other end of this hunt."

***

Within a few hours the mountain range receded and shrank into a thin, almost indistinguishable ribbon at the edge of the horizon that lay behind them now as the two sleds made their way steadily north. The desert stretched out in all directions, a sandy carpet unrolling endlessly to the horizon. Their speed was nominal and now and again on the desert floor a rock or a gully distinguished itself as they passed by, but for the most part, the scenery was uniformly nondescript. The continuous line at the edge of the sky and desert made it seem like the sled wasn't moving at all, and the sameness of the scenery had a hypnotizing effect on Nik.

Her fear receded somewhat, and her mind focused now on her current situation. It was strange to ride like this on the sled. Although the sled's field protected them from the desert heat, the shield itself was not visible to the eye. Just like back at the crash pad on New Manhattan where she felt like she was floating alone in space, here, the field stood between the sun and the sand and the heat and the vampires and who knew what else, but it was invisible to the eye. As the desert moved along beneath them like a sandy conveyor belt, it felt like they were suspended above it, traveling free on some magic carpet ride. Conversation was sporadic and the comm system with the sled ahead was open, so when Strober had a question or Guyal had a navigation update, it sounded like they were sitting right there in the sled's cockpit beside them. In the rear seat, Jata was asleep again. Strober said it might be a day or so before she felt like herself and sleep was the great rejuvenator.

Truman glanced back, and she followed his gaze catching movement out of the corner of her eye. Jata shifted slowly in what appeared to be an attempt to find a perfect, comfortable position. Not likely. The temperature was comfortable, but the never-ending thought of sand was now having its effect.

"I'm thirsty," she said to Truman.

Truman motioned to her feet. "Over there on the right, see that rounded cylinder? Pull out, then down."

Sure enough, she detached the metallic cup and smiled as the cool water soothed her throat. Maybe it was that she hadn't really focused on a simple drink of water for a while, but apparently there was something special about that drink.

"Mmmmmmm. Delicious."

"These things really do a nice job of processing H20," said Truman, patting the sled. "Optimal filtration and processing and the perfect temperature. Like a work of art."

Nik watched Truman review the array of readouts again before him on the sled's dash. "Guyal, anything to report? Readouts here are within standards. No anomalies."

"Nothing to report," came the reply. "These sleds are new. Wouldn't expect anything else."

"That's why I'm the engineer. We're driving these things for something other than their intended use. Just keep your eyes open."

"Truman, since we're stuck in this situation for a while, if you don't mind, can you go over again your last few minutes with Durt?" It was Strober this time. "There's something in the back of my mind that I can't seem to put my finger on."

Nik watched Truman put his hands before him as if he were standing before a crowd and telling them to quiet down. He nodded his head, and his face was tight. She knew he wasn't much of a talker, and this wouldn't be an easy task, but it was important. And he seemed curious himself. Maybe he'd overlooked something or mis-heard something in the frenzy of landing. Maybe the repetition would reveal it. It took him a minute of his thoughtful pose before he spoke.

"I'm probably thinking the same thing you are," said Truman. "That he told me something, or he tried to tell me something, but just ran out of time. I think it was as much a surprise to him as it was to me. The body does some pretty odd things when faced with a major injury. But I've been turning it around and around in my mind. Two things. First, in all our time together, there was never a time that he didn't have a plan for wriggling out of a tight space. That was just him. And second, if he did tell me something, I have no earthly idea what that might be."

"I know it sounds like we're just wasting our time, but tell us again," said Strober, "Take your time. Tell us what you were thinking, what he said, how he looked, what was up on his console, if anything. If there's anything there, we'll figure it out. And right now, we've got nothing but time on our hands."

Nik knew Strober was right. They had plenty of time on their hands. She squeezed Truman's hand, and he did as he was asked. From their reentry to shift in vector to the lifting of the cargo doors, he recounted again, and they listened without interruption, the detailed story of their pre-crash. He had a sudden thought and stopped abruptly in mid-sentence.

"Can you review the flight recorder again? See if there's anything there?" he asked.

Bam's voice joined the conversation. "I've actually been following your storyline, and I've watched the readouts here on the flight recorder. It's all here. I think you've captured it all. If there is anything, it's either got to be subtle, like a puzzle to piece together —or he just didn't get it out in time."

"Audio recording, too?"

"Yes, but to tell you the truth, there wasn't a lot to record. You all were focused on ship controls. Really just the status updates that you've told us. Nothing else. Nothing we haven't heard before."

Truman said nothing. Silent concentration. Nik watched him tilt his head as if trying to will the solution out of his brain.

"There was something else there," he said. "I don't know what it was, but something there just doesn't fit exactly. It's right there staring me in the face. I just don't know what it is. Bam, can you go back to the last thing he said? That's the only part that seems like something that's out of his character. Something he wouldn't usually say. The Latin thing."

"The Italian thing," corrected Bam.

"Whatever."

"Hang on a sec. I think I can connect the box into the sled comms," said Bam.

A long minute of silence in the sled was suddenly broken with static and a shout. Nik jumped, startled. It was Durt's voice. He was yelling to Truman for a status on the coupling mechanism. Then the screeching explosion that made her cringe. Silence again. When the voice came back on again, it had a whole different tone. It was slow and deliberate and halting. It almost didn't sound like the same voice. Nik could picture Truman standing in front of Durt aboard the dying Raven, watching in horror as his friend breathed his last.

"Madonna Mia," came the voice. It was awkward, not like it rolled off the tongue, but like it was something difficult to say.

"That doesn't even sound like Durt," said Nik.

"I know," said Truman "It has almost a ghostly quality to it. I don't think I ever heard him say that or anything like that in all the years we were together. He didn't speak any languages. Not his style. You wanted to talk to Durt, you talked his language."

"Play it again." It was Strober's voice this time.

"Madonna Mia," again filled the sleds. Slow and halting. Broken.

"Again."

They listened intently. For three endless minutes, no one said anything. Nik could almost hear the thoughts of each of them, turning the phrase upside down and inside out, trying to unlock its meaning. *Madonna Mia.* Each searching for some kind of meaning in the words. She wrestled with the words in her own mind.

Everyone heard talk of your life passing before your eyes just before death. Is that what this was? Some glimpse, some shadow of a dying man's vision, nothing more? What else could it be?

"Truman?" asked Nik. "If what you said was true about the prison, would he be concerned about the flight recorder falling into their hands? I mean, if he did have a plan for getting off the planet that he kept in his back pocket as a just-in-case plan, and none of us survived the impact, that plan—that ability to escape would be passed right along to them."

"True," said Truman. "But that's a pretty big if."

Strober agreed. "It wouldn't even have to be all of us. If just the crew was killed, we the passengers wouldn't know enough to even look for the flight recorder, much less remove it and disintegrate the ship. It would be there for the taking."

"I'm just saying that if he was concerned about his information falling into the wrong hands, he might have been selective about what he left for clues," said Nik.

"What? Like something only people who knew him could understand?" asked Strober.

"That, and maybe something that needed more than a single person's knowledge. You know, like multiple keys."

"You think a lot like he did," said Truman.

A voice came from the back seat. "They're in prison, you idiots. They couldn't just break out and go looking for a wrecked ship."

Truman turned his head. Jata was shaking her head in disgust as if their whole line of logic was flawed. Her face was still tired, but her intention was clear.

"I'm trapped in the desert with Captain idiot and his crew of fools," she said.

"Actually," said Strober, "That's not too far-fetched. Let's say for a moment that we were stranded and wanted to find the prison. We break out the sleds and make it to the LZ."

"LZ?" asked Nik.

"Landing Zone," translated Truman.

"Yes. The landing zone. The prison is surrounded by a barrier field. If you know what you're looking for, and you're patient, even the simple gages on these sleds would give you a directional bearing when they open and close."

"They turn off the field?" asked Nik.

"New prisoners, for starters," said Truman.

"Right," continued Strober, "But the prison is also a meat processing plant, so traders from the north deliver pigs and the automated Casino prisoner ships double as cargo vessels on the return trip and take the finished product off planet. I guess my point is that I think Durt knew he could get into the prison. But that would mean—"

"That would mean," continued Truman, "he might compromise the sleds and the ship."

"And the crew," reminded Strober.

"And the crew," echoed Truman.

"Why are we even listening to this pirate?" came the voice from the rear of the sled again. "The only reason were here in the first place is because of his actions. I can't believe he's still breathing."

Truman turned again and faced Jata.

"Yes, the reason we're here is both because of him and thanks to him. We're here and not either floating in space or in the next world yet because of his cooperation."

He extended a finger and pointed it at her. "You in particular should understand that. He saved your life, not once but twice. Now don't get me wrong. I've wanted to kill him a couple of times since I met him, too. But until we get our situation sorted out here, I need all the resources I have. If the time comes, and he needs killing. I'll do it myself."

Strober said nothing.

The conversation went dead again. For the rest of the afternoon, in fact, conversation was sparse as the tiny sleds made their way northward over the seemingly endless desert. They were no closer to figuring a way off the planet than when they first stepped into the enclosed sleds. Nik could sense the heat coming off the desert sand, although she couldn't feel it, thanks to the sled's protective field. Invisible as it was, it enclosed and protected them as securely as if it were made of composite shielding. On all sides of them, the desert extended and fused with the horizon, the heat blurring the division between the two. The only measure of progress was the growing shadow of the sled that grew taller in the sand beside them as the afternoon progressed. The constant sitting was becoming unbearable, but the heat of the desert made it impractical to stop. They couldn't leave the protective cocoon of the sleds without putting themselves at risk. Truman said the standard strategy for crossing the desert was to move at night and seek cover during the daylight hours. But in their case, the night was the only time they could actually exit the tightness of the sled vehicles, stretch, sleep and regain some semblance of muscle flexibility from the cramped quarters. They might be able to change to some more practical approach as they reached the desert's higher latitudes, but here, driving in the heat was the only thing that kept their pace. Stopping every few hours might be more reasonable at night, but there was no sleeping in these things, and with the heat so extreme here, a daytime travel break was not an option. So on they went.

In the rear, Jata snoozed. Nik felt she'd like to do the same, but the feeling that had been building on and off for hours finally reached a point that was at first insistent and then unbearable. Nik tugged at Truman's sleeve. She mouthed her desire silently, hoping he could read her lips and her need. His puzzled expression said otherwise. She tried again without success, finally leaning close to him and whispering it.

"I have to pee."

She knew her face displayed genuine distress and felt a momentary flash of anger as he let a smile escape.

"What's so funny? Can you stop?" she asked sharply. She pleaded with him, mouthing silently, "I really have to go!"

He shook his head and pointed at the second digital readout from the end of the console display. She looked at it momentarily, her eyes squinting, not just from the sun, but trying to make sense of the number 160.

She shook her head. "That can't be how fast we're going. I thought you said these things would only do about 30 kilometers an hour."

"Temperature. It's 160 degrees outside here. We can't stop."

"But I can't hold it forever," she cried in disbelief, her voice a wail of discomfort.

He smiled again. "You don't need to. I'm sorry if this is new to you. Just go in your seat. It's all part of the sled's recirculation system that captures and repurposes all our moisture. The sweat that evaporates off of us. Everything."

"Everything?"

"Pretty much. It's actually quite efficient. The air we're breathing, the water we drink. All part of its closed system."

She looked at him incredulously.

"The water? The water I drank? I drank my own pee?" She tried her best to get the concept through her mind.

"No. Not yet. But you will later. The sled has a little storage capacity, but it is recycled for extended job site stays on construction sites."

"So what I drank wasn't pee. It came from someplace else?"

"It came from New Manhattan. But there's a strong recycling program there, too, so it's hard to tell where that water's been. When you drink it, you're only borrowing it anyway."

Part of her wanted to express her revulsion, protesting a part of modern life she'd never really thought about before. Mentally, she fought the whole concept of water recycling and reuse, exclaiming her disgust and her outrage to herself. But that part of her was fighting a losing battle. In an instant she relented and surrendered. The facial contortions of indignant protest gave way to an expression of relief as she embraced the reality of space travel and another of its various requirements. She sat back in her seat and just let it happen, doing her part. Making her contribution to the water supply.

Truman reconnected the comms with the front sled that he had discreetly disconnected when he'd heard Nik's whispered plea.

She thanked him silently with her eyes.

Silence reigned again. Until it didn't.

A loud peal of laughter broke the silence of the sleds.

It stopped for an instant, and then rang out again.

Truman looked at Nik for clarity. She looked right back at him, reflecting the same quizzical look he gave her. Out of the corner of his eye, he caught movement and turned.

Jata was a awake now.

12

TEA

TEA SERVICE WAS A SHOW. A treat for the eyes. Especially true since these eyes had never seen a Kulian tea service. Cotel watched with unwavering eyes as the metallic tea cart that appeared as a single solid object of metal began to disassemble itself, mechanical arms appearing from behind opened plates. What seconds before had been a dome of highly polished silver metal was now an ornate serving table, the spider-like arms and servos that put on the complex transformation were now a part of the finely crafted cart before him. In the back of his mind, he knew in practical terms that the actual service of tea need not be so complex to be functional. All they were really after was a nice cup of tea. But the mechanical artistry demonstration left him staring at the cart, trying to undo the process in his mind and identify which of the decorative corners before him had been that initial mechanical arm. He stared intently, but the perfection of the cart as a newly formed object was too precise in its formation, and shortly he gave up trying. His companions were staring, too, each with a smile as they watched him watching and inspecting the cart.

"Amazing," he said slowly as he looked up and realized he'd been as much a show for them as the one they'd offered him. "Simply amazing."

"You know we have this same quality of mechanics on the

ship," said Ruzilan.

He nodded. "Yes, but our ship systems are optimized for their actual purposes. This was—"

He trailed off. "This was a—"

Ruzilan finished his sentence for him. "Yes. This was a show."

"A show-off, more like."

"True enough. A show-off. We thought you might enjoy it."

The girl was serving with a practiced hand, and Cotel watched as the steaming tea filled cups bearing the Three Standards mark.

"There are seven different variations for the transformation," she said. "The motions are dependent on the type of tea you select. This is our most popular."

A show-off it was, and were he in their shoes, he'd be showing it off, too. This was their source of national pride. The mechanicals he'd brought home as kitchen support were impressive enough, but like the ship systems, there was little unnecessary flair to their function. They chopped or ground or washed or steamed or whatever they were supposed to do without fail, but they didn't transform like this. This was something special. "I did enjoy it. But I guess you can tell that, can't you?"

"Wait until you taste it," said the girl.

In fact, as she mentioned it, he focused on the aroma of the tea that had been masked by his selective visual focus. It was sweet and floral with an odd edge of some spice to it. He couldn't name it as it was something wholly new to him. Kulian tea and Kulian food in general was something Mudson children were told about and then shared with one another from the time they learned to speak. Children's tales told before bedtime always characterized the foreign food as poison or as having some destructive properties for the story's hero. The Kulian food would blind the hero or confuse him or something similar. Always with a different twist, but always warning the youngsters of the dangers of the taboo food.

The teacup on the table before him, the aroma became more intense, and he breathed in its exotic charm.

"Let it rest a minute," said Ruzilan, "You'll scald your mouth."

Cotel closed his eyes and reveled in the aromatics of the tea.

The girl had spied another customer and acknowledged with her tea wave.

"Go on dear," he heard Ruzilan's mother say, "We'll see you a bit later."

With the girl off to perform her next service, Ruz's mother broke the conversation into a new vein.

"Mr. Cotel, this is wickedly rude of me, but I need a few minutes alone with my son."

It wasn't a surprising request, and as he was about to acknowledge his assent, Ruz spoke up.

"No, Mother. Unless he has a real problem with it, I'd like him to hear what you have to say."

The woman looked up skeptically into Cotel's fair features and light eyes. She didn't say anything, but seemed to be making her best attempt to read his mind from his reaction.

Cotel shrugged. "Far be it from me to intrude into whatever matters you need to discuss," he said, "But Ruz and I share a special relationship. We rely on one another. More than once, he's saved my life."

"And you mine," replied Ruzilan.

"So for Ruz, I don't mind, but I'd be just as happy taking a stroll in your beautiful park here."

That seemed to satisfy the woman, and she nodded in understanding.

"There are two kinds of sons, Mr. Cotel. Those who break your heart, and those who don't. Me? I have both. My number one son," she said nodding at Ruzilan, "is not my eldest son. No, my eldest is my husband's son, through and through. This one is mine. He is dedicated to service and to making our country a better place and to making our family, well, a better family."

She patted her leg beneath the table.

Cotel heard not the expected slapping sound of a thigh, but a more solid thud. The limp, he remembered. The leg was another Kulian wonder. This was where Ruzilan's service and dedication lay.

"I have the ability to walk around today, thanks to my number one son. I lost this leg to disease when Ruz was a boy, and I always made my way around thanks to a helper cart. I didn't mind in the least. The boys and their father talked about nothing but replacing my leg for years. At the end of each of their deals was a brand new leg for me. But it never materialized. I didn't mind. I figured it was all talk anyway. But Ruz—little Ruz here," she said, reaching across the table to caress his face lightly. "Ruz put his mind to it. Don't get me wrong, Mr. Cotel. The leg matters nothing to me, but Ruz achieved something more than his older, supposedly smarter brothers could."

Ruz was obviously proud of the compliment, but at the same time, embarrassed to play the part of a Mamma's boy in front of his superior. Cotel realized the truth of his struggle was to overcome his painful shyness while becoming an ever more central player in the stability of his family.

Ruz closed his eyes and shook his head, as if he couldn't believe his mother would do that in front of someone he respected so highly.

"C'mon. Out with it; you only compliment me like this when you need something."

Cotel noted he didn't say it as if it were company or ship business, as if he were in the presence those he worked with. Gone was the professional demeanor. No, this was a family discussion, and he was included as if he were a brother or an uncle. Part of the family. And in a way, he guessed, he was. After the invitation and now this induction, he'd suddenly become a part of the family's inner circle. Not something that usually happens with a Mudson citizen. Ruz was himself now, and his personality took on a new dimension.

She nodded. This time without smiling. As her words formed, her features became a mask of concern.

"It's your brothers." She paused. "Again."

"Of course it is. It's always them. How much this time?"

"They don't need money. In fact, I think they're making too much."

Ruz nodded. "Haven't been by in a while, have they?"

"Not in weeks. And they're sending me things. Things I don't need. Things they can't afford. Something's wrong."

Ruz turned to Cotel.

"My two older brothers are brilliant. And I'm not saying that with any kind of sarcasm. They are bright and always full of what you might call entrepreneurial spirit. But along with that, neither of them have any patience or discipline. So they spend a lot more time talking their way out of situations than they do talking others into them. They're not twins, but they might as well be, with my father when he was alive, rounding out their third. Always working angles and never really having much success for any extended period of time. And that's where I would come in. I went to work for someone else, and my steady, predictable work has always saved the day."

He stared off across the park. The tea girl was in the middle of another service, and Cotel could sense Ruz's conflict. His life was surrounded by opportunities, but bounded by family presumptions and fear. Fear of what others might say or not say. He was just too sensitive for his own good.

"Too much money?" he told his mother, "Well, that won't last for long. They'll be busted flat and knocking on your door within a few days."

"That's what I thought, too. But people talk. I listen. This time they've outdone themselves."

Ruz rolled his eyes, but said nothing.

"They're working for Picek. At least, that's what I hear."

Ruz snapped his head toward her and narrowed his eyes. "How long?"

"Oh, I don't know. It's got to be weeks now."

"Idiots." He shook his head in disbelief. "Damn idiots."

Cotel picked up the edge of fear in his voice. *This wasn't overcoming shyness fear. This was lose-your-head fear.*

"There's more," she said, her voice suddenly quiet. "Bodies are showing up in the sea again."

"Mauled?"

"Almost unrecognizable."

***

Some things in the universe never change, and at least for the present, Simms' post in the tower room seemed to be one of them. Grinder made an unconscious half-turn as he entered the tower room, looking for the girl who was always here by his side before he realized what he'd done. *You couldn't be in the tower room with Simms if you've been skewed to death in the meat processing machinery now could you?* He looked at Simms again, just to see if he noticed. Of course he'd noticed. It was Simms.

"I keep doing it myself," Simms said. "She really became a part of me. I even ask her questions from time to time before I realize she's not here anymore to give me those flippant answers that only she could give." His eyes traced the floor to the chair where she'd sat for so many of their days together here, and a sad smile crossed his face.

Outside, the desert view had dissolved into just a faint remnant of the visible horizon. Almost total darkness surrounded them, with only a few faint lights from the complex below reflecting the ghostly shapes of the buildings. The scene was so familiar, it wasn't even a scene anymore. A prison in complete darkness looks the same as the desert that surrounds it. And out here, even though their prison walls weren't visible, for the most part it didn't matter. Even if they could deactivate the force field walls, they'd still be stuck in the middle of nowhere. Nowhere to run and no way to survive in the burning desert. Claustrom's sun could cook a human.

Simms spoke. "It wasn't one of the cooks, was it?"

Grinder shook his head, confirming.

Of course, those on the cook staff would be the first suspects on anyone's list looking for a Casino-backed killer. They'd have to give the Casinos more credit than that. But that was where the inquiry had to begin. Sometimes the most effective killers were those hiding in plain sight. Anyway, it hadn't been the case, but they hadn't yet ruled out the possibility of more than one Casino assassin in the prison population.

"In the past year, we've replaced three head chefs. Not because they're poor chefs, but because it's a hell of a job. I never paid that much attention to how they operate, but they take turns. They've got an unbreakable key program, so only one of them at a time could have had access to the Warden-adjacent spaces, so it was all of them or none of them."

Simms nodded, his eyebrows raised. "Our meals are fairly standard, but you'd think that with three different hands in the galley, we'd take some notice when they swapped places. Shame on us for overlooking such an integral part of our culture here. I think I'd actually like to tour our galley. Never really thought about it before."

He paused for a moment, collecting his assessed thoughts.

"So unless they've all come as a team, the cooks are cleared. I'm satisfied. Anything interesting in their arrival times or backgrounds?"

"Nothing I could see. Two of the three have been here around two years. The older one's been here five. Nothing suggests any prior acquaintances.

"I don't think either of us thought we'd find anything there, but it would have been easy to overlook, so a good place to start."

Grinder nodded. *Thorough they were*.

"What's next?"

"Mechanics."

"I'm liking that much better as a possibility. Any of the new arrivals mechanics? I don't think so."

Grinder agreed. "Not a one among the lot of them. Sometimes we get lucky and some real talent shows up. Standard load of pretenders this time."

"Except Vee"

"Except Vee," he repeated. "You figured they'd sneak someone in, someone you didn't know anything about?"

"I was sure of it."

"Worst undercover op ever, if that was their play. So you took his hand off. Was that it?"

"Call it an insurance policy. Hard to blend in; hard to focus; hard to do anything when your primary hand is sitting in a stasis bin."

"You saved it?"

"Sure. Saves me some time and him some pain if he turns out not to be a plant. When the time comes, of course."

Grinder shook his head in disbelief. "You *still* think he's the guy?"

Simms smiled. "Nah. He's not the guy. But he's clever, and he's come up with some refinements to my rough plan, so my decision to take it was still the right one."

Grinder said nothing as a retort. *Neither the time nor the place.*

"Mechanics it is, then. I'll let you know what I find."

Now it was Simms who lapsed into silence. He nodded as he stared through the darkened tower window into Clastrom's darkness. Grinder knew not what the dangerous and powerful mind mulled, but knew better than to ask and exited the room. The multi-level staircase took him five minutes to descend, and he opted for the surface transit between buildings. The sweet desert air, though still hot enough to soak him in a sweat as he crossed the complex grounds, was helped somewhat by an evening breeze. Within the hour, the outside air would become downright cool. Not that he'd notice. He slipped back inside the arena and made his way to his cell. He had some more inquiries to make, but he was tired and needed to give it some space. His inquiries were standard, and the inmates expected it from him. Grinder, the emissary of the Wiz. But too many questions in too little time had a way of chilling the quality of cooperation and answers. He knew how to work this community, and sometimes the best way to work it was to not work it for a while. And that was his plan for tonight. He'd wait. One of the two things he was truly good at.

***

The laugh confused Truman. The desert-scape, with the exception of the color shift before them brought on by the approaching evening, remained unchanged and unblemished as it had for the past hour. And the hour previous. And the hour before that. Beside him, Nik stared ahead into the unchanging landscape, but apparently she, too, was confused by the laughter. Her head tilted fractionally as she scanned the horizon before them. *Was there something funny or ironic out there that eluded them?* Jata was bolt upright in the seat behind Nik. Her head was moving side-to-side as if looking for something. Concern and fear directed her motions, and he heard her speak for the first time in hours. It was a single word, just back from the edge of her near-death sleep, with a hoarse edge to it. Like her throat was being used for the first time.

"Vampires?" she croaked.

Truman suddenly realized her fear and smiled. He couldn't help himself. The laughter was contagious and the woman in the back seat was only half awake. Probably just awakened from reliving the morning's paralyzing nightmare in the sand. He felt sorry for her. She'd actually learned a valuable lesson for them all. She also now had a new experience associated with a laugh, Strober's laugh especially. Next to him, Nik was smiling, too.

It wasn't really funny, but it was kind of funny.

"Where are they? I don't see anything," came the pleading voice from behind them. "Why can't I see them?"

"Alright. Enough already," said Truman, "Strober, you've scared Jata half to death here."

The laughter still tinged the edge of his voice as Strober

responded.

"Sorry," he said. "Is she OK?"

Truman turned his head and looked at Jata with pity, her features still wide-eyed with fear. "No vampires. Not in here, anyway. Just a crazy pirate."

Jata shook her head as if to shake off the sleepiness that fogged her mind. She nodded in understanding.

Strober's voice continued over the sled's comm system. "I'm feeling hypnotized by this never-ending sand parade all afternoon, and your story of the crash is running forward and backward in my head. Over and over again, with all kinds of improbable fantastic possibilities. I'm seeing each one of us conspiring to crash the ship. Small groups within our ranks banding together. It's an endless program playing over and over, most of it making no sense. And making less sense as the day wears on. I fall asleep thinking about it. I wake up, and it's still running. But now, instead of Durt speaking some random phrase in a foreign language, it's some frail white-haired old lady flying the ship. She's saying all the same things Durt said. The flight recorder played his words back to me, but my half-awake brain played them back with this old woman's cracked voice. I see her sitting there in Durt's seat. She has these old reading glasses around her neck on a necklace so she won't lose them. Just like I've seen in some of the old films. Her hair is so white, it's blue. She's wearing an apron like she just came out of the kitchen, and she's annoyed that she has to do everything. She's barking orders and she's flying the Raven, and she's blowing her nose and stuffing the tissues into her bra."

Nik was shaking her head and grinning at the mental image. Truman had no idea how this helped them, even if it was entertaining.

"And then at a certain point, she gives up. Like it's useless. She throws her hands in the air, and I hear her say those words. Madonna Mia. But it's not English. It's like in her mother tongue."

"Latin," said Jata.

"Italian," corrected Bam over the comm system. "It's Italian."

"Yes," said Strober. "It's Italian. But she doesn't say it like we say it. She has an accent, like you'd hear it in a film by someone who has grown up saying it. It just flowed off her tongue like we might say something like *son-of-a-bitch*. But her language. Her way of saying it. Her accent."

He paused for a moment. Truman listened. Now he was intrigued. Strober was a master storyteller. He just couldn't make out where the story was going. It had to be going somewhere.

"And then I think to myself, Strober, you've heard this before. Where have you heard it? Was it a film? There's something in the back of my mind I just can't dislodge. I love movies, and I've seen thousands of them. So I just sit here and start imagining films I've seen, but the more I try to remember, the more damning it gets. It doesn't come through. It's a blank. Something you may not know about me is that I spent some time on this planet a few years back."

"Now there's a surprise," came the sarcastic voice from the back seat.

Strober took it in good humor. "I know. A pirate in prison. You're all shocked into disbelief. It wasn't for that long, but one of the benefits of being locked up there is access to this unbelievable library of films and books. When I wasn't sleeping, I was addicted to seeing as many as I could."

"And Madonna Mia. Was that one of the films?" prodded Nik.

"That's what I was trying to remember. In fact, I remembered the phrase from a few different films, but not a one of them made any sense to me as to why it would sound familiar. And then it comes to me. And it's not just the words themselves, but the old tongue. The native language."

He broke from the flow of his film memories abruptly and seemed to start a fresh new dialogue. Truman didn't like what he called open loops. They were annoying, and this was one of them. He followed the new storyline nonetheless.

"There's a great northern sea that connects the planet's

indigenous population here."

"Yes, we know. We *all* know." came the voice of Jata. "It's called the Great Northern Sea."

Truman felt Jata's hand on his shoulder as she whispered. "Let me kill him. Just stop the sleds, and let me kill him now."

Truman smiled and shook his head.

Clearly it was rare, but Jata had a sense of humor, too.

"Strober, if this wild tale of yours goes on much longer, as much as I'm enjoying it, I'm going to kill you myself," said Truman.

Strober continued, undeterred.

"But they don't call it that here. They have their own names for everything. Even this planet. We call it Claustrom. It's our invention. What we call the Great Northern Sea, they call Namia. And they have a word that describes it. It's Mado."

"Mado?" questioned Nik? "That's not a word."

"You're right Nik, it's not a word. It's an acronym."

"What, like a local dialect?" asked Truman in true engineer form. He was unimpressed. "I'm telling you Strober, you'll have to do a lot better than that."

"It's an acronym. It's an abbreviation for an organization. Governments are phenomenal at coining these words. I think it stands for Mapping, Discovery and Observation, and I didn't hear it. I *saw* it. It was on one of the maps of the planet."

"Damn." This time was Guyal. "He's right. It's on the digital maps. But I never made that connection. I always spelled it out, you know, M-A-D-O."

"So Durt wasn't saying Madonna Mia," said Strober, "He was saying MADO Namia. That's two clues in one. I think he was telling us to check out the map of the Great Northern Sea. I'm betting that was his clue. That was his plan."

"And with the vectors—" said Guyal.

Truman was silent.

Beside him, Nik nodded in understanding. "Pirate, yes. Crazy? Maybe not so much."

The tenuous line of logic that Strober must be drawing between some mumbled final words and some kind of escape plan had to be just that, Truman thought, a tenuous connection. And if it didn't make sense, then, at least in his mind, it couldn't be true. Beside him, Nik had other ideas. Always the optimist and not ashamed of what she didn't know, her face lit with a smile, waiting impatiently to hear how the story might unfold.

"That's an interesting coincidence, Strober," said Truman, "But it doesn't really help us. What we need is a way out of here, not some smart-ass language puzzle."

"Truman. I've got to admit that I didn't know Durt at all. Only really by reputation. But let me ask you this. Was he one for a smart-ass language puzzle?"

It was true. If there was anyone who was, it would have been Durt, not that that made any more sense than it had before, though.

"How well do you know the history of Claustrom?" asked Strober.

"I don't know. Probably as well as anyone." *A lie, of course.*

Truman couldn't stand history. Never made a lot of sense to him how it might help anyone. Not that it was terribly difficult as it was nothing more than memorization of names, cities and events when it came to examination time. Once his education was complete as a young man, he ignored it and promptly forgot any history of significance. It couldn't put food on his table or repair a ship's power plant.

History belonged to the past. A good place for it. He wasn't fooling anyone, but it didn't matter. Strober could have his fun. Not that they had anything else to do.

Strober continued. "Five centuries ago this place was a frontier planet. The first hyper-gate gave us access to this system. Midway came first, with its commercialized applications and this, the system's other habitable planet, became a military outpost. The expeditionary defense forces established a presence here to watch over any potential threats, and of course, defend Midway's commercial interests. They were here to explore, assess and defend. They were most successful at exploration, identifying the second hyper-gate within a decade, but after finalizing their assessment that, in fact, it was a portal to the edge of the galaxy, and there was nobody out here but us, they had little motivation to continue their service as a defensive force. The military force was down-sized and returned to Earth. But—"

Jata interrupted from behind in her predictable annoyed voice. "Yes, yes, we know all this. What's your point?"

"What you may not know is that only about half of them returned to Earth. Down-sizing meant they'd be out on the street, for a lot of them, at least, so hundreds of them elected to stay. They'd lived there for decades already. They arrived as a single fighting unit, but by the time Earth pulled the plug on the need for them, they'd already carved out a life here. Rich, fertile lands with no Earth government to speak of. So they stayed.

"Why did they break off flights from here?" asked Nik.

"For a while they had regular supply ships, but when Earth decided there was nothing here they needed, they became fewer. Not that the community here cared. Most of them saw this as a perfect Garden of Eden. They lived off the land and evolved in the way they chose. Then, when the first prison went into the desert here, the ships stopped altogether. Only flights onto this planet are the automated prisoner transports and the occasional entertainment shows from Midway. Place has been quarantined for centuries."

"Still waiting," said Truman. "How does this help us?"

"Say you're leaving behind half of your people. What does that mean?"

"You wouldn't strand them," said Jata. "Nobody left behind. They'd leave them a way off."

"Exactly. They'd leave them a way off, an escape hatch. Legends in the military community are all over the map. Some say half the military fleet of fighters is still here someplace. Like a stash of some sort, if trouble ever came up. Others say just a few ships remained. In any case, whatever decision was made, it was considered to be in the military intelligence realm. Those kinds of things don't make the headlines. You can't go back to any archive and look them up. And after a few generations, the truth fades into legend. Which is where we are now."

13

PEACHES

AS DARKNESS CREPT into the desert and the long shadows thrown by the sleds faded, the outside temperatures fell. Each hour they drove north took them further from the perils of the prison and the desert and closer to the milder climate of the north. Nik heard grid numbers from Guyal as she'd flirted with the edges of sleep again. Truman had been right. The combination of stress and gravity and whatever else thrown in on top had made her constantly sleepy. Not that it mattered as her brain calculated the numbers automatically.

How often had she told herself that she could do her number crunching job in her sleep?

She'd never had the occasion or desire to try, just a saying really, but her brain seemed to miss the constant stream of numbers that formed her livelihood. Time and distance and velocity. They became a picture in her mind of the sleds moving northward, making time away from the perils and toward…toward what? The only way off the planet was behind them. In spite of her protests to the contrary, she had looked forward to the excitement and glamor of Midway and the subsequent return to Earth, and in their absence, she felt a sense of loss, of disappointment.

What would Mother say? "You drag your pretty little ass to the end of the universe, you know what you're in for. You get what you deserve."

She could hear it as if she were sitting next to her like Truman was, his eyes always forward, immobile. There really wasn't an end to the universe, and if there were, she certainly wasn't anywhere near it. But she took the point. Her mother was a pro at that. Stating the obvious, anyway. Stating something everyone already knew, then acting all high and mighty, like it was something you said constantly. A number of things had drawn Nik into a New Manhattan rotation. She could have worked in any major Earth city, and still might. With her resume and her experience now, she had the flexibility to choose her career location. But escaping that overbearing righteousness had to be near the top of the list. She done what, she presumed, her mother had wanted to do before she came along and surprised the both of them. She didn't talk of it often, but it was there, that underlying feeling that she should have done something more for herself than get married and raise a daughter. Certainly she had the mental capacity. What she didn't have was the perspective. All of her time was spent looking backward at what might have been and looking forward to what hadn't happened yet. For Nik, having children and raising a family was always a part of her planned future, but Mother's bemoaning her daughter's unmarried status wasn't as much a cry of her failure in her married-mother social circles as much as it was a cry of loneliness for the grandchildren she so desperately needed to validate what had become her own life choices.

All things considered, now that she'd been to Mother's so-called end of the universe, maybe it wasn't such a bad idea. How much and how many of her choices were made, not to follow her own desires, but in an effort to meet expectations of others?

Impossible to tell sometimes as one melded with the other, but in spite of all those reasons for leaving, there was a giant reason for returning. She missed Mother. Evaluation and reevaluation of what's important in life sometimes brought her in a full circle. The things she needed the most in life were staring her right in the face, and she'd missed them until now. Brushes with death, she imagined, had a way of doing that.

Outside, darkness now looked down on the sleds from a ceiling of stars that peeped at them from above. She watched Truman touch the console before him, and the warm, sweet smell of the desert blew into her face as the sled's field deactivated, and they settled onto the sand. She stood and stretched and caught a glimpse of Jata's awkwardly sprawled form now asleep in the rear seat. As she stepped out of the vehicle, she heard voices from the other sled, a conversation punctuated now and again by what she presumed were utterances of relief as their bodies rediscovered freedom of movement. The utility light from the back of Guyal's sled illuminated the array of containers stacked on its cargo deck. He pulled one free and stepped back. Instinctively, she walked toward him, realizing at the same time, both what was in the case, and that she was incredibly hungry. He set the case down on the sand and opened it. She looked over his shoulder at a bright array of colored panels. The case's inside cover doubled as a display screen. As he played his fingers over the various selection options, the corresponding meals flashed across the display. It wasn't the three-dimensional meal renderings that were common on New Manhattan, but a compact, ruggedized version of the same technology with a functional 2-D screen.

Guyal turned an inquiring eye to her.

"What'll it be, young lady? Steak and lobsters? Onion soup? A nice juicy cheeseburger?"

While it all sounded unmistakably delicious, she was in the mood for comfort. "Peaches and cream, please."

Guyal nodded as his finger searched and pressed.

"Peaches and cream. Superb choice," he said as a pill-sized morsel was deposited in the receptacle below the display. She retrieved it and popped it into her mouth.

"Take your time with that one. Enjoy," said Guyal.

She nodded, saying nothing, but patting his shoulder in thanks as the delicate flavors saturated her mouth and senses. *Wow. Better than sex. Almost.*

***

The hum was always there. The sound of their confinement. When the machines weren't online it was the sound of the barrier field. It was all part of the environment, unnoticeable at first because it was so all encompassing. Grinder knew the sound didn't come from the field itself, but from the aging field generators. Generators no one had the will to replace. They worked, according to Casino thinking. What was the point of replacing them? If the hum annoyed the prisoners, then so much the better. It was a prison after all and not a luxury resort. Eventually, they'd have to be replaced, but as long as they served their function of providing a barrier wall, there was little need to make the effort.

The sound was always there. Day and night. Night and day. Until it wasn't.

And when it wasn't, it meant prisoner transport, or in today's case, it meant circus rehearsal for the circus performers. For prisoners, it meant a show. One of the benefits of being confined in a Casino-subsidized prison was that even those of the lowest caste of Casino citizen, were still considered an aspect of Casino society. About once a year, Midway's entertainment branch reinvented itself for the benefit of its guests from Earth. A trip to Midway was never disappointing and because the entertainment experience evolved on a regular basis, the inbound flights were always overflowing with players with sweating palms and bulging pockets. On the return flight, their pockets empty but their conversations full of their Midway adventures, and now as perfectly trained Casino marketing agents, they would ensure the unending flow of Casino contributors.

Grinder remembered. It was a another life when his name wasn't Grinder. The adventure of space travel. The thrill of just walking through the city on another planet. The amazing meals. He'd been too young to gamble, but there were plenty of adventure games and rides to suit him. Some people spent their lives planning and saving for their next Midway fantasy. *Nice life, if you could get it.* He'd thought about that trip from time to time, but life, reality, and his failure to live up to his own expectations had somehow distorted his youthful vision of the planet. The series of decisions that landed him here played forever on his mind.

Would a different path have been a better choice? Would he ever have a chance to tell his story from his point of view? Would it matter?

The silence was delicious. It wouldn't last long, but the barrier field would be down for the next two hours. The actual passage of the transport vehicles that made their way south from the remote landing zone took only about a minute or so to cross the barrier, but along with ushering in the show materials, portable field generators, staff and performers and whatever else it took to put on a Casino-worthy show, maintenance bots took that opportunity to run offline diagnostics, replace parts and make necessary calibrations to the five barrier units.

This was where the Warden earned his keep—even if the Warden wasn't an actual human. Aside from the monitoring duties of prison and meat processing data, the Warden took prisoner inventory. Prisoners returned to their cells and were locked down for the duration of the operation. Bots delivering new prisoners were also programmed to hunt down any prisoners absent from their cells. No one was really sure what would happen, should a prisoner not present himself for inventory. It had never happened. Prisoners tended to look out for one another here. But no one trusted the Casinos. It was a standard part of the prisoner indoc briefing provided to incomings before their arrival, but the actual consequences were left unspecified, with the presumption, that it wasn't an action, or a violation, that would be taken lightly. Bots were usually a little too efficient for any trial an error, and in gray areas like these, the bot programmer's sense of humor was much more likely to benefit her standing with peers than with the prisoner in question.

It had been a long day, and with the extreme external seasonal temperatures, the arrivals took place in the evening. For Grinder, lockdowns were a time of solace. The locked cell door didn't bother him in the least. The wonderful silence offered a doorway to sleep. He smiled and surrendered to it.

***

The three days in the sled that followed were uneventful and, for the most part, indistinguishable from one another. Sand without end had a way of playing tricks on the eye. If he never saw sand again, it would be too soon. After checking and rechecking the simple dials and gauges for the hundredth time, Truman finally gave up looking for any patterns of variation in the sled that might reveal a defect that would leave them stranded. The temperatures now allowed it, and they were now making regular stops every six hours. They traded seats now and again for variation and to try and find a different position or a new thread of conversation to pass the time. Ultimately, they returned to their original seats, wandering travelers in the desert, with those seats the closest thing to a home they had.

The plans of what to do once they reached the great northern sea continued to elude Truman. *Still too many variables.* He was in charge, and he was moving in the right direction, or so he presumed, but how to be sure? He knew he couldn't be sure. *That was Durt's job. He was so cocksure of everything.* And pretty much, he always turned out to be right. This was not Truman's area of expertise or even competence. His specialty was fixing things that existed, not anticipating things that didn't. Thoughts of doubt wrestled in his mind constantly. True enough to his own assessment, though, much of the endless sand trek was spent sleeping. The sled temperatures were comfortable and the planet's gravity did a number on them. The direction of the sleds were aligned and directed at a single point to the north, and the constant sand horizon and passing sand beneath the sleds had a hypnotizing effect on their collective minds.

Next to him, Nik kept up a regular stream of conversational inquiry, asking about stories she had heard of Truman and Durt and then laughing when he reconstructed the actual events that the stories were based on. Truman was game to relate their adventures, but each one would trail off with a wistful gaze ahead. Jata became less sullen, although he thought the attitude came with the personality. He answered her practical questions and ignored the baited ones. Not that he always caught her intention, but after the first one, a sideways glance at Nik's expression became his proxy. Women were fickle from his point of view, but the sled time was teaching him a thing or two about them, whether he liked to admit it or not.

It wasn't until the afternoon of their fourth day that it happened. Later, Truman would wonder why he hadn't anticipated it, taken some measures to prepare. Mentally at least, if nothing else. The conversation had returned again to their progress, with Guyal consulting his instruments intermittently and Truman making his calculations. Nik was reviewing Truman's numbers when he heard an odd, puzzled tone to her voice.

"Truman?"

He looked over at her, but she was staring straight ahead. She'd adopted his standard stance for thinking.

She paused for a long moment, rubbing her eyes as if to clear away the grip of visual paralyses.

"According to what we've been saying, we have another five or six days of this before we reach the mountains."

Truman nodded. "More or less. Why?"

"When should we actually be able to start seeing the mountain range?

"I don't know exactly. But Guyal should be able to tell us. Probably tomorrow; maybe the next day."

"I think I see them now."

Truman, doubtful, looked up, finding the horizon with his

eyes. Sure enough, there was a distinct shadow above the horizon that hadn't been there last time he'd checked.

"Good eyes, Nik."

He hit the console intercom.

"Guyal. Eyes to the horizon. Can you give us a range from your planet data?"

Guyal's voice came back after a pause, thick with sleep.

"Hang on. Let me check it out."

Behind him, Jata had popped up and was scanning the horizon, too.

"I see it," said Jata. "But that doesn't look like five days off. Are you sure about your calculations?"

Her voice and her question grated on Truman so much that he cringed. He was about to respond and shut her down following a glance at Nik, but what he saw was not what he expected.

"I think she's right," said Nik, still staring forward. "Either our velocity is wrong or our maps are off. We're a lot closer than five days."

Truman looked up, ready to put their eyeballing theories to rest. But they weren't wrong.

Guyal's voice came back, less sleepy, but puzzled nonetheless.

"Truman. I have the scans and maps in front of me, but there's nothing there. I mean, according to the instruments, there's no mountain range. We shouldn't be able to make them out visually for another two days.

Give me a minute, let me run diagnostics."

"Don't bother," came a new voice to the conversation. Strober had been sleeping as well, but his voice had more of an edge to it than just sleep. "It's not a mountain range."

"What are you talking about?" asked Nik, indignant. "Of course it's a mountain range. What else could it be?"

"No mountain range," he repeated, more urgently this time. "It's a sandstorm."

***

January was smiling. Jan, for short, sat between Grinder and Simms. Grinder admired her creation. Her handiwork. She'd had a hand in the set design, and a solid day of non-stop effort by her and her team had created a new vision. It made his exit from lockdown more than a relief. She and her staff had transformed the sterile, static cell blocks of the arena into what would soon dazzle Earth's rich and famous. They'd pay through their golden noses for access to the stone seats they now sat on. The Casino considered this a dress rehearsal, but to the viewing audience, the dress rehearsal moniker made no difference. There were no mistakes or retakes here. The dress rehearsal was about the timing. Set up and tear down. Intro and finale. It needed to be timed and orchestrated perfectly for Casino scheduling. Only so much time was available, and every movement was choreographed distinctly to this end.

With the stage set, the arena was no longer the arena. Grinder squinted his eyes and turned his head to try and reimagine in his mind what the arena looked like before the circus stage was set. The circus here was nothing new.   Each year—sometimes in half that time, depending on when new show concepts were hatched on Midway—it had a new twist. Sometimes it was just subject matter, but other times—and this was one of them—they'd harness the technology of field manipulation and object rendering in a new and unique way. What the eye saw had no relationship whatsoever with its staging grounds. The layers and floors of side-by-side cells on the opposite side of the arena had disappeared into the stage scene. On the side of the prisoner audience, the semi-circle of cells that remained had transformed into an open gallery of terraced stone for the viewing audience, an open amphitheater in the early Earth style. He shook his head in wonder. They had outdone themselves.

Out of the corner of his eye, Grinder caught unexpected movement. A lone standing figure moved about in the seated crowd, a buzz about him of raised hands, whistles and curious eyes. He turned to Jan with curiosity in his eyes.

"Popcorn," she said.

"Real, organic popcorn? I don't believe it."

"Nor should you. But you couldn't tell the difference."

Grinder knew she was right. Molecular manipulation had made the foodstuffs of film legend available again, and while it wasn't cheap, it was certainly more feasible and cost-effective now than finding and cultivating arable land.

"Taste-wise, we're there. We're still experimenting with its structure to replicate exactly its substance. Like everything else here, this is a testing crowd."

And the crowd responded. The novelty of popcorn, a first on prison grounds, was having its desired effect. It was first tasted, examined and consumed. Without fail, the creative minds next tested its airborne properties, tossing it at one another, some even trying to catch it in their open mouths. Grinder winced as he saw pieces bound for the floor. The waste of effort, he thought, to create something that amazing that would wind up underfoot like dirt and sand. He shook his head. But bounty and waste were both a part of the Casino culture. If the crowd reaction was any measure, their playful boredom was a welcome break from the banality of the daily prison routine, maybe not so different from Earth-side vacationers on Midway.

Beside him, Jan was immobile. Only her eyes moved as she watched the crowd intently. She was part coordinator. Part psychologist. Part marketer. Which elements worked? Which elements would create the draw the vacationers couldn't resist?

Grinder followed her gaze, taking a mental inventory. Animated and happy, some of them looked like different people, their faces transformed from the ones he watched over and spoke with each day. Excited. Anticipating. The prison culture and attitude was now on its head. He was smiling, too, without even realizing it.

He spotted Vee two rows up and near the edge of the terraced, stone-rendered seats in animated conversation with one of the younger female inmates. She was tossing popcorn at his face, and he caught one now and again. Vee caught his stare after a bit, and waved a greeting. Grinder waved back. *Lose a hand; get a girl?* Whatever animosity he'd harbored before seemed to have disappeared. For the moment, anyway. He shot a sideward glance at Simms. Simms was watching him, too. But he wasn't smiling, and he didn't wave. He seemed to be studying Vee from a distance. While Jan's motives were transparent to him, Simms' never were. That's what made him dangerous.

On the ground before them stood a traditional market scene with three tents, one primary with two supporting tents on either side of it. Behind, an open desert stretched its sandy reaches into a distant horizon. The detail on the tents was exquisite, with the front tent reflecting a sewn patchwork of fabric, thanks either to the intricate programming of the render or an actual handmade set piece. Either way, it added depth to the desert scene.

A warm breeze and the scent of the desert blew into their faces. A thousand or so voices that made up the prisoner audience buzzed in as the effect became apparent.

"Is that a synthesized breeze, or are you taking it from outside?" asked Grinder.

Jan smiled her appreciation. "What do you think? It's our call to order."

"I think I can't tell. It smells just like stepping outside, but you wouldn't short us here would you? Because you have to recreate it on Midway."

"No one knows what the desert smells like better than this audience, so you're our sniff test."

"Amazing," said Grinder in wonder. "It doesn't get any more authentic than this."

To Jan's left, Simms was silent. You'd think he'd be more enthused to see his girl, thought Grinder. He supposed the Wiz had his reasons, his thoughts, his schemes. He always did. That was just The Wiz. He was usually well tuned into that frequency of thought, but he'd let it go for tonight. Tonight was not about scheming, it was about experiencing. He liked Jan, and despite her many female assets and charms, he was more attracted to conversation with her than anything physical. Part of it was the lockdown and the endless drudgery of their prison existence. A new perspective helped ease the psyche immensely. The other part was that fine line between being an engaging conversationalist with Simms' lady friend and creating the kind of jealously that left you looking over your shoulder and then one day, without warning, dead. Simms' mind was elsewhere tonight. It wasn't the first time, and he'd done a visual check already to make sure he wasn't overstepping. A nod from Simms and a silently mouthed "thank you" confirmed it.

They talked incidentally about show preps for another minute or so, but there wasn't a lot more time for talk. He wasn't sure if he heard the pounding and rumbling first, or if she involuntarily touched his arm first. It came from nothing and then it was everywhere. The market scene in front of them turned to chaos, vendors and shoppers alike, running out of the tents, the ground vibrating beneath them. In the audience, prisoners looked at one another. Some stood up, searching for the nearest exit. Beside him, Jan's face showed concern and worry, her hands gripping his forearm on one side and Simms' on the other. An earthquake?

The tents before them suddenly exploded in flames. He could feel the heat on his face, and he sat back involuntarily. Jan laughed next to him, her face now transformed with glee. What had been a wall of flames before had become a ring of fire in the sand surrounding a pedestal that stretched what must be 15 meters into the air. On top stood the familiar figure of Moot, arms outstretched to the audience. The pounding was now a familiar bass line and the melody was one he'd heard before. Wow. The crowd roared and was on its feet shouting approval. Without realizing it, he was on his feet, too. That was a concert opening like he'd never seen before. He realized he was breathing hard and starting to sweat. Next to him Jan was beaming.

"Now that's how you open a show!" she shouted to him over the music.

14

ELEPHANTS

THE ELEPHANTS MARCHED in a column. Here and there one got out of line, and its rider would reign it back in. Perfectly synchronized animals would look like the field rendered objects they were. Grinder realized this was the next step in programming. Here and there he imagined, performers from the crew were interspersed with the rendered actors, but for the life of him, he couldn't pick them out. He couldn't tell the difference. To the audience, it looked as if a military column of elephants were being driven into the arena. This certainly was the next step in performance programming. If programs could fool the human eye, there was little of the valley left between actual and perceived performance. The elephants split into rows, then turned back on one another, becoming a single formation. It wasn't flawless, but almost. Just enough flaw to make it real. Above the din of the stomping feet and the occasional trumpet came the shouts of riders, urging their mounts to perform. The scent of the animals now permeated the arena. Gone were the sweet smells of the morning desert. The stands shook with movement of the beasts and their performance. Involuntarily, Grinder caught a pungent whiff of the elephants and grimaced. Beside him Jan smiled with satisfaction. Around the audience, the smell of the performance had similar effects. He'd never seen an elephant before—except news reports and in films, of course. He knew their shape and their gaits, but little else. He was riveted. The elephants paraded and drilled for another ten minutes before reforming as a column and departing just as they entered, a small elephant trailing the final rank, attempting to keep up with the larger animals ahead, a comical close to an impressive show.

The big cats were next. Big cats here were an apt description, not in comparison to a standard house cat, but in comparison to Earth's big cats from the forests and jungles. They were a mixture of breeds, from the dark and shiny coat of the black panther to the eye-dazzling flash of the Bengal tiger, an odd assortment of orphaned strays a million miles from home, or that was the intent, Grinder guessed. But their grace and power were only part of their intrigue. It was their size that impressed the audience. One paw of the black panther was the width of the trainer's chest. The feline forms towered over him as he cracked his whip and encouraged the cats to jump and balance, sometimes in pairs, other times as a group. The trainer seemed to have trouble with one of the pumas. It distinguished itself as the one cat that wouldn't stoop to the level of the performer, lashing out frequently with snarls and paw swipes. He agilely dodged each time just beyond the reach of the giant paw with its extended claws, until he misjudged. The cat seemed almost surprised, but wasted no time in tossing its human trainer head over heels vertically into the air, the man screaming and twisting as he fell helplessly into the mouth of the giant puma. A collective intake of breath and a wince of sympathy pain escaped the audience as they heard the scream silenced by the crunch of bone as the giant teeth closed on the human. Not a sound escaped the audience until the trainer reappeared from behind the puma that still licked its chops, and the crowed applauded, laughing as the performance's sleight-of-hand became apparent, and both the trainer and the rendered puma bowed in unison.

Even Simms, on the other side of Jan, was enjoying himself. He was on his feet like the rest, whistling his appreciation and waving his one hand in the air.

Jan turned to Grinder. "Our latest generation gives us a whole new dimension to the show," she said. "Your mind believes what it sees. Even if logically, you know it's not possible for you to be seeing a column of elephants, you see it. Add in the sensory perception of scent and vibration, and you can't help but be taken in, even if it's only for a moment."

The crowd was still whistling and stomping as the trainer, and this time, all of his big cats took their second bow.

"You had me with the first elephant. I've never seen anything like it."

"It's not the renderings that make you believe. It's the imperfections." Jan was bubbling. "You're so used to presuming that rendered objects are always perfect, and they always follow clean symmetric patterns. This new generation of organic animators have pushed our performance art into a whole different universe."

January was one of the most attractive women he'd ever met. Green eyes, sharp features and a body to die for. He glanced quickly beyond Jan to Simms as those words crossed his mind. No, he didn't want to die for her, he reminded himself. He was on babysitting duty. *Focus*. Not that it mattered just now, though. Simms' demeanor had changed again. His faraway look returned, and his gaze was forward.

The applause faded and Grinder followed the direction of Simm's gaze back to the arena. He'd missed the transition. The big cat set was gone. In its place was an ocean. The sand at the base of the stone seats was now seawater, and from his perch, it was as if they floated above its surface. A pair of prisoners with ringside seats moved down to dangle their feet over the edge. Waves rose to cover their feet and knees before receding again. He heard them whoop with delight. It wasn't every day the ocean came to the middle of the desert.

On the horizon, he saw what Simms must have been looking at

moments before. He made out sails on the horizon. The top masts of a sailing ship were visible. He stood transfixed. A strong ocean breeze now blew across the viewing audience. He could taste the sharp smell of salt as he breathed in deeply, closing his eyes and reveling in the experience. When he opened his eyes again, there was something new on the horizon, a second set of sails pursuing the first. He smiled in anticipation. A naval battle? Was it even possible? Why not? he thought. If you can render giant cats, a battle at sea should be well within the realm of possibility. He heard a distant boom and felt its thump in his chest and smiled again in anticipation. His heart beat faster. The two sets of sails grew in size at the edge of the horizon, one square-rigged warship pursuing another. The crowd watched in awe. The 19th century age of sail was familiar to most of them, thanks to the prison's comprehensive film library. Coincidence. Or not, he thought, as the role of Jan's marketing strategy crossed his mind. Her attention was not on the ships, but the audience. She'd clearly seen the show to distraction and helped create its tension and choreography. She understood as well as he did that within the prison population was an avid subculture that watched films from this time period, probably more times that she had. They discussed strategy and power and politics of the era. He'd sat in on a few, but their level of detail in each of their discussion topics was beyond his attention and interest level. There was something about this age, though, that intrigued him, and he'd watched the full collection of films, even if the majority of that collection was available only in the ancient 2-dimensional format. Now what lay before him, this was...well, this was the real thing. His mind was convinced. They had balcony seats to the approaching battle. He tried to make out the flags that flew from the ships' masts.

***

Nik's eyes were stuck on the wall of sand. For a minute silence surrounded them. Mechanically they stared at something they'd never seen before. The sleds drove them ever closer. Nik heard herself whisper. "Truman, what do we do? Is this it?" Truman looked back at her. It wasn't a face of concern.

"We'll be fine. Just delayed, that's all."

He touched the intercom on the console.

"Guyal, I'm watching you. Putting down on your lead."

"Down it is," came the reply, and Nik watched as they followed the lead sled into a hover and then a downward float to the desert floor.

Strober's voice came over the comm link. "How much longer do we have before the sand locks us in?"

Nik watched Truman as he took another look at the approaching line. "Its size still looks about the same. Hard to tell from this perspective. Just keep your eyes on it."

Guyal took a guess. "Probably less than 10 minutes, but that's not a scientific opinion. Just a navigator's sense."

"Ration generators. How many did you take from the ship?" asked Strober.

"Two. I stowed one in each of the sleds," said Guyal, "Why?"

"According to your estimate we have precious little time to retrieve them from the cargo and move them inside the sled's cabin. Unless you have a way to dig around in your cargo from inside."

Silence.

"How long could the storm last?" asked Nik, her voice rising and tinged with uncertainty.

"Anywhere from a few hours to a few weeks," said Strober. "Depends on the storm. I remember one time—"

Truman cut him off. The urgency in his voice matched Nik's expression. "Do it. Do it now," he said tightly. "They're utility carts, not fancy transports. They don't work that way."

As he was talking, Nik watch him find the field console button. The protective barrier dissolved, and a desert blast slammed into her face. She grabbed her seat in surprise. It was hard to breathe. Outside the temperature had dropped significantly, but the heat remained oppressive. She figured they could stand it, but not for long. Next to her, Truman jumped out and made his way to the back of the sled.

"Where is it?" he shouted over the wind to Guyal. Nik could see him pulling containers left and right. "They all look the same!"

Without a word from the back seat, Jata had launched herself out of the vehicle and now stood beside him, grabbing containers and pointing. In front Guyal pulled the case from the night before off the top of the sled's containers and made his way to the rear sled. Nik watched as he hurried by. She was sweating from the heat, her discarded flight suit top no longer playing its protective role. Her shirt was soaked just by the short exposure to the desert heat. Guyal was sweating, too, the moisture beading and dripping off him. And every drop of moisture seemed to attract and trap sand. Their faces were now covered with a thin layer of sand, it stung her eyes and she squeezed them closed. A black case flew over the cargo area and thumped into the back seat. Seconds later Truman and Jata were back in their seats. The cabin field reactivated and everything went silent again. She looked up at Truman and then back at Jata. Both were panting like animals, Jata with one hand on the case beside her. Their prize.

Beautiful, she thought, as she tried unsuccessfully to brush the sand from her face and forehead. The sweat had caked it on, and all she was doing was pushing it around, scraping her skin.

"Just give it a few minutes," said Jata. "Let it dry and then try again."

Nik nodded and turned to Truman again. "How long? You know we can't stay in here for weeks."

Truman shrugged. "Anybody's guess. We don't have much choice."

"Can't we drive out of it?"

"Too dangerous. We do have our own protective field here, but we're still vulnerable to the laws of physics. Remember the explosion and how we flipped after the hyper-gate? Sandstorm will do the same thing. We could be caught up and blown anywhere it well enough pleased. Our best bet, if we have a best bet, is to stay burrowed here in the sand until it passes."

Nik closed her eyes. With her eyes closed, it looked the same in her mind as it had before, the endless sand spread out in all directions away from them. The sound was the same. Rather, the silence was the same. The wind was clearly screaming now, but within the sled's field, it was as calm as a quiet desert evening, like their first one under the stars. Fair enough, she reasoned with herself. Can't really do much about it. She had no idea what she'd do if this went on for weeks, or even more than a day or so. There were a number of things she didn't want to think about right now. With all the scramble in the last few minutes, her heart had calmed somewhat, and in spite of her racing mind, she felt a yawn coming on. Truman must have had a sympathetic thought, as she watched him stretch his arms out and yawn. He, too, must feel another sled-cramped nap coming on.

When the sand wall hit, two things happened, almost simultaneously. The abrupt force of the wind twisted the horizon, driving it down into the sand. And it got dark. Like night. The density of the sand blocked out the sunlight almost completely. Safety lights near their feet and on the side of the sleds threw an odd green light. She could make out shapes, but not much more. They'd need better lighting than this if they were to break out the rations later. After all that had happened, at least that was something to look forward to, she thought.

Behind, she heard Jata stretching as well. They were tired. It was dark. Sounded like a perfect opportunity to go to sleep. And it was, until it happened.

Nik would remember this moment later as a critical turning point that transformed her from a quiet hopeful passenger to a resigned and fearful woman. It could be worse. That's what she always said. She had quite a knack for putting things into perspective with that phrase. It could be worse. It was bad, the whole crashing a spaceship thing, and she guessed she ought to be thankful for the fact that she was still alive, but she didn't feel very thankful now, and she was just about to feel less thankful.

Through the darkness of the screaming sand came a flash of light. She blinked her eyes, not sure what she had seen. It flashed again, this time stronger. She looked over at Truman. Who was rubbing his eyes, probably wondering if he'd seen it, too.

"What the hell was that?" came the question from the back seat.

Truman was on the intercom. "Guyal. Confirm."

Guyal was back on the comm link immediately. "Truman. Affirmative. Confirming sandstorm lightning here."

"Oh no." whispered Truman.

"Just hang on tight, and keep your fingers crossed," Guyal said.

Truman shook his head. "Won't do a damn bit of good. Huge amounts of energy in the storm, and we sit here operating two independent energy fields. Energy has to go somewhere. One or both of us will be toast."

"Be positive. Maybe we'll get lucky," said Guyal.

"Only one kind of luck on this planet. Let's just say the wind's not blowing our way today."

Nik knew Truman had been wrong before about things he wasn't familiar with. But he wasn't, she thought as she took his hand, gripping it. Not this time. She was frantic. Shaking.

Beside her, Truman was quiet. Saying nothing and nodding his head from side to side. Denying it. As if he couldn't believe it was happening.

She squeezed his had tightly and shook it back and forth. "What do we do? Truman, What do we do?"

"The only thing we can do. We die."

His pronouncement stopped her in her seat, frozen.

The silence shattered a moment later with a brilliant flash. Nik felt her hair stand on end as the energy crackled around the cabin, and in an instant everything changed. A million things happened at once. The lightning hit interrupted the field generator. It went dead. Nik screamed, but the sound of her scream drowned in the full fury of the storm as it crashed into their unprotected sled.

***

The wind died. Grinder felt the change on his face, and he saw it in the eased heel of the ships before him. The fresh breath of salt air that fueled the ship-on-ship pursuit died away. A light breeze remained, and the pursuing ship, a bit smaller than the lead ship, used its maneuvering capability to its advantage. He could now make out the crew and hear their shouts as they closed the distance between them and their prize. Again, the chaser cannon from the forecastle, the front deck of the pursuer, spoke in its demanding voice. Shots cracked, and Grinder was able to make out sharpshooters from the rigging of the larger ship, firing back at their attackers. An attempt, he presumed, to take out their command and control. One of the shots hit home, and he watched the figure behind the ship's helm collapse. But the impact of the shot was negligible as another sailor stepped up immediately to take his place. Its gun ports open and its cannon extended and ready for action, the smaller ship tightened sail from its downwind course, swinging wide, then catching the breeze on the other side and maneuvering to a new course that would bring its firepower to bear on the stern of its opponent. The larger ship began a maneuver to take an evasive course and protect its vulnerable backside, but its size made it slow to respond to the light breeze. Its rudder was hard over, but it made little evasive progress. Behind it, the smaller ship glided in behind and began its devastating attack. Canon fire thumped through the audience, fire spewing from the big guns as one after another their canon balls ripped into the after-structure of the ship. Smoke billowed and engulfed portions of the ships from view. The acrid oder was heavy, and Grinder could make out the human sounds of battle, the excited roar of the attackers and the screams of the wounded.

Beside him Jan was in action. Her gaze, as before, was not solely on the battle. Instead she divided her attention between the progress of the fight and the reaction of the crowd. Her head snapped back and forth. She knew the script inside and out. She knew when to expect reaction and was judging her own assessment against an audience who had no idea what to expect next. And then it happened.

Judging by the flag, if he remembered his history correctly, the larger ship flew the French flag. Red, white and blue, it streamed less proudly from its after-mast, now that the wind had slackened. The other ship, though, flew no flag. Its sails were a patchwork of canvas, sewn and re-sewn, as if stitched together from its own scraps, day after day, its battles constant, and its crew forever on the brink of the next battle. Unlike the hull of the French ship that reflected the ocean sun brightly as if its planking were fresh, its mettle yet untested, the hull of the flag-less ship, like its sails, was a patchwork of various types and shades of wood, probably scavenged from its less fortunate opponents. Despite its dismal appearance, the ship handled the wind sweetly, and its crew made the most of the vessel's potential.

January was biting her nails next to him. Something big must be on its way. The show was engaging, and he was a huge fan of Earth's age of sail, but if she was going to impress the Casinos, there had to be so much more than just a show. The wind and the aroma of the ocean were spectacular ideas, but apparently there was more. The whoosh overhead startled him, but the explosion that followed above and behind the crowd took him out of his seat, the blast of heat and force from an errant cannonball, knocking him to the terrace's stone aisle in front of his seat.

The crowd screamed in fear and shock. From behind him he heard a moan of pain. A blood-covered figure, his arm off at the shoulder stumbled through the crowd, then fell motionless. Red-hot shards of the exploded cannonball were visible here and there, making their own contribution to the smoke, thick now from the battle below. The audience was frightened and vocal, shouting and moving away, crowding what had been the entrance, but as he tried to make out the exit doors, Grinder realized the entire area had re-rendered. There were no exit doors.

Next to him, Jan was clapping and shouting, not in fear, but in exultation. "Yes!" she shouted into the air.

Pandemonium had broken out in the crowd. He heard crying and fighting and shouting, all mixed into a single fearful roar.

Next to him, Jan was shouting something in his ear. The crowd noise was so dense, he had a hard time making it out. He looked at her straight in the face and read her lips as she shouted. He shook his head to clear the confusion. Then he understood.

"It's all part of the show." She said it again, and she couldn't contain her enthusiasm. "It's all part of the show."

As if on cue, the armless spectator now stood up, both arms intact and raised over his head. He repeated Jan's words.

"It's all part of the show."

It took a few minutes for the chant to be picked up across the thousand or so spectators, but as it did, shouts of fear turned to wonder. In a corner, some began to applaud, understanding they'd been fooled by the reality of the theater. Now the crowd roared with approval. They were on their feet, shouting and watching with renewed enthusiasm the ongoing battle below their terraced seats.

The two ships maneuvered against one another, each with clear advantages and disadvantages. The smaller ship, now with a black standard of skull and crossbones hoisted, easily outmaneuvered the larger and more powerful French battleship, which, to its own advantage, outgunned its pirate attackers.

The battle raged on between the ships, each raking the other with devastating broadsides, splintering rails, and perforating sails and sailors until a deadly shot to the French ship scored a direct hit to its mainmast. A distinct murmur of awe rose from the crowd as the mast toppled over the side and into the sea.

Shouts of enthusiasm from the pirate crew made their way to the crowd. French sailors scrambled to cut away the mast's lines, and men poured from below the decks of the massive ship to crowd the rails in anticipation of a pirate boarding.

Grinder could see the French officers motioning their men away from the rails. They shouted and waved, but to no avail. The length of the ship was solid with men, their cutlasses and pikes in the air anticipating the fight ahead.

Just meters away, the black-flagged ship had another strategy in mind. Its crew abandoned their topside positions, leaving only the gun crews visible.

"Oh no," Grinder said under his breath. "Go back. Go back. Go!" He was as engaged as the French officers. "Don't you see what they're doing? He shouted. "You're all going to die."

And then he heard the command, high and shrill.

"Fire!"

The black-flagged ship's guns all spoke at once, a withering barrage of metal and powder and smoke and death. Then silence. The crowd watched as the smoke dissipated, revealing the devastation. On the deck of the French ship, nothing moved. Where a minute before stood a shouting mass of energy and patriotism now lay carnage. Piles upon piles of immobile bodies, as if they'd all just gone to sleep. A hush spread over the crowd with whispers here and there.

Then a shout rang out. A standing figure near the center of the audience stood and pointed.

"Look at the horizon."

Grinder, squinting, checked out the horizon. It took him a moment for his eyes to focus and to translate the shapes he saw there.

They were sails. A lot of sails. What looked like 30 or 40 separate topsails. The French fleet!

The crowd sympathies turned in a heartbeat.

"You better run," came a shout from the crowd, echoed with a roar of audience approval.

The black ship's crew responded immediately to the lookout's "Sail Ho!" transforming from a fighting force to an escaping force.

The captain's commands echoed from his post behind the ship's wheel, shouting at the top of his lungs while peering through his long scope at the approaching sails. The ship hoisted a full press of sails, a wondrous sight, and caught what little breeze there was, moving the ship away from its dismasted opponent, now dead in the water with little movement on board. A sudden gust of wind hit the audience with fresh sea air, the black ship heeling and picking up speed as the scene before them dissolved into black.

The crowd exploded with shouts and cheers. January was first among them, jumping and dancing and shouting. An unbridled success. She leaned over and kissed Simms. Even Simms was impressed. He stood beside her shaking his head in wonder as if he didn't believe what his eyes told him he'd just seen.

"Simply Amazing, Jan," he said. "That was spectacular."

A voice echoed through the arena.

"Ladies and Gentlemen. That concludes our show for tonight. The guests are invited to join the cast for refreshments."

Nothing better than a good after party to finish the night off.

Grinder had been to some before. Some were better than others. Based on tonight's show, he hoped the after-show would be on par with the show itself.

He shot a quick glance at Simms with eyebrows raised. Simms nodded imperceptibly. A nod of thanks. Simms' next motion was to take January's arm.

Grinder smiled to himself. That was his cue and his release from duty. Not bad as far as duties go. He turned and headed to the arena's floor.

15

BACKSTAGE

AT THE ARENA ENTRANCE, what should have been an open area and a wide panoramic view of the circular prison floor, its tiered balconies of inmate cells looking down on it from above, had become a thicket of greenery. Plants like he'd never seen before. The growth was so thick that light wasn't even visible between the wall of leaves, vines and branches. This was something new. The post show was always interesting, but this was a new twist. Grinder reached out and ran his hand over a large heart-shaped leaf. It was huge, and he could feel its cool moisture on his hand. Like some plant right out of one of Earth's restricted forest preserves. But this was different. He paced back and forth. A few yards away, he saw others in his same state of curiosity. Examining, touching, looking for a way in or a way through to see what, if anything, lay on the other side of this jungle wall.

The render was exquisite. Where here, a few minutes before, he'd seen water and the grand finale of the staged naval battle, now it was transformed into a scene few humans were ever allowed to experience. On Earth, few were accepted into the special corps of Park Service rangers. Special forces was more like it. They had the responsibility of growing and defending Earth's forested areas. They lived a life of fresh air amidst the divine aromas of natural plant life. And shot trespassers on sight, fertilizer for fresh growth to save Earth—that was their designated purpose. He'd heard there were some green areas developed by cities where humans were allowed, but that human visitation covered them like ants on a hill, hiding the natural beauty. There were two Earths, really. The overpopulated urban areas, which covered roughly 75 percent of the planet's inhabitable terrain, and the unpopulated, highly defended forest, jungle and farm preserves that scrubbed human carbon dioxide and enabled continued human existence. He'd never been to one, even to look at it from the outside. His time on Earth was restricted to living in the endless urban sprawl, the concrete jungle, an environment that provided everything humans could dream up, except maybe the one thing they really needed.

And here it was, right in front of him. He had no idea if these renders replicated actual plants from Earth or if they sprang from the fantasy of a software programmer from somewhere within its urban fabric, who like him, had never seen or touched a tree or a leaf or a plant or a vine.

After a couple of meters of searching, he found an area of plant life that looked less dense and pressed inside. He used his hands to move the pendulous leaves and vines from his path as he moved forward, and the green growth swished behind him, enclosing him in its leafy darkness. Within a few steps slivers of light began to appear from behind the dense foliage. The edge of the growth ended abruptly, and he squinted at the brightness of the white sand before him. On either side of him, a brilliant crescent of beach stood out starkly against the greenery of the jungle wall and sloped gently down to clear turquoise ocean waters that lapped at the sandy shore. He shook his head in wonder. Here and there along the strand, he saw women. Topless women, no less. Some in the water, others walking through the sand, drinks in their hands offering them to the newcomers, who were in the process of emerging from the jungle wall and stripping out of their prison attire. The heat quickly made its way through his clothes, and as the dampness of sweat broke over his chest, he followed suit. He stripped to his shorts and felt the sand begin to burn his feet as he abandoned his clothes in a pile and took a few quick steps to find refuge in the clear water. He looked in awe at the open ocean before him. In the back of his mind, he knew that he still stood inside the prison arena, but his eyes and mind told him differently. A few wisps of white clouds stood against a brilliant blue sky beyond.

Before he could even fathom the view, a meter or so in front of him, a head popped out of the water. The hair was short and fair and the smile was brilliant. She stood, and Grinder saw this was not one of the topless servers. She couldn't be more than a few birthdays past her 20th. Her blue bikini top restrained her well-formed chest, and there was something familiar about her face he couldn't place. It didn't matter. In contrast to the blondness of her hair, her skin was sun-darkened and well oiled. Water beaded in droplets and streamed back into the ocean. She ran her hands over her face and over her head, slicking her locks back, her green eyes complimenting the sky behind her nicely. She was still smiling. It was tinged with a sense of familiarity, and as she beckoned with a nod of her head, she sent his mind into a storm of confusion as she spoke.

"Hey you."

Those two words took him back years. The part of him that needed to maintain his cool, in-control persona responded automatically, attempting to cover his surprise.

"Hey," he said.

"Pete. It's me."

Pete. Peter. He hadn't heard that name for years. The man who was Peter Grindstaff had been Petey, and then Pete, then Peter if it was an adult conversation and Peter Tiberius Grindstaff if he had done something to infuriate his mother. But for years now it was Grinds or Grinder. This was a voice from the past. The voice was familiar and so was the face. His mind turned cartwheels, and his face was tight as if his mental energy was somehow expending a tremendous amount of physical energy, too.

"Hey," he said again.

His mind raced, putting the pieces together. It took a moment, and in that moment, slight as it was, his face had already betrayed him.

Her smile dissolved to a smirk as she watched the shock and pleasure take control of the expression he realized was now plastered all over his face. No secrets here. She stood before him now, tawny limbs dripping in the warm sun, just as she had when he was a teenager.

"Oh my God," That was it. He'd run out of words; his emotions muted his ability to speak.

She put hands on her hips and stretched backward, displaying her tight, tanned body, a live swimsuit model on the beach posing for an advertisement.

"You like?"

Their two-word conversation wasn't getting them anywhere, but he still struggled to speak.

"How did—" he began before he trailed off again.

"Sorry," she said. "I know this is a real surprise. Maybe I shouldn't have pulled it off as abruptly as I did."

Forget it. She could do the talking.

He matched her smile and reached out to her, embracing her tightly, the memories returning in a rush. He held her at arm's length and examined her more closely. *Amazing.*

"Pete, did you ever get to a point in your life where you wish you could go back and make different choices? Change everything? If you think about it, it wouldn't take much. Even a single choice to choose a different friend, a different husband. Choose a different career. Choose a different place to live. They're all interrelated. Me? I never had regrets. Everything seemed to happen for me exactly as I planned."

Yes. He remembered. *The beautiful rich girl. Family money. She could and did have everything she wanted.*

"I know what you're thinking," she said. "And I never thought about it when I knew you. When you have money, and not just a little money, but real money, you no longer need it. Strange isn't it? People give you things. They do things for you. Funny thing was, I never had any money."

He tilted his head and furrowed his brow, questioning the truth of her statement with his eyes. She was laughing.

"It's true! It was always my father who had money. His business had money. My husband had money. Lots of it. But I never had money, and for a long time, the whole concept of money was foreign to me. I had an off-Earth house. I rubbed shoulders with the rich and famous. I never gave it a second thought. I lived my dream, only it wasn't my dream. It was my mother's dream, and I was living it for her. She was living it, too, of course, but for a really long time, she told me what I wanted, and I believed her. And then one day—"

She paused, her smile fading and eyes growing distant as she gazed past his shoulder.

"And then one day my father died."

He reached out and squeezed her hand. "I'm so sorry, Rachel," he whispered.

She blinked twice, and her smile returned.

"All of a sudden I had money. I was in charge. I always thought my mother and father were happy together, that they had everything anyone could ever want in a relationship. But without him, I began to realize that it wasn't him she loved, but the person the money made him. She was in love with the lifestyle. And she didn't skip a beat. Like me she had no clue about money, but unlike me, she had no aptitude for it. I took control of the family money, and even though she encouraged it, she resented it. She remarried a few years later and hasn't said two words to me in years."

He shook his head. "Money changes everything and everyone."

"You got that right. My peckerwood husband thought he

needed something more than me, so I took all of his. Maybe he's happy now with this whore girlfriend."

He shot her a look.

"I'm serious," she said, a half-laugh still in her voice. "He met her at a company gambling retreat on Midway. She actually was a whore. He probably needs something more than her now. Anyway, with all the money in the world, you'd think I'd find a way to be happy. As it turns out, not so much. I was alone. I partied. I traveled. I partied. The business ran itself really."

"Business?"

"Asteroid exploration and mining. It's huge. Turns out, I have quite the business sense. Sense enough to draft a company constitution and hire some smart people to run it. But anyway, there I was; I had everything, but I didn't have a clue what I wanted. I was never alone, but I was always lonely. I tried all kinds of drugs and treatments, none of which were healthy for me, until I finally hit on it. I needed to go back in time."

He looked at her quizzically, an eyebrow raised.

She laughed again.

"Not really go back it time," she said, "But aside from putting me in an early grave, you'd be surprised what all that money can do."

He looked more closely at her face. There were subtle differences. Knowing now who she was, he compared the new Rachel with the teen Rachel from his memory. Her cheekbones were marginally sharper and her nose made less of a button and more of a statement. These differences had disguised her at first glance, but her voice and her eyes, those green eyes couldn't hide for long. She smiled with them. He swam in them momentarily, his teen infatuations reignited. There was something else. Time had a way of pulling tricks on the mind, but her body seemed to have evolved as well. Or was it just his memory? It didn't matter. She'd been hot then, and she was hot, maybe hotter, now.

She said, "Nice, eh?"

Damn the two-word exchanges.

He said nothing as he gazed up and down the curves of her tanned and glistening and no doubt expensive shape, nodding wordlessly.

"Not that. This."

It wasn't her body she was referring to, but the larger environment. She was extending her hand, beckoning to the rendered beach scene behind her.

He stepped back and surveyed the scene more closely.

"Sure. It's a beautiful beach." He stopped his sentence short as he realized two things, one after the other. This wasn't just any beach. He looked back at her quickly, her green eyes nodding in anticipation as his mind raced to catch up.

"Bahamas."

"Do you remember?"

As if he could forget. It had been his teenage fantasy, and then it had happened. The girl, the beach. The rest. He'd remember those two weeks for the rest of his life. And here it was again, but it caught him so unaware, he hadn't even recognized his own fantasy. Now he turned a circle in place, a 360-degree gaze as he drank it all in again and realized his second thing.

This was her creation. This was her way of going back in time.

That's what she told him. Money changes everything.

"You been sittin' on some sugar?" she asked in her faux-cheesy pickup line voice that no one but her could pull off. Her eyes twinkled. "'Cause that is one sweet ass."

He was still catching up. "You did this."

"My vision and my, what would you call it? My substantial resources."

"Of all the possibilities in the universe, you chose a two-week teenage boyfriend? I don't believe it. You were my fantasy. I was your— well, I don't know what I was, but certainly not your fantasy."

"You're right," she acknowledged. "You weren't really what I wanted, but the more I thought about it after you left, you were what I needed most. You were intelligent. Loyal. You knew exactly what you wanted. You wanted to make a better world, a better life. For everyone. It wasn't terribly realistic, but you were so serious that your life had to make a difference, that it was the one thing I kept coming back to over and over. Plus, you weren't bad looking either. So now I'm unencumbered. Free. And no offense to you, but part of me wanted to see if I could do it. Could I track you down? And if so, what would be my play? I do have to admit, I was surprised to find you in prison."

A momentary shiver of fright streaked through him, and he froze. But she was being earnest like she'd never been earnest before, and she continued, non-stop.

"But I figured, what the hell. I'd done things when I was my other self that should have landed me in prison. To me it didn't make a bit of difference. So there I was. I had this random whim about reinventing myself. And then I thought, why stop there? Why not follow the inspiration to its conclusion? And once I had the idea, I also saw some potential for some side benefit, and not just for myself. Well, actually, a good portion for myself, but it wasn't just about the financial benefit. I was stretching my wings and my connections. It's amazing what people would do for me when I asked them. The ideas just started to flow."

She was talking quickly, one thought on top of the other as her explanation spilled out of her mouth. His looks had never hurt him, but that was never something he thought a lot about.

"Look where it got me," she finished.

She looked at him, saying nothing for a moment.

How much did she know? How much information had her substantial resources purchased?

"I thought about it forever. I obsessed over it. My carefree life went on with its ups and downs. And when I was down, I'd rewind my life and obsess over the decisions I'd made. If I could go back, what would I do differently? And each time I did that, I'd come back to you, and your insistence that your life had to matter. At a certain point, this became possible. The Casinos are forever searching for new ideas. New fantasies their Earth guests can't say no to. This one's mine. It seems to be working well now in its test phase."

"None taken," he said.

She'd been on a short, excited little journey with her mind, and she looked at him oddly.

He clarified. "I don't take offense at not being the central inspiration for your project. In fact, this just might be the biggest stroke my ego ever got. In my life."

She raised her hands above her head, grinning as she twirled around in the ankle-deep water, a wet victory dance. "Yay, me!" she said. Her smile dazzled him.

"Look, Peter, and this is only if you're interested, I want to go back and give us a chance. If you're interested, of course. A proper chance. Not like before. My vision is a lot clearer than it was last time we were together on a beach."

Was she serious?

Because if she was, everything in his life, what was left of it anyway, was about to change.

"So, you know I'm in prison, right? You know that's not something you just buy your way out of."

She looked back at him, like he hadn't heard anything she'd said. She shook her head slowly as she spoke. "I wouldn't be so sure about that one. But listen to me. You're stunned. You don't know what to say. I'm sorry, Petey."

She changed the subject abruptly.

"C'mon," she said with a sly smile. "I want to take you to another world."

She had probably said that before. Or maybe that was just wishful thinking. The Bahamas had been another world. And they had been together in another world. And when a teenage boy and his girlfriend are alone on a beach, there's only one possible meaning that would run through his mind. It wasn't rocket science.

Anatomy, maybe, but for him, it had just been a whole lot of magic. Now he wasn't so sure what she meant as she tugged his hand, urging him forward toward the end of the beach.

She was right. Up and down the beach now, the prisoner crowd was laughing, drinking, gawking. This was a whole new level of after-party.

"C'mon, she said again, taking his hand, "I want to show you something."

They walked hand-in-hand through the shallow water. They didn't say much, just enjoyed the sensations of the beach revelers, the hot sun and the cool ocean waves tickling their feet. In his teens, this would have been heaven. It certainly was now. A 10-minute walk landed them at the end of the strand, the white sand ending abruptly with the dense wall of jungle meeting the lapping ocean. She pulled him on with her hand.

"Back into the jungle?" he asked.

She winked at him. "This is the best part."

She parted the hanging green vines with her left hand, dragging him behind her with her right.

He couldn't let go. Not now. Not ever.

He held up his hand before him as they made their way through the foliage, missing only an occasional branch or leaf that slapped his face. As before, darkness closed in, with only a dim outline and a cool damp sensation of a new environment ahead.

The dense jungle ended abruptly, and he caught his breath as they stepped onto a wide bamboo platform. Below them the ground dropped away to nothing. They were near the top of a canopy, the jungle floor 40 or maybe 50 meters below them. He stopped short, jerking her enthusiastic stride to a halt and drinking it all in.

Above them, the canopy served as their rooftop. Here and there, it let shafts of light through to the jungle below. She hadn't been kidding. This was a whole different world. Maybe he should pay more attention to what she was really saying. The whole sweet ass thing had thrown him off mentally. She played well to the school boy fantasy. It was always hard to tell. Anyway, even if he was just being paranoid, and living in a prison will do that to you, playing closer attention couldn't hurt. Even in this hell-hole, he still had a lot to lose. He wondered again just how much of his history she had uncovered. She seemed to have done it so easily. And did he really believe her story that he'd been the inspiration for her life-changing decision?

Once upon a time he believed in living a life that mattered. A life that made a difference. cMaybe he still did.

Sometimes that whole concept of life's meaning got lost here. But he was here, and he was still alive, and that said something about his instincts. He looked at her again, this time with fresh eyes and a bit of skepticism. She looked back. It didn't help. Whatever was on her mind was reflected clearly on her face, and what he saw were thoughts of sincerity. It had been decades after only a few weeks, but there were a few things he knew instinctively. This was one of them. She truly believed what she said.

Before them a rope bridge stretched out from the edge of the platform, a hundred meters if it was a centimeter. Suspended in the air, it angled up slightly and ended in some kind of tree house structure. It was hard to make out details at this distance, but it was a mansion compared to his cell, the cell he'd be back to quickly enough.

She scampered ahead of him out onto the bridge, nothing but boards and ropes and air between her and the jungle floor below.

She nodded with a tilted head toward the tree house, her hands out, balancing her delicious form between the rope bridge's twin suspension lines that connected the house with the platform.

"You wanna sleep over?"

"No snakes, right?"

"Of course not," she said, and her eyes feigned a hurt look that quickly melted into a mischievous grin. "Well maybe one."

He couldn't help but smile. He wasn't sure how much sleep

they'd be getting. He stepped forward to grasp the support line himself as he stepped onto the bridge. The bridge was swaying now with her forward motion. Backward actually. She had turned and was now making progress toward the treehouse, backing away from him.

"We don't have much time. You better hurry."

She was taunting him.

He watched her receding figure as he took his second step, more quickly this time.

"You'd better run," he called back.

She did.

16

PLAN

THE DAY WAS GONE. Grinder was exhausted, and he'd made no more forward progress today than he had in his past two weeks of inquiries into suspects for the assassin. In the aftermath of the circus and Rachel's departure, he'd gone through service people, access, paybacks. All angles considered. No results. He was usually pretty good at this, at reading people and situations, but this time was different. He was no closer today than the day of the murder, for that matter. And now, again, he'd have to make a no-progress report to Simms. With all the innovations and design capabilities, you'd think they could build some kind of floor transport mechanism in these award-winning structures, he thought. The stairs were a bitch at the end of the day, especially today.

The Wiz sat in his usual position, surveying the evening desert scape. He didn't move a muscle in his entire body, with the exception of his eyebrows which raised together, a silent questioning expression.

"Just another bunch of dead ends," Grinder told the eyebrows. "It really shouldn't be this hard."

Simms nodded. "Not your fault. We need to reexamine our assumptions. They must be flawed. I didn't tell you this, but I set Vee on developing an escape plan."

Grinder stopped short, surprised.

"We agreed he couldn't be the guy, but should you trust him to figure a way out of here with an escape plan?"

"Who said anything about trust?"

Grinder smiled with the corner of his mouth. "How long has he had?"

"It's been three days, but he came to me with his plan this morning."

"I'm not sure why having him develop a plan for you is the right play."

"You could be right. But think about it from our point of view. Our collective point of view. We need two things. We need to finger an assassin, and we need to decide on an escape plan."

Grinder laughed out loud. "You still think there's a way out of here?"

The eyebrows raised again and turned to address his question. He realized too late his spontaneous outburst of laughter might have been too much. Enough to annoy or insult Simms. But Simms was smiling.

"There are a number of ways out of here, I just need to choose the right one."

Grinder gave him a doubtful look.

"Here's what he wants me to do," continued Simms. "As it turns out, Vee is something of an art prodigy. Sculpting is his special talent. I've handicapped him somewhat, but his new girlfriend has talent in that same vein. We do have a community of creative people here, don't we? Anyway, we have plenty of raw bio material from the prosciutto operation, and he's hit on the idea of face-swapping to break security. He'll make two masks. One for a paroled prisoner, the other for me."

Grinder let out a short involuntary interruption, "Ha!" before he realized he was interrupting. "Oh, sorry. It just seems stupid, over-simplified."

Simms nodded. "Sometimes those are the best plans. Have you ever been paroled?"

"Not yet."

"Me neither. But Vee has some insight into their security protocols. Parolees pass through two tiers of security in processing out of here. I don't know how many I've seen over the years, and I certainly don't know how many I've seen here. What I didn't know was that not all securitybots are programmed equally. To prisoners, they all look the same, but if you had an insight into their team programming architecture, you'd find that few, and in our case because of the low volume, only one of them is designated as a Level One securitybot. According to Vee, that is."

"So that's his crime, a little too close to security? That's actually makes a lot of sense. It's the retinals, isn't it?"

"The facial, the retinals and the fingerprints. Before anyone gets on a transport, the level-one bot verifies and re-verifies that it's releasing the right prisoner. Once complete, the soon-to-be ex-prisoners are passed along to the second tier securitybots. Now, second tier is a basic inventory protocol. In the event of an escape attempt and rundown, retinal and print scans are impractical, so the remainder of the securitybot force is slaved to the primary with just facial recognition requirements.

Grinder considered the implications. "So security is not really as ironclad as the Casinos would like us to think."

"That's what Vee seems to think."

"And he knows this how?"

"He says he wrote some codes. He's not sure, but he thinks his trespass into this area is maybe what landed him here."

"Bullshit. Casinos don't send offenders with knowledge of their security vulnerabilities into prisons they can then break out of."

"Very easy for us to say that, but you don't know bureaucracies, and the Casinos have something like you've never imagined before. On the outside, it looks all shiny and perfect, but inside, it's run by people, just like you and me. Only not as smart. They make some pretty big assumptions. And usually they're safe assumptions. Locating a prison here in the middle of the desert gives them this failsafe sense of security. Look at their record. No one's ever broken out of here. They attribute that to their impenetrable security. Truth is, life here is not that bad. They do have holes, although not very big ones. They just needed someone like me to come and point them out. I don't think they know what Vee knows. I think a computer program caught him in a place where he shouldn't have been, and he was administratively placed here. Without human intervention.

"You mean—"

"I'm sure a report was filed somewhere, but I think the significance of what he discovered has gone unnoticed. The report, along with a thousand others, is probably sitting in a second-priority queue, waiting to be addressed. Because he's here now, it's not too far of a stretch to think his removal matches the outstanding work required. Once matched, it will likely be marked as complete, filed and forgotten. The human who sits at the control panel is not the same human responsible for security violations."

"How can you be sure?"

"I can't be sure, but if there were a reported security issue, we would have seen its impact here. Updated programming, some kind of activity that we wouldn't be allowed to see."

"And it's been nothing but routine here."

"For years."

Grinder thought about it. *That was totally possible—probable even.*

"We have a couple of folks leaving on the next transport out, right?" asked Simms.

"Three actually. Smithon, Reid and Lok. Two men and a woman."

Grinder watched as the eyebrows contracted. Simms was doing a mental inventory. "We can work with that. It will have to be Smithon. Reid is a woman and Lok has strong east-Earth features and way too much—" he trailed off, his eyes searching upward for the right word.

"Body?" suggested Grinder.

"Yes. Too much body."

"So what's his plan?"

"Reid and Lok process through first. They'll be escorted to the transport. Smithon will lag to make sure he's final. Once he passes through primary security, I run after him, tackle him to the ground as if he and I have a score to settle. Response time will be fairly quick, but if we're both face down, we should be able to slip on masks without being detected. We're pulled apart, Smithon goes to isolation, I get on the transport. Done."

"If what we've learned from Vee is true, that part is certainly possible. But then what?"

"Smithon stays in isolation for the standard two months."

"Two months is not standard."

"It is now. Casino transports are the fastest money can buy, but they still have to span the distance between here and Midway. This jump? This one's going to take nearly a month."

Grinder thought it through. The jump lengths changed for each departure, as each planet traveled on its own orbit. At a certain point in the year, there was a multi-month pause where waiting for planet proximity made more sense than chasing the space between the two.

He finished the sentence.

"So by the time Smithon comes out to petition for an administrative error, blaming the bots, of course, you'll need to already be through the processing station and on your own recognizance. But what about once you get to Midway?"

"After transit, we dock with the processing station, which is in orbit around Midway. Once there, I use the facilities, drop the mask into the atomizer and put on a security shirt."

"Our brand, no doubt."

Simms smiled.

"Not perfect," he continued, "but some good work. A few minor modifications, and I'm part of the security staff. It's what they're expecting to see. Now, effectively, I've disappeared. My face is not on the local inventory for prisoners, and bots don't screen and inventory guards. I hop the next shuttle to Midway. And then —"

He stopped his straight-faced narration and smiled.

"And then, I make my way on from there."

The plan had a number of holes. "That's certainly not foolproof," said Grinder doubtfully.

"You're right. It's not. But as far as plans go, it's not bad. I've broken out before with much less."

"Then what's your concern?" He paused for a moment, pondering. "You don't trust him."

It wasn't a question. It was a statement. He wondered how Simms might react.

"Grinder," he said with a broadening grin and a shrug," I trust everyone. Until they give me reason not to. And then? Well, then I make sure they never get the opportunity to give me that reason again. Simple."

"And in this case?"

"In this case, I'm looking for a reason. On the outside, he's been helpful. This sounds like a viable plan, if his inside information is correct. But I saw him at the show, and I had a thought."

"I saw him there, too. He's seems to be over his missing hand, doesn't he?"

"It seems like it, but I wasn't thinking about his missing hand."

Grinder thought for a moment, recalling Vee's demeanor. He'd grinned and waved. That was about it. The girl he'd been with was tossing popcorn into his mouth. He shrugged. "He grinned and waved. He seemed to be having a good time."

"What did he do, Grinder?"

Grinder said it more slowly, not understanding where Simms was going with it. "He grinned," he said slowly, pausing to look at Simms with a curious look, "And he waved." He raised his hand and moved it side-to-side over his head, mimicking Vee's greeting.

"Yes, that's similar. But with one key difference." The eyebrows were up again, entreating him to play the guessing game.

He repeated the motion and said, "And he waved." Simms paused. "He waved." It was the third time that did it. *Simms had not waved with his mutilated hand. He'd waved with his remaining hand.* "He waved with his left hand. His dominant hand."

"It wasn't the wave that gave it away for me. But I watched him and the girl next to him. After she was done tossing, he took a turn. Very nimble with that left hand."

The realization startled him. "So you think he's the guy? Our assassin?"

"To be honest with you, I still don't know. Maybe. But I will find out which way his flag blows. I do know that my initial impressions are usually right—even if it was my oversight not to specify, or even consider this beforehand." He smirked slightly at his wordplay. "He hasn't been here long enough to account for the girl's betrayal. Our mole was operational way before his arrival. But this is a strategic play anyway."

"How so? If you're right, and he is the guy, how does executing this escape help?"

Simms was silent. Thoughtful. He lost his grin and stroked the bottom of his chin between his thumb and forefinger. He shook his head.

"Both ways are possible. Both perfect. We just don't have enough information."

"We certainly can't trust him. We'll just have to watch him."

"Having me escape might be playing into Casino hands. Maybe they're playing with reviving their media campaign. They keep me in here longer and go back to their "We caught The Wiz" broadcasting across all the channels. But if he's telling the truth, his inside Casino knowledge is more valuable than you might think."

Grinder said nothing, but was surprised by Simms' next

comment.

"That's where you come in."

"Me? How?"

"I'm not going to escape. You are."

He was taken aback. No way to hide that one from his face. He shook his head quickly.

"No. No way." The stunned realization crowded out his normally calm features.

"Sure you are. You're the model prisoner. No prior breakouts. Diligent. Loyal. Trustworthy."

Grinder was dismayed. "But I could get—"

"Yes, you could get an extended sentence. A year. Maybe two. That's nothing in a place like this. And they get nothing by catching you in an escape attempt, if that's their intention, which I'm still not convinced it is."

"If he is Casino, he'd smell the swap."

"Not if we waited until the final moment. I'll make him believe. We'll all be out there. But I won't make a run for it. It'll be you. And if Casino is there waiting for you, and you come back, we'll know it's him."

"And if I don't?"

"Even better. I need someone on Midway to run that end of the op. And one other thing."

He was clever, Grinder had to give him that. Clever and conniving. He gave Simms a questioning look, but said nothing.

"I need another girl."

***

The roar of the storm was incredible. Nik yelled at the top of her lungs as if her life depended on it. But it was Truman who was really in trouble. The sled's field generator was off, and they were now at the mercy of Claustrom's elements. The air was hot and dark and burning, and without the field, the sled was nearly vertical now, pushed up by the tremendous wind speed. It tilted at a dangerous angle. Truman's inert body lay half-in, half-out of the sled. Beside and beneath her, Jata had her eyes open, but was groggy, confused.

"HELP MEEEEEE!" she screamed to Jata, but she could barely hear herself. She pulled at Truman's belt. The inclined sled was serving as a wind break for her and Jata, but Truman's head and upper body were flopped outside the sled, whipped by the screaming sands.

Why wouldn't he just move himself?

"C'mon man, move your ass," she yelled at him into the din. "I can't do this by myself."

She tried again with all her strength. The engineer's girth was too much. She couldn't budge it by herself. She yelled again to Jata for help.

This time Jata responded, seeming to understand. Nik watched her wriggle out of her nearly vertical seat. Jata twisted slowly and placed her feet down on the sand in the wind shadow of the sled. The sand was everywhere, its shapeless, formless mass blocking out the majority of what light there was, raging as it blew past their grainy shadows. Truman had stripped off the top of his flight suit because of the heat, and all that remained on his back was an undershirt. She reached forward, grabbing a handful of it. Together they pulled. This time, there was movement. His body swung around and back behind the sled. As it did, Jata shoved him back into his seat and pressed forward, one foot, then two on the now angled backrest of the rear seats. As she did, the howl of the storm suddenly ceased. Silence returned, with ragged breathing and sand-drenched coughing the only sounds in the sled. They were horizontal again, and Nik didn't understand why. What in God's name was going on? It took her a full minute to be able to even speak.

"What the hell just happened?" she panted.

Jata's response was as choked as her own. "Field generator won't—"

A fit of coughing interrupted her.

"The field generator won't reset," she said again. "if its...blocked...by anything." She motioned with her head to Truman's form. "Like him."

"Oh my God. Is he alive?" She couldn't control the tremor in her voice.

Truman is our only hope. Without Truman, we're—

Well, to be honest with herself, without Truman they were all dead. They were still all tangled together inside the confines of the sled. Outside the sled the storm raged on. They could see nothing but a dark, solid wall of sand. Inside, half the sled was filled with Claustrom's sand, partially illuminated by the lights not hidden beneath its grainy layer. Jata extracted her right arm slowly from her awkward position. Her upper torso was jammed between Nik and the inert Truman, and her back legs were still propped against the top of the seat-backs in the rear.

"Be still for a sec," said Jata. "I can tell you in a moment." She stretched her right hand around, but couldn't reach Truman from that side. She shifted back slightly and reached his neck with her fingers, pressing in. Nik watched as Jata's head turned toward her, only inches away. She stared into her eyes, but Jata's concentrated focus was on her fingers. Ten seconds passed. Twenty.

Nik was whimpering. "Oh no. Truman. No."

Jata interrupted. "Got it. It's weak, but it's there."

"He's alive?"

"Let's just say he's not dead yet, but that's just judging from my limited medical knowledge. I feel a pulse, I say his heart is functioning, and he's alive, but look at us. We're in the middle of—" She paused. "Well, we don't even know where we're in the middle of. He needs more medical attention than you or I can provide. Unless you've got some medical quals up your sleeve."

Nik shook her head, tears in her eyes, saying nothing.

"There's not a lot we can do for him here. Well, maybe one thing."

Nik saw her adjust something in the rear of the sled. The seat-back reclined with Truman leaning against it, then receded and locked into the space between the front and rear seats, joining the two and creating a flat area on one side of the sled's interior. Jata pulled herself back into the seat behind Nik.

"Help me."

Together and awkwardly, they slid Truman back along the makeshift bed until his head was against the back of the rear seat. He was still unresponsive, but Nik could see he was still breathing. But she saw something else, too.

"Oh my God. Look at that, Jata." One hand was over her mouth, and the other was pointing at a bright red burn trail that snaked across his abdomen and disappeared up under his shirt.

Jata let out a low whistle. "Lightning. Truman took a hit for all of us."

"He got hit by lightning? You can't survive that can you?" she asked incredulously.

"Apparently in Truman's case you can. For a while, anyway."

Nik realized now the hopelessness of their situation. Truman needing medical attention. Them stuck in the middle of the sandstorm, on a planet that—

She stopped herself from thinking in pessimistic circles. Not one of her more positive attributes. She had a way of not being there when things got too tough. But she knew herself pretty well and focused on her options. There had to be some way to help.

"What about a medkit? Don't we have one from the ship?" she asked. Her voice was still high and squeaky. Scared.

"We do, but we can't access it until the wind takes a break. Let's hope it's fully stocked.

Nik closed her eyes, folded her palms together and said a silent prayer. It was a prayer for the end of the storm. It was a prayer for medical supplies. It was a prayer for a way out of there.

Mostly, it was a prayer for Truman.

17

ALONE

IT WAS JUST SHORT of four hours later, according to the sled's console display, when the light changed. It didn't happen all of a sudden, but over the course of a few minutes so that it wasn't immediately evident. They'd been silent for what seemed like forever, each lost in her own mental gyrations. Nik figured Jata was thinking her way out of the desert by practical means. Like coming up with options and plans like Truman might do.

Truman? Who knew what Truman was thinking, if anything.

He was still unconscious, comatose. Marginally breathing. She and Jata had swapped seats, and Jata spent a ridiculous amount of time studying what little data was available in the sled's console. Nik took the rear seat near Truman's prone form. She was figuring a way out, too. But it wasn't practical, and it wasn't real. She imagined herself back in her office, maintaining her steady and responsible eye on inventory and cash flows. It was all logical, and it made sense to her. She was somebody there. People counted on her. It was nice to be counted on. Here? Here she might as well be dead for all the good she did. She didn't want to be dead, but the little control she'd been able to exert over her life by professional competence had no bearing here. Not that most people would be any different. Were she a musician with a gift for playing an instrument or a chef from Midway's ritziest restaurant, she'd still be in the same place and have the same sense of helplessness. Maybe her mother was right. She should have stayed home. But she couldn't wait to run away and show her mother how far and how fast she could run. Show her how smart her little girl really was. And she'd done it. In fact, she couldn't have run much farther than the edge of the known galaxy. But what had it gotten her? Nothing but grief. She could hear her mother's voice in her mind. That simple, small-town, all-knowing, all-annoying voice that always started with, "You know," followed by a pause, and then a parroting of whatever useless drivel was spewing from the information services or from the mouths and minds of her friends, if you could call them that. No, on second thought she didn't really miss that.

That had been a valid reason for running away. Maybe a valid reason for her professional success. But was this her reward for her hard work? The universe couldn't possibly be that cruel and stupid. People were like that, sure. But somehow this all had to make sense to her.

She wondered where she had made a misstep that could warrant something like this. Truman was her answer. That seemed selfish, but in her mental process, that seemed true enough. If he could recover, he'd know exactly what to do. Or not, she thought. Durt had known exactly what to do and look where it got him.

Was that her fate, too? Her bones cleaned and polished by the sun and winds and buried by the sands on a distant planet?

Then she noticed the light. Truman's features had just a bit more clarity now, and she watched his shallow breathing. "Oh," she said simply. "That's different."

In the front, Jata didn't look up from the displays she was checking for the thousandth time as she spoke.

"What's different?"

"It's a little bit lighter, and the sand looks, well, different."

Jata now joined her upward gaze, sitting bolt upright. She twisted her head in a couple of different directions. "Yes!" she exclaimed.

"What is it?"

"That, Nik, is the color of the afternoon sun. It looks like the storm is breaking."

Nik looked up again with renewed interest. She looked up at the console display. She was right. It was late afternoon. The Claustrom sun would sink to the horizon, changing the whole look of the desert.

Within a minute, the storm was gone. Disappeared as quickly as it had come.

Jata pressed the console's field control and climbed out of the sled, easing her cramped legs onto the sand, and stretching her arms over her head. Nik followed suit. Her legs and arms and neck. Probably even her hair needed to stretch out. The evening air was warm and sweet, the burning heat now tolerable.

Jata didn't waste any time. "Give me a hand in the back here," she said, walking around to the rear of the sled. "Let's get the medkit out and see what we have to work with."

Together they began pulling off the top cases. The containers were all a similar dark gray color, but in varying dimensions. They tossed cases into the sand.

"What does it look like?" asked Nik as she tossed a small thin case aside.

Jata shook her head and said, in what Nik took to be a tone of exasperation, "I don't know, Nik. I'm thinking it will be the one with the big red cross on it."

Nik was thinking how stupid she must sound. Then she saw it. Medium-sized grey case, just like every other one. But the cross wasn't red. It was the same color as the case itself, with the cross and its surface raised and roughed and readily identifiable.

"Here." She said, pulling it from between a couple other cases and putting it behind the sled on the sand.

Jata's eyes lit up. "That's the one." She pressed the edges and the top popped open. She made *uh-hu* sounds with her closed mouth as her eyes made an inventory of the case. She reached down inside the container's lower compartment, her eyes and face now showing concern.

"Crap."

"What? What is it?"

Jata rummaged again, then sat back, resigned, her butt in the sand, her head shaking.

"No medbelt."

"No medbelt?"

"The one piece of equipment that could save Truman, and it's not here."

"What does it do?"

Jata pursed her lips, pausing a moment to take a deep breath. "It's a belt that generates a stasis field. Basically if you're hurt or sick, you can put the patient in stasis—freeze him, until you can get him to medical help. It's the one thing we need the most."

"And we don't have it?"

"And we don't have it," echoed Jata.

Nik was devastated. "No. I don't believe it," she said, the shake coming back into her voice. "It's got to be here somewhere. We can't just let Truman die here."

Jata was standing now. Gazing around the desert scene. Silent.

"What is it? There's something else isn't there?" Nik was now staring uncertainly at her still and staring form.

"Where are they?" asked Jata, hands on her hips and stomping the sand. "Where in the hell are they?"

"Where's who?"

"The other sled," said Jata. "It's not here."

***

"It's a win-win situation."

It was Simms again, trying to poke holes in his own plan. "You're the only one who has a downside, and that downside is an acceptable one, yes?"

Like he could say no to that. Maybe before the circus he had a lot less to lose, but now with Rachel on the line, and Simms knowing. Hell, Simms was probably the mastermind behind her appearance here. Devious son-of-a bitch. But what could he do?

Simms was right about the risk, Grinder thought. What Simms assessed as his risk, anyway. Prison standards for non-violent first-time offenders might pick up a year or two, certainly subject to an assessment of his offense. Maybe they'd even thank him for pointing out the hole in their security matrix. If it turned out to be true, of course. But the more he thought about it, the less likely it would be for him to gain anything from a failed attempt. But if it did work, Rachel was on the other end of the deal, so that was something. A new wrinkle and a new opportunity.

"You're right, Wiz. I guess I've grown accustomed to this place. A year or two. I could do it standing on my head."

Simms nodded in approval.

They were back in the tower, like most evenings. It was a different dynamic without the girl here, but the desert was still the desert. The view never changed. Time dragged on. It was storm season and storms came and went. Cooler temperatures were on the way. Fresh shipments of animals were arriving. They'd try out their latest plant innovations. The transports that brought new arrivals also brought equipment for the plant. Equipment and parts manufactured to their specifications by on-planet craftsmen, and transported to the landing zone and installed when conditions made it too hot to keep the animals alive. It was a season of work. This was a good season. Always plenty of activity. Days passed quickly. The prison population truly took pride in the design and operation of their machines. There was plenty of commercial potential here for an independent. Except the Casinos would never let that happen.

"One thing I don't understand."

Simms said nothing, but raised his eyebrows.

"I turned this place upside down. For weeks. I know we have a pile of suspects to review, but I eliminated every logical one. If someone here is a Casino mole, It's a damn magic trick."

Simms said nothing.

But it wasn't silent. In the background, the music was there again.

"Sometimes I lose track," said Simms. "Saturday again?"

"Rehearsals as usual. Tuesdays and Saturdays. There's something about those melodies that get inside your brain and won't stop dancing around."

He nodded. "It's good for them. Takes their minds off—" he paused, looking at the prison compound through the tower window, "this."

It was what he wasn't saying that was understood. Gina had been a huge Moot fan. Tuesday and Saturdays and any ad-hoc jam session, she'd be bouncing on her toes, her eyes happy and inquiring. You'd know what day it was, just by her bounces. Simms would nod and smile, and she'd be off as fast as her little feet could bounce her down the tower stairs. Grinder knew Simms never really liked the music and railed against it now and again, but he understood its importance. So he allowed it. What Simms didn't know was something he'd never share with Simms. Something he'd uncovered in his investigation. She'd been a fan, but she'd been a lot more than that, too. She might have been Moot's favorite fan, at least on some nights when she couldn't control her passion. No one said anything overtly. Mostly nods and whispers because of who Simms was. They didn't want to be on the wrong side of that one.

"I keep going over it in my mind," he said, half to himself and half to Simms. "I can't disagree with Vee as a prime suspect, but there's no way he had access to make any communications."

"But there were communications made."

"There had to be."

"Which means," Simms paused in thought. "You said you eliminated every logical suspect. And that means we need to look at who are not the logical suspects. We need to look at our whole approach. And Vee is just too damn unpredictable not to be a suspect. We have to think beyond our own standards of logic. It has to be something else. Something we're not seeing. Sophisticated electronics? Something that wouldn't trigger the comm flags?"

Grinder shrugged. "Re-screening is a standard part of any medical check, and I personally watched each one of his. He didn't do anything special. Didn't make any attempt to override any security protocols with the medbot. He just sat there. I thought the same thing."

"The other, larger issue is that he hasn't been here long enough to develop relationships and pass along useful information, so while I know there's something about him, I also get the sense that he's not the guy. It doesn't all quite make sense yet. But it will."

They lapsed into silence again. The only sound, the stops and starts of the musicians. Sometimes they'd play a song twice or three times in a row—just to work on their timing or maybe a new ending. He wasn't a musician, so they all sounded pretty much the same. But like Simms, the music itself with its catchy melodies and its haunting vocals reminded him of the girl as well. Gina had known she was burned. She was deep cover. He'd figured her for a prison or Casino agent when he'd taken the transmitter off her. Somehow she'd been betrayed. Not that it was uncommon, especially in her line of work, but to take out someone that close to Grinder had to have two things. Balls and motive. He figured they were right on the motive. A direct line from Grinder to the guilds. Any guild. That was certainly a dangerous path. The only other possible hand behind that brazen of a killing would have to be a personal motive. And that was impossible to get his mind around. Anyone who opposed the Wiz had a way of disappearing. The universe was full of motives with revenge on their collective minds. Still. He let it go for a while.

You could drive yourself crazy, he thought. Someone had done it. And if it wasn't Vee, the assassin was still here, hidden in plain sight among the thousand or so incarcerated. Unless—

They sat for some time without speech. The music came to a

blaring crescendo and ended with a final shout from the cymbals. A few voices from the band straggled through the sound system, and then it was silent again.

There was one possibility he hadn't considered.

Approach from a different angle. Yes.

He looked up at Simms, also lost in thought. The sun was gone now and only the whiteness of the odd-shaped prison exteriors reflected the ground lights into one another. As he did for hours and days, Simms surveyed the scene. His eyes had gone blank. He was looking inside himself. Searching for his elusive solution. Was he having the same epiphany?

"Wiz, I've got to check on something."

Simms didn't move. He didn't acknowledge the comment. He did that sometimes. He left the man to his thoughts and his darkened prison yard. A brilliant, intelligent, dangerous man. A psychopath.

18

TRACKS

NIK CRIED. She couldn't help it. It was just too much, and she wasn't that strong to begin with. She hadn't said much of anything as the sun sank beneath the desert's horizon. Her back to the sled and her face to the shrinking sun, she wouldn't eat. She sipped water in her silence. Jata assessed the pair of them as pretty much the same. Truman, unconscious and on his back in the sled, and Nik, conscious but silent, her ass in the sand, and her forlorn gaze at the desert panorama of evening hues, had about the same practical use as that desert thing that had left her paralyzed.

It was up to her. Truth be told, it wasn't pretty.

She could just drive off in the sled and leave the two of them to the will of the desert. She might have considered that, if she knew where she was going, but with that many variables, it just wasn't motivated. Not that she liked to admit it, but Truman's assessment about keeping the pirate alive and thinking applied to this situation, too, and he had been right. A time for everything, she reminded herself. She was tired and felt her own energy ebbing as the stars above began to reveal themselves. She sat down next to Nik and tried to think of something funny. Just in case. She kept her eyes peeled for any sign of those vampire creatures, blinking away sleep, but the next time she'd blinked, the sun was up, warming the desert sands for another day. Truman showed no sign of change, and after some discussion, they both agreed that the only help for Truman now lay in the impossible task of locating the prison and then finding their way in. The sunrise gave them their bearings, and after a fairly one-sided discussion, they'd pointed the sled east and departed.

For the most part, their view looked exactly as it had for the previous days. Endless hours of sand. Boredom. Sleep. The same circular discussions.

"How can we be sure we're going the right way?" It was Nik again with the same question she'd asked that morning.

"We can't be sure. I told you before. This is our best guess."

"I still think their sled got buried in the sand. We should have stayed to look for them. To dig them out."

This discussion again, too.

"Look, their sled might be buried in the sand, but it wasn't buried in the sand near us," she told Nik. "If there were two sleds next to one another, they'd both be buried or neither one would be. The only explanation that makes any logical sense is that when the sled reengaged after the lighting strike, we must have lost purchase in the sand and been blown along like a beach ball."

"But we were just sitting there." She wasn't talking to anyone in particular. Just trying to explain it to herself.

"Yes. That's what it felt like. But remember when we were just sitting there and flipping through space on the Raven? Same thing. The sled gives us our own grav field, so even if we're blown like a feather, it wouldn't feel like it. And with the sand blocking out the sunlight, we had no point of reference."

In fact, now that she thought about it, the wind speed had been a good clue to that.

"While you were watching Truman, I watched the wind speed drop off while I was getting familiar with the console. I thought the storm was letting up, but this would explain that, too."

Nik's eyes were big again.

"But with that wind speed—" She trailed off.

"It's a bunch of variables. We don't have Guyal's map or brain. We have ours and whatever data is in that thing," she said, nodding at the console.

Based on what she knew, finding the prison in the desert was a pretty low probability. All the answers probably lay in the other sled. Or in Truman's now mute brain.

Conversation fell off again until about midday when Nik shrieked.

Jata jumped and craned her head back sharply to see surprise and joy on Nik's face. But Nik wasn't looking at her. She was looking down at Truman. She followed her gaze.

His eyes were blinking. He was staring straight up into the sky. But he was awake. He let out a muffled groan.

"Don't talk. Just rest," said Nik, patting his chest. "Oh, Truman you gave us quite a scare."

"He's still giving us a scare, Nik."

"At least he's awake. That's something."

That was something. Were he able to use his full mental capacities, that would be something, but she doubted that was the case.

"Truman." Nik was at it again. "Truman, I don't want you to say anything. Just listen. I've been dying to talk to you, so I'm just going to talk a little. And you listen. But don't say anything, OK? No, don't answer that."

Jata rolled her eyes.

So Nik recounted their story in her own girl-style of storytelling. Pretty flowery. Lots of extraneous details, thought Jata. But the story was there.

"So we don't know if we're going the right way, but we're going East, because really the only way to save your life is to get you some type of medical assistance. And the only place on this planet that has that is that damn prison. So if we can find it, that's where we're going."

Truman said something unintelligible, and started to protest by sitting up, but then fell back on his back, unable to even make that simple move. He was grimacing, his face a mask of pain.

Nik scolded him. "Truman!" she said sharply. "Stop that! You're not doing yourself or anyone else any favors by doing that. Just rest, you pig-headed engineer."

Truman seemed to understand the gravity of his situation, and tried to speak again.

"What was that? Jata, I think he said *cracks*. Did you hear it? Does that make sense?"

"*Tracks*. It sounded more like he said *tracks*."

Truman made another largely unintelligible sound.

She looked again at Nik. "Something, something, Gods" is what I heard for the second one. But that doesn't help us. I thought he might have something practical. He's just complaining."

Nik was silent for a moment. She had a thoughtful look on her face. "Gods. Something, something. Gods," she repeated, like she'd heard it somewhere before.

"Oh, she suddenly exclaimed. "Oh, I know this. He's not complaining. I know what he's trying to say."

She looked down at Truman. "I've got it, Truman. I've got it. We'll keep our eyes out."

Nik was off an another unhelpful tangent, thought Jata.

"It's the Plate of the Gods, Jata. That's what he said."

"OK. But what does that even mean? How does that help us?"

"The Plate of the Gods is a ridiculously priced ham. It's cured ham. They call it prosciutto. It's on New Manhattan. It's on Midway. It's on Earth, but only in the most exclusive places. They let on that it's farmed and produced on a mysterious farm someplace on Earth, but actually, the pigs are raised here, in the north, and the meat is cured in the desert. At the prison."

"So... find the tracks—"

"Find the prison," finished Nik. "If they bring ham south for curing, there has to be a mechanism for its transportation."

Jata nodded, surprised.

"Ooooh," crowed Nik. "I did get one!"

"Yes you did. Good for you, Nik. That one just may be a lifesaver. But that only works if we weren't blown too far east. We'll keep going east until we hit it. But if we're past it already, we're going the wrong way. We would have passed it in the storm. Who knows how far we could drive in the desert. Could be forever with the speed of this thing."

Nik frowned as a thought dawned on her. "Does this console thing save its numbers?" asked Nik.

"Theoretically. But I have no idea how to access it."

"Show me the basics. If I can get wind speed differential and add in a time factor, I'm betting I can guess more or less. Probably enough to find the answer to whether we're over the tracks or not."

"You some kind of math whiz or something?" Jata asked doubtfully.

Crying Nik had become smiling Nik. "I wouldn't say wizard. Anyway, it doesn't matter. Just show me what you know about this thing."

Nik climbed up and over Truman, pushing his legs to the one side of the reclined seat. The two of them hunched over the console side-by-side, demonstrated for Nik what she had been able to learn from her use of it. The controls were standard, so the fundamentals of operation were the same. Nik said what they needed was in the history modules. Something she'd never had the need or desire to use. Within a few minutes, she made up her mind. She didn't seem like it, and she never would have guessed it based on her initial impression, but Nik *was* some kind of a whiz. Within minutes, she had the numbers she needed and was running calculations, both on the console and in her head.

"Pain in the ass," Nik mumbled as she worked the console screen methodically. "2D screens. Utilitarian by design. Pain in the ass by accident."

In under ten minutes, Nik had her answer.

"Right on track," she said with a satisfied smile."

"So we didn't blow over it?

"Pretty sure not. Our speed and time in the storm wouldn't put us past it."

"How pretty sure? What level of certainty?"

"I'd say 75 percent. Maybe 80."

"Based on your outside estimate, when should we see it?" asked Jata.

Nik's eyes were closed again. "Factoring in our drive distance," she said. "Tomorrow morning would be the earliest and tomorrow after dark, the latest."

"So just to be sure we don't drive by in the dark, we'll stop when the sun goes down."

Nik nodded.

The next day passed slowly, and when the time came, they might have driven right over their target, were it not for her lookout stance, thought Jata. She'd realized the length of tracks would form a more identifiable signature in the sand than would the width. She gave Nik the front seat and the forward watch with her eyes on the lookout to the east as they made their way in that direction. She faced south, so together they had one lookout with eyes straight ahead and another with eyes perpendicular.

True to Nik's word and her math calculations, it was late afternoon when her brain triggered her mouth into action.

"Stop!" she shouted, in something of a screech. She hadn't spoken in hours and the sound was almost inhuman.

Nik jumped and slammed her hand into the console control in a single, jerking movement. More methodically now, she slowly navigated the sled in a semi-circle and came back over what looked like, at first glance, to be a ridge of sand. Her eyes were wide and unbelieving as she turned her face.

"My God. I didn't even see that," she whispered, "They don't look like what I had in mind for tracks. We could have driven on forever."

"One for me," said Jata with a smile.

The sun was low, and the exterior temperatures, according to the console readout, were bearable. They parked the sled on the sand ridge and got out to take a look. The ridge's only distinguishing feature was its uniformity as it stretched to the horizons, both north and south.

"Which way from here?" Nik was asking from her standing position on the elevated mound, kicking away the sand and revealing something solid, metallic maybe. The evening sun lit the side of her face with an orange glow.

"We need to go north."

Nik put on her confused look again. "North?" she asked. "But that's away from the prison."

"We're lucky. If we'd hit the track north of the LZ, I don't know what we would have found. Traces in the sand get covered up pretty quickly by the desert."

"LZ?"

By the look of Nik's face, she knew she hadn't helped relieve any of the confusion. She'd have to spell it out.

"LZ is a landing zone, remember? I know we talked about it. And before I say anything more, let's agree we get something to eat and start in the morning. I'll explain better on a full stomach. We can't just drive to the prison and knock on the door. We want in, we need to be riding on one of their supply vehicles. They're on schedules. They're expected. And authorized. We drive up there right now? They're prisoners. You think they could open the gate?"

Nik was nodding her head, the wheels turning inside. She was talking to herself now, almost under her breath as she walked to the back of the sled. "North. In the morning." She turned abruptly, a quick smile on her face.

"Two," she said, in a thankful and maybe a little more respectful tone. "That's *two* for you, Jata."

***

Grinder was impressed. It had been good information. Vee's escape plan went off just as planned. The improvised scene of anger took no one by surprise. In the prison no one knew anything and everyone knew everything, and certainly the bots couldn't be surprised. Their security protocols executed as programmed. They scanned the masks and sorted them appropriately under their programmed directives. Vee's work on the masks was masterful. Even what he anticipated would be a foul odor of dead pig, paint and chemicals turned out to be nothing. The pleasant smell of the desert sand muted the mask's scent of assembly. If necessary, he could have worn it for a lot longer. But it wasn't necessary. Once loaded onto the transport, they no longer had any reason to be checked or guarded. For all practical purposes, they were now free men catching a lift to Midway. The three of them took seats on the spartan transport car. The bots, their mission completed for now, filed themselves into their respective storage lockers and went dormant. They'd be useless crates of metal and composite until a signal reactivated them for their next cargo shipment coming the other way.

While the better part of the day was spent mostly in silence as the transport sped north toward the landing zone, what little talk there was focused on the meals they would eat, the places they would go and the people they would visit. He learned a lot more than he needed to know about his fellow parolees on that first leg off of Claustrom, but he was happy to do it. He shared some of his own plans. Some of it true. Some of it bullshit. He didn't care one way or the other. They were fine as traveling companions, but they wouldn't be buddies for life, so the effort at expanding their friendship or even at conversation, aside from sharing their shared convict bond, was really a waste of time.

At the landing zone, theirs had been the third of three railed transport cars. The other two stood empty, awaiting their next cargo. Parts. Equipment. Actually, now with the cooler season upon them, those things would be overflowing with pigs on a regular schedule. A fourth vehicle rounded out the LZ's vehicle inventory. It was smaller with a big fat nose and an odd tail. He presumed it was used to clear sand from the rails, but had no idea how it actually worked. The circular rail turnout mirrored the one on the prison ground. A single rail line with a circle at each end. That certainly didn't win any architectural awards, but it was practical. It split the difference between the prison and the planet's population to the north. It maintained a dead zone between the population and the prison and served as an avenue of barter. It had its own security standards, as if the desert itself wasn't enough.

But they weren't there for the cars. The flat rectangular area situated to the right of the circular rail and the transport that sat upon it was one of the most beautiful sights he'd seen in a long time. His ride off the planet. Its shape and function normally threw a chill of terror into its soon-to-be passengers with one-way tickets to Claustrom. But not today. It was going his way. He guessed that when not in use as a prisoner transport, the ship was used for other duties as needed. What he needed at the moment, aside from a ride off the desert floor, was some seat other than the metal one he'd used for too many hours. God, his ass could use some padding. If he weren't in such a hurry, he'd have plopped down right there on the sand just to rest his swollen hind quarters. He needn't have worried. The ship must at least have the occasional need to carry some pretty heavy VIPs. Onboard the transport the forward compartments were palatial and well appointed. Large leather sitting chairs with a bar full of options he hadn't seen in ages. He might have a smoke after the stasis wore off, not that he really liked it. He preferred to drink it and presumed such a well-stocked bar would include a number of recovery options.

Hell, maybe I should just skip stasis and spend the weeks it would take to get to Midway's processing and release station drinking my way through the bar. They'd probably figure someway to stick me for the tab. Yeah, welcome back to reality, Grinder.

The hospitality bot had scanned them in, run through a brief of the cabin's amenities and promptly disappeared. Perfect. He stashed the mask in his bag, walked behind the bar for a scotch and planted himself in one of the chairs. It looked and smelled like leather, but he was sure it was a Casino illusion. Matter manipulation. But what did it matter? He'd presume it was real leather and enjoy the experience. The other two were off exploring the contents of every drawer and closet. He didn't have the energy. He took a sip and sat back in the plump seat, closing his eyes and reveling in the luxury.

It wasn't until he opened his eyes and focused that he realized that weeks had passed. The luxury chair was, in fact, a stasis pod. Slick. His time on the planet had put him off his game. He checked his surroundings quickly. The stasis display was to his right, and his bag was on the deck to his left, just where he'd left it.

He grabbed his bag, slipped his mask on and went to look for the other two. They'd found seats at the other end of the cabin similar to his, but they were moving slower than he was. Taking their time. Bullshitting between themselves.

"Move it," he said, as gruffly as he could. They were no longer under his authority. They knew it and responded indifferently, stretching arms and reaching for cigarettes. "They won't open the hatch until we're all awake and ready. Sorry," he said, changing his tone. "I just have a lot of catching up to do. I'll be at the bar."

In fact, he was only partially through his single malt, or a reasonable facsimile of one, by the time they were ready. He downed the remainder, and the trio headed for the hatch.

Out of nowhere the same hospitality bot from before reappeared. Grinder had no idea where it had filed itself, but there it was, wishing them a great day. The bot provided out-processing instructions, most of which were already taken care of virtually, just the obligatory out-processing retinals they'd take before allowing him to descend to the planet. He rolled his eyes and walked out into what appeared to be a lounge area. Services, no doubt, for the human passengers who used these same ships. He ducked into the men's room, leaving the other two to follow the bot's directions for a ride down to the planet. He didn't need anything there but the atomizer. He stripped the mask from his face, watched it "woof" into particles. In practical terms, now both he and the mask had disappeared. He pulled the shirt from his bag. It was a heavy work shirt, and with a couple of motions he pulled it inside out.

"There you go," he said under his breath, "official Bureau of Prisons staff."

It actually fit pretty well. He tossed the bag over his shoulder, exited the restroom following the bots' direction for the retinals, but took a left for the staff entrance instead of a right for the scan to exit. No one stopped him. Out of the corner of his eye he caught a pair of security bots moving down the passageway. Inventory incomplete. They were about to have a problem. He, on the other hand, was about to be done with his problems. By the time they figured out—

He stopped abruptly. He'd turned the corner inside the staff entrance and come face-to-face with a crowd of Casino security guards. Not official federal staff like his shirt identified him as, but low-budget, poorly trained rent-a-guards. Five of them. All of them smiling. One of them, the biggest of the group, wasn't really smiling, but leering. Son of a bitch. Vee *was* the guy. The kid had taken them in without the blink of an eye.

The big guy had his security club out and was beating it into his hand. Big stupid grin plastered all over his face. Doing some kind of dopey dance.

"Welcome to Midway, Mr. Wiz. You just got another one-way ticket to hell."

He was coming closer, still wielding the stick. In the right hands, that stick could do some damage. Too bad for the guy, his hands weren't the right ones.

"Simple case of mistaken identity. I'm not your guy," he said, raising his hands, "But I tell you one thing. You come any closer with that bat, and I'll stick it up your ass."

It seemed to amuse the big guy, his leering face out in front of his big awkward body. He came closer.

Grinder changed his mind. No reason to stick it up his ass. His years of prison life condensed into his right fist and promptly out through a right hook, finding a sweet spot on the left side of the big guy's chin. It dropped him to the deck, his huge form landing more awkwardly than his jeering dance had been. He figured the remaining four would rush him, but they all took a step back. He realized suddenly they weren't chosen for their combat skills. Maybe they weren't even guards. This wasn't an arrest, he remembered. This was supposed to be a media event. He looked at them again. Sure enough each one could pass for a film star. Even the big guy who was now kissing the floor. He smiled. Their media event wasn't going to go well.

"Who's next?"

Three of them stood their ground, not moving. A fourth scurried off around the corner and within seconds returned with a bulkier, uglier version of the guards. He wore the same uniform, but carried himself like a security professional might. Mr. Big was stirring again and making his way to his knees. It was OK. He didn't need to fight them. He raised his hands in the air again and directed his comment to the new arrival.

"Simple case of mistaken identity."

The guard smirked and shook his head. "They told me you might say that, so I've got my little girlfriend here to tell me the truth," he said, patting his hip and taking a retinal scanner from its holster. "You can't fool her."

Grinder shrugged. The game was up. He'd wrecked their show, so it was back to business.

The guard approached, scanner in his right hand. "You can put those down," he said nodding to Grinder's raised hands, "but I wouldn't make any sudden movements. You don't want to scare me. Just relax and we'll get you on your way."

He believed him. That's the way a security professional worked. Everything calm, a certain Zen feel to the whole operation. The guy was calm and did his job. The bright blue light flashed in his eyes momentarily.

"See, that wasn't half bad, Mr. Simms." He was smiling as he checked the scanner's readout. An easy day today for him. Until it wasn't. His brow furrowed, and his smile disappeared. He touched his left hand to his ear and spoke, apparently summoning the A-team. He reexamined Grinder, checking the readout, then his face. Like it was something he couldn't believe. It wasn't making sense to him. His lips moved, but no words came out. A couple of "um's" and then an "ah" as if he was trying to regain his composure with the right words.

Grinder didn't mind the words he came up with. In fact, he expected something similar.

"Holy shit."

Grinder grinned broadly now. The A-team showed up, one taller and the other stockier and solid, both just as ugly. They said nothing but repeated what the first one had done, verifying what the retinal screen told them.

"What? What is it?" The big guy was up on his feet again, and apparently wondering why the three weren't giving him the beat-down of his life.

The tall one spoke. "Mr. Grindstaff. We are sincerely sorry for the inconvenience. You're right. It looks like a simple case of mistaken identity. We had no idea you were a federal prison officer."

19

DEPUTY

THE OFFICE BUILDING of the Bureau of Prisons on Midway was much nicer than the one on Earth. While the Earth-side building was utilitarian—federally contracted and approved—it was more like a prison than any type of business environment. Here, things were a bit different. Proximity and policy can have that effect when used in the right combination, Grinder thought to himself. The Casinos had a vested interest in maintaining positive relations with the Bureau here. It was the Bureau that kept their money flowing, keeping would-be adversaries of their cash-flow objectives off-planet and enabling their prison enterprise, a nice feather in their Casino cap. The architecture of the building reflected that appreciation. Grinder guessed it took up an area nearly the size of the Claustrom prison complex, its regal columns on the outside and courtyards and gardens on the inside overflowing with luxury. Every convenience was provided, with no practical reason to leave the complex. Living quarters, restaurants, pools, spas, even a theater. These amenities made a Bureau assignment to Midway the dream assignment in the prison's career system. And here he was. He'd only been here twice before, once as a child, and then once on his way to his Claustrom assignment, but now he was going to take some time to enjoy it. Sure, Claustrom wasn't an Earth prison, but he'd been undercover, and that counted for a lot. His entry retinal scan had actually been of some use, as it now guided him to his quarters, which seemed huge. Anything would, he guessed, after spending that much time on the inside. They reminded him of the transport ship, the sheer opulence. But then this was Midway.

He'd poured a drink and was enjoying the latitude of deciding what to do next when a soft female voice decided for him.

"Mr. Grindstaff. The Deputy Director." It was a pleasant voice that seemed to come from nowhere and everywhere in the apartment. He looked toward the apartment door. The Deputy Director appeared behind her desk, rendered perfectly in the open space between the bar and the door. It was Williams and she was smiling. He liked Deputy Williams. A good woman. Successful in a federal career that had taken most of her time and energy and left her plenty of gray hair, a number of extra pounds, and those distinctive glasses. Realistically, she didn't need the glasses, but a distaste for any robotic surgery left her with this alternative, and he couldn't imagine her without them.

"Look, I'm sorry to bother you, but I have a couple things I need from you. Then I'll cut you loose for a couple weeks. Or whatever you need."

Grinder looked at the glass in his hand. This was the good stuff. This shouldn't go to waste.

"Say an hour?" he said to Williams.

Williams nodded with a smile and clicked off. The render vanished and returned the apartment to its former state. Which was something. The leather furniture, the stone floors, the stocked bar.

He found fresh suits hanging in the bedroom closet. Less of a closet, he thought, and more of a clothing store. He could get used to this. He took his time and a bit of a scenic route to Williams' office. An hour would have to be a guideline rather than an actual measure of time. It would take him some time to adapt to this new environment, but adapting would be a pleasure. He smiled to himself. The gardens, the fountains, the food, the service. Everything was new and unbelievably different from what he'd grown used to on Claustrom. He didn't know if he could go back. After that stint, he shouldn't have to. For a while anyway, and then only if he requested it. At this moment, however, that was the furthest thing from his mind. He strolled through the complex at leisure, drinking in the sights, sounds and scents, and after a complete walking tour, left the gardens and living area behind him, and made his way into the heart of the Bureau's operations. Office after identical office seemed eerily similar to the cells of his most recently departed assignment. He shook off the feeling and found Williams' office on the third level.

Good natured as always, Williams looked up and motioned him in past her receptionist, who apparently was expecting him, and said nothing. He went to close the door, and raised his eyebrows as if to ask that was what Williams wanted. It was.

"We didn't really expect you, but it's great to see you," said Williams. "So, fill me in with the latest."

He recounted the recent weeks following the girl's assassination and their coming up against a brick wall identifying the killer."

"She was one of ours, you know."

He didn't, and his face showed it. "Simms said she was from one of the guild families. No one relies on the Casinos or has as much conflict with them as the guilds do. I didn't know."

Williams nodded. "She was that, too. She came to us from the families. Odd career choice for one of them, but it worked well for us and for them as well."

But not for her, he thought, but said nothing.

"As you know, the Casinos love the whole ham operation."

"Prosciutto," Grinder corrected her.

"Whatever. It's partly profit, but more status. It's the fact that they are able to provide no-kidding live meat, not the near-meat they manipulate and sell across the planet. So they like Simms just where he is. And," she paused to punctuate her point with a wave of her eyeglasses, "they want to keep the families out, even though under their status agreements, this is something that would normally fall under guild authority. Because it's off-planet and governed both by federal prison regulations and the cultural no-contact authority with the local population, the prison and its operations are something of an exception."

Grinder nodded. He knew all this, but interrupting the Deputy Director would get him nowhere, so he kept his mouth shut and listened.

It was like Williams had read his thoughts. "Sorry. I guess you know this already. Forgive me. What can you share from your up-close and personal experience with Simms?"

"Aside from his hatred of the Casinos, he was genuinely distressed by the girl's," he paused, "by Gina's death. My suspicion, and his, were on this new kid, Vee. A lot of things didn't add up. Simms sensed it immediately and had his hand removed."

Williams was shocked. "Removed? Like cut off?" Her face clenched with disgust.

He nodded. Made it look like an accident. A maimed assassin couldn't do too much damage. He promised to replace it if the kid turned out to be loyal. Meantime, he becomes the kid's best friend and gives him a task to figure out a way through security."

"And that's why you're here."

"Exactly. I'm sure now the kid did it. He had inside information on security protocols that we exploited. Vee thought he was planning for Simms, and the Casinos would be on the other end ready to catch him in the media spotlight, refresh their marketing campaign and extend his sentence."

"Clever."

"But I rained on their parade."

"You're the wrong guy."

He smiled again. "You should have seen their faces when the retinals popped up for them."

"So the kid's the killer?"

"We know that here, but Simms doesn't. My escape plan was

the test of truth. If I return."

Williams nodded and filled in the rest. "If you return, you'd pick up a little more time, but you'd know the kid was it," She thought for a moment. "And if you don't come back?"

"If the plan was valid and worked out as planned, I'm on my way to meet with the guild families for another prison plant."

Williams shook her head. "It's not just for the ham, then is it?"

He didn't correct her this time, but nodded instead. "He confided in me about the breakout, but not about what he would do once he broke out. There was always some kind of plan in his mind. In some way, I know that it's got to end with his revenge on the Casinos. He's got a one-track mind. He's brilliant, don't get me wrong, but he's focused. So I thought the same thing. There's got to be something more he was working on. But now—"

He raised is hands. "Now I'm here. And with only a suggestion of a motive. Not much of a success, I'm afraid."

Williams put her hands to her temples and rubbed, rocking back and forth on the luxury of the executive chair, compliments, he knew, of a self-serving Casino.

He, too, was silent for what seemed like a long time, his eyes closed, his mind thoughtful.

Finally she spoke. "You can't go back."

Williams was adamant, and there was some finality in her voice. *Good*.

Not that he wouldn't go back in a heartbeat to complete the job, but Williams was thinking the same thing he was. Or at least he thought so.

"You go back. The kid winds up dead, and you're back to zero. We'd have to start all over again. Sounds like the wheels to whatever he's up to are already in motion. No, we play this one out."

"Fair enough. I'll get started."

Williams raised her hand as if to curb his professional enthusiasm. "Not so fast, Grinder. Penetrating the guilds is not a spacewalk, and I need you to get your head right before you try on that new hat."

He nodded. The Deputy Director was right. And he did have a few things he wanted to do. Walk, drink, sleep, Rachel.

"There is one other thing, and then I'll be on my way," he told Williams. "The kid is not the mole. That threw me for a loop for a long time. There have to be two of them. Two Casino insiders on Claustrom—the kid assassin sent in for the kill and then the mole himself. Someone who's been there a lot longer."

"So who's the mole?"

"That one stumped me, but I had a notion just before I left. I need you to get linguistics to monitor the prison feed Tuesdays and Saturdays."

"Seems pretty random." Williams was doubtful.

"We eliminated everyone. And I mean everyone. Timeframes, proximity to communications, electronics. Everything. Nothing made sense. Then I realized they must be two separate individuals. One feeding information and the other sent to kill. To break the comm link. The only real possibility is Moot."

"The rock star?"

Grinder nodded. "Those nonsense lyrics that make up jam sessions? I think you'll find they aren't nonsense, but regular reports."

Williams gave a low whistle. "What language?"

"God if I know. But I'd bet they're not any standard language. Probably something archaic. A dead language, maybe. His rehearsals use the same music, but I bet a stay on Claustrom, that he's singing those weekly rehearsals, not about love or pain or heartbreak. He's singing his messages, his prison updates, right to the ears of his Casino handlers. They must have something on him. Something serious."

"Right under our noses all this time?"

"Under our ears. I can't guarantee it, but it's certainly worth checking into."

Williams nodded. "Linguistics it is. Now for you. I want you to take the time you need. I don't have a clue how long that is, but I'll rely on you to make it the right amount of time. Then, if you're up to it, I think you know what your next assignment is."

"Another girl?"

Williams smiled. "Yes, another girl."

***

The prosciutto was divine. Jata had never eaten it before. It wasn't something a woman of her practical means could reasonably afford. But now that she'd had a taste of it, she knew it was something she would have to have again. It wasn't just the taste, there was a whole euphoric feeling that went along with it as it was digested. She felt wonderful. No wonder it cost so much. She wondered if she'd eaten too much. After their time in the desert, over-eating would probably play havoc with her digestion. So be it. Right now she felt good. She stood next to the man they called The Wiz. He was giving her a personal tour of the prison's processing facility. It was odd and creepy, all the machinery silent and inactive, but they were having a pleasant conversation. He didn't seem so dangerous. He was telling her the story of the prison's most recent intrigue, the killing of one of the prisoners. A female. A friend of his.

"I had this modified by one of our more talented guests here," he told her. "So when I find her assassin, he will suffer the same fate that she did."

At first she thought it was a sword. It was about a meter in length, a cylindrical dagger, maybe a half-inch in diameter at the base, shrinking to what look like a wickedly sharp point at the other end. He held it by its odd-shaped handle and waved the tip of the conical sword about in the air in front of them.

"So it was a man?"

"Good point. Allow me to clarify. So that *he* or *she* will suffer the same fate. This is the very point that caused the death. And in this very spot."

He motioned to a piece of equipment that had a bed of sharp

spines that looked very much like the one he held in his hand.

"I had it removed and modified for my personal use."

"I thought this was a prison. You made it here?" She was certainly missing something.

"No," he said, extending his arm and motioning to his head with its tip, "I made it up here. In my mind."

That was only part of the story, she guessed.

"And then a friend who does fine work in iron and steel finished it off for me. Here, try it out."

He offered it to her, and she took it in her hands for a closer inspection. She felt its weight and hefted it for a moment. It was more of a dagger than a sword, its intent to pierce and widen rather than to hack and cut. It was a good weight, but she didn't know what to think about the contraption at the end where the standard grip would be on a normal sword or a saber. She gave it a couple of swings, but couldn't get a good grip.

"I guess I don't know how to handle this model very well," she said. "You must have some kind of technique."

"Some technique, indeed," he said extending his hand. "Do you mind?"

She handed it back to him, then watched as he took it. She'd noticed his lack of a left hand before, but not thought a lot about it. Hard to fathom what went on in prison, and especially one like this with such an arsenal of mechanized cutting tools. After a couple minor adjustments, he attached it to his stump with a clamping motion, the mechanism neatly displacing what should have been his left hand. *That's why its odd design made it difficult to handle. It's a grip for a man without a hand.*

It was a perfect fit.

"That's some weapon. You're left-handed, yes?"

"Sadly, no. But I plan to be more so soon. It looks good, but I'm terribly awkward with it. Much more so than I thought I would be. I'm struggling with the clamp, too. Part of it is brain coordination, but part is also muscle development. For now, I just need to practice."

She watched him standing there. From a certain perspective, she could picture the things he might do. She wondered just how much of what she'd heard about him was true.

He caught her looking and smiled. "I know what you're thinking. Am I the monster you've heard so much about? Hard to say, I think. They don't bring me in to consult on their marketing campaigns, so I don't know my own reputation very well, but I imagine they take their own poetic license."

She nodded. *It was a marketing campaign after all.* "They do," she confirmed.

"One thing you should know about me. I value loyalty above all else. That's the honest truth. I've done a lot of things, but I think loyalty is the human trait I admire most. Aside from that, I don't let anything get in the way of what's right. I've been wrongly imprisoned for a number of crimes that either I didn't commit or that I committed, but got a lot more time than I deserved because of who I am. They've used me beyond what's reasonable, and I won't let anything get in my way of putting things as they should be. Back in balance." Then he winked at her. "I won't lie. I've done things that deserve prison time. And I've done plenty. You?"

She looked him in the eye. "Aside from the fact that this is the first time in my life I've been inside a prison, I still think we probably have something in common, Mr. Wiz."

"Just Wiz," he said. "No need for the Mister."

"I'm a lot like you, Wiz. I believe there are two kinds of people in this life. Those who are willing to do what it takes to get what they want, and those who don't have the guts. And I'll be honest with you. I have little respect for the second group."

Simms nodded in understanding, then changed the subject.

"So tell me again about your trek through the desert. You said you had something for me?"

Jata paused for a moment, considering which parts to tell and which parts to keep to herself.

"So here's what I want," she told him conspiratorially. "I want a tier one mansion in high-Earth orbit. The information I have, if you can use it, and I think you can, will more than cover that. I do believe you'll do as you say, and anyone with your history of, what was it you said? Bringing things into balance? Someone who has a plan for taking on the Casinos might consider it pocket change. For me, the information won't do me any good unless I trade it for something that does."

Simms twisted his head toward her.

"It's funny," he said. "There must be some kind of divine wind blowing this year. I plot my way out of here for years, and when I'm finally ready to make my move, my old friend Truman shows up with a ride. I don't really need it, but I'll take it since it's here. Things just got marginally easier."

"You and Truman are old friends?"

"Well, that's not entirely true. Larson and I were acquaintances before we—"

He trailed off.

"Whatever you were, you're not anymore. Killed on impact. Truman buried him in the desert."

"Sorry to hear," said Simms. He was neither smiling nor frowning. No emotion showed. "I was looking forward to catching up with him."

"Not in this life you won't."

"I'm sorry, you were going to sell me something?"

"Yes, of course."

So she related the story of the two sleds, the abandoned military presence, the vector conversations.

When she finished, he was silent. She watched him consider the information. Nodding and stroking his chin as if he were having an internal, silent discussion with himself. He stared at her hard for a moment longer and then burst out laughing.

She jumped. Not the emotion she expected from him. And in the back of her mind the sand vampire was ready for another attack.

He calmed down after a minute and apologized. "Sorry. That old legend. Don't you believe it."

She tried to play it off. "I didn't really believe it. But Truman did. And he didn't really think you two were friends."

She caught the feigned surprise in his response.

"Really? After all we went through, him and Durt and me and—"
Again, he trailed off into silence.

"He figured if we came here, we'd all die."

Simms shook his head. "I find that hard to believe. But tell me, if Truman thought it was true, what did they find? Not that I believe it's worth anything more than maybe a couple more laughs."

So she went back over it again, it a little more detail.

"What about the second sled?

She shrugged. "No idea. We got separated in the sandstorm. Lost maybe. They could be driving around out there now looking for us."

"So this secret location? What did he have, some coordinates or some ancient map?"

Now she understood he was playing with her. She gave it another try. She had good knowledge. It had to be worth a bundle to the right person.

"It's underwater. And I don't need the coordinates. I've got Truman. Look, Wiz. I do apologize. I guess I thought you'd be in a much better position. I'm afraid I've misjudged you."

Simms didn't smile at her comment, but she watched his eyes reflect his amusement.

"For a guy in your position here, revenge on your mind and knowing who you are. Shit, just based on what you've told me in the last few minutes, you've got significant resources and options at your disposal. The only thing I can think is you're just not ready yet. It has to be something huge because it's the Casinos. I figured, what the hell, I have this information that I can't use, but a working combat vehicle on a flight-denied planet? I figured that's worth, at a minimum, what I'm looking for."

She stopped short, realizing he might have taken her words as an insult.

Again he considered. "There is certainly opportunity for power for those willing to take it. And yes, hypothetically, a combat-ready ship or two would certainly move up our timeline. Who else have you told about this?"

Yes, she thought, in how many pieces would the pie have to be divided? He wasn't insulted. Like her, he was counting.

"Well, presuming no one in the other sled survived, just the four of us."

"Four?" he asked, leaning in and lowering his voice in his own conspiratorial tone. "Are you sure it's four?"

Then the ham caught up with her. She had eaten too much and too quickly. She winced at the sudden twinge of heartburn. "Yes," she gasped, "You, me, Nik and Truman." But as she said Truman, she realized his face had changed from conspirator to something darker. His eyes were cold and curious, and she followed his gaze as he looked down and realized with horror that it wasn't the ham giving her heartburn, but the meter of sharp cylindrical steel, extending from his left hand. She hadn't even felt it go in.

The pain intensified, "Why?" she whispered. "Why?"

"You betrayed the crew that brought you in from the desert within a day," he whispered. "I don't need you. I could never trust you. No loyalty. That's too bad. Plus—"

She was losing focus. She couldn't speak. She heard him, but she couldn't respond. She crumpled and collapsed on the floor. The life draining from her, she looked up into his face hovering above her.

"Plus," he finished, his face only a blur now, "I needed the practice."

20

WATERBORNE

THE HORIZON WAS NOW SIMILAR, but markedly different from
Guyal's perspective. The mountains had become visible a few days
before, growing ever larger and more distinct as the desert floor
transformed itself from barren, endless sand into the more
uniquely textured high plains of Claustrom. The uniformity of the
color spectrum for the previous week made the greenery, as it
began to show itself, all the more brilliant. Now and again, a bright
splash of violet, buttery yellows and even a spark of crimson here
or there turned his head. He couldn't help but point out the first
few bright sprays of color that jumped out of the landscape. Eye-
candy for monochrome eyes. He stopped after his third time,
realizing he was annoying himself as much as anyone, but he
couldn't help his eyes darting then fixating on the odd and unique
floral variations of the planet. More than anything, this marked
progress, and their progress was good news.

They needed some good news after losing contact with the
other sled. Half their crew gone. And now he was in charge, a crew
of the most polar opposites he could imagine. A bright rich kid and
an unpredictable pirate. He had no idea what to expect. The
dangers of space travel were always there for every pilot or
navigator or engineer or even passenger, for that matter, who
ventured into space. But the engineering and safety standards that

brought them across the galaxy, not just once, but for a lifetime of trips without incident, had pushed that to the deep recesses of his mind. He figured he wasn't the only one who felt that way. Besides, he was a natural. For him, the job was easy. The only downside was the family separation, but he figured had he stayed with an Earth-side career, the time devoted to a successful career that would support his sizable family would require even more separation. Up to work before them. Home after them. A few stolen moments here and there. It was true he was gone months at a time, but when he was home, he was home. He was there for long stretches of time to visit, to enjoy. To laugh. To cry. To live. The kids loved the fact that he was a pilot even though he wasn't. Officially anyway. Technically, he could fly the ship. Every crew member could. It was a fundamental requirement of being flight crew. Even if he'd only done it a few times, for them, he was a pilot.

The son or daughter of a pilot was someone special on Earth, and all things considered, they had a comfortable life. He wondered about them now and again, but separation was always painful for him, so he tried not to think about his wife and their six children living their lives. Looking up at the sky with hope and anticipation on their minds. *When's my Daddy coming home? Don't worry, sweetie. Certainly not until you finish your dinner.*

The mountains were imposing. As the ground began to rise toward them, he'd identified a probable route through the barren rock cliffs that faced the desert. The sled's nominal grav field kept them stable, but didn't give them the luxury of actual flight that might shortcut their journey with a quick hop over the peaks ahead of them. It made its way over rock as easily and transparently as it had over sand, and as they crested the mountain pass, they entered a whole new world. Not a world of rock and sand, but a world now of expansive water, the scene transformed into lush shades in the blue green spectrum, a mix of rock and forest and water beckoning them on. The forest decorated the northern slopes and descended to meet the northern sea below them. He couldn't help himself.

He'd set the sled down for a stretch and drank in the cool breeze that wafted the scent of trees and plants. It triggered a faint memory of family picnics in the camping areas near the restricted forests on Earth. The indigenous plant life here was Earth-like with its own unique strain of trees and plants. Its odor was reminiscent of a forest he remembered, but different somehow.

Now the planet's northern sea stretched out before them as they made their way across the water. It was calm and quiet with only a minor ripple of breeze here and there in its azure beauty. Not unlike the sand that spread out before them on their trip north, the water now stretched endlessly to the horizon.

Strober sat beside him with Bam behind, the medkit beside him on the rear seat. He'd been concerned about their seating situation once they left the pass.

Was it wise to have a pirate sitting next to the pilot?

Not that he was doing much piloting. He was doing more sitting and staring at the scenery. But Bam had wanted the extra space to review the contents of the medkit and get familiar with the medbelt. Their plan was to use the medbelt as a technique to retrieve the ship, should they find it. The belt generated its own protective field and would serve nicely as a diving apparatus. He smiled. *Who were they kidding? They sounded like his kids and a game of exploration.* The kids were so inventive with their ideas, he thought, zooming around the galaxy in their imaginary spaceships. What they were calling a plan to get home was a lot like those kids' games. He wondered how long they'd carry on the charade. For now, it didn't matter. They were all caught up in the surreal atmosphere of the foreign planet. When faced with impossible situations, sometimes the mind had to become inventive. For the time being, they were safe. They had food and water. And they had a plan.

Bam wasn't a big contributor to their conversations and spent a lot of time behind his glasses. As usual, he was silent now in the back seat, the only sound came from the various components as he inventoried the case's contents and fiddled with the belt.

Guyal looked over at Strober who looked as bored as he felt himself. First traveling over an ocean of sand, and now across a desert of water. *What was left to see? Or say?*

"Can I ask you a question?" he asked Strober, an offering of some focus other than the waterscape and the mountain range that now shrank below the horizon behind them.

Strober smiled and looked genuinely relieved.

"You want to know how I could do the things I do? How a seemingly principled man could choose a criminal path?"

"You do seem quite principled. And intelligent," he added. It sounded like he was tip-toeing through a social minefield, attempting not to gaffe in conversation. *Would the man take offense at such a line of questioning?* But he was sincere. He was sure it would be an interesting story.

Strober seemed to sense his sincerity and nodded.

"Thanks. That's a nice thing to say to a guy who marooned you in a desert."

"To tell the truth, without your help, we'd probably all be dead or dying. So I figure there's probably a reasonable and rational side to you."

"I like to think so. But being reasonable and rational doesn't always work out best for me." He readjusted himself in his tight quarters, his eyes gazing upward at the open sky.

"At one time in my life, I was on the top of the world. I had everything a man could want. Of course, that's been a few years. I was a young man then with the world to conquer, or at least explore. My family farmed in the Midwest. It was the family business and had been for generations. My old man was a magician on the farm. He had this sixth sense about him when it came to farming. When to plant. What to plant. He knew the trading markets inside and out and had a real knack for killer harvests at just the right time. He could grow a cornfield on bare rock."

He shook his head "It was back-breaking work for him and his team. Don't ask me how, but he could figure a way. He always figured a way. Farms that didn't do so well? He'd buy the farm, keep them on, and I'll eat my boots if he wouldn't turn those fields as green as a grasshopper's belly."

Guyal smiled at the words. Thinking about the farm seemed to make him talk differently. Different words. Words you might hear growing up on a farm.

"It wasn't just the land, or anyone could have done it," he continued. "It was his passion and his know-how and his energy that flowed out of him and into those crops. Nobody else could do it like he could."

"One of a kind, it sounds like."

"One-of-a-kind he was. No one would argue that. I worked with him for a few years, but I didn't inherit the magic or passion from him. It didn't matter. His operation was huge and he needed someone to take care of the business side. My inventive side ran more toward stories and tall tales. They called it sales. I called it bullshitting, and I was king of the bullshitters. I'd spin up a yarn so fast it'd make a sheep's eyes spin. Which worked out fine. Me and the old man. What a team."

He paused, a smile on his face, still gazing into the expansive blue of the sky that was not nearly as bright now with the evening advancing.

"Until—"

He swallowed and the smile shifted perceptibly. Guyal no longer saw the joy of youth, but the cynicism of humanity.

"The Casinos?" prompted Guyal.

"You're goddam right, the Casinos," he said, his eyes now thin and full of anger. "The Casinos had become the business of the world. While the rest of the world was enamored with the latest travel and vacations and entertainment, the Casinos were buying up whatever they wanted. It tended to go in phases. Long before we were around, they'd bought themselves some key government officials. They couldn't control the federal system, but they didn't need to. Just one at a time. Kinda subtle, you know. Pay as you go. I never really paid a lot of attention because it didn't have a major impact on me. For me, life was good."

Guyal had a thought. "Was it the New Manhattan project?"

"I think so. Not sure really. Could have been anything, their focus of interest was pretty random most of the time, but far as we could tell, that was the one real thing that made sense. They wanted to be able to supply and then design self-sustaining environments, but there wasn't a world organization they could have that had the know-how to make that happen. The biological guild was too principled for any amount of money. So they made their own. Bought their own, more like it. Guyal, you know how to fuck up a good thing?" he asked.

Guyal shifted his eyes in question, but said nothing. Strober wasn't really looking for an answer anyway.

"You combine and consolidate. Establish standards and stomp out innovation. The government specializes in shit like that. But this wasn't the government. This was a tyrannical consolidation designed with one goal in mind. Profit. The whole settlement concept is amazing. Simply amazing what they've accomplished. But it's not for everyone. In fact, it's not really for anyone. Just a few elites with nothing better to do. But the people who can afford to buy space there aren't the ones who need it on Earth. And they —"

He stopped short.

"Sorry," I can't tell the story without getting all wrapped up in it."

There were the beginnings of tears of anger in his eyes, and he blinked repeatedly as he spoke.

Guyal understood. "They took your farm, didn't they?"

"They called it eminent domain. Actually, that was the government's language. They probably just called it minor acquisitions or some shit like that. They gave the old man a place in the city and a pension. They took his land as part of their minor acquisition program. Gave him peanuts for his family's generations of work. A year later he was dead. It literally killed him. All the folks he supported over the years got the same thing. They did OK. They tried to talk some sense into him, stop by and talk or whatever. It was like he had no more incentive to live. What's the point in doing anything, he figured, if it was just getting confiscated in the end. They should have just come to his door and shot him. That would have been less painful."

Guyal understood. He didn't need to say anything. He nodded his head thinking through the story himself.

Strober continued. But it was like a different person talking now. Cold and flat. Gone was the youthful exuberance and colorful language of his nostalgia. It was almost a whisper.

"So when the opportunity to pull off something like this came along, who was I to say no? It wasn't my idea, but it was a brilliant one, and I was happy to play along. My inherited talent played well into the scheme. I've got to tell you. I don't know who is behind the thefts. Always very cleanly done. Everybody walked away a winner. Except the Casinos. And I was fine with that. I'm less bitter now than when I started, but as I get older, sometimes there's nothing I miss more than those years together with the old man."

Now he cracked a smile, the nostalgia washing over him again. He put his hands behind his head and gazed skyward again. Guyal figured he didn't see the sky. At least not the one over Claustrom.

                            ***

The handheld might just be the most valuable tool they had. Guyal had put it through its paces and then some. Its mapping capability and the vector information from the flight recorder were not a perfect match, but in a question of meters versus kilometers, the differences were manageable. The weather held for their four-day crossing, but began to shift that morning, the clear skies above obscured by threatening clouds. Increased wind whipped up the worst surface chop they'd yet encountered. The sled wasn't made for over-water travel, and any wind it encountered tossed them off their target track. He'd thought about taking them underwater, but knew that would compromise their speed and progress. By now, they were fairly close to the spot indicated by the intersecting vectors of the flight recorder. Data integrity here was a joke. All they could do was to guess at what might lie beneath them.

In the back Bam was silent still, but not hiding behind the glasses. They'd found their way to a resting spot atop his head among his tangled hair. He looked out at the growing storm as if he could see something. What had once been calm and inviting now threatened.

"Is this the place? Are we here? How can you even tell?" Bam asked, peering out of the various angles of the sled as if to find some type of landmark in the angry gray sea.

"As far as I can tell, we're pretty close," said Guyal, shrugging. The only real way ahead was to dive and begin some type of standard search pattern on the sea floor, he thought. And that was a tenuous plan at best. The ocean floor was a lot like the desert. Way too much area to find anything without a landmark.

"I'm going to dive and see what we can see here. I've got to be honest. I don't have very high hopes. We might as well be searching the desert for the other sled. At least there, we'd know there was something to find. Best we can do here is run in circles until we exhaust our capacity to run in circles."

Strober looked at him for a moment. "Rudimentary tools? Maybe that's all we need."

He looked at Strober with an inquisitive glance. "Why? What do you have in mind?"

"I'm just thinking, that if there is something down there, it didn't get down there by accident. If it's been hidden for hundreds of years, then it's not something that could easily be found."

"But we're here on a planet with no flights on and off, but through remote-piloted vehicles. How much thought would you need?"

Strober shook his head. "Don't think about hiding the ship

today. Think about hiding the ship in *the* day. The day when it was a military outpost. The day when a ship might need to be hidden."

He understood and nodded as such. "Go on," he said.

"So it had to be out of sight, not only from external eyes, but from sensors, too, Right?"

"That seems logical."

Behind them Bam was silent, but following the conversation and listening intently.

"So where do you stash a fighter so it's away from prying eyes? Not everything vanishes from vision below the surface. What's the ocean depth here?

Guyal shook his head. "I don't know. A hundred meters, maybe more.

From the air, wouldn't you be able to make out a vessel sitting on the seafloor?

"Sure. Maybe. What's your point?"

"If this isn't the place, then it doesn't matter. But if there is something down there, and we follow Durt's theory, then there has to be something special. Something pretty unique about this specific place. The reason it was selected."

"He motioned to Guyal's handheld. "That thing have sub-surface info on it?"

"Sure. Why?"

"Pop it open and let's have a look at what's down there. What makes this place so special?"

He complied with the request, more out of politeness than anything else. He found it hard to believe that the charts of the ocean floor might give them any clues to the whereabouts of some so-called fighter.

He manipulated his scanner and caught something out of the corner of his eye from the back of the sled. It was Bam.

"Here, use these." Bam offered up his glasses again in one hand, and in his other he offered a thin silver cylinder dwarfed in the palm of his hand. "insert this into your output, and put these on," he said moving the glasses in the direction of Guyal's head.

He put on the glasses and within a minute he was transfixed. He'd used them initially to look at the flight recorder that first day in the desert, but the readout from the handheld offered a new dimension to the digital maps inside. No wonder the kid was hiding behind these things.

"Use your eyes to focus on the selection you want and hold them there. It's a little tricky at first, but you get used to it."

He was right. It took him a bit of getting used to, but it was fairly easy once he got the hang of it. He opened the planet's terrain map from the archives and awkwardly, but surely, moved his eyes to their approximate location.

"What about numbers?" he asked. "I don't see an input for coordinates."

"Blink twice," said Bam. "Not like you've got something in your eye, but slowly. Mechanically. Or just say the numbers. The audio interface should pick them up."

He did both. The first time he blinked, it was too fast and nothing happened, but when he tried again, more deliberately this time, the screen filled with a number pad, and he watched them self select as he read off their current coordinates. The view defaulted to sea level, so the view was nothing but an open ocean view. Instinctively he tilted his head down as if to look under the water. The glasses responded. He was swimming virtually underwater. He presumed the surface beneath would be reflective of the water above. Flat and unremarkable. He was wrong. While he hadn't been too far off on his initial guess about the depth of the water below them, he was amazed at the topography of the sea floor. Ridges and dips. Peaks and valleys. Maybe Strober had something after all. But it wasn't clear like he had hoped. There was no clear hiding place.

"Anything unique about this place?" asked Strober.

"Actually, it's all unique. It's not flat like I thought it would be. Here take a look."

As he took the glasses from his face and handed them to Strober, the sled suddenly went dark. Outside the wind and sea had picked up significantly. It was an odd feeling. The sled was upside down in the water, tossing and turning with the waves, but for them, thanks to the grav field, they sat immobile, with only their transparent view telling them the true story of their condition.

Guyal reached forward and entered a pair of commands into the console. "Let's make sure we don't get blown too far off our target," he said.

The light from outside dimmed as he intentionally drove them beneath the surface. The sled's interior lights came up. The water was crystal clear, and while visibility was limited by the day's cloud cover, they could make out the outline of some of the sea's underwater terrain.

"You're right," said Strober from behind the glasses. "It's not a simple hiding place. Maybe that's why this makes sense. Too many hiding places. But it's not that deep. A ship overhead, even with a standard scan capability, could easily penetrate to this level and identify its unique, non-organic shape."

"So this isn't the place," said Guyal. *He'd been right. They'd been playing a kids game of exploration.*

Srober took the glasses off and handed them back.

Guyal waved them away. "Have a look around with those," he said. "I'm going to put us down on these exact coordinates and start a standard search pattern. Play with those things and see what you can see. Find us a target of opportunity."

They sat in silence, Guyal and Bam watching the shadowy subsurface formations and Strober, glasses on, navigating a virtual view of the surrounding area.

"There," said Guyal a few minutes later as he maneuvered the sled to a standstill on the bottom. "We're right on top of both vectors here."

The transparent shield of the sled gave them an unrestricted view of Namia's hidden floor as they peered outside. He wondered if there might be sea-life here, but saw nothing but underwater boulders, formations and depressions. On their right side, a relatively flat area broke up quickly into a rocky ridge, beyond which were a number of small peaks reaching probably halfway to the surface. On their left side, the view was similar, with shorter, smoother formations leading toward a single thin peak that reached almost to the surface, an odd alien landscape.

"Crap. This thing is defective." It was Strober. He tapped the glasses a couple of times with his finger as if to adjust them.

"Let me have a look, Stro." It was Bam in the back seat. "You don't adjust them mechanically like that. It's all virtual. What's the matter?"

"I don't know what I did, but the renderings are gone now."

Bam took the glasses back, replaced them quickly on his head and was silent for a moment. Then he sat back on the rear seat and began to move his hands in front of himself.

"What's with the hands?" asked Strober.

Guyal shrugged.

Bam ignored him for a moment and made a few additional gestures.

"You navigate the program with your eyes," said Bam, removing the glasses. "You can control them with your hand motions, too. And with your hands, you can review and manipulate the code."

He looked at Guyal and asked curiously. "Where did you get this map?"

"It standard issue. Public access, I guess. Online archives. Pretty standard software for navigators for hire."

"What's wrong with the glasses?" asked Strober with a smile. "Was the free software too intense for your glasses?"

"The glasses are fine," Bam said flatly. "But here's what's interesting. See that thin peak there in the distance? North and west of that peak, on this map anyway, is an extremely even surface. It doesn't look like the rest of the ocean floor. At least on the map, anyway. And when I have a closer look at it, to explore it with the glasses, there's nothing there.

"What, like a big hole?" asked Guyal, already putting the sled in motion.

"No. Not like a hole. Like a vacuum. There's nothing there. No coordinates. No topographical information. Just black."

Strober whistled softly. "Not like there's a hole, then. More like it was removed."

"Removed?" asked Guyal.

Bam offered his theory. "I'm betting this information is hundreds of years old. Probably mapped by the military group, the outpost that was assigned here. Who would have had better access? Part of their expeditionary surveillance duties, maybe."

"Doesn't make sense to me," said Strober. "If you wanted to hide it, you wouldn't leave it blank like that, you'd fill in some random data that made it look like the rest of the ocean floor around it. This just looks like a big black hole."

"Only if they had that level of sophistication. If they were military, likely they deployed a mapping drone and sent the whole package home for intel review and logging. Might even be there was a mapping request after they'd abandoned their military mission, say from the AME."

Bam squinted, not understanding.

"Administration of Maps and Exploration," filled in Guyal. "It's the larger parent organization that, at one time, included MADO. The functions of MADO still exist within AME, but MADO has been renamed, it's only real legacy is on the maps it created. So anyway, the AME says, *Hey, you don't have a military mission there anymore, so how about declassifying the scans and sharing with us?* What do you think they would do? There's no longer a threat, so they go in, rip out their hidey-hole and pass it along. Minimum effort. Almost no risk. Who's going to Claustrom to look for something that isn't there? It actually kind of looks like a glitch. I wonder if that's what Durt was betting on."

The sled moved a lot slower under water than above it, but by now they had made up about half the distance to the thin peak. The gray weather above wasn't helping their visibility much, but their discussion had reasoned them into a much better state of mind, and no one seemed to notice. Guyal wasn't convinced that they'd actually find something, but this was certainly an interesting development. Something truly coincidental. Another few minutes along the sea floor, and he steered up and over a ridge just west of the peak. At the base where the peak met the sea bottom, Guyal judged it to be less than 40 meters in diameter. Above them now, it stretched upward toward the grey surface of the sea like a pointing finger.

As the sled made its way over the ridge and past the finger, he understood why the map was scanned as it was. They'd sent the mapping drone down here, and it had done exactly what they'd asked it to do. What they saw before them was nothing. Black. The sea floor dropped vertically below them. It didn't reflect on the map because there was nothing there to reflect.

No one spoke.

Guyal brought the sled to a stop. They floated there in the stillness. Silent. Suspended over a huge hole in the crust of the sea bottom.

21

FAIRWIND

THE MEDBOTS WERE AMAZING. While Truman felt like he'd been in and out of his right mind for a month, it was really only a few days. The floating face above him resolved again into clarity, but it was different this time. He felt something warm in his hand and the face was smoother, more friendly.

"Nik," he whispered hoarsely as her face came into full view.

The face smiled and shushed him, one finger to her lips. She held his hand and brushed his forehead.

"Truman. We almost lost you," she said, leaning over and whispering in his ear.

Odd. He felt like hell, but he didn't feel lost. He remembered being in the sled. A sandstorm. A long series of surreal dreams. And now here. In prison. Had he not made it clear that this was a place they wouldn't come out of? He steeled himself.

"Nik. What are we doing here? I told you coming here was a bad idea." He said it in a low voice with concern. *Not that he was scolding her. She was here with him, wasn't she?*

She was practical. "Coming here, Truman? Coming here saved your life. I know exactly what you said, but lost in the middle of the desert with you incapacitated and incoherent. It really narrowed our options. We figured our only way out of here was with you. Which meant, the only way out of here was—" she paused. "It sounds stupid. But the only way out was to break in."

"How in God's name did you do that?" he asked, genuinely curious. "You get close enough with anything that flies, and they go into lockdown—if the sled's grav field is big enough to make a dent in its threshold, that is—not that it really matters as it's a damn desert out there, and if it doesn't, they couldn't let you in if they wanted to.

"We found this place that Jata called the LZ. You know what that is?"

Truman nodded.

"The landing zone, right? So we figured we'd just wait there until something landed."

Truman put his hand to his head. "How long was I out?"

Jata was pretty good with the medcase. She wanted to put a medbelt on you. You know, put you in stasis until we could get you some medical assistance, but looks like we lost the damn thing in the crash or the storm or somewhere anyway. You picked up some kind of desert infection. We kept the fever down best we could, but you were a raving lunatic there for days."

He shook his head. "I don't remember most of it."

"That's probably best. You were pretty disturbed."

"So you're at the LZ. A ship landed?"

"Nope." Now she was smiling again. "It was pigs."

Now he was confused. "Flying pigs?"

"No, silly. Pigs from somewhere in the north. They drove them down in these—I don't know what they're called. Some kind of mechanical transport vehicles. The pigs got out of them and into these railcars that were there. Remember, you told me about the prosciutto? Anyway, I think they thought we worked for the prison. They didn't really say anything to us. We climbed in with the pigs. You were almost more trouble than you were worth," she said playfully. "When they saw what we were trying to do, they thought it was funny. I couldn't believe how strong they were. They were only about yay high," she said extending her hand out to indicate, maybe three-quarters of her standing height. "They pitched in and closed the doors behind us. You should have seen their faces when we unloaded at the other end. And that guy, Simms. He doesn't seem so bad."

Truman looked at her narrowly. *That's exactly what she was supposed to think. Innocent until the very end.*

"You just don't know him very well, yet. Give him a chance." Then he had a thought. "Where's Jata?"

She looked at him again, still playful. "Don't worry about her. She's fine. You just get rest up and get better. Mr. Simms said he didn't need her, and that he was sending her home. I told you he's not as bad as you make him out to be."

Truman thought about it. Sending her home could mean a lot of things. Especially if it was a lie. He was pretty sure where she'd gone. It wasn't to meet her pilot. It was to meet her maker. It would be a warning to him. He'd try and keep Nik in the dark as long as he could. She'd be his insurance policy. He could hear Simms already. *Play along, and I won't hurt the girl.* Hell, he wouldn't even have to say it, he thought. Anyone who knew how to pronounce his name would infer it.

When he was done, Simms would kill him. No, scratch that. Simms would have someone else kill him. That was more his style. While she watched, of course. After that, who knew? He knew it didn't matter.

As he already knew what would happen, it was pretty hard to surprise him. In this case, it wasn't a matter of what. It was a matter of when. He now held the keys. Even if he didn't have a clue about how he'd use them. Simms might be more ruthless, but he was at the end of his rope. And that made him dangerous, too. Not a thought he'd had very often.

Nik left him alone for the rest of the afternoon. He napped on an off and was visited by a medbot a couple of times. He drank an odd-flavored soup that made him sleepy, and by the time he awoke, he felt like a different person. Younger. Energized. He surprised himself as he hopped out of bed. The stiffness and the burning was gone. He was full of energy. He hopped around a bit.

Damn. I feel great.

And then Simms entered.

Truman couldn't help himself. He lunged, but quickly caught himself. "You son-of-a-bitch," he snarled.

Simms looked mildly taken aback, but he smiled. "That's good, Truman. Looks like you're fully recovered. Now we can talk. I told you before I had a proposition for you. As it turns out, this may turn from a good day into a great day."

Truman responded. "And if I didn't tell you before. You go straight to hell."

"Maybe. Maybe one day. But not today. No, Truman. Today you've done me a great favor. And you'll do me another. You know I've intended to break out of here from the day I got here."

Truman nodded. "No big leap there. We figured as much."

"And in fact, I could have, but I wasn't ready yet. Some of my best work is just ahead. I needed a team and, well, I have one here. But I also needed a ride off. We're very close to finalizing a plan to engage with our partners to the north. But yesterday," he said with an feigned aside to Truman, "and you're going to love this. Yesterday, while you were napping, I had a nice discussion with your friend."

"Nik?"

"No, the other one. Odd name. Jata, yes?"

"Jata. Yes." His eyes narrowed suspiciously. "What did you do?"

"I did you a favor," said Simms with a shrug. "She sold you out for a share of, let's just call it a larger piece of pie. I'm surprised she didn't betray you sooner."

He thought about it for a moment. He wasn't sure she hadn't, but if she was to blame for conspiring with Strober, she wasn't very good at it.

Simms went on. "She told me the sad tale of Durt. And what a hero he was. I believed her. A traitor's tongue is free when it's fishing. I am sorry to hear that. You know I had plans for him."

"Of course you did. You have plans for everyone. But I'm still not sure what favor you did me."

"I saved you from being betrayed, Truman. She changed sides in an instant. Not five minutes into the conversation, and I had everything I needed. I barely even had to ask. No loyalty there, Truman. And without loyalty, what's the point of anything? She wanted a nice place orbiting earth. I let her have it."

"You killed her, didn't you?" he hissed. He wasn't surprised at all. Predictable. He feigned shock with his eyes. "But you told Nik that you—"

Simms interrupted. "I told Nik I sent her home. And I did. I did send her to another place. She told me she wanted what she deserved. She was a traitor. I gave it to her."

Truman wondered at the cold-blooded calculation. Apparently his thoughts were transparent to Simms.

"Are you afraid of me, Truman?"

Truman looked him straight in the eye. "Not even a little," he lied.

"You should be. I don't let anything or anyone stand in my way."

He said nothing. It might be true, but there was a lot of that in him, too. And he had one other advantage, he thought. Simms might be a cold-blooded killer, but he was a predictable cold-blooded killer. And that was something to work with.

"So here's what I need you to do. Jata told me about your little trip north and a lost frigate. Ring a bell?"

Anger rose in his throat, and his face betrayed him.

She double-crossed me, that ungrateful bitch.

Simms smiled.

Truman realized something else. In spite of her betrayal, she'd given them a bargaining chip they hadn't had before.

He still wasn't convinced that there was anything at the end of their so-called treasure hunt,   but if Simms thought it was worth something, then they now had some kind of leverage. Yes, he thought, the ship might be real or imagined, but either way, it might help get them out of here.

Another aspect occurred to him. A military ship in the hands of someone like Simms? That was something he hadn't even considered. It was a threat not to just them but to just about everything. He thought about what he could do himself with that capability, if his motives were ill-intended. If he wanted to exact revenge, that ship could offer a huge portion of it. Then he multiplied his worst thoughts by magnitude of ten. Or something like that. No, he decided, it wasn't going to happen. Somehow, Simms had to be stopped.

"So, we've moved our schedule forward, thanks to you," Simms continued. "It's a little earlier than I'd planned, but since you've come with such a generous offer, and it's a perfect night for it, I've made the decision to compress my schedule."

"After you, Truman," he said, motioning with feigned politeness.

Truman noticed now that he'd held the stump of his missing arm behind his back. It was an odd stance, but probably an unconscious habit he'd developed since losing his hand. But as they moved toward the door, he realized Simms carried some type of sword. Carried wasn't the right word. It was attached, but it wasn't a sword. It did have a sharpened tip to it, but there was no edge. Useless for hacking or cutting. Still, in the right hands, it could be deadly. He wondered if it had served as Jata's instrument of death.

With Simms prodding him from behind, the pair exited the prison's sick bay and made their way to what seemed to be the center of the outdoor compound. Outside it was dark, the heat of the day dissipated. The odd-shaped white structures of the prison reflected the compound's security lights, throwing monster-like shadows and an eerie glow onto the scene before them.

Truman had a hard time making it out at first. He recognized

Nik crouched down in something that looked like a big box. A second figure moved about near her. Spread out on the ground next to the box was what appeared to be a pile of brilliant white cloth. Sheets, maybe? But it was some kind of material that shimmered in the reflected light. No one else was around. Behind him, Simms was narrating for him.

"Truman, do you know what we do here?"

"Ruin lives?"

Simms chuckled. "Among other things, I guess. No, we enrich lives. They call our product the Plate of the Gods. You're right, though. We do ruin the lives of a lot of pigs here on the planet. But that's what they're made for. The product gets shipped around the galaxy and sold for astronomical prices. We take what we want here. But we're also very frugal. We often make creative use of the parts that aren't shipped out of here."

As they neared the others, he realized Nik wasn't crouching. She was bound and gagged. Her eyes were wide and scared, and she shook her head from side-to-side as he approached as if to throw off the gag and scream for help or to warn him away. He had no idea how Simms had directed the other prisoners away, but aside from the four of them, the prison's central area was deserted.

"Here we have a basket formed of pigskin. It's large enough to support the four of us. We've made ourselves some lines from the same material, and see this?" He motioned with his metal skewer to the pile of white fabric, "this is compliments of the Casinos. This material is unbelievably strong. They put on quite a show for us. And for some odd reason," he said with a smile, "they misplaced the fabric for one of their tents. They were pretty creative. They came with this, and they went home with some of our prison sheets. I think they're still scratching their heads."

Truman had to wonder at the genius and simplicity of it. There was only one missing element. And then he saw them. A pair of tanks that, he presumed, likely contained methane. A pig by-product, no doubt.

Simms was looking at the sky. Cloud cover masked the night stars and there was a bit of a breeze. Something they would need to rely on, he figured. It was out of the south, too. That explained the compressed schedule. He guessed it didn't happen that often. He watched as the kid Simms called simply "V" set about for preparation. He, too, was missing a hand.

What was this, some kind of criminal club?

But even with one hand, within a couple of minutes he was ready, and with an assent from Simms, he lit the end of the tanks, and Truman watched as the big white balloon slowly took shape and loomed above them. Nik was already strapped into the pig leather basket, and the kid had rigged a type of support harness that secured the skewer at the end of Simms' arm close to Nik's mid-section. Probably positioned next to her heart so that any thoughts or plans of throwing Simms from the balloon were quickly forgotten as such an attempt would leave Nik with a leaky heart. Simms didn't even have to say anything.

Truman climbed in beside him.

"I trust you've checked out my harness already, so let's just agree to get along for now. You're an engineer and should be able to quickly grasp how to fly this thing. Doesn't have to be pretty, but I'd make it as pretty as possible, were I in your shoes. Wouldn't want me to slip and—"

He didn't finish the sentence. But he didn't have to. Truman understood and nodded.

"You know, Truman, I'd drive. Or I'd have Vee here drive, but we're a bit short-handed." He burst out laughing at his own expense. Vee joined in, too, the two of them tickled with their own ingenuity. Truman smiled grimly. His eyes were on Nik, cowering beneath the threat and the point of sharpened steel, eyes wide and body shaking. He was having a hard time finding anything about their situation humorous.

The balloon worked surprisingly well. Much better than he expected. It cleared the prison grounds without incident, and the wind pushed them north. Beneath them the metal of the tracks wasn't too hard to make out, even with the overcast sky. Their eyes adjusted to the dim light and only now and again did Truman need to make a course adjustment with the makeshift steering jets they had rigged. The wind stayed with them as they floated north. Were it not for their particular situation, the ride might have been more pleasant, a smooth, airy ride. But Nik was tied up under threat of death, and Simms would not shut up and rambled on and on about whatever came to his mind. He bragged about his time at the prison, how he'd had this planned for a long time, but wasn't really ready yet. How he'd made contact with a group from the northern manufacturers, the same ones who provided the equipment for their curing setup. Once in a while, Vee would interrupt with some inane comment that seemed to annoy the annoyer, but Simms ignored him for the most part.

When it happened, it was so quick that it was done before he even realized it. Vee was more surprised than anyone. It was dark, and in a flash, the skewer was out of its cradle, inside of Vee, and then just as quickly back it its original position. What should have stayed inside of Vee was now dripping darkly onto Nik. She screamed, a muffled scream that made its way with difficulty through her gag. Then silence. Finally, Simms had shut up. A look of complete surprise covered Vee's face. His eyes wide, seeing but not believing.

He sputtered, incredulous. "But. But I thought—" were the only words that escaped his mouth. He didn't or couldn't say anything else.

Simms pulled him close. It was a low growl, but Truman heard every word. "You know what this is, don't you?" he said, nodding to his skewer. "This is the same piece of metal you used in the assassination. It found its way home. You killed with it. And now I've done the same. This brings revenge and balance. I will share this moment with her family on Midway. He who lives by the sword should expect nothing less."

Truman watched as Simms shoved him. Final understanding of Simms' words replaced Vee's perplexed expression, but only for a moment before he sagged, stumbled and fell headfirst into the darkness of the desert below.

22

MESA

STROBER FINALLY BROKE the silence with a single word.

"Shit."

Guyal considered and agreed that it was the right word.

"Now what?" he asked.

"So really what we have here is an answer isn't it?" said Strober "We've got a legend from history. We've got maps with anomalies to support it. We do the visual, and what do we see?" He wasn't really looking for an answer that he didn't' supply himself and went on to answer his own question. "We see the anomaly explained. You've got to admit it was pretty coincidental. But now we know. There's nothing here."

"Clearly," said Guyal, the disappointment obvious in his voice. Like the others, he'd been caught up in their game of exploration. And now it was done. Game over. Time to quit and wash up for dinner. But there was no going home now. What did they have to risk now to get a ride off the planet? He guessed it was back to the prison. He was certain their affiliation with Durt would be easily discovered and strictly dealt with.

Yes, shit was the right word.

"Let's go," he said, a tone of finality in his voice.

"Wait a sec." It was Bam in the back again.

He rolled his eyes. "Now what?"

"I'm just thinking here. What if our conclusion is the one we're supposed to come to? What if the hole were the actual stash place, and we walked away because we thought our clues were compromised and our coincidences just too much. Now that would be clever. That's just the thing an intel group might do."

"Bam, you're not just thinking. You're over-thinking," said Strober. "I think we've spent enough time here. Time to get on with the next plan."

"Humor me. I'll make it worth your while. This really is something of a geographical anomaly. We're here. Let's take a look. You don't have any physical restrictions on this sled do you?"

"None physical. Just mental ones," said Guyal, his voice suddenly tired.

"OK. Just satisfy my curiosity. Then we'll go."

Guyal nodded his head and set the sled in motion with the console control.

"Sure," he said.

This time they descended vertically. The grav system and shield would serve them well even here. They could, if they had the depth, dive for miles beneath the surface, the same as if they were submerged in just a few meters of water. He switched on the sled's exterior lights. Above them, now, instead of the grey sky, they saw the sheer vertical cliffs that formed the edge of their anomaly. Even though the sled descended vertically, the grav system made it feel like they drove forward in an upright position. The light reflected off the rocky sides, leaving everything else in darkness. They dove down and forward.

"Any way to tell how deep we are?" asked Bam.

"Not in this thing. It would strictly be guessing."

Bam nodded.

It was Strober who noticed the difference first. "Is there a current that's pushing the sled sideways?"

"Again, Hard to tell in this thing. Why do you ask?" But he saw what Strober was talking about. Above them, the sheer face seemed a bit farther away than it had a minute before. He stared at it for a minute to see if he could tell if it was them or something pushing the sled away from the underwater cliff sides. Then it became clear. Ahead of them, the wall took a decided angle upward. They peered into the depths as the wall inclined up and away from them. The rock face they'd followed down ended abruptly. The darkness below now surrounded them on all sides except the ceiling that extended forward above them.

"It's like an undersea bottle here," said Bam in awe. "And we're through the neck right now. It's like a sub-ocean down here. God knows how big the inside of this bottle is."

Guyal put the sled into a circular pattern, keeping eyes open, in the absence of any sonar capability. All directions were the same to them.

"Any bright ideas on which way?" he asked.

"The perfect place," said Strober.

Guyal wasn't sure what he meant. "Perfect?"

"To hide a ship. Not visible from above. Marked by a unique underwater formation. Maybe it wasn't supposed to be hidden after all. They did want to be able to retrieve it, didn't they?"

"That still doesn't help with a direction."

"Oh, I think it does."

Bam agreed from the back. "I think he's right."

Strober continued his thought. "The only marker we have to distinguish that jagged opening down here was that peak. That thin little peak. Put yourself in the place of the pilot in charge of stashing his ship. He finds this hole in the floor, and he needs a way to mark it, so he—or someone else—can find it."

Bam picked up his conversation. "Yes. So I'm the pilot, and I can't very well erect any type of sign, so I have to use a sign that's already there."

"The peak," said Guyal.

Strober nodded. "The peak."

"Which means, the most probable direction is this side of the bottle. The side the peak is on."

Guyal was done second guessing. He was done hoping. He was afraid of being disappointed again. He said nothing but put the sled on a new course, the rock still overhead, but their direction as best he could guess, aligned with the thin peak and now parallel to the water's surface above. It seemed to go on forever, but within the hour, they were able to make out something in front of them. The color of the sides of the huge underwater cavern were markedly lighter at this depth. Almost a dirty white color that easily reflected the exterior sled lights back to them. The sides weren't smooth as a bottle might be, but were jagged with ridges and shelves, like a giant hand had crushed the cavern and left it crunched and crinkled. As they approached the vertical side, Guyal put the sled into another circular pattern.

"Eyes open for any—"

"Anomalies," came the quick response from Bam.

Guyal nodded. "Anomalies. Yes."

They missed it on the first pass. The lights disappeared into the darkness of the cavern behind them as the sled rotated, and as they passed their light over the white wall in front of them, the brightness of the reflection left them temporarily blinded. But when Guyal reversed direction, between the time their eyes went from darkness into the bright reflection, they all saw it. Guyal held his breath as he slowly maneuvered the sled's lights to bear on the direction his dead reckoning sense told him was due north. They were parallel to the cavern's wall. The clarity of the water, even at this depth, combined with the reflective properties of the wall revealed the anomaly. They could make out a flat-topped mesa extending outward from the wall's sides in the distance. Silence filled the sled as Guyal set a course. The mesa grew before them, its size immense. The odd white protrusion extended outward from the wall, an oddly shaped mesa formed by natural geological forces of the planet. Still no one spoke.

The sled drew closer. The top of the formation was unusually flat. Nature was funny sometimes. Its size was impressive, too. Not just a small irregularity in the side of the bottle, but its own formation that extended up from below, like a flat-topped mountain connected to the sheer rock face they now traveled beside. He was no geologist, but the mineral activities that shaped these billions of years in the past were a wonder to look upon.

"Holy shit. Check it out." Strober, again, had added the correct modifier.

Holy shit was right, because there, at the edge of the mesa it stood. No mistaking it for anything else. No natural mineral or organic formation. It was a goddam space ship. Just sitting there peacefully as it no doubt had for centuries. The clear waters offered an unrestricted view of the thing as they approached.

"How can there be no bacterial growth on that thing after all this time?" he asked, realizing the answer himself as soon as it was spoken. It was a stupid question, but it was too late to take it back.

"Force field shield protects it from just about everything," said Bam. "It's beautiful. An Aldrin class. Originally a combat vessel, later it took on research and transport missions."

"How the hell do you know that?" asked Strober.

Guyal was curious, too. Of all the things a kid should know, this didn't seem to be one of them.

Bam smiled. "My latest flight combat release." He tapped the dark glasses atop his head. "It's been centuries since we built any decent military designs. Everything has to do with practical and commercial designs. For combat? It's always these whacked out, unrealistic combat designs fighting in a conceived universe packed with different types of invented monsters. It got so overdone. I had this idea to stop being so unrealistic. Fantasy based, I guess is the right term. I wanted a real experience, or as close to real as I could get. You get my game, and you pilot these planes as if you were really in them. Same specs. Same controls. You pick the plane. You pick the mission. That's where I get creative. I've got a number of battle scenarios and a number of bombing and raiding missions. I have one where you take out the entire Casino complex on Midway."

So that's why he spent so much time behind his glasses. Made sense, Guyal thought. Maybe he shouldn't be so quick to judge.

Strober was impressed. "What about this one? Have you flown it?"

"It's a fairly common airframe, but its use in my game is more utility than fighter. Like a multi-purpose plane. I have flown it a few times to check it out, but its capabilities are limited on most of my missions."

"Maybe you add a mission where you break into one stashed in an undersea cavern."

Bam smiled.

Strober continued. "So what's next? How do we get into this thing? Password? Secret frequency?"

"Two options. They may have it set in their secure mode. If so, we'll have to go back to the surface, and I'll have to come back with the med belt. You'll need to propel me. I should be able to open it manually from underneath. If it's not in secure mode, it may be rigged for quick escape. If so, it may be sensitive to our grav field. There's a lockout chamber in the back for in-space transfers. My guess is that it would work the same down here."

Guyal circled around the ship and approached it from behind. Its bulk dwarfed the sled. It was the size of a building. He didn't see anything that looked like a mechanism to open the rear door, so he shrugged and pressed the sled forward, making contact between its shield and that of the Aldrin. At first nothing happened. Then the ship came alive. A strip of lights above them blazed on, illuminating the sled with an almost unbearable light. He kept the sled pressed against the back of the big ship, his eyes locked on the ship's huge hatch before them and watched for an opening. They sat there for a moment, unmoving, bumped up against the bigger ship.

"Something's wrong," said Strober.

Guyal glanced sideways at him for a second. Strober wasn't

searching the back of the ship, he was looking out of the sled and down at the mesa beneath them.

"We're pushing the ship," said Strober. "What the hell is going on?"

Both Guyal and Bam checked the outside of the sled at the same time. Sure enough, Guyal had the sled pushing against the hull in a forward direction. And below them, they watched as they made progress over the mesa's surface. Instinctively, Guyal maneuvered in reverse and then to a standstill. The distance between them and the ship increased.

"We're not pushing it," he said. "It's moving away."

"*What*?" cried Strober with a shout. "How is that possible?"

More lights on the ship came alive as it moved away from them.

"Follow it," urged Bam. "Close as you can."

But Guyal was already pressing the controls and pushing the sled forward. Within a minute he'd achieved the sled's maximum underwater speed and was not making any progress toward the ship. They watched in despair as the ship slowly picked up speed and pulled away from them, growing smaller until it finally disappeared into the darkness.

***

The restless Namian sea had calmed itself somewhat by the time the sled broke the surface. The waves were shorter, and the wind not nearly as evident. But the sky above remained a gray ceiling. They searched the horizon for some clue, but as they expected, found no trace of the Aldrin. Endless sea and sky. Countless options. Guyal shook his head.

Why had they even thought they could be successful?

This state, the position of dashed hope that they were now experiencing, was maybe worse than if they hadn't come so close to actually snagging the vessel. They had found it, though. That was some kind of experience. A piece of history. Vanished. Returned to some other hiding place. A ghost now, just as it had been before, the intended state of those who hid it there at one time. They sat for some time in silence. The waves of the sea beneath them formed their infinite variations, a shifting and ever-changing waterscape that both distracted them and held them entranced.

"You know," said Bam from the back, but Guyal tuned him out. He talked on for minutes, trying to convince them and himself that they weren't lost, that he had a number of ideas. It was like a flood gate had opened. For days he said nothing, and now he had to catch up with himself. Talking about everything. Talking about nothing. Talking to everyone and to no one. His voice droned on in the background, an odd almost hypnotic combination of the visual ocean and the rising and falling of Bam's voice.

That's when the idea hit Guyal. He reached his hand behind and made a simple request with a single word. "Glasses," he said.

Bam stopped talking and handed them over, a hopeful look on his face.

"What is it?" he asked. "Whatcha got?"

Guyal didn't answer. The glasses were still connected to his handheld, and he maneuvered the software with his eyes. Bam had been right. What was awkward initially was now easy, and he was able to quickly fly up and over the rendered landscape of the Claustrom map. He zoomed in. He flew over. He dove beneath. He continued like this for a few minutes until he found what he was looking for. He smiled. Not so unrealistic after all. If he was right.

By now his crew-members were beside themselves. He was always the doubter. He wasn't the wild idea guy. So if he had something. He *had* something, and they were both exhorting him to share.

"So I was thinking, if we tripped a security device, what would be the most logical return spot?" He didn't wait for them to respond. "Home, right?"

They agreed.

"How much do you know about mapping drones?"

Bam began reeling off a list of models and technical specs.

Guyal shook his head. "Impressive, but not really useful. My idea is a lot simpler that. They're usually small, inexpensive. Most are or were traditionally thought of as disposable. If you lost one, you'd send out another which would pick up where that one left off. The other shortcoming, and it's related to its low budget nature is its—"

"Range!" said Strober, in unison with him. He was shaking his head enthusiastically now. He got it, too.

"Yes, its range," he said. "Those things have a limited range, so in order to map a planet, you need to carry these things out and allow them to do their mapping. Deserts, mountains, hills, lakes, seas. For most of them, you have to take the drone out to the area you want it to map, set it on its pattern and then recover it."

"Or abandon it," said Bam. "But why do you think they'd use drones? Wouldn't the ship systems do the same thing? Maybe better?"

"Maybe. But I'd bet that mapping wasn't a military objective. I think it was probably an AME request. Think about it. This is a military outpost. Their mission here is to serve as an exploration and defense force. They're Earth's outer perimeter. They've explored the planet, found no threats, and have their focus on the other planets and potential threats in this star's system. What possible military benefit could they gain from mapping the planet? If they scan with their ship systems, it becomes part of the military intelligence system. You'd never get it out of there in any useful form. I'm betting AME was probably under pressure from mining and development interests, so they likely shipped out their own equipment, and asked the military to deploy them as a favor."

They followed his logic and urged him to continue.

"So, in the absence of any threat, the military is usually pretty open to supporting federal agencies' requests. They ship out the drones and the project goes into action like a military duty rotation. The drones log hours, so they have to ensure they keep them in the air for the agreed number of hours. But flying around the planet deploying these things is a duty without any particular payback for them. So, and this was my thought, the drones spend a lot more time in the air around the outpost where they just flip the switch and these things fly off and do their thing. Not using up military time, and not sending them around the planet to sit there and wait for it to be done. Obviously there was a lot of that, too, because we have a fully rendered map of the planet.

Bam shook his head. "That's all very interesting speculation. But how does that help us here today?"

"When a drone overflies an area for mapping, it's set to gather a certain level of detail. If it's set on its same path a second time, it doesn't skip over what it's done before, it adds additional data. More detail. So I thought, if my idea was valid, not only should I be able to see an area with a lot richer detail. I should also be able to see a distinct border that would mark the edge of the drone's range, and the center of which would be—"

He paused and watched Bam's puzzled face melt.

"You son-of-a-bitch. You found it didn't you?" laughed Bam.

Guyal handed the glasses back to him. "Check it out for yourself. It sticks out like…well, it's pretty clear. I think you can see where we're going. I've got us headed in that general direction. We should see the northern coast tomorrow sometime, and presuming our assumption about it being recalled to its home-base is correct, it's not more than a couple days away.

23

SHORELINE

THE MORNING DAWNED BRIGHT and clear. Gone were the clouds. The wind remained, sprinkling an active, sparkling texture over Namia's surface. It was a cheerful site, and were it not for the close quarters, the days on end in the sled and the cramped, sore muscles, it would have been a perfect morning. They sighted green hills that afternoon and vectored the sled in a northwesterly direction, traveling parallel to the shoreline about a kilometer distant. Now that they were familiar with the glasses, they took turns zooming around the handheld's planet map and walking through the virtual Aldrin, a lot more certain now that the ship would soon be in their hands.

According to their calculations, the center of the more richly detailed area was at the mouth of a river in a well protected bay. Nothing on the map suggested anything to hint that an outpost had been there at one time. After the centuries, he expected nothing would be left. If the Aldrin were called home, it would probably sit there on the shore, patiently waiting as its program had directed.

By the third day, the three had a difficult time containing their enthusiasm. The weather held, and the reflected sun had a marked effect on Bam's tweak of the shield's transparency. Now programed for optimum light levels, the tinting darkened the shield to match the light for optimum visibility. In the desert that had been a blessing, but here as they tried to distinguish the features of the shore, the shifting, reflected light became something of an annoyance. Finally, Guyal switched off the tinting feature, and they squinted eagerly across the short span of water, their eyes picking out oddities on the shore. While the colors of shoreline approximated what they knew on Earth, the shapes of the plants and trees were uniquely alien, as if their basic building blocks were the same, but they'd chosen alternate and separate paths of evolution to best match their need for propagation on this planet.

"There, that's our landmark. Straight ahead," said Bam. He had the glasses and he peered over the top of them, as they sat perched on the middle of his nose. In this position he could see both the map and the view ahead.

Guyal followed Bam's pointed finger, but couldn't make out anything through his squinting eyes.

"You're right. There on the horizon. Just barely," said Strober.

Sure enough, a dim outline of a tall rock formation just offshore appeared as an odd shape where the water met the sky. According to his handheld, the entrance to the bay lay just north of it. It grew larger over the next hours as they drew closer, and they examined its unique form. It was large enough to support a few Claustrom trees at its top, but the ocean and the wind, over millions of years had reduced what was once a mighty peak to a giant piece of abstract art, a landmark and a welcome sign to a protected bay they wouldn't soon forget. Its bulk dwarfed the sled as they passed between it and the green shoreline.

Past their landmark, they steered the sled east and entered the bay of their destination. The channel opening was not that wide, its north cape less than a kilometer from its southern mate. For the water surface, it made a noticeable difference, the water protected and quiet as they scanned the opposite shore.

It wasn't difficult to identify their destination. The hills beyond the tree line parted distinctly, presumably for the river. The water here was much shallower, and they could easily make out the ridges of white sand on the bottom of the bay a few meters below.

They were about midway across the bay when Strober pointed it out.

"Do you see it?" he asked? "Look at that break in the sand."

He had seen it, but not recognized it as the ship. His eyes told him it was a large rock, but as they closed the distance, the detail became clearer. Their theory had been correct. The Aldrin was recalled and beached at its home port.

Bam punched him in the shoulder and let out a whoop. "Nice work, navigator! That's our ride home."

He didn't mind the punch. In fact, he appreciated it. But his exuberance was interrupted.

"Hang on," said Strober. "There's something else. What's that?"

He was right. There was something else. The area around the Aldrin was moving slightly. Like it was alive.

He echoed Strober's curiosity. "What *is* that?"

Bam had the answer. "It's people. It's a crowd of people."

As the sled approached the shore, he realized Bam was right. But it wasn't what he might have expected. And it didn't make a lot of sense.

How could there be people here in the middle of...well, in the middle of nowhere?

Here in a wild remote corner of the planet were maybe a hundred people. And they weren't really curious about the Aldrin. They were actually dancing. Gyrating about in celebration. In his logical mind it didn't compute.

"What the hell is going on?" asked Bam. "Who are they, and what are they doing here?"

"They're ghosts," said Strober. "I wouldn't believe it myself if I weren't seeing it with my own eyes." His jaw was open and his eyes stared at the dancing mass of people. He was shaking his head like he wanted to say something but was overwhelmed.

"Looks like people to me," said Bam.

Strober recovered quickly. "Of course they're people. But just like there were stories about a lost fleet of ships here, there were stories about a tribe of hunters, too."

Guyal looked at Strober curiously.

"You know about the descendants of the outpost here. They asked and were approved to stay here on the planet once their defense mission was no longer deemed critical. There was big defense downsizing. Within the community that stayed here, there were two primary groups. One farmed in the western fields and the other mined in the eastern mountains. They set up a regular route of trade using the sea as their trade route.

"And the ghosts?"

They're not really ghosts. But as it turns out, the mineral elements here contain substances not found on Earth. I couldn't tell you what they are, but what they do is facilitate mental development. Beyond anything we're familiar with. They get it through their food sources. That's one of the reasons the prosciutto here is so sought after. It has an actual euphoric effect. In the east, they process their foods to the point where it has almost no effect, but for the farmers, it's a fairly common trait for them to have expanded mental powers. It's now in their DNA. It varies from person to person, obviously."

"So what, they could read minds?"

Strober nodded. "Some can do just that."

"But what about these—" He paused, not knowing exactly what to call the group dancing on the shore. "These people?"

Strober shrugged. "To the best of my knowledge, they've rarely been seen. Again, just legends and stories. I never really believed they existed. Supposedly, there was a small group within the military community who wanted to live off the land. Apparently plenty of wild local game in the north here. They're supposed to be able to appear and disappear at will. Like ghosts."

"Well, they're certainly appearing now," said Bam, checking out the circling mob as they drew closer.

Guyal suddenly grabbed Strober's shoulder. "What...is...that?"

He couldn't believe his eyes. The crowd had parted slightly. In the center of the circle he saw what looked to be a cat.

Beside him, Strober was speechless, too, his mouth open.

It was a cat. Or it was cat-like anyway. But it was no ordinary cat. It sat serenely in the midst of the dancers with what looked like a smile on its face. It was lying down on the beach, stretched out as if totally relaxed. For a moment, the alien feline raised its tail, maybe the length of three men lying end-to-end, then replaced it in a more comfortable position. By now, the group had spotted the sled, and the crowd waved them in with big smiles and open-armed greetings.

"Do you think it's safe?" A closer inspection of the cat gave him no clear answers.

"Look, we don't have much of a choice. They seem friendly," Bam said uncertainly. "They're not going to eat us, are they?"

Strober smiled. "Let's hope not. But no sudden movements, OK?"

Guyal and Bam nodded in unison. In silence. Guyal nosed the sled onto the beach and shut it down. They stepped out as it settled onto the sand.

The demeanor of the crowd changed suddenly. It went from wild dancing to silent, prone, bowing. The trio looked at one another, surprised and mildly amused.

Each person was dressed differently, a unique mix of skin, fur, feathers, bark, wood and bone. A large male dressed more opulently than the others approached the trio alone.

"Welcome. I am Tofar." His voice was deep, and it had an odd quality to it.

Strober took the lead, pointing first to himself and then in turn to the others beside him. "Strober, Bam and Guyal," he said.

It was a breach of protocol, Guyal knew, but he allowed it and watched, fascinated, at what happened next.

"Your arrival has been foreseen. We are honored to be a part of your quest."

The voice was clear, but Guyal had watched him closely and his lips hadn't moved.

What kind of trickery was this? Was this their mental power?

Tofar continued. "This ship of our ancestors, we offer to you as our gift."

He motioned behind him, and a second male stepped forward, this one slim and bony and ancient. Were it not for his skin, he'd be a walking skeleton. He said nothing, but looked at them intently. Dark eyes stared out of their sunken sockets. He wasn't smiling. He wasn't angry. He was focused. Guyal felt an odd tingling sensation and shivered involuntarily. He saw Bam and Strober do the same.

The skeleton nodded in assent. Now he smiled. It seemed like the wrong expression for him, but Guyal felt a wave of relief. Tofar was smiling, too, and a third figure approached, this one a female. She walked slowly with purpose. Her fur and feather clothing hugged her figure closely. In her hand she held a slim tube, maybe the width of a finger. She extended it before her as she approached. The piece that extended above her hand flashed a purple light intermittently. She stood before Strober, then bowed low and extended the flashing tube before her.

Bam whispered in wonder. "The remote recall." All eyes were focused on the tube as they realized what it was. This truly *was* their ride home.

What happened next left them stunned. Guyal wondered what Strober might say. Some words of gratitude? Something about their quest to get the hell off this planet? But he didn't say anything. When they looked up to thank their newest allies, there was no one there. They stood alone on the beach in the shadow of the Aldrin.

For a minute no one said anything.

Strober finally broke the silence. "I told you so. Ghosts."

Bam recovered first. "C'mon. Let's get aboard." He took the flashing cylinder from Strober and moved toward the ship.

Strober stretched out his arms and his tight muscles. "I could really use a couple of days here at the beach."

Guyal disagreed violently. "Are you crazy?" He moved his face closer, his eyes earnest. "Did you see the size of that cat? We need to just get the hell out of here. Now."

Strober grinned. "You're right. God knows how long that thing stays docile. Looks like it eats a lot."

Behind them, a mechanical whir interrupted their conversation. They turned to find an open hatch in the side of the ship, its opening filled immediately with a grinning Bam.

"C'mon. Let's go." He motioned to the pair with his hand. They wasted no more time and boarded the ship, the hatch sealing the beach behind them. The interior of the ship was dim with the low green safety illumination lights. After the brightness of the beach, it was a cave in comparison, and Guyal used his hands on the side of the passageway to guide him as his eyes adjusted to the interior of the Aldrin. It wasn't unfamiliar to any of them, each having spent a good deal of time exploring the virtual model.

They made their way forward to the navigation and combat center. After their cramped journey from the Raven over the past weeks, the interior of the Aldrin was palatial. Guyal stretched his arms and held them there, just because he could. Suddenly he felt tired. The weight of fear and adventure and their journey made him realize he hadn't slept well in—

He shook his head. He hadn't slept well since they'd left New Manhattan. But this was a victory. He'd won his game of exploration. You can't really celebrate victory by going to sleep, but, he figured, maybe this time he'd make an exception. Anyway, officially, he was in charge of these two, so he had at least a few more obligations.

The cockpit looked more like a betting table at a casino than a combat environment with a central circular console and tactical seats placed around it. He took a seat and activated the navigation and combat control, first waving his hand over the table, and then, when that got no response, manually pressing its center. The table came to life. Its center elevated slightly, and the smooth black surface split into eight plates, each forming a triangular piece of the combat console. By hovering his hands over the now-energized screens, he was able to scroll through combat, security, logistics, and navigation readouts with his fingertips.

He stopped on the nav menu and began to review its functions. He looked up at what he thought must have been a couple minutes later to find Bam staring at the security screen.

"Guys, check this out," Bam said without looking up.

Guyal looked up from the nav station. Bam had the security system up and was running through its screens as if he knew it inside and out. Actually, by now, he probably did.

"What's the last thing you remember about that crowd on the beach?"

Strober shrugged and answered. "We were standing there, the three of us. And I was looking at that thing." He motioned at the purple cylinder sticking up out of the side console, next to the central control table. "I look up again, and I'm staring at beach and trees, and I'm blinking to make sure of what I'm actually seeing, which is an entire crowd of people vanish."

"Me, too." said Bam. They both looked at him. He nodded his concurrence. "That's exactly what happened. So here's a different point of view."

He pressed his screen, and the security cam that had captured them from the ship's view played back on the angled view-screens on the table before them. It wasn't a particularly well-framed shot, but it was clear enough to show the three of them standing side-by-side. The screen played back their interaction and the presentation of the purple cylinder.

"Yep. That's us. Your security cam works. So what?" said Strober.

"Just wait. Watch. Now."

The camera caught the completed presentation, and then something odd. Guyal didn't realize it at first. He remembered staring at the cylinder, but on the video they were still staring at the cylinder. Their host had turned around, his back to the three of them, and was now addressing his people, his hands in the air. The crowd listened. Some nodded in agreement.

"I don't remember any of this," said Strober. "I looked down. I looked up. They were gone."

The host was done talking. The crowed milled around for another minute or so and then walked off into the trees beyond the edge of the screen, the big cat ambling slowly in their midst. The three of them were still frozen on the screen, staring at the cylinder. After a minute, they looked up and then at one another.

"And, we're back," said Bam.

"Strober's right," said Guyal. "They're ghosts." He was running through all the possibilities in his mind. He was on the beach again. He was staring at the cylinder. His mind was wired, but he was so tired he couldn't think straight. He looked up. They'd asked him a question, but he'd been too engrossed in his thoughts to even notice.

He shook his head as he realized what he'd heard.

"Say that again," he said to the two of them seated at the table beside him.

"I said, how soon can we take off?" asked Bam.

It was clear the excitement was still buzzing through his veins. Strober watched him. Curious now of his response.

"Look, we're not going anywhere without the rest of our crew. I don't know what you had in mind, but I'm ranking officer here, and I cannot in good conscience abandon them."

Bam looked ready to argue the point, but he stopped short. And nodded his head. "You know what, you're right. But if they're lost in the desert, even with this ship, we don't stand a chance of tracking them down. The desert's just too big. And well, to tell the truth—"

He didn't have to tell the truth as his unfinished sentence implied. If the other sled had been compromised, the only thing they might turn up would be bones—if they turned up anything at all. They all knew it. No one had to say it.

"I've been thinking about it," he told them. "And keep in mind, my primary duty is to them. We now can look after ourselves. So, like it our not, here are what I see as the most likely possibilities. First, and this is worst case, somehow they lost their way, and they're driving around in the desert. If that's true. There's no practical way to track them down. Desert is too big and too much time has passed. We could spend years looking for them. Not practical. I think that's a low probability knowing Truman's in control."

Bam and Strober both nodded their agreement.

Guyal continued. "Aside from that, and I put myself in Truman's shoes, what are the only other possibilities?"

"Prison," said Strober, "That's certainly one."

"It might be their smartest move. If they could get the sled close to the prison, it might set off a field proximity alarm on Midway. A security team might already be on its way. I'm not sure about the barrier wall's sensitivity. If that's the case, it's not our concern. We've got comms now, so they'd show up on our sensors once they broke the atmosphere. And we haven't heard anything on the glasses have we?"

Bam confirmed with a shake of his head. "Silence."

"So, according to this thing," he said, his hand once again over the control table, "based on planetary position, had that been their play, they would have launched—" he paused, making the time calculations in his head. "How many days since the storm? 10 days? Two weeks? Presuming they were able to find the prison, although I have no idea how they'd do it, but I don't put anything past Truman, two weeks into what should be about a two-month passage, that gives us another six weeks before they show up with their fancy toys. But it's also six weeks that—"

"That we could be looking for them, too," interjected Bam.

Guyal nodded. "It would give us a chance to put this thing through its paces."

Bam smiled and nodded, his attention focused on the multitude of controls and capabilities around him. Strober was not so quickly pulled from the conversation.

"But based on what we know about Truman, that's probably a pretty minimal possibility. You took extraordinary measures to avoid the prison."

"Durt made the mistake of underestimating Simms once. He carries..." He stopped short and corrected himself. "He carried that reminder with him to his grave."

"The scar?" asked Bam.

Guyal nodded.

"He didn't say so in so many words, but I think they figured it was likely that Simms had schemed a way through the security system. Us showing up and asking for help would be the equivalent of him signing a death certificate for all of us. He could take care of himself, but the rest of us? We'd never make it out in one piece. And Durt couldn't allow that."

"So if they're not at the prison," Bam said.

"I think there are three choices they would have had," said Strober. "If we rule out prison, then there are only two others."

Guyal agreed with a nod.

"The location of this ship and," Bam was shaking his head. "And I don't know."

"Tiron," said Strober. "It's the largest of the Claustrom cities."

Guyal agreed. "That was my thought, too. Now Truman could have a much better memory than I give him credit for. He's another one you never want to underestimate, but he didn't have any of the tools we had. The flight recorder." He motioned to Bam's head. "The glasses. My handheld. No, more likely than not, if they didn't choose the prison, Tiron would be their next logical choice."

He realized he'd been yawning almost constantly through their conversation. All of them were virtually on the edge of collapse, the adrenaline now finally draining from their systems. He suppressed another yawn.

"I've vectored us back to our spot on the map. The hole in the sea." He looked at Bam. "This thing has a proximity alarm, too?"

Bam nodded. "Full sensor suite. The interface is like an antique, but it's functional."

"What we need most is some down time. Keep in mind, we're under federal mandate not to interfere with non-flight cultures. So we can fly, but only at night."

Strober shook his head tiredly. "Who would know? Who would care?"

"There's a little thing called a flight recorder." He raised his eyes at Bam who confirmed with a nod. "It'll be open for inspection and scanning on return to Midway. Now, we spent a lot of time and energy to get this thing. We don't want it confiscated for something stupid. Especially you," he said severely to Strober.

Strober raised his hands in defense.

"You're right. Take it easy. We do need some sleep."

Guyal continued. "I don't know what their shipping lanes are, so we'll submerge in that general area. See if they show up. If not, we'll double check the pass we came through. If they were on our tail and had the same basic direction, that pass is the most likely candidate for passage. If we still have no sign of them, we make our way to Tiron, have a look around. If there are foreigners, we should be able to pick up on that fairly easily."

"And if that doesn't work?" asked Bam.

"If that doesn't work, and we still have no comms with prison security, we go down to the prison and ring the bell ourselves."

Strober nodded.

"We could go do that tonight."

Guyal was exhausted. "You do what the hell you want," he said, standing up and pushing himself away from the circular table. He was done playing nice. "Nav systems are set and locked. I can barely see straight, let alone think straight. I'm going to find a bed and sleep for a really long time."

24

CIVILIZATION

THE MOUNTAINS FORMED in the distance against the edge of Claustrom's desert. At first they were shadows. Outlines in the haze. But as jagged peaks and severe ridges became visible, their shapes embodied a sense of foreboding.

The ride was excruciating for Truman, both physically, as his renewed energy was cramped in the sled again, and mentally as well. He occupied the front pilot seat while Simms sat directly behind him next to Nik, his skewer cradled and directed at her.

Just knowing how close the point was to severing Nik's life was a big part of it, but Simms also loved to talk. It was like he hadn't talked to anyone in years. And Truman listened. Nik was scared and cried a lot. Mostly to herself.

Maybe he should do something stupid. Make him kill Nik. At least she wouldn't have to listen to his blather.

He scolded himself for his thought. It wasn't practical, and he wasn't thinking like he should. He was thinking like Simms wanted him to. Simms' genius was not in his practical understanding of combat or torture, although the constant stream of one-way conversation made a pretty good case for the that. No, Simms' consistent success and power came from his knack for intimidation. Constant. Irrepressible. So much so, that at a certain point, the mental defenses of his opponents cracked and crumbled, sometimes unconsciously and other times overtly. Raised hands. White flag. You win. I surrender. He was certainly persistent, and because of that, he was ultimately successful. In spite of the voice in his head that told him to just do what he was told and everything would work out fine, he knew that the intimidation only worked if the intimidated participated in the process.

Ignore the intimidation. Make it an engineering problem to solve.

Even though he hadn't said a word in hours, in his mind, he'd disagreed mentally with pretty much everything that came out of Simms' mouth, shouting out his silent resistance with all his willpower, but it did him no good. In fact, it played directly into Simms' technique. Keep this up, and you'll have no choice but to surrender, he told himself, and he was stunned with his realization. It was true. And that realization shifted his focus to a new strategy. Simms had finally talked himself into a stupor. He never really slept and would jump awake every few minutes, his skewer sometimes jerking dangerously. Then he'd smile and start in again.

They'd drifted the balloon northward until the track ended, where they'd put down. There, along with some transport railcars, sat their sled. Out of place. Just waiting for them. He'd wondered as they'd put down how they could make their way in the desert without navigation instruments, but realized shortly that the southbound pig transport had left a trail clear enough for a blind man to follow. The sizable mounds on either side of the sand trench would make for easy navigation, even at night. As day broke they returned to an endless panorama of sand, but its shape was different from inside the north-facing trench. The sand walls on either side blocked out the direct light of morning sun.

The absence of Simms voice prompted him to glance over his shoulder at Nik in the rear seat. The gag was gone now. In fact, the gag hadn't really been practical in the first place. More to minimize distraction during their pre-flight with the balloon he thought, and of course, the ever-present intimidation factor. But he was surprised to see her smiling again. He raised his eyebrows in a silent question to her and nodded toward Simms, seated behind him and out of his line of sight. She shook her head, closing her eyes momentarily and tilting it to one side. He read her well. Simms had his eyes closed and was asleep. Good.

Her wrists were bound, but she still had movement of her hands, and had something. He couldn't quite make out what it was. Women had a whole separate dimension of women things they carried around with them to which he remained oblivious. Sometimes in their purses. Sometimes in their pockets, if they had them. Apparently she'd dug some little woman tool out of one the recesses of her flight suit and was working diligently against the skewer harness.

Her face transformed instantly, again on the edge of tears. He heard Simms clear his throat behind him. He watched her furtive glance and pitiful expression keep an eye on Simms. After a few moments, apparently satisfied, she looked back at him, her eyes now bright with the challenge, and shot him a broad smile.

He brought two fingers to his eyes and then made a walking motion with them as if to say, "watch for the right moment, and then we'll make a run for it." She nodded. She was already there. And she seemed to be enjoying the challenge. He shook his head with wonder at the realization. It wasn't just on him. He didn't have to be the only player, the only hero. As a team, they'd be a lot stronger and have much better success.

What held them at bay? It was the skewer. Simms' weapon of poetic justice had served its poetic purpose, but that was about it. It wasn't well suited as a practical combat weapon. It's point of attack was limited, and while deadly at point blank range, its actual level of threat dropped off sharply after that. Actually, the more he thought about it, the higher his spirits rose. He stole a glance at Nik and gave her a quick wink. She nodded and went back to her efforts. Where she'd been terrified before, he could tell she was genuinely excited now.

The mountains loomed larger before them as they made their way north. The sled moved excruciatingly slow, but it moved as fast as it could go. He made sure of that. But with a one-handed maniac sitting behind you holding you hostage, time changes and takes its own sweet path. Days became nights and then days again.

The uniformity of the path they followed north was uninterrupted three days into the northward trek. But on the morning of the fourth, something was different. It appeared first as a dust cloud on the horizon that resolved slowly into some ungainly looking vehicles that made their way directly toward them. Truman pulled the sled up and over the side of the trench and set it down in the sand a hundred meters off or so.

"Those are the things I told you about," said Nik from behind him. "They're some kind of pig carriers.

They looked like no vehicles Truman had ever seen, but they seemed to fulfill their purpose in a practical way. In front was the power. Its huge mechanical tracks moved the machine forward, tossing sand in its wake as it crawled forward through the desert. On its top was another set of tracks, immobile. Backups maybe. Truman marveled at the size of the procession. Three rectangular containers followed the lead crawler and another crawler unit, this one backward facing, trailed at the rear. Because of the trench, he was unable to make out the wheels or tracks beneath the vehicles, but just below the top tracks of the crawler units, he saw figures inside. They didn't seem to notice the sled parked in the sand watching their southward progress. He made out figures in the rear unit, too. And these figures were much more animated. He could see one pointing and motioning. Another then stood beside him to see what the first had seen. Both then dissolved into what appeared to be laughter. Truman furrowed his brows, not understanding what they would find so amusing. Then he saw they'd shared something. A bottle maybe? Ah, he thought, they're drinking. He wondered if they might not see mirages on a regular basis, given their task.

"A shipload of pigs."

Simms was awake and staring at the transport machines.

"A what?" asked Truman.

"Well, half a shipload anyway. Prison facilities have a limited capacity and can only process so many pigs at a time. There are no storage facilities, so when the pigs do come, they have to maintain their shipping schedule. And they don't come directly from Tiron. They're raised on grazing lands farther east and come in on transport ships. It's really quite an efficient system."

Once Simms was awake and intrigued, he started in again.

At a certain point, Truman's mouth got the better of him. He couldn't help himself.

"Man, you sure talk a lot. Of all the things I'd heard about you, that was never one of them. You chatter like a little girl." He realized once he said it that he probably shouldn't have. That Nik might pay for his loose tongue. But Simms just laughed.

"Right you are, Truman. I've been thinking and scheming since the first day I put my foot in that prison. And people, especially prisoners, wouldn't know what to do with a happy attitude. Not very useful in my opinion. A smile and a laugh, a sincere one, mind you, doesn't intimidate. So the last few years have been brooding and planning and intimidating. And then you come along and gave me this sled and accelerated my plans immensely," he said gleefully. "I have a rapt audience here. And it doesn't matter what I say. Deny me, and I'll have fun in my own way, taking my Durt Larson pound of flesh from the two of you. Give me what I want, and, oh I don't know. Maybe I'll just strand you back in the desert or something. You found your way out once. Maybe you'll do it again."

He put on a faux surprise expression.

"Oh, I've let the cat out of the bag. You thought I'd be fair and do what I said, didn't you?"

Truman shot a quick look at Nik. The fear had returned. Quickly. Unmistakably. Apparently that's exactly what she thought.

She probably didn't care for some ancient spaceship anyway, even if they could find it. What she couldn't fathom, and he had no intention of explaining to her, was how dangerous Simms could be with a ship in his hand and a chip on his shoulder.

Then he went off on another tangent, telling them, as he had a number of times before, as if he couldn't contain his excitement, of their intended destination. He'd called it the loading facility. Apparently, it was the location where pigs were loaded on for their final ride south to the prison. Truman envied the pigs.

Sure they were going to die. Everyone was. But they didn't have to listen to Simms as they drove toward their final destination. Lucky bastards.

Simms' approach was to drive directly to the facility and ask for Picek. It was his contact, and considering the relationship, probably not a nice guy. Presuming he was a guy. Sometimes with these names, it was hard to tell. Then, he told them, that is where Truman's talent would come in. They'd make plans to travel to and recover whatever was located in the cross hairs of their secret location. At that point, he inferred that all would work out well. He knew what that meant, too. Everyone was going to get what they deserved. In his assessment, obviously.

Time stood still as desert melted into high plains. The low native plants and vegetation marked their departure from the endless sandy ocean. Here and there they began to see signs of civilization. No people at all. An empty building here, a road carved there. The main road was well worn, and even at night, they made good progress.

As it turned out, at least for the initial part, things went just the way Simms outlined. There wasn't much of anything south of the city. Some abandoned mining efforts that either hadn't panned out or had panned out and then petered out. No, the only thing of value south of the city was the road that led south to the prison. And based on the activity they encountered, which was none, it was a single-purpose highway.

When at last they arrived at the loading facility they'd heard so much about, they found the entire complex consisted of four rectangular warehouse structures, presumably Truman guessed, for parts for the transport they'd seen, and a large area enclosed by a retaining wall. Based on the wall height and the condition of the ground it fenced, it was clear a shipment of pigs had passed through recently. The place looked abandoned, but Simms insisted it wasn't. Probably just awaiting the arrival of the next shipment, he said. Based on the schedule of the last departure, it would be more than a week before the transport returned for its next load.

Truman circled the perimeter of the place and came to what appeared to be the facility entrance on the north side. The main road stretched northward, presumably into the city of Tiron. A closed iron gate greeted them, and with no one in sight, Simms directed Truman to shut down the sled and motioned Nik to get out in front of him, the harness maintaining the point of his skewer in deadly proximity.

He prodded her toward the gate and yelled.

"PICEK!"

Silence.

"PICEK!" he repeated at the top of his lungs and listened for some kind of response.

Still no one answered.

In a quick motion, he undid the harness and quickly reattached it to the gate, placing the business end of his steel extension at the base of Nik's throat in warning.

"Don't try anything, Nik. I like you, but I don't need you as much as you think I do, so be still for a minute."

She swallowed and nodded, not saying a thing.

With Nik secured to the gate, Simms began to drag the end of his arm extension across the vertical bars that kept them out of the complex. The resulting sound was an odd ringing with an almost musical quality to it. He walked to the edge of the entrance and then would spring back at Nik, bringing the metal to within millimeters of her neck or chest.

"Ha!" he would shout, and Nik would shudder, waiting to be pierced.

As it turned out, Simms was right. The place wasn't abandoned. His racket raised what was likely the duty mechanic or the duty guard. Maybe he was both. He was short and round and surly.

"Whaddya want?" he barked.

Again Simms repeated his code word, *Picek*. This time quietly and with an edge.

The guard looked at him narrowly, his eyes full of suspicion. "What do you want with Picek?"

Simms wasn't one to be trifled with, but he understood that he must communicate his basic message. He motioned to the sled.

"Truman, switch on the sled for me."

Truman, still in the front seat of the sled obliged, and the sled floated off the ground to cruising level.

Simms pointed to himself.

"I'm Simms. Get me Picek."

But the man wasn't looking at him. His eyes were still locked on the floating sled. He shook his head and rubbed his eyes. And then an understanding came over his face.

"Picek," he muttered. "Picek. Yes, Picek."

He looked at Simms in sudden fear.

And that was the moment.

Nik lunged back suddenly, the remaining strands of the harness snapping, leaving the leather straps hanging from the iron gate.

Truman quickly understood their opportunity, steering the sled north, away from the loading facility and toward Tiron. Nik was running for her life. Step, step, step and jump, her face a mask of physical effort.

Simms was astounded. He froze momentarily in disbelief, then broke into a run, chasing the retreating sled. He stopped after a few steps, seeming to realize he didn't have any chance of catching up with his prey.

The guard watched in amazement as the sled moved off, the man in front and the woman suspended above the vehicle as if she were floating there and flying forward.

A minute later Truman cut the sled's power, and Nik dropped over the seat beside him, laughing. Truman immediately reengaged the sled and continued their retreat.

Nik slid into the sled's front passenger seat. She was exuberant.

"I can't even describe how I feel now," she said, flashing him a smile. "I've been trembling for days now. I just knew I was going to fall asleep, or he was going to jerk the wrong way, and that would be the end of me. And then, BAM!, we're out."

Truman smiled at her exuberance. He was a bit surprised they'd been able to escape so easily, but maybe he'd overestimated Simms.

"You know they'll scour the planet for us."

Nik turned and looked at him, a puzzled expression on her face.

"Truman, we're in a shielded sled. This is a backward, flightless planet with what, swords and guns probably for weapons. What are they going to do, shoot us with arrows?"

While her point was valid, he couldn't shake the sense they weren't out of danger. Certainly, though, they were better off now than at any time in any recent memory.

"They have Simms at their helm. We'll need to watch our step."

Nik considered for a moment and shook her head in agreement. "We need to find the others."

Truman shook his head. "No. I think it's the other way around. They'll need to find us."

Truman sobered at the conversation. "If they're alive."

Nik repeated the phrase to herself, processing it. "If they're alive?"

Then she looked at him and slapped his chest. "Don't think like that!" she scolded. "Of course they're alive. Maybe they're still looking in the desert for us."

"I wouldn't be. It's just too big. With their limited capabilities in the sled, they could search for years and not find something this size. The range of the communication signals in these sleds is limited to about as far as you can see, so, if you were them, scouring the desert wouldn't be your primary option."

"So if you were them, what would your primary option be?"

Truman looked out at the changing landscape as he considered the question. The low-growing vegetation had given way to Claustrom's own alien brand of bushes and trees. The ground beneath them was no longer sandy, but the trail was well worn. Well-traveled. He had another thought.

"We should get off this road. At least for a few hours."

Nik was puzzled again. "Why should we? What could they do?"

"Look, we might be impenetrable to their primitive tools, but they could certainly trap and contain us. Lock us in a sturdy building or keep and sooner or later we'd have to come out."

"They wouldn't know that. They've never seen something like this before."

He gave her a look as if she had overlooked something.

She realized what it was. "Oh yeah. They have Simms."

That thought on his mind, he steered the sled into an opening beside the dirt and stone road, crawling between trees and over undergrowth. It didn't take long for them to lose sight of the road. He set the sled down at the first opportunity and stepped out, stretching. Some of Nik's resilience returned again, and she hugged him tightly in the shade of the odd looking trees above. He felt the softness of her body and her delicate kiss that took him far from the forest floor. Then he pulled back. It was refreshing to be able to simply stand free for a few minutes, to breathe in the planet's air around them. It wasn't the scorching air of the desert. It was a comfortable, almost cool environment.

She looked at him, a satisfied look on her face. She knew they couldn't stay there for long, but it was a respite for now.

"So where do we go?" she asked.

Truman continued his thoughts from the road.

"So, if we're in the desert, they don't know if we're dead or alive, and they can't find us with what they have. So they won't look. They know me. Well, Guyal knows me. I made it clear we couldn't go to the prison."

"But you did go to the prison."

Truman nodded in agreement. "Yes I did, but they know what I said and not what I did, so they wouldn't look there."

"You don't think they'd go looking for that thing about the old ship, do you?"

He shrugged. "I think it's a stupid fantasy, but I might. Just to have a look, you know. Presuming they're alive."

He raised his hands in defense as Nik gave him a sharp look.

"Of course, they're alive," he said. "They have the coordinates, and Guyal has a planet scan map. A ship would have a lot more capability. Actually, given our, and their, last known position. I'd probably check it out first. The closest option really."

Nik saw the logic. "And then?"

"Then probably Tiron."

Nik's eyes popped wider than normal, if that was even possible.

"Do you really think so?"

"It's what I would do."

She smiled broadly, and her smile dissolved slowly into a yawn. "I need something to eat and—"

She stopped abruptly as she looked into his eyes.

Truman would really liked to have had another kiss, but stifled his own yawn and raised a finger. There was something on the edge of his senses. Something that shouldn't be there. The woods were quiet but not completely silent. He wasn't an expert by any means. Few people on Earth were forestry experts. But the woods he'd had experience with were full of sounds. Birds, bees, other insects and animals going about their individual little lives. But this forest didn't seem to hold much of those sounds. Here an there was an odd snap or crack as the wind brushed the trees. But now there was something else. An odd, almost metallic whine. He cocked his head as he focused. He saw Nik caught it, too. It was louder now. It built quickly to a crescendo, almost like a giant, angry bee, that screamed at them and then faded into the distance.

He looked into Nik's eyes and saw her dread return in a flash.

"It's them isn't it?"

"They haven't evolved wired or wireless communication yet, but they do seem to have a knack for vehicles."

She shook her head in wonder. "What the hell was that?"

"Hard to say for sure, but it went by us on the road. I should think it's some form of high speed vehicle. Two-wheeled, maybe."

"A motorcycle?"

"Could be. And by the sound of it, a lot faster than we could ever muster in this thing."

"They know we're missing."

Truman nodded grimly. "And they know we're coming."

25

PIERSIDE

THE SUN WAS ALREADY BEHIND the mountain peaks that served as Tiron's rugged backdrop. Dusk was giving way to a night that would soon dissolve the outline of the mountains into full darkness. For three days, Strober had explored the port area, crisscrossing its rails and businesses and warehouses. It seemed the safest and most likely place to get information. While the city was full of life, it was also full of Kulian citizens with their short and distinctive statures. He'd find it difficult to keep a low profile there. But the port was different. Here, those physical variations were expected with representatives from across the realm working the docks and the ships. Plenty of work to be done with much less notice paid to what appeared to be some kind of a fisherman or dockworker.

He'd covered his flight suit with a discarded blanket the first evening, which he then traded for an unattended coat and hat. Now he looked much like many of the other sailors in the port area, taking care of their business. His task of the day, like it had been since their arrival days before, was to gather information. Arrival or whereabouts of strangers was likely to be the topic of gossip and speculation. While he rarely asked any questions, he did position himself near pairs or groups in conversation, nonchalantly eavesdropping for a hint of what he was in search of. After dark, he'd slip into the crowded bars for an hour or so, allowing the alcohol, or whatever it was on this planet they used to forget their troubles and loosen their tongues, to assist him.

The Aldrin was submerged in the bay, away from logical shipping lane traffic. He'd taken the sled and stashed it beneath a nearby pier, borrowing a derelict rowboat that looked as if it hadn't seen service in years, but remained serviceable. At night he returned the rowboat to its mooring line and returned to the ship. The Aldrin had provided them with additional sensors and a remote communications capability. He suggested they scour the city at night with the ship, but Bam now had plans for it and Guyal was unwilling to put his license at risk by breaking the federal non-intervention protocol that forbade future technologies from contact with the planet's inhabitants. He figured it wouldn't make a difference anyway. Were the other sled in the city, they'd likely shut it down overnight. They could fly right over it and not know it was there.

Onboard Bam and Guyal familiarized themselves with the Aldrin's capabilities and listened in with him as he eavesdropped. He was their eyes on the shore. Actually their ears. The visual component was a bit of a giveaway here, so the embedded earpiece had to suffice. Through it, they kept up a constant stream of chatter. Some of it was even helpful.

By the third evening, he figured the worst. No talk or gossip even remotely helpful, and he'd returned to the ship discouraged, ready to recommend calling it quits and switching from a rescue to a recovery, but this morning, something had popped. He'd been right. He didn't even have to eavesdrop to know something was up. The standard talk of weather, shipping and loading speculations were replaced with animated groups talking excitedly. Some talk of a flying woman and a man with a sword for a hand and a name repeated, Picek, a name the groups seemed to hold in some reverence. The conversations were repeated and shared and stretched throughout the day, and now as he made his way from one bar to another, he was sure they'd been right. The other sled and its crew were here in Tiron. They had to be. Despite the fact that the day's search yielded nothing but sore feet, he still had no real plan to scour the city. He did, however, have a renewed spring in his step that evening as he headed back to the Aldrin. He crossed the rail line and made his way through the warehouse complex that stood between him and the shipping piers. The light in the area was dim, but as his eyes adjusted to the growing darkness, he caught an odd shape and retreated quickly into the shadows. He slowed his gait marginally and felt for his knife. He'd seen no violence in the past few days, but this was the port area, and it paid to be prepared. Something about the shadow was out of place.

It didn't move like a dockworker or a thief might move.

His impression was not one of ill-intent. There was hesitation. There was fear. Not someone who wanted to relieve him of his valuables. Someone like him. In the shadows. On the run. He silenced his steps, backtracking slowly and silently. Sure enough, the shadow materialized a second time. Now he was taking no chances. His knife flashed, and he held its point to the exposed neck of his shadow. Something was wrong. There wasn't a struggle. Hands were up in the air. And something familiar. Shit, it was a flight suit.

"Strober?" It was a shaky fearful voice in an incredulous tone.

Srober knew that voice. The shadows had disguised what would have been a dead giveaway in the daylight, but his subconscious had picked up on it.

"Truman," he whispered, and the realization made him laugh.

"How in the hell did you find me? This is impossible."

Strober stashed his knife and brought himself face-to-face with the engineer.

"You should *not* be hanging around in alleys surprising unsavory dock workers. You could get hurt."

Truman had regained a bit more of his composure now. "You should watch yourself, pirate. Someone might take that thing away from you and stick it up your ass."

Strober bounced away with a laugh. "It sure wouldn't be you, tubby."

Truman caught him by the arm and pulled him into a bear hug. He whispered into Strober's ear. "I wouldn't be so sure of that."

Strober was powerless and didn't put up a fight.

"You got me, man."

Truman pushed him away, laughing.

"I've been searching this place day and night for any sign of you. For days. I was in the process of writing you off when you finally decide to show up. Guess it was just a matter of time. Where are the others?" Strober asked, giving up his mirth for a more serious question.

Truman's momentary smile dissolved immediately. "Jata is dead. Killed by Simms."

Strober closed his eyes and bowed his head for a moment, a pause before his next question.

"And Nik?"

"Nik and I escaped, but now—"

"Now?"

Truman recounted quickly an abbreviated version of their prison break and northward trek.

"So you left Nik and the sled to get some intel about us?"

Truman nodded. "We agreed that I should go as I look a lot more Kulian than she does. And that she should keep the sled powered up and secure until I got back. In this world, it's pretty much impervious to anything. So I eavesdrop on a few conversations in the port area, listening for any hint of you, and what do I hear?"

Strober grinned. "You hear about yourself."

"Exactly. Guy with a sword hand and a flying woman." He shook his head in exasperation. "So I go back to check on Nik, and she's gone. Her, the sled, everything. Gone. Not a trace. I don't have a clue where she's gone, so I come back to the port area, just to hide out. Maybe hear something."

"You don't hide very well, do you?"

Truman nodded with a wry smirk. "Yeah, thank God for that. What about you?"

Strober's eyes narrowed, still smiling. "You won't fucking believe it."

"That wild, lame idea of yours with the ship?" Truman snorted.

"It certainly was wild, but it was anything but lame. We found it."

"Fuck you."

"It's true."

"I don't believe it."

"To tell you the truth, Truman, I found it, along with a lot of other shit, pretty hard to believe, too. But chew on this."

He reached up and fished the audio transmitter out of his ear and handed it to Truman.

Truman took the object from him and examined it as best he could in the shadows.

"Go ahead," Strober told him, motioning to his ear, "put it in."

Truman obliged, not sure what to expect. His eyes shot wide open.

"Guyal?" he asked in amazement. "Where the hell are you?" He listened for a moment. "Kicking back in an Aldrin-class frigate? You can't be serious. I find that really hard to believe."

He watched Truman exchange a few more words, then began pulling him toward the piers.

"C'mon, Truman. Stop bullshitting and move it."

Truman fell silent as they walked, listening to updates from Guyal. As they rounded the corner of the warehouse area, the port lights lit up the sides of a pair of transport ships moored at the first two piers. Strober had stashed the rowboat at the end of the piers. He could have kicked himself for his distraction, but the place was now deserted as they made their way past the transports that towered above them, and his mind wandered to their next steps.

He couldn't wait to continue his conversation with Truman, but Truman was in his own distraction, his eyes focused straight ahead, and his mind focused on a point somewhere beneath the bay.

The net that dropped over them took them by surprise. Completely.

There were two of them. One was of the short, round Kulian stock they'd become accustomed to in the port city. But the second was different. The second was tall and fair. Best guess, he was taller than either of them. They struggled within the confines of the net, but only for a short time. They were unprepared for the trap, and in short order, they were bound, marched aboard the second ship and left alone in what looked to be a cargo area. No cargo was in sight, but the locked iron hatches kept them restrained, nonetheless. One of their captors had said something about thieves before leaving them, apparently to find some higher authority.

Truman was still connected to Guyal with his earpiece, but said the connection was tenuous. He moved his head to try and find a position of clarity. Apparently unsuccessful, he looked at Strober.

"Thieves? Why would they think we're thieves?"

Strober shook his head and then stopped, thinking they were probably right. "I bet it's the rowboat."

Truman raised his eyebrows, questioning.

"I couldn't very well park the sled out front, so I found this derelict boat a few minutes row from here. And I borrowed it." He shrugged. "I put it back each night when I'm done. Someone must have reported it."

"So now we're boat thieves."

"It shouldn't be too hard to talk our way out of it."

"Let's hope not. Who the hell knows how serious of a crime that is here."

It was at least another hour, maybe more, before the doors opened again. They exchanged stories and tried moving about for better audio reception, but with little success. When the door did open, it wasn't the two from before; however, they had statures similar to their captors. One was short and round, the other tall and fair-haired.

They took some time inspecting the prisoners. The tall one paid particular attention to their clothing. He touched Strober's coat.

"I should think this is not your coat, is it, friend?" His eyes were a piercing blue, and he studied Strober's features carefully as he waited for an answer.

Strober assented with a nod.

"Nor the cap. And if my colleague here is right, there's a small boat nearby that does not belong to you either. Am I correct?"

Again, Strober nodded.

"But this," he said, as he touched the fabric of Truman's flight suit. "This is a fabric I'm not familiar with at all. And its design. You're neither Mudson nor Kulian, are you?"

Truman said nothing.

He looked at Truman with the same penetrating gaze and said simply, "You're from Earth."

Strober was immediately puzzled. From the point of view of an inhabitant of this planet, Earth might be a legend or a myth. With the no-contact order in place for centuries, he wondered how he might be so sure. The simple and direct statement begged an alternate explanation. To someone familiar with flight suits, that would be an automatic assumption, but a local here? Save for his size, Truman could pass for a Kulian citizen. He stopped in mid-thought.

Of course. He was Mudson, and he had their thoughts at his disposal.

He remembered the tingling sensation from the beach.

Another damn mind reader.

He shivered just thinking about it.

"My name is Cotel," said the tall one. "These crimes are of little importance. I'll return the coat and hat," and he extended his hand.

Truman willingly shed the clothes and handed them over.

"You return the boat," he continued, "and just walk next time."

Strober nodded, sheepishly.

"Now that that's settled, I do have a proposal for the four of you."

A look of surprise streaked across Truman's face. He'd tried to contain it, but his surprise couldn't be disguised.

"It seems we have a common concern."

Strober watched his face change from surprise to understanding. Truman's voice was no more than a whisper, but that was all it needed to be. "Picek."

Cotel agreed. "Picek."

***

The castle overlooked the river and the valley below with despotic satisfaction. Its high perch dominated the landscape, with sheer stone walls matching the abrupt cliff edges and punishing faces that served as a natural barrier for both friend and foe. The brilliance of a waterfall peeked out briefly before plunging to form the river that ran its course hundreds of meters below, its roar rumbling constantly beneath the working sounds of the castle. Nik's view from the castle was much less foreboding. A large grassy meadow painted with wildflowers here and there framed the lower end of her view. Green forested ridges descended toward the city in the distance with the blue of the northern sea beyond.

Were she not a prisoner, Nik would have enjoyed it more, and were it not for her damn presumption that a quick stretch outside the sled wouldn't do anyone any harm, she wouldn't even be a prisoner. In spite of how worried Truman had been for her, she'd gone ahead and done it. She'd been careful.

Who was he anyway, her mother?

But he'd been right, she thought, forlornly. She'd checked the area completely to make sure no one was watching and then shut down the sled and climbed out just for a minute of glorious stretching, working out a cramp that had been building for hours. Up and down, touching her toes and feeling the pleasure of stretching muscles. And that had been it. Something hit her, knocking her to the ground. Someone had been watching and waiting. Silently and patiently.

She'd known from that moment she was fucked. And not in a good way. They'd thrown her and the sled in some type of transport vehicle with a pair of stinky, leering locals with bad teeth. Ugh. She didn't know why they tied her up. She had no place to go or to run to. The last leg of the journey had been the most painful. Miles on foot. She kept falling with her hands bound behind her back, and they seemed to rather enjoy grabbing her and putting her back on her feet. They never talked to her, but whispered sometimes between themselves. Apparently now she was property of this Picek guy. As she looked over what she might normally consider a picture-worthy landscape, she thought about tossing herself over. If she could fly, it would be no problem. But she couldn't. Not any more. She'd flown halfway across the galaxy and now? She figured she could probably fly for about six seconds before the castle's parapet broke her silly little neck. At least she wasn't tied up any longer. Simms and Picek were not too far away. Deep in conversation, and unless she was mistaken, enjoying immensely the view that she couldn't.

She paid attention to the conversation that drifted to her through the mountain air. Simms had made a gift of the sled to Picek. He'd teach him how to operate it and offered technical help in a number of future projects. Apparently they'd already laid some kind of plans, which, presuming he'd made contact through their pig delivery network, would make sense.

What Simms wanted from him was the support to mount an expedition to explore and recover a ship somewhere in the Namian sea. She actually agreed with the laugh that came from Picek. Picek was more interested in what they were going to do with her and why they hadn't started yet. The one word that came back was predictable. Leverage. Simms told him that if they had her, then the other one, the valuable one, the one called Truman, would be here shortly. The Tiron streets were his, and his men were out in force. There was a sizable price on Truman's head. He was certain that soon enough Truman would show up either as a prisoner or a hero to rescue his girl. He said they could count on Truman to be stupid like that.

Simms had a different look to him now. He'd cut off his long, white hair, dressed in Kulian attire and now had a sheath for his steel skewer. It was slung over his back to keep it out of the way when it wasn't in use. But every time she'd seen him, it was in use. He liked to motion with it, to lean against it. To make his points with it. Now, he had it by his side, its point making a scraping sound on the paving stones of the castle. He looked somewhat ridiculous, but she'd seen him use it, a recent addition to his wardrobe, she figured, as he was sometimes awkward with it. He kept it up, nonetheless.

Their conversation complete, she was herded back inside the castle. The doors in the castle were not equipped with handles, but rather had remote mechanical mechanisms that opened the door automatically when pressed, and then closed. While it looked like an electric door, a low mechanical whir said otherwise. They didn't stay. Rather, they pushed her into her cell without a word, leaving her alone and allowing the door to close on its own behind her. Aside from the door she'd entered by, the room offered a single barred window to the view below, and at the opposite side of the room, sat another, much larger door, formed of thick, solid wood, its bulk reinforced with straps of black iron. The door didn't appear to have hinges, and she wondered to herself how it worked. On either side of the door sat the head of a lion or something lion-like anyway. Probably intended to represent some type of animal, some real or mythical cat from this planet. Worshipped maybe. Feared certainly. The heads were formed of metal, and the intricate design work was impressive. That was it. No furniture. Nothing but her, a stone floor, two locked doors and emptiness. She gazed out the barred window. She couldn't even toss herself into the next life here as she could have from above. She blinked back the tears as, her back against the wall, she collapsed slowly to the stone floor.

26

UNDERGROUND

TRUMAN SAT ACROSS the low table from the ship's captain. Calm and fair-faced, there was something familiar about him. It wasn't in his features or his appearance, and for a few minutes, he couldn't put his finger on it. Then he realized that it was Durt. People were naturally drawn to Cotel, and he took it all in stride. No anger. No animosity. Just a cool calm with an answer for everything. Like Durt. For Truman, it was different. Placed on his shoulders, the burden of leadership was a challenge. He knew machines and programs and fields and systems as they were limited and predictable. People, on the other hand, seemed to have an unlimited number of variables, like a flawed program or a ship out of control after a power surge. These were things beyond anyone's control. But Durt never had a problem seeing through them or managing these kinds of variables.

He did what he said he would do. He'd predict what would happen, and it would happen. Not that it had helped him in his last time at the helm.

He closed his eyes and shook his head silently.

Got himself into a bit of trouble there didn't he? But they'd all walked away, even if he hadn't. And here they were now.

He realized that this, or something like this, had been Durt's vision. Find that ship and get the hell off the planet without haste.

They had found the ship, but now there were complications.

There were always complications.

The bar was deserted with the exception of their party. He wasn't sure if that was by design or by chance. Of all the bars on the waterfront that greeted, enticed and ultimately served the odd collection of sailors and the port area's specialized force of laborers, this would not have been his first choice of venue. The shipping and warehousing complex of buildings and structures stood between them and the docks, and across the rail line that ran along the dock area was an extended row of lighted establishments. Bars and grills and merchants providing services, only some of which he could identify. This place was neither well lighted nor well advertised. No sign displayed what might be available for purchase. Up a narrow alley and down another. Now that he was here, he was pretty sure he could find it again, but he would never have looked here in the first place. There was also a stench to the place. It wasn't overpowering, but it was there, a dampness that indicated their proximity to the sea. They'd descended a carved stone stairwell, and they now sat beneath the city. Quite a feat, he thought, this close to the water. No, this was not a place you'd come to enjoy the atmosphere. This was a place of secrecy, of isolation and conspiracy. It was perfect.

The dark ale on the table before him had a curious and delicious edge to it. It seem like forever since he'd just sat and visited. A different universe. Well, a different part of the universe, anyway. Around the table in various stages of conversation sat his shipmates, Guyal, Strober the pirate, and one of the richest men on Earth. He'd figured a guy with that much money and power would have personality issues in a situation like this, but you'd never know he wasn't just another crew member. He seemed to love this role and played it well. He didn't want to be Bam the heir to a mining fortune. He wanted to be Bam the pilot or Bam the technician. He could be any of those things because no one cared on this planet.

Apparently Simms didn't know either. Because that could be trouble.

He understood that this role was also a practical defense mechanism. Pull down the glasses, and he was just another kid plugged into his own virtual reality. Probably hard to live a normal life with a name and a fortune like his, he thought. Not that his was a normal life, but Bam seethed a quiet confidence.

A sense of entitlement came standard with an inherited fortune.

Seated with them was their latest ally, Cotel. This was Cotel's choice of establishment. He supposed they might have just met on the ship, but Cotel had insisted on meeting them in the port area. Now dressed in their local attire, most of which was ill-fitting, they looked much less like off-planet intruders and more like a band of marine laborers. Cotel had introduced the final members of their group as Ruzilan, his engineer and Tagren, Ruzilan's brother. Ruzilan was polite and quiet. Tagran was anything but. He ranged between excitable, happy and nervous, all in the space of a sentence. The group had been subdued, almost furtive on their alley walk, but once inside, they'd met the real Tagran. Right now he was in the middle of his animated phase.

"I tell you what," he said. "They've got this city locked down tight." He looked at Truman. "And you, my friend, you are some wanted man. I'm responsible for keeping an eye on this part of the port section. I'm Picek's eyes here. Reporting you could make me rich. And not reporting you could make me—"

He faltered a moment, fear quickly clouding his eyes and changing his bright tone abruptly, "dead."

Truman wasn't surprised. That explained their specific rendezvous point. He moved his gaze to Ruzilan who looked embarrassed, and then to Cotel again who raised his hand, motioning for calm.

"Easy, Tag. No one here is going to kill you. Not even Picek."

Bam repeated "Pie-check" a couple of times and shook his head with a smile, as if he found it hard to believe that was an actual name.

Truman's eyes went to the man behind the bar who provided them drinks. He cleaned glasses and his equipment studiously, maybe too much so.

Tagran saw his questioning gaze and picked up on it. "Don't worry about him. Zosac is one of us. You're secret's safe here."

"Maybe Zosac wants to be a rich man," pointed out Truman. He looked again at Cotel.

"Maybe we all want to be rich men," said Cotel. "But more importantly, we all want to be free men. And in many ways, especially in these days of Picek, many of them can no longer say that they are free men. Traditionally we Mudson do not share or support or even associate with the Kulian people, but my colleague has shared with me what might be called a family problem. I am here with you tonight to help see what I can do. To offer what help I can to resolve these problems."

Behind the bar, Zosac carried the look of a haunted man. His defensive posture was the dead look on his face that would bring no controversy. He was of standard Kulian stock, taller and slimmer than most, and only streaks of his dark hair still clung to his balding head. The expressionless dark eyes gazed at Truman, now aware he'd become the center of conversation. He spoke, but only a few words. As he did, his eyes flickered with a spark.

"Anyone who Picek wants as much as he wants you is a friend of mine."

Truman raised the glass of ale before him toward the barkeep in a salute. "Thank you, friend."

Cotel smiled and nodded. "Truman. I know you and your crew have a military aircraft. We'd like your assistance in, how should I say this, alleviating the Picek problem that troubles our cities and our families."

Truman started to speak, but Bam, seated next to Truman, interjected sharply.

"No way. We can't."

Cotel turned his gaze to Bam. "I know. You have a code. Like a non-intervention code in the affairs of our planet here. But this is a rare opportunity. Never before have we had this type of capability or support."

Bam shook his head. "No, that's not it. I mean, aside from that policy. We don't have the capability you think we do. I've gone over the ship from top to bottom, inside and out over the past few days. I know what should be there, and we don't have what you think we have."

Truman turned a curious glance to Bam.

Guyal nodded in confirmation.

"It should have nukes, phase-plasmas, and conventional weapons for on-planet combat. But it doesn't. It's been de-weaponized. Now it's like a surveillance ship or a trainer. It meets all of its original nav and engineering specs, but they stripped off all of its offensive capabilities. It's real purpose when it was stashed, was not as an operational combat frigate, I think, but as a last resort. A taxi."

"A ride home," said Guyal.

Cotel paused for a moment, at a loss for words.

"It doesn't matter," said Truman. "We have our own little problem as you well know."

"The flying woman." It was Ruzilan. He'd been silent for the conversation, but his mind was sharp, and he followed the conversation directly.

Truman smiled, thinking of Nik suspended above the sled, a look of exhilaration on her face.

"Yes, Nik, one of our crew."

The group was silent again, but Truman's mind was turning. The edges of a plan were forming.

"I think we're going about this the wrong way," he said. "This is not an explosives problem. This is a Picek problem."

"And a Simms problem," added Strober.

Truman agreed silently, lost in thought. "So tell us about Picek," he said as he looked up. "What's he like? What are his vices? What are his weaknesses? How do we get to him?"

"You don't," said Tagran in a flat voice. "They say he's made of iron. The same iron that comes from the mountains. He doesn't know anything about mining though. He knows about pain and weakness and greed and—"

A troubled expression was getting the best of him.

"You know," he continued. "If you visited our city, and you didn't live or work here, you'd never know it. Life goes on, from an outsider's point of view. But every little piece of business, from our famous tea to our rail lines, construction and manufacturing—he has a piece of everything. His people are all over the city. Even I'm his people now. We, our family I mean, are really riding the poverty line, and I thought I could do a few jobs and get us back on our feet and now—"

He looked up at the crowd. "Now he *owns* me."

Guyal offered the obvious solution. "You could always quit. Poverty is certainly preferable to slavery—I would say anyway."

Tagran countered defensively. "You don't understand. It's not that easy at all. There's a significant penalty for leaving this kind of service. Say I don't show up for a job one day. He doesn't worry. He puts out the word for me, and my brother, who isn't under Picek's thumb, is entered into service, forcefully. When I'm located, and it's never a question of if, but when, I lose something for my weakness. Usually fingers first, but it depends on the offense. Might be a hand or a foot, but not usually because that makes me less productive. Ears and eyes and." He looked down. "other things, too. Or, if he decides I'm not worth the trouble, his favorite thing is to watch people being dismembered and devoured by his giant cat."

Truman watched Guyal and Strober exchange surprised glances.

"He has a chamber in that castle. Two doors; one for the

prisoner and one for the cat, a big one. He's got viewing ports in the ceiling. They're recessed so the prisoner can't tell he's being watched. He's a devious bastard, actually. Anyway, so I got invited to see a show like that. Not an invitation you get to turn down. And not even that I wanted to. I had no idea what kind of a show it would be." He put his hand over his mouth. "It made me sick." His eyes were wide and nervous again as he told the group. "No, really. I physically got sick. After I'd seen it, I knew there was no way out, knowing what I knew. And I figured the next time I sat there, it wouldn't be some random prisoner, but my brother or my mother or—"

He stopped his story abruptly.

Truman was lost in thought again. "No offensive weapons," he said to himself and repeated it under his breath. He turned to Bam. "What about the defensive array?"

Bam nodded. "Standard array."

"Infrasound?"

Bam looked at him with a curious expression. "Yes," he said slowly. "There is a separate module specifically for infrasound, but I have no idea what that even means, or what it does."

Truman said nothing, leaving Bam with a mystified look on his face.

Across the table, though, Strober picked up on the question and posed one of his own to Tagran.

"What about ghosts? Does he believe in ghosts?"

Tagran gave him a thoughtful look. "Not ghosts, no. At least I don't think so. But he's very superstitious. A lot of the uneducated folks are. Especially in the mountains where mines are dangerous and simple miners pass on tales. So, ghosts no, but monsters with claws and flames? That's another story." He looked at Truman with an amused smile. "Don't get me wrong. There's plenty of weird crazy shit in these mountains, but this story is one that everyone in Kulan knows."

Ruzilan rolled his eyes. "That's kid's stuff. No one believes it's real. The mountain monsters are a myth. A legend."

Tagran shrugged. "Say what you will, brother. I think the same thing you do. I'm just telling you what people say about him. They say his father was killed in the mines, and his mother was a nomadic. Never worked, you know. Begged, stole, swindled. They say he grew up fearing the mines and hating everyone else."

"Sounds like someone we know," said Truman, "The two of them should see eye-to-eye."

He leaned over and whispered something into Bam's ear. Bam was attentive, and nodded his head, agreeing.

"Tagran, what about mining supplies? Can you get your hands on explosives? Fuses? Things like that?"

Tagran gave the group a doubtful look.

"We don't need much."

"Sorry. I don't really have access to anything like that. I can't without—"

Truman understood. "You can't without the risk of losing your fingers, can you?"

Cotel was staring at Bam again. "You're considering destroying the castle? But that doesn't make sense."

Truman looked closely at Cotel and then turned his focus quickly to Bam. The blue eyes of the fair-haired Cotel had sensed what Bam was thinking.

He hadn't seen that one coming. He could see, but apparently, he couldn't interpret what he didn't understand. Their whispered plans were probably clear as day in Bam's mind, but without a frame of reference, Cotel, the native planet dweller, couldn't comprehend things he'd never seen before.

Now it was Bam's turn to smile. "Not the castle, Cotel. The empire."

Cotel shook his head, still mystified.

"It doesn't matter," we can still work it without the pyrotechnics," said Truman. "Might not be as effective, but it will still work."

A sound from the back of the bar reminded them that they remained attended. Zosac left his cleaning duties and joined them at the table.

His tired face hung in a dejected expression as he shook his head and apologized.

"Forgive me for my eavesdropping."

His old friend Cotel and his newest friend Truman both assured him there was no reason to apologize, and he nodded his thanks.

"I may be able to help with—"

"Explosives?" interrupted Bam excitedly.

He was always doing that, thought Truman.

Zosac jumped at the word as if even acknowledging it brought a penalty, but confirmed with a nod.

"I have no guarantee," he continued. "I can promise nothing, but I may be able to help. I will meet one of you. Just one," and he looked at Cotel, "here tomorrow morning. If I can be of help, I will. If not, you have my prayers and my apologies."

Truman nodded solemnly and stood up slowly. "Thank you, Zosac. We appreciate what you can do. We, too, will be of help. If we can. You have my word."

Zosac bowed and returned to his bar.

***

In fact, Zosac did help. The package was small, but adequate for their intended purposes. And it wasn't Cotel who'd returned for the meeting in the morning, but Truman. He thanked the gaunt, haunted man profusely and assured him, that whatever the outcome, there were two things he knew for certain. That with or without their off-world help, the will of one man could not bend the will of thousands forever. That change had to come soon and that his help, whatever it cost him, was a part of that movement. The other thing he knew was that they wouldn't meet again. This was not his world. It was Zosac's and Cotel's and the rest. It would be up to them to find their own balance. His world was out there, and he motioned to the sky. He needed to get back to it.

Zosac said nothing. He nodded and waved farewell, and then he did something Truman had not yet seen him do, and figured he hadn't done in a long time. He smiled.

The package tucked under his arm, Truman pulled his hat low and melted into the morning port activity.

They'd spent a good portion of the night going over the Aldrin, Bam explaining what he knew, and Truman asking incessant questions. They'd pored over maps, and at Strober's suggestion, after midnight, they'd made a darkened ship surveillance run, adding scan detail to Guyal's planet scan map, now resident in the Aldrin's combat control. Piece by piece, they'd put their plan together. Its objectives were simple. Retrieve Nik, minimize planetary intervention and get their asses to Midway. Those were their agreed upon primary objectives. Personally, Truman had a couple of additional objectives, but he kept those to himself. They were objectives of opportunity. He'd share them if and when he needed to. He smiled to himself, realizing that was something Durt might say.

As they planned, Truman handed the package off to Strober and headed back through the warehouse complex, following the same path they had taken the night before. He wouldn't walk fast. Just matter-of- factly. He figured it wouldn't take long. He was right. Within a few minutes, like clockwork, Tagran came into view. At first recognition, Tagran's face froze. Complete surprise. Then he began shaking his head, trying to be discreet to anyone who might see him, but being anything but. He tried unsuccessfully to direct Truman away with his nervous, twitchy eyes. Truman strode toward him with deliberate steps, and with each one, Tagran's eyes and level of concern grew.

"What the hell do you think you're doing?" he hissed at Truman between clenched teeth. "You can't be here. You're going to get us both killed."

Truman fought back his uncertainty and used a low soothing

voice like he sometimes did when he talked to his ship. To make this work, he needed a smooth operator, not a nervous freak.

"It's fine. Just relax. I'm here to make you famous. Maybe even rich."

That did the trick. Tagran's face shifted colors from disturbed to curious.

Perfect.

Truman continued. "You're due back at the castle this afternoon, yes?"

Tagran confirmed with a nod.

"That's what I thought. Now, what is your security protocol?"

Tagran didn't understand, and his puzzled expression said so.

Truman clarified. "What alarm are you supposed to raise if you see me?"

"I shout, *thief*! and under local law, anyone nearby must help detain you. Law enforcement responds, and you're arrested."

"And then turned over to Picek?"

He nodded. The mention of that name made him shudder.

"Who gets the bounty?"

"Hard to tell, Truman. A little here and a little there. Lots of folks involved."

"So, maybe no one?"

Tagran shrugged. "Could be. No one would see what anyone else got, if anything. And no one would dare to ask."

"But what if one man captured Truman and presented him in person in front of everyone. He'd be obligated to pay wouldn't he?"

Tagran saw where he was going and talked it through to himself. "If Truman was captured and no bounty was paid. Who would hunt the next bounty?" He looked Truman straight in the eye. "No, you're right."

Truman changed his approach abruptly.

"They're hunting Truman. Me. We, on the other hand, are hunting rats." He paused for a second, realizing his location. "Do you even have rats here?"

"Of course, we do," he said with a roll of his eyes, "this whole city is crawling with them."

"And how do you catch them?"

"Traps," he said, not really understanding the question.

Truman raised his eyebrows, waiting for the next element.

"Oh, and cheese."

"Yes, cheese. So Tagran, we're hunting rats now. Two big ones. And I'm the biggest piece of cheese you've ever seen."

27

MONSTER

NIK WAS A MESS. She'd paced long enough to wear grooves in the stone floor of her castle prison room, or so it seemed, and now sat huddled in a corner, dissolving into fits of tears now and again and then lapsing into catatonic silence. Truman had tried talking to her, to tell her he was there and that everything was going to be fine. She was beyond consoling. "I'm so stupid," was all she kept repeating. "I'm so stupid," and "This is all my fault." He'd tried his best to comfort her, but he knew the only thing that could comfort her was a way out of their situation. And right now it looked pretty grim. Their worst case scenario wasn't even death at the end of Simm's manufactured left hand. No, the worst possible outcome was to be torn to bits for the amusement of Simms and Picek, his newest ally. He could almost hear their cruel laughter now. He actually did tell her that he had what they were looking for, and that they were going to trade the ship for their safety. She didn't believe it for a second and burst into tears again. When he heard the words come out of his own mouth, he didn't really believe it himself, either, and began to feel doubt creep into his senses. So many variables. So many different choices. He'd tried to calculate odds and probabilities, but in the end he gave it up as being a useless exercise. It would work or it wouldn't. Simple as that. The details would make all the difference, but the details would have to be improvised on the spot. And that was up to him.

He inspected their rather expansive cell from end to end. The place was tight, the craftsmanship superb, and he was impressed with the detail work and the mechanical sophistication of the door that he'd entered through. He'd also taken a good look at the much larger door, which was, aside from the open air window that offered a panoramic view of the meadow below, the only other feature of interest in the room. The dark timber and iron construction described by Tagran stood there before him. He pressed his ear to its surface, but heard nothing. Overhead, beams of similar origin helped support the floor above. While he didn't doubt there were some type of view ports built into the ceiling construction, he couldn't see them, despite his efforts. Maybe they'd devised some other mechanical wonder to enable the viewing of a cat feast. And maybe he didn't care. It didn't help him one way or another.

He and Tagran had ridden the Tiron rail transportation as far as it went, and then made the remainder of the trip on foot, with him ahead and Tagran following behind with a stick, driving him mercilessly forward, for the benefit of anyone they met along the path. The bruises made his back tender, and the night he'd spent on the cold stone floor hadn't given his muscles any relief.

It wasn't until he saw the light change hue through their cell that he realized he'd been there nearly a day already. He paced again for a time, thinking and waiting and expecting.

It wasn't until nearly nightfall that the door opened and Simms entered, a very different Simms from the one they'd abandoned south of the city. He now dressed in the rougher local clothes, well cut, and clearly of animal skin origin. He looked every bit like the crime lord he'd sided with. And Picek was there with him, larger than the majority of Kulians he'd seen, but still markedly smaller than standard Earth stature. He himself was a perfect measuring stick. Where Simms was cheerful and self-assured, Picek was not. He was bearded with close-cropped hair, and he looked about the cell with a glare of annoyance like he had someplace to go or some other Picek responsibility he'd much rather be engaged in. Simms still had that stupid skewer attached to his arm, and the metallic point scraped against the stone floor as he walked about, using it almost like a cane or a walking stick. Truman caught a cringe of annoyance from Picek each time it scraped the floor. And it looked to Truman that Simms did it intentionally, taking pleasure in annoying his host.

"Truman, you look a little worse for wear," said Simms. "You could have just stayed with me and avoided all of this." He side stepped and whacked Truman's back with his long steel finger.

Truman gasped as his tender bruises sustained another assault.

"But you're not really one for doing things the easy way, are you?"

Truman watched him with ire in his eyes. "Not really my style," he said slowly.

"I understand completely. We're all prisoners of our own souls."

He came around again to face Truman, his skewer scraping deliberately over the rock surface. He brought the point to rest on Truman's cheek.

"Now, we both know what I want."

He was right. Truman did know what he wanted. That was the whole reason for coming here. But his mouth had some other ideas. His mouth was ready to tell Simms what he really wanted was a...but he didn't have the chance even to finish the thought before Simms interrupted.

"Ah, ah," he said, shaking his head and clucking his tongue. "I know what you want to say, but let's not waste my time or yours. You never know just how much you have left."

His face changed to a scowl in a flash as he again pressed his steel tip against Truman's cheek as an exclamation to his point.

Truman couldn't believe how sharp it was. He hadn't even felt the point, but he could feel a drop of blood run down the side if his cheek.

Bastard.

"Careful," he said evenly to Simms. "You'll make me lose my memory."

Simms said nothing, but took a quick step back and stood side-by-side with Picek who had a scowl of his own. He then turned quickly on his heel, taking a pair of long steps and with his extended steel, pointed it, as he had for days on end in the sled, at Nik's heart.

Nik didn't even flinch. Inside, Truman's soul screamed at him to do something. To save the girl. But his face remained a stone.

No, doing nothing at this point served him better. Let Simms chew on his own impatience for a while.

"I don't know what you've done to her," he said to Simms, "but it wouldn't matter much. Look at her. She's way past being scared. You might be doing her a favor."

He watched Simms consider the fact. His right hand went to his chin. Then his expression changed. He'd reconsidered.

"I think you're right Truman," he said slowly. "She doesn't care about herself anymore. Too far gone. Maybe she's already written herself off as dead." He frowned and turned to Truman. "But you, on the other hand," he said, dropping his steel to the floor with a smile, "you're a different story."

He moved toward Truman, but stopped short as the sound of a fist pounding on the smaller, exterior door, interrupted. The door to the cell swung into the room and revealed a shouting and commotion just outside the cell.

Truman watched as the door guard protested and struggled to hold back a familiar figure. It was Tagran. But it wasn't. It looked like Tagran, but this man wore a beard and longer, unkempt hair. He had the same face and the same wide eyes, but these eyes weren't reflecting the nervous eyes that Tagran had used so frequently in the Underground. No, these eyes were wide with fear. The eyes of a disturbed man. It was Tagran's almost-twin, and he was babbling with a voice caught between the edge of sanity and hysteria. Truman could make out only two words in the stream of stutters. Stopped and started words. Picek was one. The other was Dartu. Truman had no idea what the second was, but it seem to shoot fear into Picek each time it was uttered.

Picek turned to Simms with an expression of hate and fear and barked his short command.

"Wait here," he snapped, and stomped out of the cell, the door muffling his shouts behind him.

Simms turned his attention back to Truman, along with the extended point of his left hand.

"Dartu?" asked Truman, "What the hell is Dartu?

Simms shook his head with impatience. Damn superstitious son of a bitch," he said. "Dartu is what they call that fairy tale monster he's obsessed with. Waste of time." He shook his head again as if to clear his thoughts and return to the business at hand. He spent an uncomfortable amount of time staring out the cell's now dark window until he finally seemed to come to a decision.

"Listen up, Nik," said Simms in a matter-of-fact tone as if he had to explain things to a child. "This is your man. Actually, he's a poor excuse for a man. He got himself caught, and that is, if I may say so, a pretty crappy job of rescuing you. But he does have one item of redeeming value in that big fat bald head of his. He plays his cards right, it might even be worth the pair of your useless lives. I can't decide. I've changed my mind a couple of times already."

He replaced the skewer tip on Truman's cheek, and Truman heard Nik let out a little scream behind him.

Truman raised his hands. Sometimes it was really hard to follow Simms' mood and personality shifts. He had to be careful.

"OK, Simms. Take it easy. You're right. I do have something you want. Yes, you're right, I know exactly what it is. More accurately, I know exactly where it is. But I need a couple of things from you."

Simms smirked, another personality emerging. "Really? Do tell, Truman."

"First, and this is critical for you, this is between you and me. Not between the three of us," and he motioned to Nik's huddled form in the corner of the stone cell. "Just you and me. You take her back to Tiron, and release her. You just let her walk away."

Simms stared at him and said nothing. No expression.

Hands still in the air and his right eye on the steel tip an inch away, he continued. "Then I want a solid meal and a real bed. I'm tired and sore and," he pointed with his raised right hand to his own head, "not really thinking straight. If you want to safeguard those coordinates, I wouldn't be so free with the point of that thing. One wrong move and I won't remember much of anything."

He shrugged as his finale. "That's it."

Now Simms was smiling. "Everything for the girl, eh?" he shook his head as if he couldn't believe he'd actually said it. "Done," he said abruptly, dropping the point from his cheek to his neck.

He stared into Truman eyes, as if trying to judge the risks inherent in his offer.

His stare broke off suddenly as the door opened behind him, and Picek entered the room again.

By now, the twilight of the evening had vanished, the cell's outside light now replaced by some type of weak electric light in the ceiling. It wasn't strong enough to light the cell well, but it did throw an odd, yellowish tint over the room and gave what he took to be Picek's normal scowl an additional menacing aspect.

Instinctively, Truman took a step backward.

The same wild eyes that Tagran's brother had displayed before now shone from Picek's face. In his hand, he gripped an odd-shaped metallic pistol.

Then Truman felt it, too. A sick feeling in the pit of his stomach, a darkness and the edge of fear like he'd never felt before. He broke into a cold sweat. Nik screamed. Something was terribly wrong.

Picek rushed to the barred window and looked out. He was shaking now. He raised his pistol and shouted at the top of his voice, "Take that you black monster. You stay the hell away from me."

Truman heard two sharp reports. Then, as if in response, a blast from outside the castle shook the cell, and he felt the impact inside his chest. The explosion did two things simultaneously. First, it lit up the sky and turned the barred window into a frame that silhouetted the outline of Picek's head. Second, it woke him up to what was happening. He realized it wasn't that something was terribly wrong. It was terribly right. He'd miscalculated the effects of the infrasound to the point where he'd forgotten about it completely, the feeling of fear was so intense. A dark, misty shadow of something caught the corner of his eye and then passed through the wall. He couldn't believe what he was seeing. What he could believe was an intense desire to escape from this room and anything associated with it. The figure of Picek, his pistol still raised, turned away from the window and toward them in what seemed like slow motion. Simms stood beside Picek, fear reflecting on his face as well, and as he watched, Simms narrowed his eyes and seemed to will the fear away from his features. Fear was screaming through the very being of Truman as he realized in this situation, as in many others, the man who had best control of his emotions might best respond first. Clearly, Picek had no emotional control. None. As he turned to face Truman and Nik behind him on the floor in the corner, now wailing at the top of her voice, his expression was not one of words, but of action. Truman realized his own bulk was the prime target for Picek's next shot. Picek raised his arm to aim his weapon directly at Truman. His mouth was open as if to say something, but the fear that pierced all of them didn't allow him to actually form words, just an open-mouthed cry of silent anguish.

Truman heard a long, drawn-out, "nooooooooo." The sound of despair. But it wasn't from Picek's mouth. It came from Simms. He watched Picek's face shift from fear to complete surprise. The realization came to Truman at the same time it came to Picek. The bright piece of jewelry now protruding from his chest was not an accessory, but the tip of Simm's steel finger. Picek took a single, faltering step and pitched forward on the stone floor, the metal gun skittering across the stone floor before him.

Truman stepped sideways, shaking.

Simms advanced toward him, the bloody skewer in front of him, any fear now vanished from his face, replaced by hot anger.

"This is your doing," he hissed. "I don't know what it is, but it's one of your tricks. Let me tell you something. I told you this before. In a few months, I'll have these fuckers building flying machines. You probably don't even have any damn coordinates. I'm to the point now where you're less an annoyance to me dead than you're a benefit to me alive, so I'm just going to poke your heart out now before you invent any more problems for me."

Truman backed up again, but the point of Simms steel followed quickly and steadily, its point at the base of his neck as they stood face-to-face. He realized that now less than a meter remained between his back and the giant cat door behind him. He had no more retreat steps left to take.

He kept his focus on Simms' eyes.

This was it. No mercy or hesitation there. Time for a diversion.

"You might have my life, but I have something you don't, Simms."

Simms smile transformed itself into a twisted sneer. "Yeah, what's that?"

Truman watched the eyes. The eyes told the story, and the eyes said Simms' death thrust was imminent, but his curiosity needed to be satisfied, and he waited impatiently for the answer.

"Both hands," Truman said.

That did it. The eyes engaged the brain and the brain engaged the left-handed thrust. It was as forceful as Simms could make it, something Truman had counted on. Twisting aside, the blade caught him on the side of the neck, ripping a superficial patch, but as it passed, Truman caught the shaft with both hands, stepping back and adding the full clout of his additional force to the already powerful thrust. It buried the sharpness of the skewer deep into the side of the wooden door.

Now it was Simms turn to be surprised.

Sticky blood dripped from Truman's neck wound, but the pain was a benefit. It helped him keep his focus. With his right hand, he swung around and smashed his hand into the head of the metal cat figure on the right side of the huge door. As he had hoped, the door swung inward, dragging the attached Simms forward as he stumbled after his poetic skewer. Pulling was of no use, and the hand that might have been used to release the attachment from the end of his arm was now flailing out of control, trying to find purchase or balance.

The putrid scent of death and decay escaped the cat chamber, making it hard to breathe, but it wasn't enough to stop his pre-planned second motion, a forceful sidekick with his boot into the stumbling hip of Simms, the bulk of the giant door now pulling him into the interior of the chamber. The kick sent him sprawling to the floor. Inside the chamber.

Truman moved quickly behind him to jam his hand into the second metallic cat figure on the left side of the door and watched as the door changed its course immediately and closed, with only the steel skewer keeping the giant door from closing completely. He watched as Simms tried to lever the door open again, and he saw fingers peek through in an attempt to reopen the closed door.

A fearsome growl from within froze the clawing fingers momentarily, and Truman watched first the fingers and then the skewer disappear inside as the door closed completely. An unearthly scream followed. A second was cut short. It sent another jolt of fear through Truman's heart. He stood and stumbled to the barred window, now panting. In the darkness outside, flames from the explosion still flickered in the darkened meadow below. It reflected light on a great beast that now sat in the meadow. He stared uncomprehendingly. Wings, a tail. He couldn't believe his eyes. It was a damn dragon. Picek's monster. Fear petrified him again as he dropped to the floor and scrambled to the gun that lay in the corner of the cell near Nik. He picked it up and pointed it at the exit door. Shaking. Frozen there. Waiting.

Within a few minutes the fear subsided and exhaustion took over. And when the door did open a few minutes later, he didn't have the energy to pull the trigger even if he'd wanted to. He saved the last of his senses for the head that appeared from behind the door.

"Thanks, Strober," he gasped at the familiar face that swam in and out of his vision. "Let's call it even."

28

Dig

THE SUNRISE WAS BEAUTIFUL. But it was the last sunrise on Claustrom any of them hoped to see. The view was familiar but markedly different with a few scattered cargo cases beneath the overhang of the Aldrin's hull serving as makeshift chairs. Truman sat on the fender of the cargo sled as the group sipped what coffee they had left and shared what cigarettes they could muster. The long shadows of the sheer cliffs behind them that had sheltered them after the Raven's crash were gone now. Only the shadow of the low ridge to the east painted the form of what they all knew to be Durt Larson's grave in a misty morning shade. But it wasn't a conversation of sorrow or grief.

"Hand to God," Truman shared with the group, "When I looked out that window onto the meadow, I saw a damn dragon. And it wasn't like I blinked, and it was gone, or I thought it might be something that looked like a dragon. There was a huge, scaly dragon just sitting there in the meadow."

Guyal had a half-grin on his face but didn't say anything.

Nik agreed with Truman. "I saw something, too. But it wasn't a dragon. Some kind of monster with this one, giant white eye. I figured it was something they gave me to confuse me. Some type of drug, I guess. And I saw some other shadowy things, too. But I had no clue as to what was real and what wasn't by that point."

"Infrasound," said Truman. "Remind me never to use that shit again."

"Why not?" asked Guyal with a smile. "It worked didn't it? We're sitting here drinking coffee and pretty much intact."

"Infra-what?" asked Nik curiously, "What is it? It's something we did? With this?" she said, motioning to the ship above them.

Truman raised his coffee to Guyal. "Guyal actually. He was the only one behind the field. The only one who didn't feel its effect. The rest of us were either willing, or in your case, unknowing participants."

"You should have told me."

Truman disagreed. "Wouldn't have done anything but confuse you. You were a wreck."

Nik acknowledged his point. "Yeah, probably. But what was it?"

"It's part of the ship's defensive system," said Truman. "It sets up this low frequency vibration. Right around 19 hertz. Humans can only hear down to about 20 hertz. It resonates, among other things, our eye sockets. There was a lot of controversy when this frigate was made about opening up doors to other dimensions. Phantom appearances. Got outlawed with the exception of its military applications. And since we haven't had military applications for centuries, we've pretty much forgotten about it. Different people see different things. Usually, because the vibration triggers a fear response, it manifests the things you fear most."

"You're afraid of dragons?" asked Nik, smiling. "You even ever seen a dragon?"

"No. Not until last night anyway. We were in a castle. I think maybe it was what I was expecting to see. The mind works in strange ways. I'm sure Picek saw his monster, though."

Bam was listening, but hadn't said a thing. His back on the sand and his feet up on a crate, he was shaking his head. Truman figured he must have seen something he just couldn't get his mind around.

"Anyway," said Truman changing the subject, "we've got a good long trip ahead of us. We looked at charts, and we've missed our close launch window. Our quickest transit in this thing, will take us a good three months.

"Bam, I know you've missed your Midway launch."

Bam perked his face up, and this time it had a smile on it. "This baby has given me a whole new perspective," he said.

"Guyal?"

The big navigator popped another breakfast strip into his mouth and smiled. "You know, I just may give up navigating for a while. The kids will never believe the stories I have now, but that won't stop them from asking me to tell them. God knows I'll never get, and—" he raised both hands in the air. "Not that I want one, but I'll never get another story-worthy experience like this one."

"You ever get the urge, old man. You just let me know." It was Bam. "You can come navigate for me any day."

Guyal raised his eyebrows in surprise. "Really?"

"Got my word. But no hot-shotting. Just plain old boring business navigation."

"I think I'm about ready for some boring now."

"What about Strober?" asked Nik.

"What about me?"

Truman considered. There actually wasn't a lot he could do. As senior officer, he had obligations and requirements. He did have a few options, and he knew that while Strober's actions brought them here in the first place, were it not for him, they wouldn't likely be leaving either. He was torn.

Bam interjected. He wasn't looking at the others, but at the sunrise and at Durt's grave.

"Truman, I have an idea," he said. "We've been through a lot here, but there's a lot more out there still to do. Unanswered questions. We still got a lot of digging to do."

A raised hand motioned Bam to pause his thoughts. Truman followed his gaze to the east.

The alien sunrise was something to behold. And maybe a little too familiar by now. He downed the remainder of his coffee. It wasn't bad, but somehow in the molecular manipulation, it left the tinge of a manufactured aftertaste and reminded him he'd been stalling. The sooner he got to it, the sooner they could leave this place behind them. He stood, closed his eyes and took a deep breath, still for a moment. Bam was right, they did have some digging to do. But first, he had some digging of his own.

"Hold that thought," he told Bam as he stood up and stepped into the sled that had served as his coffee-drinking seat.

His mouth was tight, and as he closed his eyes again, he felt Nik's hand slip into his.

"It's OK," she said. "I know you can't leave him here. None of us can. I'll go with you."

Without another word, Truman powered up the sled and steered it toward the shadowed rock pile. He felt Nik's eyes on him, watching him closely as they glided eastward. He thought his expression was probably clear to her. He felt grim with the distasteful task ahead, but couldn't help thinking of his time with Durt. He formed the edge of a smile.

He maneuvered the sled behind the rocky grave and took the shovel from the cargo deck, the sled now resting on the rough surface at the base of the ridge that stood between them and Claustrom's sun.

They took careful steps, Truman using the shovel as a staff for balance and Nik using Truman. Slowly and deliberately, he got to work.

"Why didn't you use one of the mechanicals?" she asked. "This will take you forever."

He said nothing, but continued to move rocks with the shovel and at a certain point, let the shovel fall to the ground, and on his knees, began moving rocks with his bare hands.

Nik watched him curiously and then kneeled beside him to help. Even if he was dead, it was still Durt. Truman heard an unintentional gasp escape her lips, and he caught a glimpse of the flight jacket fabric she'd uncovered beneath her last rock. She stood up suddenly and she grabbed Truman's shoulder for balance.

He watched a range of emotions cross her pretty face. Disgust, surprise and confusion. The last one remained.

"But—"

At a loss for words, she was looking and pointing at Durt's right hand that extended from the flight suit sleeve. Truman watched her face for a moment longer. What she had expected to see was the mummified, sand-dried hand of a dead man. What she saw was most decidedly not mummified and most decidedly not dead. She was dumbfounded.

He leaned forward and removed more rocks, quickly uncovering the real reason he'd chosen that spot. It was an uneven rock formation that left something of an overhang, a little stone pocket. Durt's body wasn't really buried in stones. It was lying in a small stone cave and the rocks had hidden him from the elements. A few more stones uncovered his secret.

Nik couldn't help herself. She pointed. "Is that—" and then stopped.

Truman realized she'd never seen one.

"Yes. That's a medbelt."

"The one you needed. The one we couldn't find. Because—"

"Because he needed it more."

"And you left him here."

"I left him here to save his life."

"And you didn't tell us?"

"Couldn't take the chance. I could've sworn to the ends of the galaxy that he was dead, and Simms wouldn't have believed me. But if he heard it from you or—"

"Or Jata," she said softly.

Truman nodded, "Or both."

"Then he would believe."

He stood up and took a step back for a moment, his shovel balanced upright, its handle on the rocky surface of Claustrom and its blade pointed toward the alien sky. Durt's body, still in stasis from the medbelt, had a peaceful expression on his face, in spite of the object protruding slightly from his chest. Beyond them, the Aldrin lay poised for takeoff. The crew had finished their morning break and were once again engaged with the activity of reloading and packing.

"Welcome back, buddy. We got you," he said to the inert form of Durt Larson.

Nik looked more closely at the wound. "My God, Truman. Are you sure he's going to be OK? I mean that looks so serious. Do we need to get him back into the prison and the med-bots?"

Truman shook his head without hesitation as he bent over and for a closer read of the medbelt.

"The Bureau's dark as well for the next few months. No way to say who or what we'd run into on the inside. No." He was adamant. "We're not breaking into prison again."

"Why not?" she asked? "It saved your life."

He looked at her steadily. "Let's not push our luck." He motioned to Durt. "He's stable, and by the time they could alert the prison Bureau, we'll already be on Midway."

Then he smiled. Something had changed inside of him. He wasn't sure what, but smiling was something he didn't usually do. Or maybe, he just hadn't done it in a long time. That was about to change. With Nik's help, they moved Durt onto the sled's cargo deck. Nik sat close beside him as he returned them to the Aldrin.

***

"In the market for a new ship, Truman?"

The Aldrin's viewport was not nearly as generous as the Raven's had been, and they settled for watching Claustrom shrink beneath them on the tactical view screen. Not that the visual mattered that much to Truman. Their collective sense of escape was pervasive. Almost without exception, smiles of contentment flourished around the group. Guyal was lounging in the navigator's seat and Truman and Nik sat side-by-side. Durt was stowed safely in a crew stasis pod.

The question had come from Bam.

"First, my friend—"

He paused and thought a moment.

"Actually, before we went off to recover Durt, you said you had an idea, and I cut you off. You told me to hold my thoughts."

Truman made a face, embarrassed. "Sorry. I was a bit, ah, distracted."

"I know what you were," Bam said, his eyes dancing as he played with Truman. "And I don't get told that very often. Reminds me a lot of my father. I have a tendency to interrupt people, and nobody ever tells me no, so I want to say thanks to you, in fact, to all of you. I enjoyed being a part of your team. Anyway, I had this idea."

"About Strober, right?" asked Truman.

If there was one smile that was missing from the group, his was it. Strober had some things to answer for.

"Yes. About Strober," he agreed. "I think Strober died on Claustrom."

All eyes turned to Bam. They looked at him, momentarily confused.

Truman looked at Strober. He wasn't confused.

"He doesn't look dead," said a smiling Nik.

"Sure looks dead to me," said Bam. "Strober?"

Strober agreed, "I think you're right. I'm dead. Dead and buried. He placed his hand over his heart. "It was heroic, I'm sure."

Bam laughed out loud.

He looked over at Truman. "I'd like to bring him on as a consultant. I think he'd be helpful, you know, with the digging."

He turned back to Strober. "How successful did you say you were? As a pirate, I mean."

"Counting the Raven, I was 19 for 20."

"What do you think about making it an even 20?" asked Bam.

Strober looked up, considering. "I'd need resources. A new

identity."

"You ask a lot for a dead man."

"So kill me."

"Oh yeah," said Bam, "Strober is definitely dead."

It made sense to Truman. He had no issues avoiding the investigations and months of federal interviews that were sure to follow. He could make sure Durt got what he needed and, well, it never hurt to do a favor for the richest man on Earth. A new start for Strober? Actually, it was a new start for all of them. He saw only two problems. First, Strober needed a new name and a new identity. Second, and this was his own problem, the Raven had been his baby, and he'd traded her in for a newer model. It would take some getting used to as he knew virtually nothing about Nik. But he wasn't worried.

Claustrom, by now, had shrunk to the size of the rest of the stars on the view screen.

Nik touched his arm. "So of all the stories you told me, you never told me what Durt did to create such hate in Simms."

He kept his eye on the screen for a while before letting Claustrom fade out of focus. Their course was set. Midway was on the other side of Sol II, and they had months to figure solutions to both problems. And stories of Durt? Yes, there would be time for that, too.

He looked over at Nik and smiled again. He was looking forward to it.

About the Author

JAMES SLATER

For more information about the author and for updates on
the sequel to Claustrom, visit:

www.jamesslaterbooks.com

Copyright © 2016 by James Slater

www.ingramcontent.com/pod-product-compliance
Lightning Source LLC
Chambersburg PA
CBHW051332250626

47155CB00007B/2569